RAPALLO'S SHADOW

WFernie

WILLIAM FERNIE

Rapallo's Shadow by William Fernie

First published by Fernie Publishing Limited, 2024

ISBN: 978-1-7395881-4-4

Cover design and interior design by Paul Palmer-Edwards.

For more information visit: **www. ferniebooks.com**

For Katherine & Hannah

CONTENTS

CHAPTER ONE

As far as Tom Munro was concerned, Alice had died after her fall onboard the SS *Ferris Star*. He had mourned her loss only to be told some weeks later that she had not died at all. Now he was travelling to meet her at the third or, was it the fourth attempt? He had struggled to cope with his emotions, which were compounded by the perilous state of Ferris International Airlines, his other dream.

Tom decided it was time to make a move. He sloshed down a third whisky, banged his glass down determinedly and pushed through the heavy wooden doors and out of the smoky London public house to catch a bus.

He thought about how he would react to seeing her again. Alice was someone he had loved and then lost most dramatically. He had been devastated. His life had stalled as he mourned her death. Everyone around him had been sympathetic and benevolent and keen to offer advice. But he had pushed them away as if determined to suffer in his dark despair.

Now he was about to see Alice again. Fit and well by all accounts except for a limp. He was still confused. He felt quite sick. He wasn't sure whether it was nerves or his excitement which made his stomach churn more. Anger and relief conflicted, brewing a bewildering concoction of feelings carried on a wave of adrenaline. How could she have put him through the emotional turmoil? Why had he been duped into believing that she had died on that miserable night at the Hamburg docks?

He blinked twice, shook the alcoholic haze from his head and looked up the street for the S-Type bus. Eventually, it appeared out of the gloom, coming to a halt with a long howling squeal in response to his raised arm. He smirked at the bold whisky advertisement he saw on the side of the bus: "Don't be Vague. Ask for Haig". He chose a front seat on the open upper deck to clear his head.

The bus moved off, and he immediately regretted his decision. It wasn't quite a pea-souper yet, but the smog was settling in the still air. Charles Dickens, he recalled, had described the meteorological phenomenon in his novel, *Bleak House,* as soft black drizzle. He tried to clear the soot from his eyes and decided that the lower deck might be preferable. He stood, turned carefully and staggered back along the top deck, lurching from seat to seat, grabbing each well-polished seat handle one by one. Negotiating the stairway proved even more difficult now as the bus swayed and jolted on its journey. The numerous whiskies didn't help.

He pushed his way into the crowded lower compartment. The locals looked at him. He imagined their thoughts; nobody in their right senses would be on the upper deck in this weather, probably a tourist, worse for drink, not a Londoner or something similar.

When settled, he indulged in his favourite pastime when travelling, people-watching. He noted the usual attire of the menfolk, most in baggy, care-worn, tweed suits and an abundance of flat caps. Not many women were abroad in the gloomy smog. Still, those who had ventured forth were a little more colourful and wrapped tightly in heavy coats, with many sporting fashionable, bell-shaped cloche hats. He tried to guess what they did for a living and where they might work and decided on office work in banks and shops, probably.

The bus continued along Horse Guards Avenue, headed east towards the Thames, then turned along the Victoria Embankment. It slowed to a walking pace, the yellow headlights of the oncoming traffic casting ethereal halo patterns, the beams barely penetrating the smog. Alice's note had just mentioned Westminster Bridge. It was vague, as always, he was not confident from previous experience that she would be there. He wondered why he bothered.

When the Palace of Westminster slowly materialised, he decided to alight as the bus was barely moving. He walked east to survey the entire extent of the bridge. He could only see a few feet, so his search would be difficult. The road was packed with a chaotic assortment of horse-drawn coaches, chugging motor buses, cyclists and carts of all shapes and sizes struggling to progress in the poor visibility. The traffic was almost at a standstill. He could not see across the road to the other side of the bridge and decided to walk along one side and return on the other. That way, he would not miss her. Why couldn't she pick a more specific meeting place? So typical of Alice. Was it a sense of humour or a penchant for her mysterious clandestine world?

He had not anticipated the dense, chaotic pedestrian traffic on the bridge. He battled his way through the crowd, his head swivelling this way and that as he checked every shape that bore a vague resemblance to Alice. On several occasions, he peered at a vaguely familiar figure only to be confronted by a shocked, then irritated expression. He started to tire of apologising. His first pass of the bridge proved fruitless. He crossed to the other side, dodging around clods of horse dung and all manner of vehicles. He held his hand to his face in the pungent exhaust smoke. 'If Alice isn't here, she's just making a fool of me', he muttered.

'Here we go again', he mumbled as he set off to do battle on his return trek. This time, he decided to stick close to the cast iron balustrade, running his gloved hand along the barrel-shaped handrail to guide his progress. He ploughed his way through the pedestrian onslaught. They had probably decided to escape London early to avoid the worsening weather conditions. He had all but given up when he noticed a figure leaning casually against the balustrade. He recognised the shape, the pose; something just told him it was Alice. His heart leapt. 'Alice?' he said as he peered under her hood. He'd forgiven her already.

'Of course, it is you daft thing!'

Tom stood up straight and sighed, his head sinking to his chest. The mixed emotions returned with a vengeance. He remained silent and blinked hard to stifle a tear, shaking his head in disbelief. 'God, you are a one, Alice. Is that all you have to say?'

'Let's go somewhere a little quieter,' she instructed with a prod in his chest. 'You need a stiff drink. I know a little pub just off Bridge Street. It's not too far. Come on.'

'Steady on, a pub?'

'Yes, of course. It's a better class of public house. Quite suitable for us women folk now.'

Tom followed as Alice made off at her pace despite a noticeable limp. At Whitehall, they barged headlong across the traffic flow. Tom felt it necessary to act as a traffic policeman as they crossed to the pub opposite the Houses of Parliament, a favourite haunt of parliamentarians, according to Alice. Tom sprinted ahead and opened the stout wooden door. Heads turned, and expressions varied as women were still barely accepted in public bars but more so in London.

They found a cosy corner table under welcoming wall lights. Tom scanned the busy surroundings and noted the heavy oak panelling and preponderance of mirrors, etched glass and elaborate lighting. 'This'll be fine,' said Alice. 'We need to catch up.'

Tom sat with his back to the wall so that he could survey the comings and goings, always part of the entertainment in a pub. He was still in a "dwam", unable to believe that he had finally met up with the elusive Alice. 'I'll say,' he said in a noticeably exasperated tone. 'Let's start with what happened on the *Ferris Star.*'

'Ah, that'll be difficult. I can't remember anything about that. Can you tell me? You were there.'

'Didn't Harry Price and your people at SIS tell you?'

'Harry wanted you to talk it through with me. See if it jogged my memory. You know that he's a little sensitive about us. "Our relationship", he says. C has made it very clear that there is to be no flirtatious behaviour amongst his staff, no fraternisation, no shenanigans.' Alice giggled and then looked serious. 'Harry's a good friend to you, Tom. He felt terrible about the deception.'

'Damn it, Alice. They told me you had died. I couldn't even go to your funeral. Do you know what I went through? I lost you. It nearly killed me. I don't know…'

'Thomas Munro. I can only say sorry, but I couldn't do anything. I didn't know that I was that important to you.'

'Maybe you're not now,' Tom mumbled.

'Look, C wanted everyone to believe I'd been killed. To live to fight another day,' he told me.

'That's not funny, Alice, let me get those drinks. Are you still drinking whisky?'

'Yes, please.'

Alice watched Tom push his way to the bar. She smiled and shook her head affectionately, knowing that her need to return to work surpassed all else, and resolved to discourage him. She was too young to get serious; settling down was just not for her. Their recent activities in Berlin had only just started to reveal the truth behind the German subterfuge. They had to get to the bottom of it, something she was most determined to achieve.

She was momentarily distracted by the leering looks from fellow drinkers and dared a cheeky smile and an impudent wave until Tom returned.

'Please don't antagonise them, Alice. I want some peace and quiet, not another pub brawl. Do you remember that escapade in Hamburg?'

'Yes. We came off all right, didn't we?'

Tom carefully placed the drinks on the table and looked more relaxed. 'I suppose we did. Here we are. I'm ready for a whisky or two, ' he said.

'Me too. Cheers.'

'Welcome back. From the dead, I should say,' said Tom with a sigh. 'This is so strange.'

'We need to put that behind us. As I said, I had no idea what C had planned. They just wanted to ensure Colonel von der Lang knew I had been killed that night.'

'Was it Heinrich Wolf you were arguing with on the *Ferris Star*?'

'As I said, my mind is still hazy, but I believe it was.'

'I chased him, or whoever it was but he got away. It

was dark, so I couldn't be sure either.'

Alice thoughtfully sipped at her drink. 'I hear you managed to get some hard evidence from the Colonel's flat. Pasha's letter proved that the Reichswehr was in discussion with the Russian military?'

Tom cocked his head to one side. 'So, you remember that?'

'Harry and C told me.'

Tom sat back and took a good-sized gulp of his whisky. Alice unintentionally mimicked him, and they smiled when they put their glasses down. 'Yes, we need to move on now. What are your plans, Alice?'

'Get to the bottom of this deception. Get better hard evidence and stop it.'

'That's a tall order Alice. We might get the evidence, but I wonder if anyone can stop it.'

'That depends on what we find. And why shouldn't we stop it?'

'What *you* find,' said Tom, thrusting a finger at Alice.

'So, you're not going to help? You're still on the SIS books, as it were.'

'Maybe, but I'm needed at the airline even more now. We're struggling.'

Alice frowned. 'I see. You must be worried.'

'I certainly am, but we need to keep trying. We've put so much into the business. I need to find out how long Sir Reginald Ferris will put up with the drain on his finances,' said Tom, eyeing his empty glass. 'Another drink?'

‘Definitely, but you must keep a clear head if you’re flying tomorrow.’

‘True, but only if this smog clears, and I don’t expect it will.’

The barman was in much demand on Tom’s second visit to the curving, rather congested bar. He had time to reflect on his conversation with Alice. She hadn’t changed and was obviously intent on continuing the hunt for evidence as before. He turned to look at her. She smiled back with a wave. He thought again about her demeanour. Pragmatic, determined, a little cold, perhaps. She still had that indomitable glint in her eye, and he still found her attractive. The few occasions they had shared a bed popped into his mind. He grinned and wondered if it would happen again. In common with the recent months since his demob, Tom’s thoughts danced back and forth between his airline aspirations and Alice’s intelligence work. Was he going to be sucked into that again?

Tom carried the tray with the whisky glasses and water jug back to their table. ‘Here we are.’

‘Do you think the airline will keep going, Tom?’

‘I hope so, and I’ll keep trying. Sir Reg is a determined man, and he calls the shots. But it isn’t viable in its current form, so I’ll find it difficult to argue that we should keep it going. Large subsidies are the only workable solution. But the government isn’t interested. Some people in the industry are talking about amalgamating all our British airlines into one.'

'Would that work?'

'It could. But I've just got to keep Sir Reginald Ferris on my side, which means Ferris International must be financially viable. Right now, it's not.'

'Is there too much competition?'

'Very much so, and the European lines are subsidised. We're not.'

'I remember you crowing about that before.'

'Crowing?'

'Well, you did a bit. When are you flying again?

'As I said, tomorrow or whenever we can get airborne after the fog clears. We fly from Croydon now. It's a much better airfield. We've got a couple of offices with storage for mail and cargo and some overnight accommodation.'

'Shall we go back to my flat? This leg is still hurting a bit. It tires me out. I've got some things to tell you. Not here.'

Tom cranked his boyish smile up to full beam.

'Don't get too excited.'

'I suppose your leg'll get in the way.'

'Thomas, behave yourself.'

'Look, I plan to return to Croydon for the early flight.'

'We'll stay at my place then. I have a nice settee. We need to talk. Might need your help again.'

Alice's ground-floor apartment was neat, with a single bedroom, a small, rather tight kitchen and a living room with a coal fire. It felt temporary: a little tatty and the groaning front door needed attention. No clutter or personal knick-knacks were evident.

'Have you been here long?' said Tom flippantly, looking for photographs or any further clues to the enigmatic Alice. He knew she had lost her parents in the War, during a Gotha bombing near Liverpool Street station and her brother, an RFC pilot, had been killed in France. Other than that, she was enigmatic but fascinating. Tom felt that he could understand why she was so focused and determined. Her way of dealing with her loss. Her entire family. He could understand if revenge was the driving motive, whether she admitted it or not. He turned to see Alice massaging her thigh. 'I could do that,' he suggested impudently.

'Cheeky chappie.'

'I expect you'll take a while to recover and get fighting fit again.'

'Yes, I'll be getting fit as soon as I can. Not long now.'

'Have you got a new job, another... project?' said Tom, searching for the correct terminology.

'Well, I still need to finish with Germany. It's far from resolved, as you know. If anything, it's getting more urgent.'

'What do you plan?'

'Can't say...'

'Yes, I remember, need to know.'

'Another whisky?'

'Why not.'

Alice spent nearly an hour describing what the SIS knew about German activities post-war, particularly the movement of Fokker aeroplanes out of Germany.

Tom looked puzzled. 'I just find it amazing that they got away with it. From your description of events, it's pretty clear that the German and Allied authorities knew what was happening. In the case of the Allies, they just ignored it. There seems to be a reluctance to punish the Germans any more. You could say it is almost a policy of appeasement.'

'I agree except for the French, who are determined to see the Versailles Treaty reparations paid in full. You and I know much more is happening behind the scenes, in the shadows. It will be my job to find out what is happening in these shadows. I plan to fight for that project. C will have to listen to me. You could help. Stay in touch, particularly when you know more about your future.'

'I hope it will still be *Ferris Airlines*.'

'Doesn't sound like it to me.'

'Let's wait and see,' said Tom, sighing. 'I should know soon.'

It was three days until the smog cleared, and Captain Tom Munro was back in the cockpit. He found the drone of the Rolls Royce Eagle engines mesmerising. His thoughts wandered as he flew his big Vickers Vimy Commercial to Hamburg. Throughout a challenging year, he had flogged his *Ferris Airlines* aeroplanes back and forth from Croydon to Amsterdam, Brussels, Hamburg and Paris. Some of the cross Channel routes attracted government subsidies, but his company was still making a loss. They continued to operate the Vickers Vimy, but the old two-seat Bristol Tourers had been replaced by de Havilland 18s, a larger single-engine machine with six passenger seats and a powerful 450 hp Napier Lion engine.

Tom remained troubled about Alice. With some reservations, he enjoyed meeting up with her again but felt unsure about the work she hoped to take on again. He resolved to keep their relationship strictly professional; anything else would be foolhardy and emotional suicide on his part. Harry Price, his former RFC chum and SIS contact didn't want to say what was planned for Alice. He did say that she was back at work but did not say where. Tom knew that Harry would know much more. 'I'll pass on your London telephone number at Croydon,' he said, but Alice had failed to make contact again.

Tom's thoughts returned to their droning progress as they tracked up the coast from Amsterdam at a gentlemanly 90 mph. He tucked his scarf more securely into his leather flying coat and adjusted his goggles. The smell of sea air blasted his face as he leaned out into the slipstream and peered downwards. He would usually tuck down into the cockpit to seek welcome shelter behind his small windscreen, but he needed to keep a close watch on their track. He knew that some aeroplanes now featured enclosed cockpits and decided that this was the way forward, the future. The autumn weather encouraged the formation of sea fog, and he watched the ominous grey carpet of low clouds as its tenuous fingers crept inland from the North Sea and across their track. He felt a nervous churn in his stomach, knowing this could spell trouble. He recalled these feelings during the War when they had to descend through the cloud, waiting anxiously for the ground to appear.

Tom's mechanic sat alongside, enjoying the view. He was a new lad oblivious to the perilous state of their airline and the threatening low cloud, his face beaming with evident enthusiasm. Despite a determined effort from all, *Ferris International Airlines'* financial prospects were grim. The usual problems prevailed: subsidised competition, challenging economic conditions throughout Europe, and a government with its head in the sand. Not in the clouds, Tom thought with a sarcastic smirk.

'That doesn't look too good, Captain, the fog,' shouted the mechanic.

'Oh, that. We'll have to press on,' said Tom with a poor attempt at indifference. In minutes, the Vimy was enveloped in a dense stratus cloud, the airflow drenching their coats and goggles in a fine mist.

'This wasn't forecast,' said Tom as he transferred attention to his basic instruments and the rapidly disappearing view of the ground. 'We should be able to climb above it. It's a sea fog.'

'I can't see anything. How do you know where we are?' said the mechanic as the roar of the engines increased.

The Vimy rose from the cloud within minutes, and Tom settled his machine on their north-easterly course to Hamburg. He was very familiar with the vagaries of European weather. He knew they were in trouble if the cloud continued to Hamburg. His altimeter would be inaccurate now, and he hoped the cloud would not extend to the ground. He shivered at the thought and felt the need to reassure his companion. 'I normally just follow the coast if the weather's bad, but in these conditions we maintain our course and…' Tom pointed at the clock on the panel. 'Using our estimated flight time to Hamburg, we should be in the area in, let's see, 45 minutes.'

'OK, I'll look out for the coast.'

'I don't think you'll see it. It should be on my side. What's your name, by the way? Sorry, I've forgotten.

'Reg Bailey, Captain.'

'Well, Reg, I hope we can find Hamburg. If you get any sight of the ground, sing out. We might need to put down somewhere.'

'Won't we get stuck?'

'Hopefully not.' Tom said curtly.

The *Vimy* droned on just above the fog bank, Tom peering downwards to glimpse the ground. He felt embarrassed and worried in equal measure. A pilot of his experience should have read the forecast correctly, such as it was. He started to consider a field landing when they reached the Hamburg area. Alternatively, they could turn inland, where the fog might be dispersed. It would have to be a big field, and if he got down, would they get off again? He imagined the company's reaction when he called to say they were stuck in some muddy field. And what about his eight passengers? He had landed out a few times before, but he didn't want to consider that situation, not quite yet.

He was tired of straining into the grey drizzle and the need to clear his goggles when his mechanic shouted.

'It still seems solid. Do we go down into it and hope for the best?'

'Yes, we descend very slowly till we see the ground, then I decide what to do. I know the Hamburg area quite well, so when we know where we are, we make our way to the aerodrome at Fuhlsbüttel. I hope we get a break in the cloud, though. So, keep looking.' Tom noticed that his mechanic's beaming enthusiasm had gone. He thought about another alternative; he could try breaking cloud over the sea. That could be disastrous if it went wrong, as they didn't carry life jackets. Still, they wouldn't risk colliding with buildings or anything too solid.

'By my log, we should be near Bremen now. There's an aerodrome to the south-west of the city. Can you see any ground on your side?'

'No, nothing. Just that continuous grey covering. Looks all soft and fluffy.'

'Ah, yes… well, we've got about 45 minutes of fuel now. Some time to stooge around at Hamburg, then we'll need to go down and try it.' He shuddered at the thought of descending blind into the cloud but knew they had no choice. He could not afford to run out of fuel; that would be disastrous. He estimated they had 30 minutes of fuel remaining when his calculations put them over Hamburg. 'Right, Reg, we need to go down. I want you to yell out when you see the ground and anything recognisable or distinctive so that we can work out our position. I hope we'll spot the River Elbe.'

'Yes, sir.'

Tom turned northwest, hoping to break out of the cloud clear of the city. He knew that if he found the river, he could work his way towards the aerodrome, which lay due north of Hamburg. He thought briefly about his passengers, glanced across at Reg and attempted a reassuring smile. He suddenly felt a crushing sense of responsibility.

He shook himself into the present, exercised his fingers, then placed his hand on the throttles and slowly pulled the levers back. The throbbing roar of the Eagle engines reduced to a dull rumble which reverberated through their seats. Tom lowered the nose for the descent, moving his feet on the rudder pedals to re-balance the machine with the engines at idle. He swallowed hard and tried to relax his tense grip on the controls. He looked across at Reg once again. 'Here we go, good lookout now.'

'Yes, sir.'

Tom could not entirely rely on his altimeter, but it was the only indication he had of their height. It indicated that they were 2000 feet above sea level when they began their descent. The cloud seemed to accelerate as they neared the solid-looking surface, a glistening, snowy landscape now as the sun had broken through overhead. A pretty picture, but a deadly trap if it extended to the ground. The wispy cloud tops zipped by before their cockpit was immersed in a dank grey world. Two pairs of eyes strained as the altimeter wound down. 1500, 1200, 1000... 'When we reach 500 feet, I need to slow our descent and feel our way,' Tom mumbled. 'The ground's here somewhere. Anything on your side, Reg?'

'No.'

'That's five hundred feet, Reg. I'm heading west and levelling off.'

'I can't see a damn thing. We might hit the ground.'

'Just keep looking, damn it.'

CHAPTER TWO

Harry Price rose from the large oak table and walked to the first-floor bay window, which overlooked Melbury Road. Since the move from Whitehall Court in 1919, West House had been the secretive and nondescript headquarters of the British Secret Intelligence Services. An autumn gale had stripped the remaining leaves from the silver birch trees in front of the large detached townhouse, and traffic was now quite visible on the road. He watched the stream of vehicles for a few minutes before returning to the table to rearrange his notes for the second time.

His boss would not like what he was about to hear. Any failure in intelligence would be poorly received. He was ready for a dressing-down. Failure was one thing, but to be duped was something else. Fortunately, their man in the British Embassy in Amsterdam had obtained a complete picture of the Fokker shenanigans, but the story was painful for the SIS, nevertheless. The boss, known as "C," had little time for inefficiency or slackness, and Harry fully expected to receive the full force of C's legendary castigations.

Harry was taking a further trip to the window when the door opened with a creak to reveal C and two other men: one fairly short with a pale, sickly complexion and the other, in contrast, a bright, dapper fellow in a well-fitted double-breasted suit and gaudy regimental tie.

'Sit, please,' said C with a casual wave across the table. 'Introductions first, I think. Harry Price will brief us on our recent discoveries. It's somewhat embarrassing, I have to admit.'

Harry nodded. 'Good morning, gentlemen.'

C continued with his introduction with an insincere grin. 'And this is... do you recognise him, Harry?'

Harry tucked in his chin and looked more closely at the pale, sickly one. 'I don't think I do, sir.'

'Well, you should.'

Harry sat up abruptly. 'Ah, I see now. You look a little different.' Harry sprung to his feet and reached out his hand across the table. 'It's Paul Drummond. The last time we met, Tom Munro had just fished you out of the Channel.'

Drummond came to life. 'Correct, and I'm still very grateful to Captain Munro and his flying skills. It was nearly a year ago now.'

C interjected. 'And this is Gerald Royale from the Foreign Office.' He peered at Royale over his glasses, a look well-known to SIS staff. 'He has some explaining to do as well. But first, Price, let's have your side of the story. Briefly now, please.'

Everything had to be brief for the boss. 'Yes, sir. I'll do my best.'

'Carry on then.'

Harry took a deep breath and launched into his

briefing. 'I think you are all familiar with the clandestine shipping of several containers of aircraft and components in contravention of the Versailles Treaty from Germany earlier this year. We let the consignment carry on, and it ended up at the Fokker works in the Netherlands, to *Nederlandse Vliegtuigenfabriek*, or the Dutch Aircraft Factory in Amsterdam. Mr Fokker is sensitive to his name being linked to his German associations and has adopted a less controversial name for his company. But that was not the end of the story. That relatively minor operation turned out to be a diversion from a much larger shipment, which was carried out under the eyes of the Inter-Allied Control Commission. By 1919, Anthony Fokker had returned to the Netherlands, attracted by a large order for aeroplanes by the Dutch government, so he set about shipping his entire inventory back to Holland by rail. Under the treaty, he couldn't continue manufacturing aircraft at his factory in Schwerin in Germany, so a return to Holland was essential.'

'What aeroplanes are we talking about?' said C.

'Mainly Fokker D.VIIs and D.VIIIs. The same type that we saw being shipped by sea from Hamburg. That was Alice Ferguson's project.'

'Yes, I know. Carry on.'

'Fokker was taking a big risk in fulfilling his contract as these aeroplanes should have been surrendered to the allies under the terms of the Treaty of Versailles.'

'So how did the bounder get away with it?' said C,

looking increasingly red.

Harry sat forward in his chair. 'That's the interesting aspect of this whole affair, sir. We are looking at some 400 engines, 200 aircraft, large quantities of steel tubing, copper and steel fittings and a host of other materials.

'How the hell did they manage to move that lot without being detected? A few heads should roll, I have no doubt.'

'Apparently, the key man in the move was Mr. Heinrich Mann, the chief of the Fokker transport department. Collecting all the material together by road was quite a task, and obtaining sufficient railway rolling stock from the German State Railway was even more challenging.'

'How do we know all this, Price? Who's the source, and can we trust the information?'

'Yes, one hundred per cent, sir. It was our man in the British Embassy in the Hague.'

'Uittenbogaart?'

'Yes, that's him. Fritz Uittenbogaart is very reliable.'

'Heinrich Mann was pretty creative in his work with appeals for help and assistance to former business friends and tokens of appreciation for wives and families such as sewing machines from the factory and surplus silk, all of which went down very well.'

'Yes, yes, but how did they get all this material out of the country?'

'By rail, as I said. The loaded wagons had to be distributed over many shunting yards, then combined into long trains of sixty or so trucks. As a result, they couldn't stay in the sidings and had to remain on the main lines. The important railway junction at Hanover had to be negotiated, and the bottlenecks at Salzbergen and Oldenzaal passed. After passing Salzbergen, the train moved on to the border where the German customs were entirely cooperative.'

'What were the Inter-Allied Control inspectors doing?'

'More subterfuge. Our clever Mr Mann put them off the scent by advising them of suspicious transport crossing the border elsewhere. So they didn't pick up on the smaller sea shipment either.'

'And we lost one of our undercover inspectors, Price?'

'Yes, we did, sir. Mr. Steven Bradley was murdered. We always suspected that he knew something. Perhaps it was the large Fokker shipment.'

C shook his head. 'But these long trains would be so obvious. Why did they not raise any suspicion?'

'The German authorities were more interested in selling the machines to raise much-needed currency. They just turned a blind eye to the trains snaking their way across the German countryside. Also, I suspect that our friend General Friedrich von Mayer at the Reichswehr had a part to play in the affair. We still need to keep an eye on Mr Fokker and the eventual destination of these aeroplanes. It could give us some clues about German plans. Remember the Sondergruppe and our suspicions about Russia, which Tom Munro uncovered in Berlin?'

'Yes, yes. What about the Allies and the Inter-Allied Control people? Do you know anything about this, Mr. Royle?'

'We did get an inkling, and you ⊠ sorry, the SIS, had raised your suspicions about the Reichswehr's Sondergruppe R project. But you mentioned that you didn't have any hard evidence, and we left it at that. We briefed the PM on what we knew, but he didn't seem too keen to investigate or stop it. One of our people just commented that Fokker was trying to recover his business interests, which was understandable. As you know, the Netherlands remained neutral throughout the war, so our government didn't want to pick a fight with our Dutch friends.'

'Typical. We need to keep an eye on Mr Fokker. Is Mr Uittenbogaart still on station in the British Embassy, Price?'

'I believe so.'

'Then make contact and let's keep our eyes and ears open in that neck of the woods. Mr Drummond will be travelling to Moscow directly, so he will watch out for any potential military cooperation between Germany and Russia, which is the sort of cooperation we suspect. As we don't have an embassy, he'll just melt into the community in his usual fashion.'

'And who will run the project, sir?' said Harry, suspecting that he knew the answer.

'Alice Ferguson, of course.'

The engine note rumbled on as they flew level in the cloud. The altimeter needle hovered around on the 500-foot mark as their aeroplane pitched and rolled in the turbulence near the ground — or was it the sea?

'Where do you think we are, Captain?'

'We're tracking northwest, so we could be over the sea. The fuel is getting low, so we've no choice. I'm going down till we see something.'

'But we might....'

'Just keep your eyes peeled and shout when you see something.'

Tom straightened his goggles, took a deep breath and eased the throttle back. Peering over the side, he didn't know what to expect: sea or open fields or, God forbid, buildings. He flew the machine instinctively, feeling his way downwards using minor movements of the controls, his eyes peering into the gloom to spot the surface. He sniffed the air and wiped his goggles almost continuously in the saturated airflow. Could they be over the sea? Reg was hanging over the other side, his head twisting and turning as he searched the grey mists for the ground.

'There,' Reg screamed, pointing to the right of the nose. 'We're going to hit it!'

Tom saw it simultaneously, a dock crane rising into the fog layer. He said nothing and slammed the throttles forward. The port engine responded. The starboard had other ideas. It coughed and spluttered in complaint. He rolled the Vimy hard to the right to avoid the crane jib whilst struggling with the starboard engine. It would not be easy maintaining height on one engine. The starboard engine had to respond. He closed the throttle, adjusted the mixture and opened up to full power as carefully as he dared. The engine coughed hesitantly. He adjusted the mixture again. They were still losing height. As Tom prepared to land on the water's surface, both engines caught, spluttered again, and then mercifully settled back into their robust and reassuring roar. 'Bloody carburettor icing, I think,' Tom mumbled as he stabilised the Vimy in the constricted space between the river and the sea fog layer just above.

Although he only had a few hundred feet to play with, Tom started breathing again and noticed the ache in his jaw from his tightly clenched teeth. He opened his mouth, exercised his jaw and took some quivering gasps of air. 'OK. We're over the Elbe. I need to get my bearings. We mustn't get into the cloud again. I'll orbit here first.' He glanced at his instruments. 'We've got 20 minutes of fuel at best.'

'Where's the aerodrome, Captain?'

'I'm trying to work out exactly where we are. That was the docks back there. The visibility could be better. I'm going to fly up the river. See if we can find the fish market. You can usually smell it. Get sniffing.'

'I can smell it already. Wow.'

'Good, let's find it. That'll be a good fix. I'll know where we are then.'

'There it is, Captain. It's on my side. Big white sheds.'

'That's it, thank God. I see it. We'll fly up the river to the docks in the city centre, then head north to find the Außenalster Lake. Just pray this cloud gets no lower. The field's just north of the lake.'

The port engine started to run roughly, attracting Tom's immediate attention to the fuel gauges. Their needles were bouncing off the empty stops. 'God, keep going. We're nearly there.'

The aerodrome only appeared once they were almost overhead. Tom blew a long sigh when the hangars came into view. He spotted the wind sock and positioned the machine close to the boundary so they could scrape in if the engines stopped. The engines were struggling now, coughing and spluttering in complaint. Tom turned the Vimy tightly onto the final approach to a landing and spotted a green light from the control tower. He didn't need any permission to land; he had no choice, he mused. The landing was not his best. He was just hugely relieved to be down. He thought he heard clapping from the passenger cabin. The engines gave up before they made it to the concrete parking apron, the Vimy rolling ignominiously to a stop in the middle of the field.

Tom sat quietly, panting like a dog, his head resting back before Reg stated the obvious.

'That was close.'

'A bit too exciting for your first flight, huh? They're not always like that.'

The passenger buildings, relatively basic wooden huts, were congested with frustrated passengers; their flights grounded by the weather. Tom, Reg, and his passengers pushed into the building; their tired, dishevelled look was unlikely to inspire confidence in the waiting passengers. Tom was arranging for the Vimy to be towed onto the apron when he heard a familiar voice.

'That was brilliant flying. Must be Captain Tommy.'

Tom spun around. 'Roth, Werner Roth by Jove! What're you doing here?'

'I'm waiting to see if the crazy Britisher manages to land in this weather. I thought it must be you somehow. Nobody else could fly in this,' said Roth, nodding toward the field barely visible beyond the steamed-up windows.

'If I'd known it would do this, I'd have stayed in bed and certainly on the ground.'

'Well, glad you got down safely. How's the airline going?'

'As tricky as the weather. You must find the same. Are you still flying with...?'

'*Deutsche Luftreederei*.'

'That's the one. Never could get my tongue around it.'

'Things are changing, Tommy. You should join us. We are heavily sponsored. I suppose that's your problem – not having any government assistance. It's essential. Even I, as a simple pilot, can see that.'

'What do you mean, join us?'

'I might be moving to a new German-Russian line

chap, all for the airline but a numbers man. He keeps moaning about our low passenger numbers.'

Tom took his time, shutting down the engines and completing his checks before taking his customary pause. He liked to savour the peace and quiet and take a little time to prepare for the transition from the airborne world to the pressures awaiting him on the ground and the customary chaos associated with the arrival. Everybody wanted his time. Most of the passengers liked to thank him for a wonderful experience, the ground staff for refuelling, unloading luggage, mail and cargo, and then the next crew for a report on the aeroplane's condition. He eventually emerged from the hubbub, pulled his helmet off and undid the belt and buttons on his flying coat. He felt hot after the incessant cold airflow swirling around his cockpit. He waved briefly to Reg Bailey, then wandered over to Daniel and his group. They seemed unusually subdued.

'We need to have a word, Tom,' said Daniel, looking unusually drawn and worried.

'Of course. What's up, Daniel.'

Daniel pulled Tom away from the group, a hand on his elbow. 'I know. I'm not very happy. I'm afraid it's over, Tom.'

'What do you mean?'

'The airline. It's finished. Father has pulled the plug. It's over. He won't finance the losses anymore.'

'Are you serious, Daniel?'

'I wouldn't joke about that sort of thing.'

'I know,' Tom said, flopping down on a bench by the arrivals hut. He fiddled with his helmet and goggles as he looked across at the Vimy and then slowly back to Daniel, who remained standing. 'For heaven's sake, sit down, Daniel. I had no warning of this. Can't we have a meeting with your father? Develop a plan and some way forward. God, man, after all our work, efforts, and blood. We can't end it like this.'

Daniel had tears in his eyes. 'Sorry, Tom, he's adamant.'

Tom looked across at Freeman, who wandered over sheepishly. 'I suppose you had a hand in this, Roger?'

'I suggest we meet with Sir Reginald,' said Roger, looking guilty. 'See if we can change his mind. I'm not sure how we can approach it. I don't have an accounting argument. On the contrary, I can only argue that we need to call a halt. I'll keep quiet. You two will need to appeal to his sense of optimism. I'll leave that to you.'

Tom shook his head. 'I don't hold out much hope. What are you doing here, Davidson?'

'I have to impound the aeroplanes. I can't let them go anywhere. Remember, they're leased from Vickers.'

Tom looked to the heavens and sighed. 'Let's arrange a meeting, Daniel. I'm not going anywhere, either.'

Tom was still trying to shake off a thumping headache as the LSWR train pulled into Salisbury station. He collected his small suitcase from the overhead rack and then opened the door onto the station platform. It was quiet apart from the hissing and gurgling noises from the locomotive. It seemed to issue steam from every conceivable gland and seal. He was momentarily distracted from his woes, watching the engine and four coaches chuff their way out of the station to disappear, trailing steam around the curve in the distance. He loved the distinctive smell of steam and oil. He likened it to aeroplanes, which also had their own characteristic aroma. The Ferris family had arranged for their driver to collect Tom, and he abandoned his pleasant musings and wandered through the archway from the station platform to be met by a smart chauffeur who doffed his cap in recognition.

'Captain Munro?'

'Ah, yes.'

'I'm to collect you for Sir Reginald Ferris. I believe Mr Daniel explained.'

'Yes, of course.'

'This way, sir.'

Tom felt like royalty in the back of the Rolls Royce as they made their way through the Salisbury traffic and south-west to Blandford Forum. He glanced across the distant rolling hills of Martin Down, his favourite playground as a child when his father was still alive. He recalled the first meeting with the Ferris family more than a year ago at their local autumn fete. Sir Reginald had enjoyed a pleasure flight in their Bristol Tourer. It seemed so long ago that Sir Reginald had agreed to fund the airline. The Rolls had a little bar in the back, and Tom found a water flask to slake his thirst. The driver turned and occasionally chatted as Wiltshire became Hampshire, then Dorset before Blandford came into view. It took a little time to pass through the town, and after a few miles of winding, narrow country roads, the grand shape of Branley House began to flicker its stately presence through the trees.

The Rolls swept around the horseshoe driveway in front of the house, announcing its arrival with scrunching tyres on gravel. As he headed for the door, Tom took a deep breath just as it opened as if by magic. He nodded his thanks to the white-gloved servant, handed over his coat and hat, and made his way up into the grand hallway, feeling very out of place in such ostentatious surroundings. He remembered meeting Daniel's sister on his recent visit and wondered if she was still around.

'Tom, my dear chap, welcome,' said Daniel in his usual effusive manner. Tom noticed his strained smile, suspecting he felt awkward about their circumstances.

'Thanks, Daniel. Have Bill and Jack Parsons arrived?'

'Yes,' said Daniel apologetically. 'They were instructed to park their motor car around in the yard. I'm afraid Father is treating them like staff or tradespeople. And you should know that Father has a shooting party tomorrow.

He suggested that we join them. And for my sake, it would be good if you could. You know what Father is like. When Father 'suggests', it's an instruction. He said your chaps can load for you, and we need some beaters as well, he suggested again.'

Tom raised his eyes to heaven. 'Oh, Daniel, that's the last thing on my mind right now!'

'I agree, but there's no harm indulging him. You never know what favours we might need in return.'

Tom's expression changed. He seemed distracted. Daniel was puzzled for a moment until all became clear. 'You met Fran when you first visited us, Tom. Do you recall?'

'Of course, I do,' said Tom, nodding his hello as Fran descended the grand curving stairway. It was excellent for making an entrance, Tom thought.

'And how is my Captain?' said Fran engagingly.

'I'm fine, all things considered,' said Tom.

'I've heard about the airline. It's very sad. What will you do?'

'I haven't given up yet. I need to do battle with your father.'

A booming voice interrupted them. 'Is that so, Captain Munro?'

Tom cringed. 'Well, forgive me, but you know what I mean, sir. We must discuss the situation; perhaps that's a more appropriate phrase.'

'Yes, quite so,' said Sir Reginald, pulling his pocket

watch from his waistcoat. 'In my study in, let's see, twenty minutes.'

'Yes, sir,' said Daniel, a little red. 'We can have a chat later, Fran. It looks like Tom is staying for dinner and the shoot tomorrow.'

'That's splendid,' said Fran with a broad smile. 'Perhaps you can sit next to me. I'll fix the seating plan.' Fran looked Tom up and down. 'Do you have …?

'He can borrow some of mine,' said Daniel.

Tom looked flustered. 'What are you two talking about?'

Daniel spoke quietly. 'We'll be in formal attire this evening, evening dress, you know, white tie. I don't expect you to have that sort of regalia in your little bag.'

'Correct. Just a change of….'

'Yes, quite. If you'll excuse us, Fran, Tom and I have a little to discuss before seeing Father.'

'Of course. I look forward to this evening. Seven p.m. in the Orangery for pre-dinners.'

Daniel and Tom retired to the library. 'My, hasn't Fran blossomed? She's quite a beauty, Daniel.'

'I know. And she has several admirers hovering in the wings. Father is very protective.' Daniel's eyebrows danced up and down mockingly. 'She often asks after you, Tom.'

Tom thought for a while before visibly making a mental adjustment. 'How do we persuade your father to keep the airline going, Daniel? If you can't tell me, no one can.'

Sir Reginald had summoned Bill Franklin (Tom's gunner from RFC days), now the Ferris Airlines sales director, and Jack Parsons, the maintenance director, from their accommodation in the outbuildings. Bill's furrowed brow was unusual for one more inclined to jesting, and Jack peered around wide-eyed at the elaborate decor. The formality of the situation precluded any welcomes other than brief hellos and nods. The Ferris accountant, Roger Freeman, was present with his usual files and bundle of papers, and Sir Reginald brought the meeting to order with a loud, 'Let's make a start.'

When all were seated, Freeman was invited to assess and report on the financial state of Ferris International Airlines, and it took nearly thirty minutes to paint a very bleak picture. 'In short, the business is making a substantial loss, and without significant government intervention in some way, we cannot continue.'

Tom tried to maintain a neutral expression as he watched Sir Reginald digesting the very negative assessment of the business. Finally, he spoke. 'Thank you, Roger. Do you have anything to say, Daniel?'

'Captain Munro and I have had a short meeting this afternoon, and we can only agree that the business is not viable in the current market conditions. We have heard talk of combining the existing airlines into one national organisation, but this is only an idea to date. Much as I hate to admit it, I can't see that we can wait for that to happen unless we are subsidised now.'

‘And you, Captain Munro. Your views?’

‘Sadly, sir, I can only agree. I’ve heard that Air Transport and Travel is throwing in the towel. Who can hope to succeed if George Holt Thomas can’t make a go of it? It’s a great disappointment to me personally. As you all know, this has been my dream for some time. And the painful quandary we face is that I know civil flying has a future. We just need to find a commercial solution.’

Sir Reginald interrupted. ‘As Roger said before we embarked on this venture, the time is not right.’ He sat tall, removed his glasses and cast his eye around the table. He spoke for a few moments, thanking the assembled company for their sterling efforts to make the airline a success. He paused when his scan reached Tom, and he nodded. Finally, he took a deep breath. ‘I have to advise that the Instone experience and that of other budding airlines confirm our own. So, regrettably, it is time to call a halt to Ferris International Airlines for the time being.’

Despite Daniel’s tuition, Tom felt decidedly uncomfortable in evening dress. It fitted remarkably well, but the wing collar and the black-capped shoes were just hellish to wear. He was still in a daze but had accepted that the airline business was just not ready to “fly” in the commercial sense. He was able to let free his emotional upset with Daniel as they dressed for dinner; he understood. “A dream shattered is a dream to rebuild”, Daniel hypothesised. Tom agreed but had no idea how his dream could be rebuilt. What now, he wondered?

Pre-dinner drinks were held in a long reception room, the Orangery. It was decorated with family paintings and some magnificent oils of the Ferris Shipping sailing ships of times of yore. Tom felt that he could take to the maritime world but his heart prevailed; flight is the boy for me, he told himself. Daniel was talking to him as they entered the room. It was crammed with about thirty or forty people, the gentlemen all in white dinner jackets, white bow ties and high-wing collars. Tom now felt that he was looking the part.

Almost immediately, he noticed a throng of young men clustered around some young ladies. Fran was amongst them and looked radiant. She was clearly the main source of the attention of these young "bloods". Daniel steered Tom away. 'Let me introduce you to my mother.'

Lady Ferris was gracious and attentive to Tom's aviation disappointment. He held himself back and didn't want to burden this noble lady with his petty woes. Dinner was served after about thirty minutes, and Tom was relieved to take a seat. He was even more pleased to be sitting next to Fran, much to the obvious chagrin of the young men who seemed determined to attract her attention earlier.

'I arranged this, you know,' she said, leaning into Tom. 'I'm very pleased. Thank you.'

'Good,' she said with an endearing wistful look.

Tom could feel eyes burning into him from across the table. 'I don't think these seating arrangements please your admirers, Fran.'

'Oh, them. They are always chasing after me. It's the inheritance, you know.'

'Isn't that a little unfair? I rather think that's not the only attraction.'

Fran cast her eyes down bashfully. 'I don't know what you mean.'

Tom smiled and gently nudged her. 'Now tell me about you—your interests, your ambitions, that sort of thing.'

'Oh, there's not much to tell. I've been rather trapped in this place, splendid though it is. Father tends to cosset me, protect me and doesn't let me… be myself. I think he is just looking for a suitable gentleman to take me off his hands. I did come out… into society, but all that did was attract the wrong sort.'

Tom nearly didn't ask the question, but he felt she was open to a wider discourse. 'What's the wrong sort?'

'Them,' Fran said, nodding discreetly across the table.

'Oh. I see that I may need to defend the damsel in distress then.'

Fran laughed. 'I might have to take you up on that.' She leaned into Tom again and whispered. 'It's quite an honour to be invited on a shoot by Father, you know.'

'Who's invited?

'You, of course. Didn't Daniel tell you?'

'Oh, yes, he did mention it. More borrowed clothes, I expect.'

Tom sighed and considered the next day's events. He was quickly distracted when his gaze fell upon the elaborate table setting. He counted twelve candles on each of the four candelabra, their flickering light illuminating the table and rosy cheeks of the quests. Sir Reginald sat at one end and Lady Ferris at the other. Silverware of all shapes and sizes and floral decorations with a Christmas theme filled most space apart for each setting. Tom counted the cutlery and wondered at the purpose of each. He knew the formality of working from the outside in for each course, but the extent of the cutlery still puzzled him. He touched the side plates and resisted the temptation to lift the plate and examine the underside.

'Fathers a collector,' said Fran. 'He's very proud of his Royal Crown Derby porcelain.' Her intuition was at work. She drew her gloved hand across the cutlery setting. 'Just watch everyone else; that's the secret.'

'We had some basic training in the RFC, but our formal dining was often in some rustic farmhouse, or a tent frequently illuminated with the flashes of distant gunfire. I was always in awe of the airmen who strove tirelessly to make our "officers mess" homely even if we did have a habit of destroying it when the evening got out of hand.'

Fran touched his arm again. 'Well, that's all gone. So, what's Captain Tom going to do now? I'm sorry to hear about the airline business.'

'Captain Tom, huh? Sounds like a storybook character.'

'I can do better than that. How does Captain Tommy sound?'

Tom giggled, which seemed to please Fran. 'A German pilot friend started calling me that. He probably was thinking of how our British soldiers were called "Tommies."'

'I think it sounds rather fun,' said Fran.

'Fun is not what's on my mind right now. You asked what was going to happen to me. The answer is I haven't given it much thought. I've only just learnt that I'm out of a job.'

A challenging main course of roast duck and the risk of dribbling the gravy gave little opportunity for conversation, but Fran and Tom swapped smiles frequently as they tackled their meal. Feeling such a positive, affectionate response from Fran caused Tom to muse over his relationships in recent times. His battle for Louisa, where he fell in love but lost out to her medical ambitions. And then there was Alice. Another independent, ambitious woman. That, according to Daniel Ferris, was where he was going wrong; "the wrong type for you, my dear chap", he had said. But love could be a divisive, truculent mistress when the "wrong types" were thrown together. He dared to admit that Alice was, again, the wrong type, but he was so powerfully attracted to her at times. He must get it right one day, he decided with another smiling glance at Fran.

The dinner came to an end with Lady Ferris inviting the ladies to "retire". Following an obvious display of the lady's finery as they made their way to a nearby anteroom, the gentlemen pushed their chairs back, loosened their ties and lit up fat cigars in clouds of smoke puffed with a gesture of liberation. Port was served, and Tom was struggling to keep up with the excesses of the evening. A year of frequent hardship in distant aerodromes or spartan accommodation had left him inadequately prepared for opulent dining. 'If you'll excuse me,' Tom said to his neighbours with a nod. 'I need a spot of fresh air, I think.'

The keen, chilly air hit Tom's senses as he tottered down the steps at the front of the floodlit house. He thought it better to stop for a moment and sat down firmly on the steps, feeling in need of a stable, stationary surface. After a few moments and with a very cold bottom, he decided to take a tour around the house to sober up. He was curious about the building. As he rounded the corner and strolled into the darkness, he could make out a long row of stables and other outbuildings and a cob-walled garden stretching far into the night. He could just see a long greenhouse building at the bottom of the garden and decided that he would explore further in the morning. He shivered and decided to head back. He turned and noticed two figures silhouetted in the floodlighting: one tall and lanky, the other, quite the opposite and carrying far too much weight. They stood, legs apart, arms akimbo, blocking his way.

The big fellow seemed to be the real troublemaker. 'Where are you going, "fly boy"?'

'Back to the dinner. It's a bit chilly, don't you think?'

'You should be used to this. Your head sticking out into the wind.'

Tom thought they were the two who seemed most perturbed by his conversation with Fran. He prepared for a bit of tussle. They were drunk, more so than himself, and drink could boost the audacity of young men. He knew he could deal with one, but two were more of a problem. 'Come on, chaps; there's no need for trouble. We've all had a little too much to drink, eh?'

Tom's suggestion had the opposite effect, and the big chap made a dash at him. Tom stepped aside and caught the man's arm as he went past. He spun him around, grabbed him by the lapels and head-butted him square on the nose. Hardly Marquess of Queensbury rules, just one of the many techniques learnt from Bill Franklin. Blood spurted into the air, and his scream of pain echoed into the night. Tom stood back and took a blow to his left cheek as the second man lunged forward. Another jink out of the way sent the man spinning to the ground when another figure joined the fray.

'Looks like you need a hand here, Tom.'

'Bill. Thank goodness,' he mumbled as he dodged another blow from '*Bloody Nose*', who had come back for more. Tom's former boxing prowess proved useful. He became lighter on his feet and efficiently dealt with the lunges from his attackers. One to one now, Bill gave one of the men a good hiding before standing back to watch Tom kick his man up the backside as he stumbled away from the fray. 'I think you've had enough, you two. Time for bed, I think?'

Bill pulled his man up to his feet and pushed him back to the house with a hefty kick to help him on his way.

'Just like old times?' said Bill.

'Yes, remember Hamburg?'

'Sure do.'

'Look, Bill, I'm sorry about how you and Jack are being treated.'

'Like menials, you mean?'

'Yes, I suppose so. Where are you eating and sleeping?'

'Servants' quarters. The dining room is down in the dungeons, and we sleep with the gods at the top of the house. It's not so bad. The staff are good to us. I hear that we're shooting or something tomorrow. I'm supposed to load shotguns. I've never seen one, let alone loaded one.'

Tom chuckled, 'You can be my loader then, you lucky chap!'

Tom clutched his forehead and stood in front of a mirror. He exhaled loudly and canted his head for a better view of his bruised cheek.

Daniel dug around in his chest of drawers and wardrobes. He looked at Tom's face like a doctor. 'I'll need to borrow some of Fran's makeup. Cover up that bruise. It's bound to raise eyebrows and questions. And you need to look the part again, Tom. Have you been on a shoot before? Handled a twelve-bore, and so on?'

'Handle a twelve-bore, but on an airfield and taking down clays.'

'A Holland and Holland twelve bore *Royal* perhaps?'

'I've no idea. We were just encouraged to develop the knack of aiming off, judging the lead, and aiming ahead of the target. You remember?'

'Well, the same applies to game shooting.'

'I assume you shoot too.'

'Of course, and Fran too. You won't believe how good a shot she is. Look, you'll do fine, but first, a bit of make-up and a good breakfast.'

The shooting party gathered by a rickety five-bar gate which bordered a long open field with tall pine trees down both sides. A cold mist hung over the field, and the beaters stirred this ethereal membrane as they made their way to a distant position to drive the birds to the guns. Bill Franklin looked bemused as he was instructed on carrying the *broken* shotgun and how to load the

12-bore cartridges. Daniel had ensured that Jack Parsons loaded for him. After suitable briefings, the shooting party began their trudge away from Branley House, and Tom was amused and impressed at how Fran strutted out confidently with the menfolk dressed from the waist up like the men but complemented by a heavy tweed skirt over her stout leather boots. She often looked back at Tom with a smile and carried her shotgun with practised ease. When it came to the shooting, Tom quickly got the hang of his *Royal* and bagged most of the birds he shot at. Similarly, Fran and Daniel performed well. Only Sir Reginald issued regular expletives as his birds got off scot-free.

Halfway through the morning, the shooting party was intercepted by two vehicles packed with hampers, and Branley House staff proceeded to serve neatly cut game sandwiches, mince pies, and hot toddies, a favourite of Sir Reginald's. Tom noticed Daniel's overtly friendly behaviour with Jack and wondered if Sir Reginald would see. He recalled Daniel's fondness for Jack and wondered if this relationship had been accepted in the family. He suspected not and winced at the thought as Sir Reginald approached.

'Enjoying the shoot, Munro?'

Tom expected Sir Reginald to avoid awkward conversations. He had effectively fired him the day before. 'Ah…yes, Sir. Very much so. Impressed with Fran's shooting.'

'Absolutely. Taught her myself,' said Sir Reginald, steering Tom away from the party. 'But Captain Munro, a word if you please.'

Tom could see that Daniel had noticed his father manoeuvring him away. He looked as if he had expected the conversation and nodded at Tom encouragingly.

'Look, Munro, I know the airline situation has been a big disappointment for you, but we all understand that conditions are not right for that line of business. For now, you are out of a job, are you not? Unless you have other plans.'

'Hardly, sir. It hasn't quite sunk in.'

'Good. I have a proposition for you then.'

'Well, I've nothing to lose now. Please carry on, sir.'

'How familiar are you with Fokker aeroplanes?'

'I've shot a few down, but otherwise, I only played with a D.VII, which we confiscated while we waited to be demobbed. It is a fine machine with beautifully balanced and coordinated controls. It has excellent turning performance…'

'That's fine. That's all I need. One of my contacts at the Fokker plant in Amsterdam has approached me.'

'I'm sorry, I don't understand. Approached for what exactly?'

'They want an experienced man to train pilots on their new range of civil machines.'

'Why me?'

'I'm trying to do you a favour, young man. It came

up in conversation, and you need a job.'

'So you know the Fokker people? And you knew about the illegal export of the Fokker D.VIIs on the Ferris Star?'

'Yes, and you should know, so did the British Government.'

Tom's expression stiffened, and he wanted to question Sir Reginald about Alice but restrained himself. Maybe Alice's report had filtered through to the government after all.

Sir Reginald continued. 'There was a strong view that we, the British Government, should not prevent the Fokker aeroplanes from being returned to the Netherlands. For my part, it was just good shipping business. And this new project is also good business for many reasons.'

Tom continued to look uneasy, and it showed. 'What new project?'

Sir Reginald became irritable. 'Look, why should I justify my actions to you, Munro?'

'I'm just interested in knowing what happened and even more interested in understanding your plans. If you want my help and participation, I want to be comfortable with the job.'

'Are you bothered about the young woman, Andrea, our shipping agent? That was unfortunate. Some German chap got a bit heavy-handed. I'm not sure why to this day. As I understand it, the Germans demanded that Fokker pay their taxes and they needed as much foreign currency as possible, hence the sale of surplus aeroplanes. And not just the machines we shipped on the Ferris Star. Would you believe it? In the end, they were shipped to Amsterdam by train. Incredible, but there you are.'

From Sir Reginald's reaction to the Alice incident on the Ferris Star, Tom deduced that he wasn't aware of Alice's SIS cover as the Ferris Shipping Agent in Hamburg. He could understand now that the SIS ploy to fake Alice's death could be helpful in maintaining a role for her. 'So, how will I be involved in this new project?'

'Right. Do you want the job or not?'

'Why don't they just employ a local pilot or a German familiar with their aeroplanes?'

'They don't want a German pilot. It will go down poorly with the Dutch people; they want someone with experience and an excellent pilot. That's you, Captain Munro. Your reputation precedes you. What d'you say?'

A shrill voice broke into their conversation. 'Tom. Come on, we're off again!' Fran shouted as she polished off her drink.

CHAPTER FOUR

The confines of Tom's home at Endless Street in Salisbury seemed incredibly cramped after the generous proportions of Branley House. On the drive back from Blandford, he meditated on his reconnection with Daniel's sister Fran and decided that she was someone he would like to see again. For the first time, a young woman had shown an apparent interest in him, a refreshing change after his experience over recent years.

Alice was often remote, distracted and just purely interested in herself and her projects. She was always kind to him, if a little snappy when challenged about her "projects". He didn't see much of Louisa as she continued her medical studies, but he was still attracted to her, although she had tactfully rejected any advances on his part. Their relationship was more like that of siblings. Tom's mother had willingly taken on the role of Louisa's surrogate parent after Sir George Foster's death. Louisa always returned to Endless Street when she wasn't engaged in lectures and hospital work at the London School of Medicine for Women. At least she was on her chosen path to becoming a doctor.

Tom was keen to talk through Sir Reginald's offer with someone. He hoped Louisa would be home. Fran would be biased. His mother was... a mother and just wanted him married and in a safe job, and Alice was never around. He thought about speaking to his friend Harry, but again, he would be biased, and there was always the risk that he might get pulled into SIS work again. He thought about this and felt that more spying work would not be too bad under the circumstances.

Surprisingly, Louisa was home. He felt his luck was in for once, and after his mother's usual grilling, he managed to move Louisa into the front room for some quiet one-on-one. 'I need to talk something through, Louisa,' he said pleadingly. He felt guilty, sidelining his mother, but they were simply on different planets.

'Oh, that sounds ominous,' Louisa quipped. 'I hope there's nothing wrong, Tom. After bending your ear over my medical ambitions, it must be your turn now.'

Tom described Sir Reginald's offer and ended his account with a note of concern. 'The trouble is, I always feel that Sir Reginald tells me half the story. There's more to his offer; I can feel it.'

Louisa shrugged. 'I don't think you have much choice. You're out of a job, and this opportunity feels to me that it could open doors. It sounds like your flying skills are much valued, so go ahead, I'd say. Do you want to run it past your mother? You'll be away from home a lot.'

'She's used to that now. Between us, we can keep an eye on things here in Salisbury. If I tell her too much, she worries. She wants me married and settled.' Tom paused and smirked. 'She feels the same about you too, Louisa, as you well know. Perhaps we should kill two birds with one stone and get married.'

Louisa poked him in the ribs. 'I think we've been through that particular possibility once or even twice before,' she said.

'Yes, I know. So, should I go ahead? Off to Amsterdam then?'

'Absolutely, and you can always write again. I did enjoy your wartime letters.'

Tom travelled by train and ferry to the Fokker factory at Veere in Zeeland, the most westerly region of the Netherlands. He had assumed he would be going to Amsterdam and was disheartened at the remoteness of his new home as he travelled from Antwerp and across the border into Zeeland. The Veere plant was originally a naval facility on the coast and flying took place at a military airfield at Souberg, about ten kilometres to the south-west. He travelled with a small suitcase, wore as much clothing as possible and topped his sartorial bulk with his leather flying coat to save space. His contact at the Fokker factory was Mr. Aart Drukker, who met him at the last station stop in Middelburg. Aart spoke good English, which seemed to be common in Holland.

His accommodation in Veere was a charming flat on top of a small bakery, which pleased Tom as he awoke in the morning to the delightful aroma of fresh baking. Better than an alarm clock, he felt. The factory comprised a random collection of warehouses, halls, hangars and huts dispersed along the riverfront, which included a wide launching ramp for the seaplane operations of times gone by. Tom shared an office with two other pilots, and became acquainted with Anthony Fokker, who frequently visited and often flew the aeroplanes. Tom immediately took to Fokker, and they spoke frequently about aeroplane handling and performance, but he was always in a rush. Tom felt like suggesting that he slow down, but he decided that was not his place. Over the first few weeks at Veere, Tom flew any machines he could. The Fokker pilots seemed to appreciate his skill, mainly as he was one of the few who had seen combat.

'We have a new machine for you to try, Tom,' said Drukker one clear blue morning.

This suggestion produced a broad smile. 'What is it then?'

'You've flown many of our types now, so it's time to try something very new. It's an F.II. The problem is, the machine is still in Germany, at our old Schwerin works. Mr Fokker wants it back in Amsterdam to demonstrate to the Dutch airline, KLM. Can you do that?'

'Of course, but I'll need to get familiar with the machine. Will the authorities let it out of Germany?'

Drukker shrugged. 'That's the problem. The Spartacus Union seems to have much power now in Germany and is unlikely to sanction the flight. It may have to be... "stolen".'

Tom felt that suspicious feeling once again. Why

should he be singled out for this flight? He recalled his strong reservations when Sir Reginald suggested the Fokker job. He didn't ask too many questions then and now felt the same caution. Intuition? He used to be amused by Louisa and Alice's so-called female intuition, but he was now convinced that it was a powerful force. He didn't question Drukker any further. 'Tell me about the F.II. It sounds like I will have to jump in and go without any familiarisation.'

'It's an exciting new machine, the future, I believe. It is a high-wing monoplane with a single engine and all-metal construction. There's space for four passengers and a two-seat cockpit under the wing leading edge. As I say, the future for a while at least.'

'And the engine?' said Tom excitedly.

'A 185 hp BMW.'

Tom nodded, his fears allayed and felt invigorated by the new work and the secretive nature of the assignment. He admitted to himself that he hankered after some excitement again. He stopped abruptly when he recognised somebody walking past in the passageway outside Drukker's office. He recognised the tall figure with an eye patch instantly. It was Heinrich Wolf, the Reichswehr officer he knew of old. Tom froze, then forced a smile.

'Is something wrong, Tom?' said Drukker, following Tom's gaze.

He answered hesitantly. 'Who's that man? He just left the building.'

'Hmm, you should keep quiet about that gentleman and stay out of his way. You won't normally see him. Mr Fokker is up to all sorts of schemes, usually to make money, but some projects are kept very secret. Just don't ask. Concentrate on your flying duties. Much safer, believe me.'

Tom couldn't hide a look of suspicion but decided to leave the subject. 'When do I go to Schwerin?'

'Tomorrow. The weather looks OK. Here's a note from Mr Fokker. I don't know what's in it, but he says it has all you need to know.'

When Tom returned to Veere, he had been away for nearly two weeks. He had the distinct impression that someone wanted him out of the way, and people sometimes responded to him as if they didn't expect to see him again. The staff at Schwerin had not been aware of the need to return the aeroplane to Amsterdam, and he was treated with suspicion and hidden from most workers at the factory. Fokker's letter had merely said that getting the machine back to Veere was important and that nobody should know of the plans, even the people at Schwerin.

'I did all I could to get the machine back, but it kept failing,' he reported to Drukker. 'The last engine problem happened when I had no chance of a decent landing, and the damage was too bad to repair, as Mr Fokker knows. He came to see the machine and arranged for it to be shipped back in pieces. I don't think he was very pleased and didn't speak to me.'

'Well, not to worry. Your reputation remains intact. In fact, as you have much experience with the Croydon journey, we want you to help with the new KLM flights. They want an experienced pilot on the Fokker F.II for the Amsterdam—Croydon route, so that's you.'

'If you think so, I'm happy to try it. I hope the machines are more reliable.'

'Good. I'll get that organised,' said Drukker. 'Oh, and there's some mail for you—on your desk.'

CHAPTER FIVE

Harry Price and Alice Ferguson felt encouraged by the resurgent SIS interest in their Russia/Germany project. "C" rushed into the room in his usual brusque fashion and plopped down with a notepad at the ready. He lost no time in getting to the point.

'As you may know, Ferguson, we have managed to get Tom Munro into Fokker employment, and he can now be instructed to keep an eye on the activities there,' said C, looking pleased with himself. 'We have no embassy staff in Moscow, as you know, after the revolution, so monitoring activities in Russia will not be easy. What do we know about Fokker and Russia, if anything?'

Alice felt particularly buoyant after hearing that she was to head up the overseas investigation into possible Russian-German military cooperation. In fact, she believed that it was inevitable, not just possible. 'I don't believe that Mr Anthony Fokker is politically motivated. I would say that he is simply interested in doing good business wherever that might be. A sharp businessman as well as a talented pilot, I've been told. As I am almost certain that the Reichswehr is involved in developing some form of cooperation with the Russians, we must monitor their movements and any travel into Russia. We will need our people to watch them in Germany and when they travel to Russia. Tracking their movements in Russia will be more of a challenge. I'm talking about known suspects, specifically General Friedrich von Mayer, Colonel Otto von der Lang and Captain Heinrich Wolf of course. My problem is that they know me, certainly von der Lang and Wolf, and they believe me dead. So I am not able to get close to these gentlemen.'

'What do you suggest? said C.

'Harry and I have discussed this. We need someone relatively free to move in and out of Russia from Germany. We have Paul Drummond in the country, but he will need some direction when we identify people of interest. We could do with a briefing on conditions in Russia. The Foreign Office people could do that.'

C nodded. 'Good idea. Arrange a briefing, Price, will you?'

'Yes, sir.'

'Are you thinking of Tom Munro for that. someone who is relatively free to move around, by chance?'

Alice jumped in and looked at Harry. 'You beat us to it. Yes, sir. We will need to get his ideas on how to do this. His best bet could be the Fokker company. He tells me that their aeroplanes and those of the German company, Junkers are causing quite a stir. The Dutch airline KLM is going to use them. I'm told it has something to do with the all-metal construction and enclosed passenger cabins.

C looked up from making notes. 'Right, Harry, get in touch with Munro, on a secure line, obviously, and see what he can suggest. Are aircraft flying into Russia from Germany yet? That could be a way of getting Munro onto the trail of the Reichswehr's people. I have no doubt that this will be dangerous work.'

'I've written to get him to call in, sir. He's been away from the Focker factory at Veere on some job ferrying aircraft from Germany. I'll get him to call from our embassy.'

C glanced back and forth between Harry and Alice. 'Good. Let me know when you have some suggestions, you two and we'll meet again. Don't delay. I want to get this moving.'

Tom called Harry in response to his letter. 'Is that Harry?'

'Yes, it is; who's calling? The line's pretty bad.'

'It's Tom Munro. Can you hear me?'

'Only just Tom. I've been expecting your call.'

Tom furrowed his brow and turned to view the office and the hallway outside. 'I have to keep my voice down. I'm calling from my office. Why the urgency? Your letter seemed quite jumpy.'

'Can't say on this line, Tom. What are you up to?'

'I'm back in Veere, but before my trip I saw a certain German gentleman at the Fokker works that I'd rather not see again.'

'Right. That's interesting if I understand you correctly. Look, wherever you are, can you call me again from our embassy? Look up Fritz Uttenbogaart and call me back. We need to talk urgently. When will you be able to do that?'

'I will have to find a reason to go to the Hague. Leave that with me. I hope to get back to you in a few days.

'Good. Stay safe and watch out. There's growing danger out there, and I fear you may be heading towards it.

'What do you mean? Sorry, silly me, need to know.'

'It's serious, Tom. Just call me soonest. I need to pick your brains.'

Alice Ferguson was prepared with a notepad at the ready as she awaited the Foreign Office representative's summary of conditions in Russia. Harry Price was also present and fiddled continuously with his pen. She expected the worst about Russia and wracked her brains for some way that she could be able to operate in Russia to track any German military activity. She was convinced this would be happening but given that she was known to the Reichswehr and was supposed to be dead, she would need to keep clear of the Reichswehr officers. The lack of an embassy or consulate meant that there would be no safe haven in Russia. She was thinking of closely monitoring the Reichswehr people in Germany and any travel they might make to Russia. This should lead them to any sites of military cooperation. She wondered if a disguise was an option, but in any event, she or anyone else would need a legitimate reason to travel into and around Russia.

C introduced Mr George Jeffreys from the Foreign Office, who looked very dapper in a smart wool tweed suit, stiff wing collar, and garish tie. 'We want a general feel for conditions in Russia,' said C. 'We need to know how easy it will be for our people to move around.'

Jeffreys embarked on a lengthy and detailed exposition covering the Russian revolution in 1917 and the years that followed. Alice found it exciting but decided that she just needed to know the conditions today and what they would face if they travelled to Moscow. Eventually, she put her pen down and glanced at C. She detected a similar impatience for the facts that were relevant to them.

C interrupted Jeffreys. 'We appreciate the complexities of the Russian situation, but we need to concentrate on what is relevant to us now. Can we please deal with that?'

'Yes, I understand. Well, the conditions are difficult in the extreme. Politically, we finally see the end of the civil war. Still, the British military and financial and logistical support for the counter-revolutionary forces does not put us in the best light with Lenin and his Bolsheviks. Nevertheless, since early 1920, the British Government has been trying to reach a trade agreement with Russia, which looks promising. From your perspective, it could mean easier movement into and out of the country. Lloyd George proposed a four-point plan: an armistice, an end to hostile propaganda, the exchange of prisoners, a mutual understanding of outstanding debts and an exchange of trade missions. I mention these details so that you can see that there should be good prospects for cover stories for your people and legitimate reasons for travel into and around the country.'

'How likely is this trade agreement?' said C.

'Quite likely, although some people are unhappy about negotiating with the Russians, notably Mr Churchill and my boss at the Foreign Office, Lord Curzon.'

'That's understandable. But what of Russian security services? The Cheka?'

'Still, an evil force to be reckoned with. A form of secret police, originally set up by Lenin in 1917 to protect the revolution from reactionary forces or "class enemies"; the bourgeoisie and members of the clergy, for example.'

Alice was busy making notes now and looked up from her notepad. 'To move around freely with these people on our heels, we must have rock-solid identities. I've heard about their methods of torture.'

'Yes, you don't want to get in the way of "Chekists". You should also know that we are receiving information about growing famine in Russia. After WWI, Lenin initially refused help for his starving people, but just this month, he has allowed relief organisations to bring in aid. Speaking cynically, this could be another route into the country for you. Organisations such as the

American Overseas Relief Organisation, the British *Feed the Children Fund*, and others.'

'We have been getting the same reports from our people,' said C. 'We probably have a good flavour of the situation, George. Thank you for your time, and do let us know if any further developments could be relevant to us.'

C turned to Alice and Harry. 'Your thoughts. Harry first?'

'Yes, sir. Are we getting any reports from Drummond? I am still waiting to receive something.'

'Good point, but nothing of any military relevance and what he does report just confirms what Jeffreys outlined. A lot of political turbulence and reports of famine.'

'Thank you. We need to start at the source of the threat, the Reichswehr. We will have the leads we need if we can track their staff into Russia. So, we must monitor and follow von Mayer, von der Lang and their staff.'

Alice responded when C glanced in her direction. 'It will be easy to set up surveillance of the Reichswehr staff but following them into Russia will be more difficult. How will they travel? Who knows?'

Harry raised a finger. 'If I might add here, Tom Munro is well installed in the Fokker organisation, and I have arranged for him to call from the embassy. He has spotted someone whom he thinks he knows. He couldn't say anything on the telephone, but I think he meant our friend Captain Heinrich Wolf. That is significant as it indicates some ongoing activity with the Germans.'

'Remind me. Who's Heinrich Wolf? What's the significance of this fellow?'

'Captain Heinrich Wolf seems to be Colonel von der Lang's right-hand man. Not only that, he's a ruffian and a tough fellow who kills when necessary. If Colonel von der Lang or the Reichswehr commander, General Friedrich von Mayer are involved in something, Wolf turns up. He's like a beacon of Reichswehr clandestine activity. Wolf tortured Munro and Bill Franklin in Berlin when they were under suspicion for spying so Wolf would recognise Tom Munro. We believe he was also responsible for Alice's accident in Hamburg. Tom will need to be very careful.'

'You need to speak to Munro, Price.'

'Yes, I hope he will be calling very shortly.'

Alice nodded approvingly. 'That's exciting news. Tom, sorry, Captain Munro might be in an ideal position to monitor German activity if Fokker is involved. The aeroplanes that Anthony Fokker shipped back from Germany might be destined for Russia.'

'Get that call into Munro, Harry, and tell me what he is learning about Fokker. See what ideas he might have.'

'Yes, sir.'

'At last, Tom. What took you so long,' said Harry, sounding unusually sharp.

‘I had to find a reason to travel from Veere. I just mentioned that I needed to extend my passport, and they seemed to accept that.’

‘Good. Well, what’s going on at Fokker?’

‘Firstly, I assume you understood my description of Heinrich Wolf at the Fokker plant?’

‘Yes, go on.’

‘All I can say is that I’ve seen him and been warned off. Something is going on, probably the supply of aeroplanes to Germany. It can only be the Special Group R project.’

‘Can you learn as much as you can? We must find a secure way to communicate with you other than from the embassy. Leave that with me. Have you met up with Uittenbogaart?’

‘Yes, seems a good type.’

‘See if he can arrange a secure telephone connection near your work or accommodation.’

‘Right, will do. For your information, I am being used to train customer airlines on Fokker’s new F.II and soon the F. III machines, which are proving popular. I’ve been flying with KLM people and heard that *Deruluft*, an air transport company, may start services into Russia from Germany. I have been thinking that route could be used by Reichswehr staff. I could follow them, see what they’re up to.’

‘Sounds interesting but dangerous.’

‘That’s what I thought. How’s Alice, by the way?’

‘She’s involved in this project but can’t get too close for obvious reasons, and not in Germany.’

‘She could always work in disguise. Take some tips from Drummond.’

‘Possible. I’ll see what Alice thinks. I know she wants to be on the front line.’

‘I’m flying some KLM services to Croydon so I could meet up with her.

‘Yes, but don’t let C think you’re getting involved with her. You know what he thinks about fraternising with staff. You know, relationships on the job.’

‘I know. Let me fish around here, and I’ll get in touch. Oh, just a thought, Harry. It would be good to have Bill back on board. He’s a good man to have around when things get tough.’

‘How would that work?’

‘Work for the SIS. I know he’s kicking his heels.

‘That’s out of the question. Bill’s American.’

‘I think I’m aware of that.’

‘Look, we’ll get support organised once we have a plan. For now, let me know if you discover anything of interest.

CHAPTER SIX

Harry, Alice and Tom met in a London safe house. Harry opened his file and took a deep breath. 'C wants me to devise a plan, and that's why we're here. It's my project, and I will head it back here. Alice will be in charge of arrangements overseas – wherever that might be. I think it will be helpful to recap.

We know that the Germans are investigating some sort of military cooperation with another power, and we suspect it's the Russians. Our evidence is not convincing enough for the government, and our job is to find that evidence and report back—no more, no less. So, the operation must be covert, invisible, with no close contact, and we must not arouse suspicions. That's a direct order from the government.

'Why the sensitivity?' Tom asked.

Harry seemed irritated by the question. 'I don't know exactly, but relationships are difficult in Europe. Everyone seems to be casting about for trade and other arrangements. The ongoing trade negotiations between us and the Russians, for example. We must accept that we need to tread carefully and that our activities must be totally clandestine. Getting back to our meeting today, what do we know to date? There are three officers of interest to us in the Reichswehr in Berlin: General Friedrich von Mayer, the Commander; Colonel Otto von der Lang, his number two; and Captain Heinrich Wolf. As you've reported, Tom, there seems to be some connection between these gentlemen and the Fokker works in the Netherlands, and now you can monitor that.

'I mentioned that I'd seen Heinrich Wolf at Fokkers,' said Tom.

'Yes, so that confirms a link of some kind, as I said.'

Alice shuffled about in her seat and twiddled her pen. 'So, we need to follow our German friends. See where they go. I'm known to the General, the Colonel, and Wolf, so I can't get too close. Von der Lang was getting a bit sweet on me, but that doesn't help much now.'

Tom smirked. 'You can always get up a disguise.'

'That's not as mad as it sounds,' said Alice. 'I just can't get too close.'

'They will travel by car around Berlin, but for overseas trips, who knows. It could be by air or train, so it won't be easy to tail them without a good-size team of people,' Tom added. 'I expect we'll need at least three people to…'

Harry butted in. 'Yes, we need people in Berlin to monitor and shadow these targets. Two or three at least, and we'll need vehicles. We should get to know their travel plans to other countries, and at that point, we'll have to set up similar monitoring of their movements in that country. We're pretty certain it's Russia, but that remains to be seen.'

Tom raised a hand. 'I think I mentioned that I may

be able to wangle a job with a German/Russian airline, Deruluft. That would get me my cover story for being in Russia. And you never know, the Reichswehr people may travel by Deruluft?'

That would be very convenient,' said Harry optimistically. 'Can you explore that further, Tom? Let me know.'

'Yes. On the Berlin surveillance work, who will shadow the Reichswehr people?'

'Our man Jim Dalton, who's already based at the embassy,' Harry replied.

Tom shook his head. 'I've met him before. He was useless.'

'Well, he's our SIS station officer in Berlin. His cover is the consulate officer which gives him excellent freedom of action. Also, he happens to know the lie of the land, is fluent in German, and is particularly adept at finding informers. He's also been watching the Reichswehr building, the Bendlerblock, and logging movements. And he's onto a couple of individuals who might be ripe for turning.'

'You'll need to be there, Alice,' said Harry. 'And the idea of a disguise is starting to be essential. You'll need to keep clear of the targets.'

'The whole disguise thing is starting to appeal. In fact, it will be essential in Germany. Leave it to me; even you won't recognise me once I'm finished, Harry.'

Harry made some notes. 'Yes, and if Russia is involved, you could be part of a trade delegation, Alice.'

Tom remembered how difficult it was to obtain hard intelligence on the Reichswehr's activities. 'I'm wondering about the evidence our ministers are going to find convincing.'

'Photographs, documents, witness statements,' said Harry. 'But photographs above all.'

'If you're flying into Russia, Tom, you should get some opportunities,' said Harry, giving Tom a thumbs-up gesture. 'Let me know about your movements and arrangements in Holland, particularly your possible job with Deruluft.'

'Will do.'

Harry checked his watch. 'I've got another meeting. I think we're finished here. Look after Tom, Alice. Show him out when you are done.'

When Tom and Alice were left alone, there was an awkward silence for a while.

'Well, Tom, back into action again,' said Alice. 'I can't wait to get back to Berlin.'

'Are you really going in disguise?'

'Yes, I'll have to.'

'I can't wait to see what you'll do. It's not as if you can cut your hair or grow a moustache.'

'The next time you see me, I will be in Berlin. See if you recognise me, eh?'

Tom's looked down at his notes and flicked through the pages.

'I know that look, Tom. What is it?'

He took a deep breath. 'When we last spoke, you talked glibly about not only finding out what the Germans are up to but also stopping it. Don't you think that's a bit ambitious? Remember what C said. Observe and report.'

Alice shrugged. 'Maybe, but first, let's see what they're up to. What are you doing this evening?'

'Back to Salisbury first, then off to see Daniel Ferris and his father, hopefully.'

'Want to stop over at my place?'

Tom's endearing smile returned. 'That would be really nice, in fact, a splendid idea.'

It was getting dark – a cold winter afternoon and Tom stood cowering against the gusty wind. He turned his collar up as Alice fiddled with the key. He leant forward and peered over Alice's shoulder. 'Are you all right?'

'Sorry, mind on other things. I need to fix this damn lock.'

'Good idea. One day, it won't work, and then you'll be in a stew. I'll have a look at it?'

'I'd appreciate that.' With a bang and a targeted thump, the door groaned open with some obvious resistance. 'There, success.'

'God, Alice, that door's in a state. It was the same on my last visit. Have you any oil?'

'Don't be silly, I'm not that organised.'

'Let me have a look at it. I don't want you getting

locked out.'

'Right, you are. I'll get something on the go. I wasn't expecting guests, you understand.'

Tom dumped his overnight bag in the hallway as Alice rummaged in her larder. He spent a few minutes examining the door. Alice's little place was just as he remembered it, tidy but lacking in identity, strangely soulless and nothing of Alice. It reminded Tom that he knew so little about her other than she seemed to be very alone in the world. Parents and brother lost in the war. He wondered what that would be like. She must have some friends. He had his mother, Louisa, Daniel and Bill. And Ferris Airlines was a community of aviation nuts who loved being around aeroplanes. That was gone now, and he suddenly felt an affinity with Alice's nomadic existence as he was also cast adrift and living a directionless lifestyle. Yes, he would like to better understand Alice's world. He decided that he would try to find out. He had tried before on their fateful trip to Finland and on other occasions but never had much success. His curiosity was aroused again.

'Look, Alice. Here's your problem.'

'What?'

'The door's barely on its hinges. Most of the screws are loose. It's dropped down and fouling. And the lock is misaligned, hence your key problems.'

'Can you fix it?'

'Do you have a screwdriver… I know. Shouldn't

have asked.'

'Don't be so quick to judge,' Alice announced.

Much jostling of cutlery and rattling of drawers didn't generate much confidence in Tom until Alice reacted as if she had scored a goal. 'Yes. Here we are. Impressed, I hope.' She grabbed the screwdriver and rushed over to Tom. He was crouched down to examine the door hinges and felt proud of his successful diagnosis. Alice knelt beside him, and he turned to take the screwdriver. They froze, both registering their closeness. Tom's face reddened. Alice smiled, and she kissed him, a long, affectionate kiss on the cheek.

She moved away with a glint in her eye. 'We'd better get the door fixed first; I think.'

Tom blew a long breath with puffed-out cheeks. 'Ah, yes. I'll need something to support the door while I tighten the screws.'

CHAPTER SEVEN

It took a long time to find a taxi at 6 am. Tom flopped down with some relief when the Beardmore cab pulled up beside him. He needed the early start to reach Salisbury in time to collect his mother's Bullnose Morris and drive to Blandford and the Ferris home at Branley House. His mother had inherited the car from Louisa's father after his death, and she took wonderful care of the little car. Tom had learnt to drive in this very car, and it held special memories for him.

Whilst travelling by train from Waterloo to Salisbury, his mind was immersed in his night with Alice. An unexpected pleasure. The last memory was of a sleeping Alice lying provocatively beneath a thin white sheet, her form perfectly and tantalisingly portrayed as if she was trying to entice him to disturb her slumber. He had resisted, grabbed his clothes and went downstairs to dress. He crept out the door with a satisfied grin as it now closed perfectly behind him.

Travelling from Salisbury, he welcomed the chilly air to bring him to his senses. He wanted to take time with his journey following his evening with Alice and to prepare for Daniel Ferris's usual demanding enthusiasm. Slow horse-drawn carts and wayward cattle helped to impede his progress. The little Morris struggled with the slow climb out of Salisbury, and the engine seemed to breathe a sigh of relief on the gradual descent down to Coombe Bissett, with its sparkling river running close to the road. In a while, he was passing Martin Down. He remembered his walks there with his father just before he died and their speculation over the origins of the mysterious *Bockerly Dyke.* Then on to Tarrant Hinton, Pimperne and through Blandford's busy market to Branley House just short of Winterbourne Stickland.

He was looking forward to seeing Daniel Ferris and his sister Fran again. He resolved to remember to call him Daniel rather than Ferris, the name he was known by on 62 Squadron. When he met Fran some months ago, the young lady surprised him with her attention. He wondered if she would behave in the same way if Sir Reginald Ferris was at home. What would be said? Tom was still very uncertain about how much Sir Reginald knew about Anthony Fokker's activities. Should he probe on that subject? He was a spy, too, after all.

He had pulled up at the front of the house, still deep in thought when he was disturbed from his reverie. 'Tom Munro. My dear chap. So good to see you,' said Daniel Ferris with his beaming smile.

'I see the sticks are gone, Daniel.'

'Yes, fully fit and ready to take on the world. Come in, come in. Let's hear all your news. It's been months. Fran can't wait to see you.'

Branley House always impressed Tom, and he noticed

the smell of fresh paint and a slight change in the colour scheme in the hallway. Daniel grabbed Tom by the elbow and towed him into one of the many reception rooms. He recalled his visit last year when Ferris Airlines had been shut down, grounded, and placed in administration. Whatever terminology he chose to think of, it still rankled. He resolved to get back into civil flying again. For now, he just had to resolve the questions about German activities. Alice certainly spurred him on, but for his conscience, he just needed to find out what devious schemes were being formulated at the Reichswehr. The thought of stopping the mysterious goings-on was another matter, but he felt increasingly convinced they should act, not just report. After all, what good had reporting done in the past? The government had simply ignored their suspicions. Not just suspicions: they *knew* something was up. Any form of intervention would take an army of people. The evidence would be vital. Perhaps they should…

'Thomas, Munro, you're not listening.'

'Sorry, Ferris.'

'So, tell me, what are you up to these days? You first, but I have some news which you might find interesting.'

'There have been a lot of changes. I can't keep up with it. As you know, with your father's help, I got a job at the Fokker firm in Amsterdam, although I have been working out of Veere, nearby. Then, I've been training new pilots on the Fokker aeroplanes, interesting machines and very much the future. They are all metal structures and British engines, more often than not. More recently, I've been seconded to Koninklijke Luchtvaart Maatschappij.'

'Good God, Tom, what does that mean?'

Tom smirked. 'I'm just showing off my Dutch language skills. The new Dutch airline loosely translated means the Royal Aviation Company. It's known as KLM now. Much easier.'

'Definitely,' said Daniel.

'I'm flying the Fokker F.II on the Croydon-Amsterdam route. It's a strange-looking machine, a high-wing monoplane sitting nose in the air on a long undercarriage. The KLM version is powered by a 250-hp Armstrong Siddeley Puma engine. The passengers have an enclosed cabin, but we pilots are still out in the draught. I've got a windscreen, but I think I'll try to get the cockpit fully enclosed.'

'That seems like a good idea, Tom.'

'Looks like I'm on the move again. A bit hush-hush, so don't say anything – to your father particularly.'

'You're not up to your secret games again with that Alice woman?'

'No, I mean, it's commercially hush-hush. Don't speak about Alice like that. She's just a spirited, independent lady.'

Daniel didn't look convinced. 'Hmm. My news might not be quite so relevant then.'

'That depends, Daniel. Go on, spill the beans.'

'Oh. Look, here's Fran.'

Tom stood smartly and took Fran's hand for a brief kiss – an almost outmoded gesture, but Tom still found it appropriate in exceptional circumstances. The ladies seemed to appreciate it, and Fran certainly did from her smiling and coy mien.

'And how is our Thomas Munro these days?' Fran purred with a very seductive look.

It caught Tom unawares. He thought she had matured amazingly in a matter of months. 'I'm keeping well, Fran, just dashing about somewhat.'

'You should come and stay for a few days. Do some shooting, play golf, and swim in the river. Not at this time of the year, of course. Have you seen Father? He'd like to hear how things are going with your flying in the Netherlands. Has Daniel told you about the amazing coincidence?'

'Ah, no.'

Daniel sat forward in his seat. 'I was just about to tell you.'

'Go on then.'

'Father is doing some business with Foster's Engineering with Robert Foster.'

'He does own the company,' said Tom.

'Well, Foster's is supplying British aero engines for the Fokker company, and Father is shipping them. It's an amazing coincidence, don't you think?'

'I suppose it is. Do you know what engines? Fosters don't make engines.'

'He doesn't seem to want to discuss the project in detail.'

'Interesting. Maybe he'll tell me being a Fokker man now – well, for the time being.'

'Would you like to speak to him? He's in his study.'

Tom felt his newly acquired espionage instincts prickle. 'Why not?'

Daniel took Tom through the house, which seemed to take five minutes, and Fran trailed along until they reached a heavy oak door. A shouty voice boomed out even with the door closed, and Tom prepared for his 'interview'. Daniel waited outside the study until there was silence, then knocked slowly and deliberately three times as if it were some kind of code.

Tom recognised Sir Reginald's voice. 'I'm busy, Daniel.'

'I've got Tom Munro with me.'

'Does he have an appointment?'

The conversation through the door continued. 'Of course not, Father.'

'I'm joking; come in.'

Sir Reginald Ferris sat behind the most enormous desk Tom had ever seen, with two carver chairs strategically positioned on the opposite side of Sir Reginald. A vast collection of books and beautifully detailed ship models in glass cases decorated the three walls surrounding the desk. Sir Reginald gestured to the other side of the room, which was clearly laid out as a lounge area in the generous study. Once they were seated, Sir Reginald rang a small bell, resulting in the bookshelves opening up to reveal a smart, bespectacled lady of mature years. Sir Reginald clutched his hands together. 'So, what are we having?'

After arranging refreshments, Sir Reginald turned his attention to Tom. 'Now tell me, how are things with your work at Fokkers?'

'All is well. I told Daniel that I would soon be helping out at KLM, the new Dutch airline, and overseeing the training of their pilots on the Fokker F.II and the F.III.'

'How do you get on with their people?'

'The Fokker staff seem distant, but that's probably the language. I'm picking it up reasonably well, but everyone wants to try their English.'

'See anything – interesting?'

'I'm not sure what you mean.'

'New aeroplanes, military machines, that sort of thing.'

Tom felt the need to be circumspect with his response. 'I am kept well away from anything military.'

'I see. Has Daniel mentioned our new project and our business with Foster's Engineering?'

'Yes, he has. Quite a coincidence.' Tom said pointedly.

'You will know I have a standing relationship for

shipping Fokker machines. Fosters was a coincidence.'

Tom decided to be direct. 'Where are the engines coming from?'

Daniel winced, and Fran shifted noticeably in her seat. They both knew there was a way of speaking to their father, and straight questions were rarely well received.

'Not at liberty to say.'

'Oh, right, I understand. Top secret then?'

Direct questions were one thing, but impudence was another in Sir Reginald's book. He looked over his half-moon glasses. 'This is not a conversation we should be having, Captain Munro. I'd avoid nosing around military matters when you return to Fokkers. It's a bit sensitive, you see. I think we should turn to another subject that should interest you, Tom.'

Tom appreciated the opportunity to change the subject, although he wanted to question Sir Reginald further. He decided it was hardly the time or place, as he could feel Daniel and Fran's discomfort radiating like the glow from hot coals. Fran had virtually disappeared into her chair.

'What would that be, sir?'

'Things are starting to move again with our British airlines. You may have heard that the Secretary of State for Air, Sir Samuel Hoare, appointed a committee to examine airline problems, particularly the cross-channel routes.

'Yes, I have been monitoring developments, but I don't think I can do anything about them.'

'Well, the report recently recommended that a new commercial organisation be created on sound business grounds, including a more substantial government subsidy—one million pounds over ten years was mentioned.'

Daniel joined in the discussion. 'What form will this organisation take, do you think?'

'From my understanding, they are talking about a national airline involving assets and personnel from the existing businesses: Daimler Hire, Handley Page, Instone and others.'

'We could have been part of that,' said Daniel.

Sir Reginald huffed. 'Except that I would have lost a lot of money.'

Tom's enthusiasm began to fade. 'Oh well, maybe something for the future. For now I have my Fokker work, but I still believe in a bright future for the aeroplane. Trans-Atlantic flying across Europe and beyond. There should be no limit once we have the engines with the power and the airframes with the capacity to carry more passengers.'

Sir Reginald stood abruptly. 'I must get on and assume you should be off back to Holland, Tom.'

'Yes, I'm scheduled to fly the Wednesday KLM flight back to Amsterdam. I can't say I'm looking forward to it. The spring weather is a devil: totally unpredictable, with frequent fog and damn cold. I will plead for enclosed cockpits despite the resistance of many pilots. I'm sure Anthony Fokker will listen. He's all for embracing new ideas.'

The Croydon Aerodrome looked particularly bleak as Tom arrived by taxi. Low cloud and light drizzle suggested he would have to delay his departure. The traffic on Plough Lane was held up by a Handley Page O/400 aeroplane, which was being towed over the crossing to the maintenance hangars on the old WWI Waddon airfield. The colossal machine dwarfed the people and motor cars congregating at the barrier. Tom gave up waiting, paid off the taxi driver and sneaked under the barrier to walk the remaining half mile along Plough Lane to the KLM office. Croydon Aerodrome had grown considerably in recent months, although the single-story, white-painted buildings seemed to be scattered haphazardly. A raised tower with a 360-degree view of the airfield had been added; a Control Tower, he was told.

As he walked up the main road towards the customs control, he saw his KLM Fokker F.II parked on the field, waiting with that familiar, impatient nose-in-the-air look. His first port of call was the new meteorological office, and the glum expression on the forecaster's face conveyed what Tom already knew. 'Low cloud all the way to the Channel. Not expected to clear until noon, I'm afraid,' he said apologetically. Another glance out of the window reinforced Tom's decision to delay his departure. He wouldn't be popular. Most passengers accepted his decision with a shrug without the need for an explanation. He could spot the nervous travellers; they looked relieved.

He needed to keep his passengers informed. He strolled into the little waiting room where two gentlemen sat reading newspapers, and a third stood looking out of the window with his back to him. The two passengers acknowledged the news of the delay reluctantly. However, the figure at the window didn't move, standing stock still, peering out over the airfield with the unflinching stare of a Buckingham Palace guard. Tom felt he was trying to avoid recognition, which would be difficult in a small aeroplane. Suddenly, Tom realised who it was – Robert Foster, Louisa's less-than-favourite uncle. He had to introduce himself. 'Mr Foster, good morning. Sorry about the delay, but we'll get you to Amsterdam just a few hours behind schedule.'

Foster turned around with a scowl. 'Damned inconvenient. This is no way to run an airline. I should have gone by train. I'll be having words.'

Tom responded to the back of Robert Foster's head as he resumed his gaze across the airfield. 'Well, it's my job to get you to your destination safely, and the weather is just not suitable until midday.' He directed the remainder of his words to the rest of the passengers, who had frowned at Foster's boorishness. 'Thank you for your patience. I'll keep you advised of any changes, but we should be able to get away at twelve.'

As the morning wore on, the low scudding stratus clouds lifted and cleared away to the north, and Tom made a slow but careful inspection of his aeroplane before supervising the loading of the baggage: post office bags and an assortment of small boxes.

When everything was ready, he waved to the KLM office to advise the passengers to board and clambered into his cockpit. As always, when flying the F.II, he offered the seat alongside him to any agile passenger who could complete the climb and would be prepared to brave the open cockpit. On this occasion, his offer was accepted, and he took some time to strap in his companion and explain the controls. The remaining three passengers chose the relative comfort of the enclosed cabin.

Once airborne, Tom climbed his aeroplane in a circular pattern around the Croydon Aerodrome checking the engine temperature and pressure for any signs of trouble, a procedure he had adopted following all too many engine failures in recent months. The F.II Puma engine was not the most reliable of power plants, and his routing to the Channel and throughout Europe overflew emergency landing grounds whenever possible. The visibility proved excellent, and he pointed out familiar landmarks as they followed the London to Maidstone railway line. At three thousand feet, they just remained clear of the developing cumulus cloud, and tucked down out of the slipstream behind the windscreen, Tom shouted out his guided tour of the Kent countryside over the engine's roar. The regular scan of his instruments and the subconscious monitoring of the engine note indicated that all was well, and he looked ahead to pick up the coastline as it converged from the right. Dover was almost visible when his routine scan triggered a response. His gaze stopped on the oil pressure. The needle was flickering its warning. The temperature was normal, but the pressure was much too low. He immediately assessed his location and checked his chart. He knew of an emergency landing ground nearby; his chart confirmed Penshurst, an old WWI field. His companion sensed Tom's heightened state of alert. 'Something wrong?' he said.

'We may need to put down. We've got low oil pressure. We're going to the Penshurst field. Yes, there it is. I knew it was near the railway line to Tonbridge.'

'Do you need any help?'

'No, it should be a routine landing as long as the engine doesn't seize.'

'I can smell oil. I can see a trail of oil on the engine on my side.'

'OK, that confirms it. We can reach the field from here. I'll shut it down when I'm sure we'll get in.'

'Won't we fall out the sky?'

Tom managed a smirk. 'No, perfectly safe. We can glide.'

His oil pressure needle flickered one last time and fell to zero.

'That's it. I'm shutting it down.'

The comforting roar and throb of the Puma engine ceased abruptly, the propeller shuddering to a halt to leave the ominous whistling of the airflow as Tom settled the machine into a glide at 70 knots. He turned south and spotted Chiddingstone Causeway sitting just north of the Tonbridge railway line, the Penshurst airfield just a field's width to the east. The heavy F.II descended quickly as Tom positioned the machine for landing into the wind, an essential requirement at their heavy weight. A tattered windsock was visible, although he had already assessed the wind strength and direction from a farmer's fire. Erring on the safe side, Tom deliberately positioned the machine fairly high on the approach. With a hefty push on the right rudder pedal, he sideslipped the aeroplane to lose height to some shouting from the cabin. He disregarded these pleas as he couldn't do much to reassure his passengers from his cockpit.

'What are you doing?' screamed his companion.

'Don't worry. Just losing height so we don't overrun the field.'

Tom straightened out from his sideslip, and the machine drifted across a dark wooded area and landed well into the field in a north-westerly direction. His landing was a little more firm than usual, but he was glad to be down. His aeroplane quickly rolled to a halt on the rain-soaked ground, and everything was quiet apart from the soft breeze gently stroking the machine.

The passenger door burst open, and the passengers tumbled out with very white faces.

'What the hell is going on?' Foster shouted.

Tom turned from his position high up in the cockpit. 'Just precautionary. Looks like we have an engine problem. We need to check it up.'

'I'll say. I have an important meeting in Amsterdam. Just get this thing back in the air. First, there was a delay, and now here we are in some field in the middle of nowhere.'

Tom unstrapped and climbed down, initially ignoring Foster's tirade. He walked around the nose of the aircraft. The left side was covered in oil streaks, and the lower cowling dripped oil onto the grass. 'A telephone, that's what I need,' he thought out loud. He walked back to his passengers to share his plan. 'If you can stay with the aeroplane, I will find a telephone to contact the company. We'll need an engineer to investigate and top up the oil.' He gestured to a large house at the southern airfield boundary. 'I'm going to try that house.'

Robert Foster was looking increasingly agitated. 'I'm coming with you. I need to make some calls, too. This is a bloody disaster.'

'Very well, Mr Foster. I hope there's a telephone.'

'Of course, there will be. Look at the place, it's a damn palace.'

Tom removed his helmet, pocketed his gloves, and set off towards the house. Foster strutted ahead, determined to spend as little time with Tom as possible. Tom caught him up and felt an overwhelming desire to be provocative. 'What's the rush, Mr Foster?'

The question brought Foster to an abrupt halt. He turned, looking as if he was spoiling for a flight. 'What's the rush? You stupid man. I have an important meeting in Amsterdam, and your bloody airline was supposed to get me there on time. Now look at us.'

'Where are you going for your meeting? I can arrange some transport, providing we can get going again.'

'Precisely. *If* we can get going again. What's your plan to get me there if that fucking machine is broken?'

'I suggest we take one step at a time. Once we get some assistance from the company engineers, we'll look at the machine and see if we can determine what caused the oil leak.'

The large grand house was more of a ruin when they reached it. Windows boarded up, and no sign of life. Foster's demeanour deteriorated to a new low. 'Fuck.'

Tom shielded his eyes and glanced to the west. 'I saw a railway station on the way in. We'll try there.'

Foster was now in a real stew, and Tom couldn't understand what could be so important. He looked fearful - scared even. He wasn't sure it would be helpful to probe any further, but his curiosity got the better of him. 'I'm sorry about this, but please relax, Mr Foster. We'll get you there, and if you can make some telephone calls, your people will understand.'

'My people, as you call them, won't fucking understand. My meetings are vital for my health if you get my meaning.'

'I can't say that I do. Where are you going? Can I help?'

'Help, don't be stupid. You're the last person in this world to help.'

Fortunately, the Penshurst railway station master had seen their arrival and was only too eager to help. 'There used to be a telephone on the airfield,' he said. 'A War Office connection, apparently, took it away last year. I see you flying types all too frequently. Feel free to use my phone.'

'Foster grabbed at the phone. 'Let me have that. I'll need some privacy.'

The station master looked askance at Foster's brusque tone. 'If you must.'

Tom interjected. 'If you want to get to Amsterdam as quickly as possible, I should make my call first.'

'I'll be the judge of that. I'm making this call now, so make yourselves scarce.'

Tom and the station master left the room before Foster banged the door closed.

'What's his problem?'

'I'd love to find out,' said Tom, standing close to the door. Foster's voice slowly increased in volume and tempo.

'Don't worry. I'll be there. It's all arranged. You've got to believe me.' Foster paused momentarily, probably listening to whoever was speaking at the other end. He started talking and shouting again. 'You've got to wait. Believe me, we can do it. Just wait till I get there.' Another short delay was followed by the noise of the telephone handset being slammed down.

'God, he'll break the damn thing,' said the station master as Foster burst out of the door and made off towards the aeroplane.

Walking backward, he turned and shouted at Tom and the station master, 'make your call. We must get going now.'

'Good God,' said Tom. 'What have I done to deserve this?' Knowing that Foster Engineering was involved in the delivery of engines to Fokker, he could feel that something very suspicious was brewing. He was clear that Foster wouldn't get that excited, worried, or even scared about the supply of engines unless something very worrying or dangerous was being planned.

It was nearly two hours before the KLM engineers arrived at Penshurst. Tom had already found that a broken oil pipe was the culprit, and it was quickly mended. 'Good thing you shut the engine down. They don't like to run dry,' was the comment. With a top-up of fresh oil, Tom got the passengers aboard, including a red-faced Robert Foster, who shot up the little step, barging ahead of the other passengers who managed a little smile at his behaviour.

Tom flew the remainder of the flight to Amsterdam without further mishap, some four hours behind schedule. He felt that they had done well by current aviation standards despite Robert Foster's incessant grumbling Before the propeller stopped spinning in Amsterdam, Foster burst out of the cabin, grabbed his overnight bag and raced across to the airport terminal building, where a car was waiting with its engine running. Tom recognised the vehicle; it was from the Fokker factory.

CHAPTER EIGHT

Tom was keen to visit the Fokker factory as soon as possible. He learnt that Robert Foster had returned to England on another KLM flight the following day. The fellow KLM pilot who flew the aeroplane mentioned unprompted that Mr Foster appeared to be very agitated, even scared. Tom needed a good reason to visit the factory as his secondment to KLM provided little excuse. He didn't need to be too concerned as he was called the following week to meet with the senior pilot. No reason was given.

The bustling city of Amsterdam was becoming one of Tom's favourites. He was accommodated in a small, cosy hotel by the *Herengracht* canal. This would mean travelling to the new Fokker works in Amsterdam North by tram and ferry across the IJ waterway. He sat quietly in the corner of the dining room and contemplated his next move. He had not been informed about why the chief pilot wanted to see him but guessed that it was another assignment change. He had enjoyed the relative routine of his flying with KLM, but he also needed something else: some excitement and a challenge. Droning along on regular routes was becoming tedious except for the regular difficulties with weather and the intense excitement of a dud engine. Fortunately, he had not experienced a troublesome engine while crossing the

Channel. He switched his deliberations to the Fokker puzzle and decided that he would need to create an opportunity to search their offices undisturbed. Still, the first challenge was to determine what offices. The design office should bear fruit, and the sales office should, too.

Surprised at how early dinner was served, he felt rushed as the waiter approached his table for his order. As he hadn't even looked at the menu, he asked for more time. His window seat provided much entertainment as he studied the traffic and passers-by. The waiter raised an eyebrow when Tom ordered a cocktail he had been introduced to at Veere, a *kopstoot.* He'd even become accustomed to the strict procedure for drinking the *Jenever* spirit from its dainty tulip-shaped glass filled to the brim with a gleaming meniscus followed by the cooling effects of the accompanying lager. To eat, he selected *rookwurst* served with *stamppot;* a smoked sausage with a selection of vegetables, which arrived promptly to interrupt his thoughts again.

He would need to assess the factory security arrangements as he was unfamiliar with the relatively new site in Amsterdam North. It had been the location of the first air transport exhibition, *Eerste Luchtvaart Tentoonstelling Amsterdam* or ELTA, in 1919 and was acquired later in the year by Fokker under the guise of his company, *NV Nederlandsche Vliegtuigenfabriek*; loosely translated as the Dutch Aircraft Factory. This name had been chosen to disassociate his company from his recent supply of

Fokker aeroplanes to Germany during the war.

Until recently, aircraft parts were made at the Veere plant and shipped to Amsterdam North by canal barge for assembly. Also, the design offices were at Veere, so Tom was unsure how much information would be at the North plant. He decided that he would learn more at his interview and started to ponder on a night visit so that he could search undisturbed. Excitement at the prospect stirred his gut, but this visceral response felt positive, something he needed. A challenge, excitement, something which Alice would understand. He wondered how she was.

Coincidentally, a young couple took their seats at the other side of the dining room, the girl bearing a striking resemblance to Alice. He felt the need to see her. He missed her but shrugged off this wave of emotion - *concentrate,* he chided himself. Despite a recommendation from a waiter to see the curtained windows of *Trompettersteeg Street* in the De Wallen neighbourhood, he felt that the so-called red-light district would be too much of a distraction for this particular visit to Amsterdam. Amused at the thought, he realised that the girl on the other side of the room was returning his smile. The man friend turned and scowled, to which Tom responded by turning away briskly. The last thing he needed was a tussle with a very tall Dutchman.

After a breakfast of strong coffee, Nagelkaas cheese, cold

meat and bread, Tom sought guidance from the hotel staff to determine the best route to Amsterdam North. Suitably equipped with some rough notes, he caught a rather odd-looking tram propelled or, more correctly, towed by a small bus. Apparently, horses had only just been replaced by this motorised tram and many other routes were now electrified. It was late morning when he set off in plenty of time for his afternoon appointment.

He took in the view from the swaying, lurching tramcar and was royally entertained by the bustling Amsterdam life: working women at street stalls in mucky aprons, children in white smocks and menfolk in collarless shirts, baggy jackets and flat caps. Ladies and gentlemen from higher classes were more formally dressed, the ladies in long bulky dresses and large hats and the men in 3-piece suits, ties and the occasional boater. They passed a hand-wound nickelodeon belting out its tunes to a small crowd who seemed to enjoy the music. Two couples danced with unruly abandon and seemed to be totally oblivious to their sniggering audience. With an apparent lack of internal space, many small shops disgorged their produce onto the street with sacks and boxes of vegetables piled against the shopfront. The lack of motor vehicles was evident, and most of the traffic consisted of trams, horse-drawn wagons, hand carts, and bicycles, all managing to avoid each other in a Dutch version of controlled chaos.

The steam ferry across the IJ left from a small wooden pier by Central Station, and the journey took just a few minutes. On disembarking, he took the hand-drawn sketch map from his pocket for the 15-minute walk to the Fokker plant. He had been once before when he attempted to return the Fokker F.II from Schwerin and recalled that he was deliberately excluded from some parts of the factory. The more he thought about this the more his suspicions were aroused. His sighting of Heinrich Wolf on that occasion had heightened his tension, and he decided that he should be on the lookout for anything suspicious or of interest to his cause.

As he approached the main gates, he could see the two large hangar-like buildings that had been the centrepiece of the ELTA exhibition. He noted a small guard post to the left of the gates. He assumed that the gates would be closed at night and scanned the fencing to their left and right. They looked flimsy and easy to overcome - a convenient covert point of entry.

An overweight guard in civilian clothing appeared from the box as Tom approached. 'I have a meeting with Mr Aart Drukker, the chief pilot.'

'Back over there on the field,' indicated the guard. 'That small building to the right.'

The flight hut overlooked the factory airfield, and Tom found Drukker in his office exhibiting a noticeably anxious expression. He looked up and forced a change in his demeanour. 'Thomas Munro, good to see you!

'Good to see you too, Mr. Drukker. It's been a while. I understand that some changes are planned for me.'

'Yes, that's correct. Take a seat, I'll get you a coffee, or is it tea?'

'A tea would be fine, thanks.'

Drukker stepped out from behind his desk to make the drinks at a table at the back of his office. He glanced intermittently over the airfield as he watched an aeroplane take off. 'That's an F.III with some improvements just taking off,' he said.

'What are the improvements?'

'More power from a Rolls Royce Eagle engine with 360 hp. Also, we've moved the cockpit to the left of the engine.'

'So, nice and cosy on the right side this time?'

'Precisely, but also much better performance.'

'I'm sure. So, you wanted to see me. I'm intrigued.'

Drukker placed a tray on his desk with teapot, cups, saucers, sugar bowl and milk in a jug with a Fokker emblem.

'You know how to serve tea, Aart.'

'I remember my time in England before the war. I had to learn fast,' Dukker said with a smile.

'Yes, as you say, I wanted to see you, as I have a new assignment for you if you are prepared to accept it. It will be a little different, and I'm not sure if…'

'Go on, "spill the beans" as we say.'

‘Well, we have a good potential order for a new airline. The problem is that it’s a German/Russian cooperative with planned flights into Russia. Mail and officials at first, but I am told that scheduled passenger flights should follow.’

Tom couldn’t believe his luck and tried to avoid looking too enthusiastic. ‘What’s it called?’

‘*Deutsch-Russische Luftverkehrs Ag*, or the much easier version, *Deruluft*.’

‘Have they planned any routes?’

Drukker shrugged. ‘I don’t think they are very sure, but they talk about Königsberg to Moscow via Kaunas and Smolensk.’

‘I’ll have to check an atlas, but this all sounds interesting. But why would I be suitable? Why not German and Russian pilots? My German is pretty good, but my Russian is non-existent.’

‘Yet again, you seem to be the man in demand. Do you know the name Werner Roth?’

‘Well, I’m blowed. Of course I do. We used to meet up in Hamburg from time to time. I remember him talking about a new airline. We didn’t get the opportunity to compare logbooks to confirm that we probably met in combat in 1918; he would be flying the Fokker D.VII, and I was flying my Bristol Fighter.’

‘Well, you might be meeting up again. Roth is the senior pilot, and we’ve been asked to supply two pilots with airline experience and familiarity with our machines.

Roth suggested you. We are negotiating the supply of F.IIs and F.IIIs, and part of the deal is the two pilots.'

Tom pushed forward on his seat, leaning on Drukker's desk. This was the ideal opportunity to get into Russia on legitimate grounds he realised, trying to quell his obvious enthusiasm. 'It sounds interesting, Aart. How would I be paid?'

'You will remain on contract to Fokker for two years. Same pay rate.'

'Don't you think I deserve a little more? This could be dangerous work over inhospitable terrain.'

'We'll see.'

Tom felt bold. 'Can I see the F.III and your other projects now?'

'I don't see why not. Leave your bag here. We can have a look around the factory.'

Apart from the many small workshops and office buildings, the Fokker site comprised the two large hangar-like buildings, which Tom had observed on the way into the factory. The doors on one hangar were wide open, and several F.II and F.III airframes were lined up along each side of the building, all in various stages of construction. Tom stopped at one F.III, constructed with the pilot's cockpit to the left of the engine.

'This one is for Deruluft,' said Drukker.

Tom wandered around the half-built machine, and once he felt he had shown sufficient interest, he asked the burning question: 'What's in the other hangar?'

'That's for military aeroplanes. I can't take you in there.'

'Oh, that's a pity. I'm always interested in how military machines are developing. We learned so much during the war, and I expect Fokker will have learned these lessons, too.'

'Yes we have,' said Drukker curtly.

Once the tour of hangar one was complete, they passed the closed doors of hangar two, and Tom managed to glance through a gap quickly. He knew the machines he saw, the unmistakable shape of the Fokker D.VII and many of them too. Drukker noticed Tom's interest just as a man squeezed his way between the doors and stopped in front of Tom. There was no mistaking him. It was Heinrich Wolf again. Their encounter was momentary, and Wolf walked on after giving a brief nod to Drukker. Tom gulped and looked at Drukker, not quite knowing how to react. Drukker broke the silence.

'You seem to know him?'

'Only when I saw him before, here. You told me to keep clear of him or something similar. You can't forget the look of the fellow. The eyepatch doesn't make him look too friendly.'

'Yes, I remember. My advice is still the same. Keep well clear. You won't need to meet up with that fellow.'

Tom's tour of the Fokker facilities included the new

design offices, but it was obvious that his visit was restricted to civil aeroplane work. A separate office behind a locked door indicated sensitive work of some sort. He didn't see any evidence of a sales office and decided it would be much too suspicious to ask. Drukker briefed him to continue flying with KLM until advised otherwise. He retraced his journey back to the hotel, thinking deeply about what to do. By the time the tram rattled its way to a stop near his hotel, he had decided to return to the Fokker factory after dark to see what he could discover. He knew that the second hangar and the *other* design office would be a starting point. As the ferries only operated until midnight, the timing of his excursion was limited, and he worried that there would be a night shift. Before returning to the hotel he made a short detour to a hardware store he had spotted from the tram and bought a torch and spare batteries.

After he had made a nervous attempt at an evening meal of *hachee*, a beef stew, washed down with a Trappist beer, he retired to his room to rest before his outing. He planned to use a bicycle which he had borrowed from one of the hotel staff. This would allow maximum flexibility. His calculations indicated that he would need to set off at nine p.m. to benefit from the cover of dark and to have sufficient time for his spying activities and the return ferry trip. He didn't sleep much, and lying on his bed, his gaze followed the pattern on the plaster ceiling rose above the lampshade. He wondered how he should gain entry to the factory site and recalled the condition of the boundary fences. It was initially designed for an exhibition and, consequently, to get people in, not keep them out. He reasoned that there should be easy access over the fence away from the lights, likely at the main gates. The alternative would be to use his pass, but this would create a record of his visit.

Dressed warmly, he decided to leave early and collected his bicycle from the rack at the side of the hotel. He rechecked his torch, then set off north alongside the *Herengracht* canal for the two km ride to the Central Station jetty. He could hear the rumpus in the nearby red-light district. It was a cold evening with bright moonlight, and he felt he could find his way around without a torch. As Tom approached the Fokker site along *Papaverweg,* it became clear that many workers were heading in his direction: a shift change. The main gates were closed, and there was no guard to check the workers in and out as they used a small side gate. This was encouraging.

As the fence to the site continued away from the main gates, it became less secure and broken in places, and entry would be easy. Tom parked his bicycle, climbed through a broken section of the fence, and decided to try the second hangar first. The internal lighting shone through the structure in places, so it was clear that work continued into the night. He would have to be careful and elected to move down the side of the building to find a door or at least a gap in the structure to see in. He stopped abruptly as a figure materialised in the dim light. Was it a guard? Perhaps, but the posture was internationally recognisable; the man was relieving himself against the wall. Tom flattened against the building, held his breath until bursting then exhaled gratefully as the man set off in the opposite direction.

A fire door at the back of the building presented the ideal entry point if it was accessible from the outside. It looked like it only opened from the inside. 'Damn,' Tom cursed. He continued his exploration at the back of the building and found another fire door ajar. It opened freely, and Tom leaned around the door frame. The lights were on, so he assumed some workers would be around. The sight astounded him. Row upon row of Fokker D.VIIs in various states of build; he counted twenty, and at least six appeared to be completed. Tom supposed this could be the batch of aeroplanes smuggled out of Germany, but their destination could not be identified as there were no national markings or even serial numbers.

There was little more to see in the building, so the design office would be the next port of call. Just as he turned to slip away, he noticed a fuselage section which was definitely not a D.VII. Something new, that was certain. A much more aerodynamic shape and the engine looked quite different from anything he had seen before. If only he had a camera. He resolved to take 'C' up on his offer of SIS "toys", which he had mentioned. He guessed that a sneaky camera would be one of the toys. Two or three men appeared just as he turned to move back into the shadows. They wore overalls and walked down the centre of the hangar towards Tom. He pulled back and listened, then decided to slope away towards the design offices.

The building, a large single-story hut-like structure, was located close to the main entrance, so he would need to be careful. It was not likely that it would be open unless it was occupied. He tried the main door at the end of the building. He remembered that this door provided access to a side corridor which ran halfway down the building, providing access to three offices: one for the chief designer and the other equipped with large drawing desks and cabinets. The corridor terminated at the last office at the far end of the passage and had a restricted access sign on the door. A tempting invitation for Tom and priority in his search for clues.

He spent little time at the building's main entrance, which was well illuminated by the gate lighting, then he started a tour around to see if there would be an open window or alternative door. He thought through his alternatives if he couldn't find an open window or door. He could force a door or break a window. Climbing through a window would be tricky; he would need a ladder. He started to wonder if his plans were a little naïve, and as he progressed around the hut, this thought became more pressing. At the back of the hut and the most distant point from the main gate, he found some storage boxes stacked against the wall below a row of windows. This raised a smile; how convenient, he thought.

He climbed onto the crates and peered in, briefly surveying the room with his torch. It was like a large hall with row upon row of draughtsmen's desks and cabinets along the walls. He felt optimistic that this room would reveal what he needed to know. Would he dare to break a window with all the associated noise? First, an investigation of the windows would be wise. A loose catch or faulty lock could be his lucky day. He restricted his search to the back windows, which were out of sight, but each was secure. He could break the window with his torch, he decided, and take the risk that the noise might alert someone. He felt lucky again and confident that this room could reveal something useful.

Following a glance left and right, he held his breath and listened determinedly for any sign of a guard or anyone else. Cringing as he used the torch to fulfil its unusual purpose, the window succumbed to its persuasive force with a loud crash. It seemed deafening. Tom winced and froze. He started to breathe again but listened intently for a minute or so. No other sounds. No running footsteps. No yells. He swallowed hard and carefully picked away the broken shards around the window frame to allow a safe route in. Once satisfied, he climbed in and down onto the floor, moving slowly and deliberately.

He poked his head out the window for a last check, peering left and right into the darkness. Once convinced that no one had heard his forced entry, he systematically searched each drawing desk. There were at least twenty in two rows. Within minutes, there was little doubt that a new machine was in the design stage. This was no surprise, as Tom knew that Fokker and the engineers were prolific designers. He found general arrangement drawings that resembled the machine he had seen in the hangar.

'Yes,' he whispered and clenched his fist as if his dart had hit the bullseye. The drawings identified this machine as a Fokker D.XIII.

He had no knowledge of this new aeroplane and was impressed with the aerodynamic lines, the faired-in engine installation to reduce drag, and the unusual bi-plane configuration. After some thought, he recalled that it was known as a sesquiplane arrangement where one wing was less than 50% of the other. In this case, and as usual for this type of design, the upper wing was larger and supported by neat V-shaped struts. He couldn't find any performance information; all the cabinets were firmly locked, and even his trusty torch was not likely to be helpful. This could be a fast machine. He returned to the drawing boards and checked each one, working down through the stack of drawings on some desks but taking extra care to avoid leaving evidence of his visit. His persistence paid off. The engine was a 450hp Napier "Lion" engine. That should produce speeds of over 150 mph, he thought.

The only information he failed to find was a customer for this machine. He hadn't seen a sales office, but a scout around might reveal one in a different building. Of the dozens of drawings he studied, not one showed any markings or reference to a customer. Perhaps they were prototypes he had seen in the hangar, and there were no customers at this stage. As he searched the last drawings, his torch suddenly flickered and died.

He stood still momentarily and blinked to restore his night vision, which had been affected by staring at the drawings. Just at that moment, he heard voices outside. Then, searching torch beams probed around the hut and into the office via the side windows. He ducked down under one of the drawing boards, which provided little cover.

He felt very vulnerable as the torch beams flashed about the room, clearly searching for something.

Was it a routine inspection, or were they after him?

They might spot the broken window, or did they hear him breaking in?

He hunkered down.

Would they come into the building and the office?

The torch beams stopped. He listened intently. If

they entered the office, the only hiding place would be behind the door.

He crawled towards the door and waited.

After a few moments, light shone under the door from the corridor. They were coming. He stood, pinned himself by the wall, and waited for the door to open.

He counted the footsteps; he didn't know why.

He held his breath for the umpteenth time that evening.

The lights went on, blinding Tom for a few moments.

The men spoke in Dutch, but Tom could understand. 'Are you sure you heard something?'

'I thought so. I'm not sure what. Glass breaking, maybe.'

Fortunately, the men left the door open, hiding Tom from view as they slowly paced the room. He tentatively leaned out and peeped around the door. The two men, security guards by their looks, were just nearing the end of the room and the broken window.

Tom decided it was time to move. He slid around the door and quietly pulled it behind him.

He tiptoed down the corridor, waiting to hear a yell at any moment.

He reached the outside door and sneaked out after a quick glance around the building and crept towards the main gate.

His route back to the hole in the fence and his bicycle seemed clear. He started with a slow, quiet gait that quickened after a few paces and this changed to a full-blown dash as he reached the darkness. By the time he reached the fence, he was spent—nervous exhaustion, he decided.

He didn't find it too easy peddling his way back to the ferry; his legs were still shaking. It reminded him of his reaction after landing from a nerve-jangling fight in his Bristol Fighter. It seemed a long time ago, but the memories were still crystal clear, particularly the sights and sounds of that awful experience in the shell crater. Over four years ago, but it still troubled him.

When he reached the ferry, he felt calmer, and the ferryman nodded as he lifted the old bicycle aboard. A slow, persistent drizzle started as the ferry reached the Central Station side of the IJ. It was much darker now, and he squinted to see his way as he left the ferry. He felt drained after the evening's activities and found his way alongside the *Westertoegang* canal before stopping to consult his map after turning down by *Brouwersgracht*, one of the prettiest canals in Amsterdam, he was told. He remembered that he needed to turn left alongside the *Herengracht* canal to find his hotel.

He couldn't read the map in the poor light and peered unsuccessfully before giving up and setting off with a wobble. He regained control just as the frantic roar of a motor car very close by caused him to glance behind. Big bright headlights and a broad silver radiator grille filled his view. Then, a violent bang. He sensed a disorientating tumbling flight through the cold dark air, distant lights rotating as he careered downward into the black void, then a splash - murky water, bubbling sounds and terrible cold ...

CHAPTER NINE

Dalton might not have been the most adventurous or bold of SIS agents, but Alice knew that he was particularly effective at finding and turning people who might be useful. His mastery of the German language was such that even Berliners could be fooled into thinking him a local. Finding someone to spy for them in the Bendlerblock, the Reichswehr headquarters, would be the holy grail, the jackpot that Dalton had been working on for over a year. An undeclared intelligence officer working in the British Embassy consular section, he could easily move freely about the city and country and was slowly proving his worth at infiltrating Berlin's dark society and nightlife. His tall, suave demeanour also proved popular with the ladies.

The British embassy in Berlin always impressed Alice. The August Orth, designed Palais Strousberg building at No. 70 Wilhelmstrasse had a chequered history. Built in 1867 for the railway magnate Bethel Henry Strousberg, it was let as the embassy for Great Britain and Ireland in 1875 following the Strousberg family's bankruptcy.

Alice had many memories of the city: the Hotel Adlon, where Tom and Bill had been accommodated (much to their delight) and nearby, the Residenz-Casino near Alexander Platz, where Heinrich Wolf and his henchmen had drugged and snatched them for questioning. She was told that the "Resi" Casino was where Dalton plied his trade in the search for his potential spies—usually women.

Dalton had not seen or met the *new* Alice, and she planned to test his powers of observation. On her arrival in Berlin, she telephoned the embassy and arranged a meeting with him at the nearby Adlon. 'I'll be in the Winter Garden,' she smirked. Their brief conversation did not mention her disguise.

Alice loved the lavish splendour of the best hotel in Berlin. Other than a plain ensemble underneath, she had dressed for the occasion with a long, elegant blue coat with a dropped matching belt and fur trim at the collar and cuffs. A fashionable cloche-style hat with ostrich feathers and practical Oxford lace-ups completed her outfit. She felt like a fraud but knew that she must play the part. She took a deep breath, stood tall and proud and nodded as the large glass doors opened as if by magic. Her appearance and demeanour were all that was necessary to pass through the reception area without being challenged.

On the contrary, some staff felt the need to offer a respectful bow of the head. Alice walked on without acknowledging this obsequious behaviour as she believed that was the required response. She had to stifle a smile and just managed to maintain her composure.

The Winter Garden was bustling with Berliners taking morning coffee, elaborate hats twisting and turning like colourful fans in time to the animated conversations. Alice was shown to a small round table overlooking the Elephant Fountain, but before long, the soft trickling of water alerted her to an imminent personal need. That would have to wait, she thought whilst absorbing the atmosphere.

She had to think again, as Dalton was late - very late. When she returned, he was circulating around the Winter Gardens, trying to look nonchalant and failing, dodging the hats like a matador. She strolled to her table and brushed past Dalton, who reacted as if to a stranger. 'I beg your pardon,' he said with a charming smile.

'You look lost,' Alice ventured.

Dalton looked surprised at her candour. 'Ah, yes. I was just looking for someone. I was late. She may have left in high dudgeon. Can I join you, then? My friend may be late as well.'

'Why not?' said Alice, returning to her table.

Dalton took his seat, at Alice's table, spreading his coat around his chair with a flourish. 'Let me get these. I might as well enjoy a coffee with a…' He leant forward for a few moments and stared determinedly at Alice, then sat back, placing his hands on the table with a bang. 'It's you, isn't it? Well, I'll be blowed. Alice, that is amazing.'

'Thank you. I was expecting you to see through my little disguise more quickly.'

'It's the blonde Aryan look that fooled me.'

‘I rather like it, but does it work?’ said Alice turning her head this way and that as if studying herself in a mirror. She leaned forward and spoke quietly. ‘Do I look credible or just made up?’

‘No, it works. It’s the heavy make-up. That does the trick; it’s so not you.’

‘Thank you. How gallant.’

Dalton looked serious. ‘Look, you won’t have heard, but something is stirring on the political front—in Europe, that is. The ambassador wants to brief us this afternoon.’

‘Am I included?’

‘Of course. You were requested by name. I’m not sure what you’ve done, but somebody has been talking to the Boss.’

Lord Edward Parkrose had been the British ambassador to Germany since 1920 and was known to be convinced that German disarmament had been successful and that there was no military threat from the country. He believed that, due to the Inter-Allied Control Commission’s efforts, it would be impossible for the Germans to conceal any military build-up.

Alice had the opposite opinion but was prepared to keep her thoughts to herself until she heard the briefing. It was difficult to believe that the vast and cavernous proportions of the Palais Strousberg were really necessary for an embassy, but she guessed it was about putting on a show. After all, the great British Empire should have appropriate accommodation for its embassy, she mused with a smirk. She had a few double-takes from the embassy staff as she accompanied Dalton; she was probably a little overdressed.

There was a significant gathering of embassy staff at the briefing, at least twenty-plus, and the subdued chitchat ended with the entry of Lord Parkrose and, Alice guessed, his secretary. They were in a relatively small room. It had a high, elaborately coffered ceiling and two substantial chandeliers that dispersed a shimmering yellowish light on the staff seated below. Parkrose stood behind a carved lectern; his secretary handed him some notes and placed a glass of water on a small table nearby. Dalton leant across to Alice. 'Looks like a long briefing...'

Parkrose began. 'We have some interesting news to report, and we should all be cognizant of these recent events. You will all be aware of the PM's enthusiasm for resolving the major economic and political issues facing Europe, and just last year, an Anglo-Soviet Trade Agreement was reached to facilitate trade between our countries. This agreement gave the Soviet government de facto recognition by Great Britain. However, this very month, a very significant conference in Genoa, planned by our PM to deal with the issues facing Germany and Russia, has been scuppered by rather surprising events.

Before I report on these events, I should say that the Genoa conference of some 34 nations was designed to develop a strategy to rebuild a defeated Germany, and Central and Eastern European states. It was also supposed to be a platform on which to negotiate a relationship between European capitalist economies and the Bolshevik regime in Soviet Russia. This was never going to be an easy task and much resisted by our French allies as they are determined to extract every last *franc* from the Germans by way of the Versailles Treaty reparations.' It was Alice's turn to lean towards Dalton. 'I know what's coming here.'

Parkrose continued. 'Now, unfortunately, Mr Lloyd George's efforts have been wrecked by the news that Germany and Russia have signed a treaty of trade and friendship at the Italian resort of Rapallo. This so-called Treaty of Rapallo has pulled Russia and Germany out of the proceedings, and the Genoa conference has lapsed into a stalemate. At this stage, I am not suggesting that this treaty is anything other than a trade agreement between two pariah states, but although I have not seen the text, I understand that it also involves the mutual renunciation of pre-war debts and Versailles Treaty claims.'

After talking for some time as if trying to justify his earlier position that Germany was more trustworthy than the French, Parkrose paused and glanced at Dalton and Alice. 'I imagine that some quarters in London will believe that there could be more behind this Rapallo Treaty - in the shadows, so to speak, but there is no firm evidence of this. No doubt there will be more detail on this event, but for now, this is a significant blow to our PM's much-promoted diplomatic efforts. I understand that the London newspapers are having a field day at his expense. As usual, please keep this news within the embassy, but report any reactions you might hear during your work to your immediate superior. Thank you.'

Lord Parkrose turned, took a gulp of water, walked towards the door and rolled his notes into a tube. He stopped amidst the loud chattering in the room and looked over his shoulder. The chattering ground to a halt. 'Dalton and Miss Ferguson, my office, please.'

Alice was not sure what to expect. The ambassador's curt instruction suggested they were in for some sort of rebuke. Dalton let Alice go ahead and into the ambassador's outer office. The secretary wore a smug look and eyed Alice up and down disapprovingly. 'Please take a seat,' she said, with a clipped upper-class accent. She maintained her supercilious expression. Alice felt like saying something to repel the subtle disapproval but could not think of anything. She knew something would occur to her later - it always did. The secretary's telephone buzzed. Dalton and Alice waited for the call from the 'headmaster'. 'You may go through now,' said the secretary. Alice smiled cordially, then let it dwindle sarcastically.

'You'll not make many friends that way, Alice,' Dalton whispered through tight lips.

The ambassador's office was more like an art gallery, the walls decorated with elaborately framed oils and watercolours. Alice was terribly distracted and wanted to look closer as she walked the twenty yards to his desk. As they reached the end of their march, Lord Parkstone rose and gestured toward a cosy collection of dark brown, well-worn Chesterfield armchairs and a three-seater settee near a French window overlooking a courtyard.

'Now, you two. I know about your mission, Miss Ferguson, and I wish you well. Dalton here has been instructed to work with you 100%. Is that clear, Dalton?'

'Yes, sir.'

'Good. But look, I don't want to know too much, and I certainly don't want any international incidents. We have worked hard to establish a good relationship with the German authorities. I don't want that destroyed by any careless activities on your part if you take my meaning. I don't believe they are up to anything regarding rebuilding their military, as suggested. Unlike the French, we should rebuild European relationships, not break them with punitive reparations. So there you have it. Go about your business quietly. Any questions?'

Alice and Dalton were unprepared for their "interview" and had little to say. Alice racked her brains and then thought of some practical issues. 'Transport, sir. We will need some motor cars and an office here in the embassy. We may need to hire a room or two for observation purposes. We will have a number, say three or four, targets to observe and tail, so we will need some good staff with initiative and a will to learn.'

Parkstone's mouth dropped. 'Some motor cars, some staff, some rooms? How many of you are there?'

'It's not so much the number involved in our operation as the number of people we want to put under surveillance.'

Dalton felt the need to chip in and felt buoyed by Alice's demands. 'If we can have three cars, that should do, sir, and we will need access to funding, some cash for general costs. I have contacts to "look after" as well as living and travel expenses.'

'Oh, very well. Speak to Francis; he should see you right. I assume your people are also contributing to this game of yours.'

Alice took umbrage and reacted without thought. 'With respect, it's not a game, sir, and I hope to prove our worth very quickly.'

Parkrose smiled. 'I like your spirit, Miss Ferguson, despite your outlandish getup.'

'She has to disguise herself in Berlin,' said Dalton. 'She is known to the people we will be watching. Just a sensible precaution.'

'Oh, very well. Just keep me informed. Nobody else knows of your role, Miss Ferguson, so bear that in mind.'

'Yes, sir, what if I'm challenged? I need a cover story.'

'True. You're working alongside Dalton in the

consular section. It's a bustling department after the war. Everyone wants to go to England.'

Alice had spent a few days finding her way around Berlin and felt quite pleased with her accommodation: a one-bedroom flat near the Bendlerblock on Eichhorn Strasse. She could stroll past the various entrances if it took her fancy. She wondered how long she would last wearing her various disguises and felt ridiculous. For this particular occasion, her disguise was very different. Not quite a "flapper", but not too far removed. She was off to the *Resi* with Dalton to meet his 'informer', a young female Reichswehr operative.

The more Alice thought about their task, the more she realised that they would need someone on the inside. Dalton's skills could be useful, but if things became difficult, she knew, from earlier experience, that she would need someone more robust. They had decided to mount a clandestine surveillance operation on the Bendlerblock, and armed with photographs of von Mayer, von der Lang and Wolf, two SIS staff detached from SIS HQ were tasked with monitoring their movements. If a pattern of movement were to emerge, two others would follow to determine their destinations, contacts, behaviour, and anything valuable. For this evening, Alice was to play the role of a colleague - an understanding and sympathetic colleague who was good at listening.

Dalton was in his element. 'Herta's desperate to

get to England,' he said, holding Alice back with an outstretched hand. 'She's in love with some English boy she met during the occupation and will do anything to get there.'

'How long have you known her?' said Alice with a doubting expression.

'I'm not an amateur at this.'

Alice was taken aback by Dalton's prickly defensiveness. 'I didn't say that.'

'Well, you sure as hell looked like it.'

'OK, I'm sorry. We need to be professional about this. This is obviously your thing, your expertise. I'll take the lead from you. Is there anything else I need to know about this… situation?'

'Just follow my lead. You should behave as a work colleague who understands Herta and her problems. I've confided in you so that you can help. She's vulnerable, but this is a big opportunity, trust me.' Dalton paused. Alice found his theatrical delivery mildly amusing, but she could see he was deadly serious. Then, he got her attention with a well-targeted phrase. 'She talks about Sondergruppe R.'

The Resi was in full swing when they eventually entered, and Alice was pleased that she had taken the precaution of taking a swift whisky before leaving her flat. She had made several appropriate adjustments to her dress and noticed that Dalton behaved gallantly towards her. His every move was respectful and gracious, the opening of doors, the open hand directing her progress and the smiles; a little excessive, maybe. But she quietly liked being treated that way and was not used to it. Even Tom was not quite so attentive, but after some thought, she suspected it was all part of Dalton's act. Alice had been to the Resi once before and had a detailed description from Tom and Bill, at least what they could remember as it was here they had been drugged. The thought put her on her guard.

'Here she is; my you look splendid,' said Dalton.

Alice was impressed. Herta was a small, petite young woman of about thirty, and although small in stature, she was well proportioned: a miniature beauty and a natural blonde. Dalton introduced her. Alice spoke briefly, noticing her excellent English. They took their seats some way back from the crowded dance floor, which bustled with energy and athletic dance moves in the style of the American swing and jive craze, which was just catching on. Dalton ordered drinks from the u-shaped bar, and they sat around a small table against the mirrored wall without the ubiquitous telephone and pneumatic communication system. Dalton didn't want them to be distracted. Alice broke the ice. 'How long have you lived in Berlin?'

'I moved from the countryside to the south side of Berlin after the war.'

Dalton took over the conversation. 'You told me you

worked in the Bendlerlock, the Reichswehr headquarters; that must be interesting.'

'It is, but I can't talk about it,' Herta said with a worried look at Alice.

'You have no need to worry about Alice here; she is a colleague and is totally trustworthy.'

'Thank you. I must be sure that I can trust you. My life will be at risk if I am even seen with foreigners. It raises questions.'

Alice glanced about for uniforms. 'I understand. Do Reichswehr staff come in here?'

'Sometimes but not in uniform.'

Alice looked alarmed. 'Surely this is a little foolish. Isn't there somewhere more secure to meet?'

'I think Herr Dalton likes it here,' Herta replied with a cheeky smirk.

Dalton shrugged. 'I can find somewhere more sedate, quiet and out of the way.'

Alice leant across to Dalton. Herta looked on curiously. 'You suppose right. We need to be able to talk quietly, and we mustn't meet anyone she knows. You know that. The next time, somewhere more secure, yes?'

'Yes, alright.'

Alice sat in the back of the spacious Armstrong Siddeley, slouched to keep well out of sight. Dalton and one of his staff, Raymond Proudfoot, sat in the front. 'Don't you think this British motor car is a bit obvious?' said Alice.

‘Standard embassy issue,’ Proudfoot replied with an impudent tone.

Dalton reassured them: ‘We’ll park well away from the flat but in view of the entrance. We’ve identified this one chap who seems to spend a lot of time with von der Lang. We’ll see them easily. If we can just get a photograph, we can see if Herta can identify him. He might be perfectly innocent, but I just feel he could be important.’

‘If he is spending a lot of time with the colonel, I agree that we must identify him,’ Alice commented whilst recalling her visit to this flat when von der Lang had befriended her. This was also where Tom had discovered the *Group R* documents and attempted to photograph them unsuccessfully. She now assumed that the colonel had decided she was not to be trusted and that Wolf had been ordered to dispose of her. This was not certain, and her memory of that night in Hamburg on the SS *Ferris Star* was still vague despite her use of all manner of techniques to recall the details. As they waited for another sighting of the colonel’s friend, Alice was thinking about her meeting with Herta and was rapidly concluding that her information from within the Reichswehr HQ would be vital.

Alice cringed at Dalton’s camera. ‘You can’t wander around with that thing, Dalton. Why don’t we park so that you can take a shot through the back window?’

‘Good idea, this should do.’

‘Pull up the road a bit. This is too close. Look, that’s them, there,’ Alice whispered as if the colonel might hear her.

‘Damn. I need to get in the back.’

Alice reached forward. ‘Give me the camera. Is it ready?’

Proudfoot pointed at the heavy camera. ‘Yes, this is the shutter. Quick, take it or you’ll miss your chance.’

‘Did you get it?’

‘Well, I clicked the clicker,’ Alice replied with a shrug.

Dalton didn’t look convinced, and Proudfoot sniggered quietly. ‘We should wait until they come out again. They’re probably having lunch or something. Then we can get a full-frontal shot,’ he said.

Alice dumped the camera on the seat beside her and opened the back door. ‘You have a go this time. Let’s swap around.’

CHAPTER TEN

Violent coughing was Tom's first recollection as strong hands grabbed at his clothing and hauled him upwards. He could hear voices as if in the distance, smelt tar or pitch, and realised that he was now face down on the ground with someone pushing his back. It was hurting. Tepid, rancid water gushed from his mouth. The taste made him retch again, and the pushing continued. 'No more,' he pleaded.

'You're a lucky man,' the voice declared.

'Where am I?'

'*Brouwersgracht.*'

'What's that?'

'A canal. You're very lucky we spotted you. You were face down when you drifted alongside our boat. We had just stepped aboard. Been ashore for a drink.'

'Tom rolled over onto his side and started to shiver uncontrollably.'

'Let's get you in front of the fire.'

He had a vague recollection of being carried from the deck to the cabin and his clothes being stripped off. The cabin's warmth was heaven to Tom's chilled body. He felt the comfort and security of a small armchair, the glorious heat from a cast iron stove and the weight of a heavy rug thrown around his shoulders. He noticed one of the men lifting the top of the stove with a gloved hand and pouring in some coal from a dirty copper scuttle. Tom wanted to give it a polish. After a few moments, when he realised how lucky he had been, a smile returned to his features when he saw steam rising from a battered pot on the stove. His senses were returning, and the shivering slowed as he glanced around the little cabin. Two rough-looking men watched his slow recovery, and his rambling thoughts amused him. They would not be the sort of people he would want an argument with.

'How did you get into the water?' said one as he prepared a mug of tea.

Tom started to remember the glaring headlights and the bang as the car hit. 'I was hit by a car. I was cycling back to my hotel. I had just set off to find the Herengracht when it happened. I should thank you two. I would have drowned.'

'You very nearly did. You must have spewed half the IJ over our deck.'

Tom smiled for the first time. 'Well, thank you again. Could you get me back to my hotel? I'm exhausted.'

The mug of coffee was thrust in front of him. 'You'll have some of this first. You need to warm up inside and we need to dry your clothes. You sure you don't want to see a doctor?'

Tom clutched the hot mug in both hands, savouring the heat. 'No, I'll be fine, just fine.'

Alice was surprised at the quality of her photograph. Dalton's picture was even better, but in both cases, the image of von der Lang's companion was excellent. The negative was enlarged, and a print was shown to Herta. Alice noticed an increasing nervousness in her demeanour. 'You seem worried, Herta. Is there something wrong?'

'Yes, This is very dangerous. I shouldn't be here. Someone might be watching.'

Dalton tried to reassure her. 'That's why we meet like this. We can change to a different café or bar every time. You suggest a place where you feel more at ease. Use our dead letter box as arranged.'

Herta lowered her gaze and nodded unenthusiastically. 'Alright.'

Dalton looked about the café then pulled the photograph from a brown envelope. 'Good. Now, have you seen this man?'

Herta looked fleetingly at the picture and at Alice as if seeking permission.

'Just say yes or no, Herta. There is no pressure. If you're not sure, just say so.'

Herta nodded, blinking nervously. 'Yes, I have. I have seen him with the colonel and the general, too.'

'Excellent,' said Dalton. Do you know his name?'

'No.'

'Alright. We just need to know his name. That's all. Just keep your eyes and ears open. We can meet again here in a week or elsewhere if you tell us with a dead letter. We check it daily, as you know.' Dalton had to prompt Herta with a questioning nod.

She responded hesitantly. 'Yes, sir,' she mumbled obediently and left as if desperate to leave the café.

Alice raised her hands in frustration. 'This isn't getting us anywhere. I'm not sure that she will be of any use to us. I feel sorry for her. She's terrified.'

'I've had everyone in the embassy look at these photographs,' said Dalton. 'No one recognises our man. I'm running out of ideas.'

'We could send a copy to Harry Price in the diplomatic bag. See if they can help.'

'Why not? Nothing ventured, and so on. I'll arrange it.'

Over the next week, the colonel and the general were observed discreetly, and photographs were taken when they were seen outside the Bendlerblock with other people. Dalton worked on another potential informer in the Reichswehr, an older man this time and with some bitter grudge against the military hierarchy. The reason for this grudge had not been identified, but Dalton was on the case. Alice met with Herta alone, believing she might be more willing to open up to a woman; Dalton seemed to make her nervous. They met twice, and more photographs were shown to her, but no names were forthcoming.

After another two weeks, Herta didn't show up for a

planned meeting. Alice had agreed to a different café, and she became worried. She waited for nearly an hour, and then, having overdosed on caffeine and become overheated under her wig, she gave up and returned to the embassy.

At their regular bi-weekly meeting, Alice felt protective of Herta. 'Do we know where she lives, Dalton? I'm getting worried.'

'We do, but we never go anywhere near our informants' homes. It's just too much risk for them.'

'Can't we visit at night, taking the necessary precautions?'

'Possible, but try another dead letter. See if we get any response. If not, we pay a visit. More disguises, I'm afraid.'

There wasn't any response to messages at the dead letter drop. Careful surveillance of the Bendlerblock at 8 a.m. and the cease-work parade of staff flowing from the building from five p.m. didn't reveal any sight of Herta; she was usually spotted then. A night-time visit to her flat close to the Potsdamer Bahnhof was arranged. Proudfoot, disguised as a railway station worker, volunteered to visit it. Alice and Dalton waited in the car around the corner, well out of sight.

They hoped that Proudfoot would not have to break in, and Alice thought through the possibilities as Dalton read a newspaper with a torch. Herta might have taken fright and had merely decided to take no further part in her informing activities. She had continued to be very nervous when they met. Dalton didn't know much about her family or relatives. She might have been discovered and warned off, or worse. They would need to be careful now. She might have been turned and be a risk to their operation. Other reasons for their situation churned around in Alice's mind when Dalton's man returned to the car looking as white as milk.

He opened the front door and sat down as if he had run a marathon, sweating profusely and breathing hard. After a few minutes to compose himself, he shook his head despairingly and turned to look at Alice. He swallowed with some difficulty. 'You need a strong stomach to go in there.'

Alice sat bolt upright in the back seat. 'She's not …'

'Yes,' said Proudfoot. 'Very much so.'

'God. How? Did you search the place? Any clues? Any notes? Anything on her?'

'Steady on Alice,' said Dalton. 'Let's think this through. We're assuming you found Herta, and she's dead? Let's start with who?'

Proudfoot still looked shocked. 'Yes, it's Herta, and her throat's been cut. In fact, her head is nearly …'

'OK, spare us the details for now,' said Dalton. 'You didn't have time to search the flat so we need to do that before light. It's deserted around here, so any volunteers?'

'I'll do it. I know what I'm looking for,' Alice said with an unusually apprehensive expression.

'I'll come too,' said Dalton. 'Keep watch, Raymond. Sound the horn if you're worried.'

'OK, but don't you think the place might be watched? said Proudfoot. 'Whoever did this must suspect or know what Herta has been up to.'

Alice paused as she opened the car door. 'It's possible, but we need to see if she has been able to leave any clues or messages. Was the door open, or did you have to break in?'

'It was open, just pulled to and no sign of a forced entry. Herta probably answered it. It might have been someone she knew.'

Proudfoot huddled down in their car, a German model arranged to be less conspicuous during their more clandestine operations. Dalton and Alice walked cautiously down the road, a single torch illuminating their way; the only sounds were the rattling bogies of a nearby goods train. Alice glanced around, taking in the layout of the surrounding roads and paths, ever alert to the possibility of covert eyes. Nothing happened, and they walked quietly to the flat entrance with a quick check behind before disappearing into a dimly lit hallway, a common passageway to all the flats in the block.

The flat was on the first floor of a three-floor building, Flat five halfway along an open walkway facing the street. Alice noticed the dead end in the poor light and realised that there was only one exit route back the way they had come; it made her nervous. Alice and Dalton looked at each other for moral support, preparing for the awful sight they knew they had to face. She wondered if Dalton would cope; he had seemed reluctant to face danger on past occasions. He pushed the door open, and they walked hesitantly through the small hallway. He immediately spotted Herta lying spreadeagled across her bed in a night dress.

There must have been a desperate struggle. Herta's face was beaten, and as Proudfoot intimated, her throat had been cut to the extent that her head was almost severed from her body. The brutal strength of the attack was evident. She lay on top of her bedding, which was soaked in her blood, a horrific ending for the slight and pretty young girl.

They didn't speak for a while until Alice broke the silence. 'We can't stay long. I'll check the bathroom. You look in that chest and bedside cabinet. I don't expect to find anything, but we must try.'

There was nothing unusual about the bathroom, and the little wall cupboard revealed nothing. Alice wasn't sure what made her do it, but she moved back into the small bathroom and closed the door. A full-length mirror was attached to the inside of the door, and there it was, in clear lipstick writing: WEBER.

'Look, Jim. Look at this. It must be a clue. Who's Weber?'

Dalton pushed into the bathroom, and they looked at the mirror together. 'That's the best we've got so far. I haven't found anything in the other rooms.'

'Have you checked her body,' Alice asked with a wince. 'Her hands maybe?'

Dalton took a breath and approached the body. He examined the hands and found nothing. 'There's blood and maybe skin under her nails. Someone might be scratched. On the face or hands. Worth noting.' He shook his head. 'I can't see anything else. There's nothing in her hands.'

Their conversation stopped abruptly as a distant car horn sounded.

'Is that our car?' said Alice.

'I've no idea, but who'd be sounding a horn at two in the morning?'

Alice made for the door. 'Let's get out of here. Wait, have a look out the window. We should be able to see the road.'

'It's the fucking Polizei. Somebody must have said something.'

'We can only go back the way we came. We'll walk straight into them.'

They stood paralysed at the door, searching for a plan. Alice tried, thinking out loud: 'Bloody hell, there's nowhere to hide. Can we talk our way out? I don't think so. Why are we here? Who are we? How do we explain that?'

'Shit, we're well and truly fucked,' Dalton exclaimed. 'Listen… quiet. Can you hear them?'

CHAPTER ELEVEN

Tom returned to his KLM duties and awaited news from Drukker. It was three weeks before he decided to call him and see how things were going. He hadn't managed to determine if his dunking in the canal was an accident or a deliberate attempt to kill him and had visited the crime scene or what he remembered of it. There were no signs of his impact with the car apart from some tiny shards of glass, a broken headlamp perhaps. He reasoned that skid marks would not appear on a wet road, but he was sure he recalled the location correctly.

His telephone calls to Art Drukker were finally successful after several attempts, and he detected that surprised tone he had noticed when he returned from Schwerin. 'Tom, ah yes, your Deruluft job. Let me see. I have some correspondence on that. I'll need to find it. Can you call me back? I'm not sure where it is.'

'I'll wait, Art; it'll be a few days until I can call again. I'm keen to get going at Deruluft. I've been thinking about it. I need a new challenge. I'll hold on…' The line went dead. Tom was used to telephone troubles, but he was suspicious on this occasion and called again. It was not answered. He decided that a call to Werner Roth would short-circuit the system. If Roth had asked for him by name as Drukker had advised, he would know the situation. Flicking through his notebook, he remembered that Roth could be contacted at the Hamburg Fuhlsbuttel aerodrome. By translating his scruffy handwriting, he could just make out the name Bernt Schmitz, the aerodrome manager.

A voice called out from just outside the Schiphol flight office. 'Ten minutes to departure, Captain.'

Tom waved a hand. 'Be with you in a minute. Need to make this call.'

Surprisingly, the call went through, and Schmitz came to the telephone after a tense wait. Tom could see the passengers boarding. Punctuality was important to KLM. 'Bernt, this is Captain Munro. I don't have much time, but I want to contact Werner Roth. Can you help?'

'I don't see much of him these days, but if you write to me or give me a message, I'll see what I can do.'

'If you see him, can you let me know how I can contact him? I might be working with him soon.'

'Very well. When will we see you here again?'

'Not sure, Bernt. I must fly; I don't want to keep my passengers waiting. I'll call you again to check on Roth's whereabouts.'

Proudfoot breathed an enormous sigh of relief as Alice and Dalton returned to the car with hats askew, flailing coats, and ashen faces. It was raining heavily now, the raindrops drumming on the car roof. 'Did they see you, the police? I sounded the horn. I rather drew attention to myself. Got worried they'd want to know what I was doing.'

Alice closed the door, and Dalton flopped down in the front, wiping his face and rearranging his hair.

'They went somewhere else, another flat,' said Alice. 'I think they were just popping in for a break. Probably one of their relatives. God, we waited there for 45 minutes, holding our breaths. I thought we were done for. Total coincidence, thank goodness.'

'Did you find anything.'

Dalton spoke with a slight shake to his voice. 'Yes, we did, but not sure what it means yet. Let's get back. I need to get my head down. We meet at the embassy at 11.'

'There's a letter in the bag from your people,' said Lord Parkrose's secretary.

Alice wasn't quite awake from her night's activities and took the letter with little interest. She met Dalton in a small, secure room and sat at the table with a sigh. She began to read with little enthusiasm before her expression changed dramatically, gritting her teeth as if she were going to explode. 'Damn and bloody damn.'

'Well, what? What's it say? Anything relevant? Do they recognise the man in the photos?'

'No, they didn't. I was certain, and I'm still certain, that the man with von der Lang is significant. I was banking on them identifying him.' Alice paused her hand rubbing her chin. 'I wonder. Could he be Weber? The name scrawled on Herta's bathroom?'

Dalton shrugged. 'Possible, I suppose.'

'It was the last conversation we had with her. We asked her to get the name of the man in the photograph.'

Tom was determined to confront Art Drukker at Fokkers. He had lost count of the phone calls he had attempted and snatched between his many KLM flights to and from Croydon. They had never been answered or returned. It was a dull grey morning when he arrived at the Fokker works, the gloom reflecting his state of mind. He was cheered a little by a young girl he passed on the way into the works. A pretty young thing despite the drab work clothes and matching headscarf. His encounter made him think about Alice and Louisa, but he decided to banish these thoughts. He had other pressing matters to deal with. He focussed on confronting Drukker.

He knocked firmly on the door, walked into Drukker's office in response to a muffled grunt, stood stock still without saying a word, and waited. Drukker was standing, hands behind his back, looking out the office window. Finally, he turned to face Tom, his expression changing from his usual, almost permanent smile to shock. His mouth dropped open, and he seemed unable to speak.

'Good morning, Art. I think you owe me an explanation,' said Tom, delivering his rehearsed statement with as much sincerity as he could muster.

Drukker struggled to respond. He brushed past Tom,

avoiding eye contact, closed the door after a brief glance into the corridor and returned to his desk. He sat down and gestured to Tom to do likewise. He took a deep breath and dabbed his forehead with his handkerchief. 'Look, Tom, I don't know what's going on. There were a lot of strange looks when I mentioned that you had been in contact. Then, I was told to ignore your calls. I'm sorry, but I didn't have any choice.'

'I can guess why that might be. Do you know what happened?'

'No. I was worried about you, but, as I said, I was told to ignore your calls.'

'Who was giving you these instructions? Who told you to ignore me? You should be able to answer that.' Tom was astonished by Drukker's behaviour. 'Why? For God's sake. Why all the secrecy? This is not like you.'

'All I can say is get yourself to Deruluft. People here don't know about these arrangements. Do that job. Get in contact with Werner Roth. Just walk away from KLM. Disappear. I'll say nothing.'

Tom could see that Drukker was terrified. He felt sorry for him and responded hesitantly. 'OK… Seems like the best plan.'

Drukker stood and thrust out his hand. 'Yes, Good. Please go. Go now. I'll say nothing. Good luck.'

Tom shook Drukker's trembling hand and turned, still stunned by his behaviour. A friend and colleague had been transformed into a quivering wreck. Why?

'Goodbye. I hope we can meet again in better circumstances.'

'Yes, goodbye and be careful. Trust no one, there are dangerous times ahead.'

Tom enjoyed train journeys, and his travel to Hamburg provided him with some quiet time to reflect on his strange predicament. He placed his small brown leather case on the luggage rack and noted that it contained almost all his worldly goods and chattels. As usual, he wore his flying coat, which wouldn't fit in his case. The weather was getting warm, and he attracted a few sideways glances from his fellow travellers. He chortled, took off the coat, and sat down to enjoy the final leg to Hamburg.

Tom was proud of his flying abilities and was always keen to do a good job, but now, this was not enough. He remembered that he had voiced his interest in doing a "little spying," but now he felt that he was becoming embroiled in something dangerous.

He knew that Alice would be fully involved in the current project and worried about her casual willingness to put her life at risk—at least, that was how he saw her behaviour. He recalled Drukker's words: 'Walk away from KLM. Disappear. I'll say nothing.' To disappear must mean one thing, he decided: someone was after him, and it wouldn't be for a friendly chat.

Tom climbed out of the taxi at the Hamburg Fuhlsbüttel airfield, paid the driver and glanced around. He noted more building works and the slow but determined efforts to improve and develop the facilities. He remembered his Vickers Vimy flights with his friend Davidson, the engine failures, and winter in desperate open cockpit conditions. At last, aeroplanes were being built with enclosed cockpits, but they were still rare. He thought that Anthony Fokker had the right ideas and hoped that the Fokker F.III he would be flying with Deruluft would have that luxury.

He knew very little about Deruluft except that a German/Russian collaboration planned flights from Germany to Russia. When Drukker had initially told him of the opportunity, he immediately thought of the potential for spying on passenger travel from Germany into Russia and that some of Alice's Reichswehr people might make the journey. It seemed too convenient, but he had given it some thought on his trip and planned to keep a secret log of all passengers. He wondered where the flights would operate from in Germany, but his priority was to hook up with Werner Roth. Tom still harboured the prospect of comparing logbooks to see if they met in combat back in 1918 - such a long time ago, he mused.

It took some time to find Bernt Schmitz, the airfield manager, but eventually, after a few enquiries, Tom found his quarry in a much more salubrious office overlooking the field. 'My, my, Bernt, this is impressive,' Tom announced to a surprised Schmitz.

'Captain Thomas Munro, good to see you again. Come in, come in. I suppose you are looking for Werner Roth?'

Tom plonked his case down with a look of relief. 'Correct. I hope you are going to tell me where I can find him.'

'You are "in luck", as you say, but I'm not sure you're going to like what I have to tell you.'

'Oh, dear. Do I need to sit down?'

'Yes, I suppose you do. Can I get you a coffee or something more refreshing?'

'A coffee will do nicely, thanks. So, do tell, where is Werner?'

Schmitz opened a drawer in a chart cabinet at the back of his office and pulled out a large atlas. He set it on his desk and pointed with a smirk. 'Sorry, this is the best we have, but look here, ' Schmitz said, tapping the map to indicate Tom's destination. 'That's where you'll find him, at Königsberg.'

Tom followed the coastline to the east along the Baltic coast from Hamburg. His finger moved over Rostock, Stettin and Danzig, then across a long coastal lagoon to Königsberg. 'This waterway will be a useful navigational feature.'

'How do you find your way around, Tom? That has always mystified me.'

'IFR,' said Tom with a smirk.

'What?'

'I follow roads and railways, IFR.'

'I should have known.'

'That's why these road maps are so useful. One day we will have proper aeronautical charts like mariners. But for now, flying in uncharted territory is just that, "uncharted."'

'The problem is you must cross this section of Polish territory,' Schmitz said, pointing at the map. 'And also, this, the Free City of Danzig to get back into German territory.'

'Will that be difficult, by train? I assume that I will need to travel by train.'

'I suppose so. I don't know of any air services.'

Tom thought about potential passengers from Berlin – the Reichswehr staff. 'Why did Deruluft set up in Konigsberg? Why not here in Hamburg or Berlin?'

'You'll have to ask Roth. It's probably because it's closest to the Russian border. There may have been problems getting permission to overfly Polish territory. I'm just guessing.'

'Right. I'll get into Hamburg for the night and explore travel possibilities to Königsberg tomorrow. I'll call you to see if Roth has been in contact. I don't want to travel all the way to Königsberg to find he's not there.'

Tom had got used to the relative luxury of the Reichshof during more recent visits to Hamburg, particularly as KLM was paying. He had second thoughts as he approached the grand edifice; the three floors and premier rooms with neat balconies would be expensive. He knew he would have to opt for a more economical room and ended up at the rear of the building with a less-than-attractive view over an industrial area. Once he had found his room and relieved himself of his coat and case, he freshened up and strolled to the Hamburg Central Station.

The ticket office clerk, a stout lady of mature years, seemed to struggle with his German until he realised, she was deaf. Her lip-reading skills were impressive, but his lips were not German, and he decided that that was the problem. He took the notepad offered to him in desperation and jotted his destination in capital letters. The clerk looked at him askance. Her speech was impeccable despite her hearing problems, and she explained that the journey would be tortuous with changes at Stettin and the Polish border. From there, everything was uncertain, but there would probably be a bus from the border to Danzig, then a train, which would probably get to Königsberg. There seemed to be too many "probablys" in her travel advice, and he felt the need to prepare for a difficult journey. If only he could fly. If only he could contact Werner Roth, he would advise. He shrugged, nodded to the impatient Hausfrau in the queue behind him, raised a hand in capitulation and paid his fare to the Polish border.

He had an early night and a good night's sleep, suspecting that it might be a while before he rested so comfortably. As a further precaution, he feasted on a generous breakfast of toast with liver sausage spread, boiled eggs and cold cuts of cured meats, all washed down with black coffee. He wondered what faced him at Königsberg, mainly as he had not been able to contact Roth. A telephone call to Bernt Smitz at the airfield didn't help, as Roth had not been in contact. Where was he to go to meet Roth? The airfield was the only option. He assumed there was one and not just some muddy field. Quite an adventure, he thought, particularly as he had no knowledge of the Polish language. That will be fun at the border.

At Hamburg, he had time to wander along the platform to look at the handsome locomotive hissing and spluttering as if keen to get off the starting blocks. He got chatting to an obvious enthusiast. They look the same the world over, he thought and was advised that the steaming monster was a Prussian P8 built at the Berliner Maschinenbau. He made a point of looking suitably impressed with this essential information before dashing off to climb aboard.

Tom took two days to reach Königsberg, arriving as it was getting dark. The train journey to the Polish border was efficient and comfortable, with a change of trains at Stettin part of the recently formed Deutsche Reichsbahn railway system, a nationally organised service formed from the pre-war regional state railways.

His recent visit to the Fokker works and the advice from Drukker had left him suspicious of all strangers. When one fellow passenger seemed to glance in his direction rather too often, he wondered if he was being followed. No one was supposed to know about his new appointment at Deruluft, so that was unlikely, he decided, and he chided himself for being so paranoid.

The journey across the Polish Corridor between Weimar Germany, and Danzig was a different matter. No trains were running, and his 50km journey took until the next day by rickety buses with an overnight stop at a bus station. His fellow bus passengers took a particular interest in their strange-looking travelling companion, one in particular, and he decided that it must be the flying coat. A strange garment on a cramped bus journey, no doubt.

With aching bones from sleeping on a wooden bench seat with his coat as a pillow and little better on the buses, he was grateful for the relative comfort on the final leg of the train service from Danzig to Königsberg.

An unshaven, scruffy-looking Captain Munro finally pushed through the front door of a small guest house opposite the station in Königsberg, dropped his bag in relief and asked for a bed for the night. The young girl in the hallway introduced herself as Anna. She checked a sizeable leather-bound book on the hall stand and looked up with a welcoming smile, just what Tom needed.

'You're in luck,' she announced cheerfully in German. 'We're normally fully booked at this time of the year, being close to the station.' After a brief evening meal in a nearby café, it was all he could do to find his way to bed to catch up on lost sleep.

Anna waited in the dining room and poured some coffee for Tom. 'You seem to do all the jobs,' Tom said as he sat down for breakfast.

'We're a family business, so I do most things with my mother and father.'

Tom struck up an easy conversation with Anna and enjoyed using his German. She was very well informed about aviation matters and proud that the Konigsberg Devenau airport was the first civil airport in Germany. She was only too pleased to tell Tom all about it. Anna even knew of Deruluft and appeared unusually air-minded for a young girl. Tom was impressed and explained his new employment with that airline.

'I would love to fly,' the girl said wide-eyed. 'Will you take me?'

Tom laughed. 'I'm not sure about that. We can't just launch into the air whenever we wish with anybody who takes a fancy to flying. One day, maybe, if you can afford it. What you could do for me is show me where I can get a taxi to the airfield. And how far is it?'

'Of course, I can get a taxi. The airfield is about five

km to the north. I go there sometimes on my bicycle to watch the aeroplanes.'

'Thank you. You seem keen. Maybe you can learn to fly one day.'

'Do you think so?'

'Why not?'

'But I'm a girl.'

'I don't see why girls can't be pilots. Maybe I can get you a flight one day. I know where you work, so let's see.'

As Tom stepped into the taxi, he caught sight of a man on the other side of the street—an odd-looking fellow with a very square face and dark black hair. He thought no more of it and reflected on the past few weeks on the journey to the airfield.

It seemed like a lifetime ago that he left Amsterdam, and now here he was on a very basic and bleak-looking field with two hangars and a small central building with a glazed control room on top. Tom paid the driver and walked to the building with a Deruluft logo. He opened the door and spoke to a young fellow behind a desk. 'I'm Captain Munro. I'm looking for Captain Roth.'

'He'll be back this afternoon. He's doing the mail run back from Moscow. We know he left yesterday. Are you the new pilot? He's desperate for another pilot. One's off sick. He's doing all the flying. He's exhausted. I'm the Operations Clerk, Ernst Adelstein.'

'Good to meet you, Ernst; call me Tom. Where are

the aeroplanes?'

'One is broken down in Moscow. One is at Kaunas on the way to Smolensk and Moscow and Captain Roth has the third on the way back now. I had a call to advise that he had left Kaunas, so he shouldn't be long. We are trying to do a daily run, but, well, you know, weather, breakdowns and sick pilots; it's difficult. That is our fleet now, but we are expecting three more very soon. And more pilots.'

Tom had a momentary thought and looked blankly out of the window. 'That's it,' he said.

'I don't understand.'

'Oh, nothing,' Tom said apologetically. He remembered where he had seen "square face" before: on the bus journey to Danzig then again when he left the taxi. Feeling that he was being a little rude, he continued his conversation. 'What machines are you flying?'

'Fokker F.IIIs with Eagle engines. Excellent machines,' the fellow added with evident pride.

'Do you know where I am to be billeted? My accommodation.'

'Same as Captain Roth, I expect, in Königsberg.'

'Right, can I get a coffee somewhere nearby?'

'I can get one for you. Black?'

'Yes, splendid.'

Tom had fallen asleep in the corner of the Deruluft Operations room when a distant aircraft engine brought him back to life. He recognised the engine note instantly: the sound of a V-12 aero engine and, in this case, the Rolls Royce Eagle, the same as in the Vickers Vimy. He shook the sleep from his eyes and turned to look out across the airfield. There it was, a high-wing monoplane. A sight that he had become accustomed to when flying with KLM.

'That's him,' said Ernst, searching the sky with his binoculars. 'I'll get the truck for the mail,' he added, rushing out the door.

Tom watched as Roth banked the machine around for his final approach. The late afternoon sun appeared through a gap in the clouds, and the aeroplane's silvered wings reflected this shaft of light with a brief orange glint. This little display gave Tom a good feeling, a good omen and like all pilots, he scrutinised Roth's landing, which was very acceptable after his four-hour flight. The aeroplane taxied across to the waiting truck, where Ernst stood ready to open the rear door and unload the mailbags as soon as the engine stopped. Tom had taken a liking to this keen young man and admired his willing enthusiasm.

Roth climbed down from his cockpit and stretched his arms high above his head. Next, the helmet came off, then the gauntlets before he turned to talk to Ernst, who was already loading his hand cart with the mail bags. Roth patted him on the shoulder. 'A good load today. Get it off into town as quick as you like.'

'Yes, sir. You have a visitor.'

Tom hardly recognised Roth, and not as he remembered him at Hamburg. He looked so much older. 'Werner, good to see you again. You look as if you could do with a drink.'

'At last, Tommy. I've been desperate to see you again.'

'Ernst told me that you are short of pilots. Well, here I am. When do I start?'

'Tomorrow, of course.'

Tom couldn't wait to get his hands on this new machine. Despite being an F.III, it looked quite different. 'Can I have a look around?'

'Let me give you a quick brief, and then we can do the details tomorrow. You can take a copy of the Pilot's Notes back to town with you,' said Roth, elbowing Tom in the ribs. 'You can read it overnight.'

'If I can stay awake.'

Roth wandered around to the nose of the machine. 'We've now got a four-blade propeller to absorb the power of the Rolls Royce Eagle engine. It produces about 240 kW, sorry for you Britishers, that's about 320 hp. Quite a bit more than the Puma engines in your KLM machines. They were 240 hp, I think.'

'That sounds right. You must have a lot better performance with that power.'

'You would think so, but most of that extra power is used to carry the extra weight. You'll see our luxurious layout in the passenger cabin; that's a big weight penalty.

If we've got a big load of mail, the seats need to come out.'

'What about the wing configuration? That's different. Is that what they call a "parasol arrangement"?'

'Yes, it sits on struts above the fuselage. I'm told it was supposed to produce better performance, but it doesn't.'

'That big propeller must take some muscle to start. Reminds me of the old Bristol Fighter.'

'That's why we have big lads like Ernst there. He can do it independently, but we mostly use two men with arms linked together.'

They continued their tour around the tail and peeped into the passenger cabins. Roth opened the door. 'See what I mean. Luxury and cabin heating, too. We don't use it unless necessary; it tends to make the passengers sick. Exhaust fumes, probably. Not that we have a lot of passengers yet, only mail.'

Tom noted the rear-facing three-seat settee at the front of the cabin and two armchairs facing forward at the rear. Little curtains and even provision for a flower vase created a cosy, luxurious atmosphere. 'You're right, it's quite sumptuous.'

'Come on, Tom. I'm dying for a drink. Let's get into town and settle you in. I have lots to tell, and... well, it's great to see you.'

Roth took Tom to his lodgings near the cathedral, overlooking the Pregel River. It was similar to his earlier accommodation: a small single bed, a wardrobe for midgets and a chest of drawers that doubled as a bedside cabinet. His living space was completed with a communal toilet and bath along the corridor next to Roth's room. According to Roth, a small dining room downstairs could accommodate half a dozen people, most of whom were salespeople.

Tom felt pleased and relieved to meet up with Roth, but his appearance took him aback: sunken eyes, pale complexion and forehead worry lines he had not noticed before. In short, he looked exhausted. He hoped that he would not end up in the same state. Once settled into his tiny room, which took little time, they had an evening meal at one of the many cafes along the riverbank. Clearly, Roth was a regular and was welcomed by a very overweight, jovial fellow who was introduced as Max. Roth referred to him as "fat Max" under his breath. They settled at an oval table by the window, Roth's normal position and they chatted about Deruluft while enjoying the entertainment provided by the diverse panoply of passers-by.

'We're just flying light cargo and mail for now,' Roth explained between welcome gulps of the local beer. 'We've got regular refuelling stops at Kaunas in Lithuania, which is about 300 km, and then onto Smolensk. That's a much bigger hop of 550 km, but we still have plenty of petrol to spare. The F.III is good for nearly 1000 km. I'm not sure that we are without a stop. The final leg to Moscow is about 400 km. We use a cruise speed of 130 km/hr, so the longest leg is just over four hours. We night-stop at Smolensk on the way to Moscow and Kaunas on the return journey.'

Tom had nearly finished his first beer, and Roth waved to Max for another round. 'I'll need to get used to these metric units again. What are the facilities like at Kaunas and Smolensk? And at the base. I assume at Moscow?' Tom looked distracted.

'What's wrong, Tom?'

'That man. I keep seeing him.'

'Who?'

'Him, across the road. The black hair and odd-looking square face. He was on the trains and buses; I remember him. Is he following me?'

Roth was surprised by Tom's reaction and attempted to placate him: 'It's probably just a coincidence. I wouldn't let him bother you.'

Tom shook his head and lowered his gaze. 'You're probably right.'

'Perhaps you've been working too hard, Tom; you seem on edge.'

Tom knew that he was just getting suspicious of anybody. Wolf could be lurking around any corner and he would probably have any number of partners in crime. He wasn't about to explain this to Rolf. 'Me working too hard. I hear you're just as guilty of that.'

'You're right there. Let's enjoy our meal,' Roth suggested, topping up their glasses.

CHAPTER TWELVE

Alice had arranged a week of 24-hour surveillance on the Bendlerblock to track the movements of the mystery man seen with von der Lang. Jim Dalton continued to work on Emil Fischer, the new Reichswehr informer known as "Fish." Dalton hoped that he would start providing information soon. Nothing had come of the murder of Herta Koch, and Fish did not know anything about it and had little to say until Dalton made a casual reference to the word Weber found in Herta's flat.

Dalton nearly fell off his bar stool when Fish responded. 'Oh, he spends a lot of time with Colonel von der Lang.'

'Who spends a lot of time with von der Lang?'

'Herr Weber.'

Dalton dug around in his inside pocket and withdrew a crumpled photo of their mystery man. 'Is this him? Is this Weber?'

'Yes, that's him.'

Alice had advised Harry of Weber's identification for further checks when Dalton burst into their office on a sweltering summer morning. 'I think we've got something.'

Alice lifted her head from pouring over Weber's

movement reports. She was losing patience with their surveillance work. 'Yes, what now? Has he gone to the toilet again?'

Dalton flashed a sarcastic smile. 'A little more than that. He's travelling. He's got a small bag and briefcase, and he's off in a taxi.'

'Do we know where?'

'Not yet.'

'Is someone following?'

'Yes, Proudfoot is on it.'

'Right. We must find out where he's going, obviously.'

'Proudfoot's onto that as well.'

'Good. Now, how is Fish getting on? Is he producing anything else?'

'We're just building his confidence and getting him to use the dead letter drop. We check it every day, and I'm avoiding regular contact now. So, we need to wait and see if he performs. We've got some good incentives for him.'

'And the colonel? Anything of interest there?'

'Could be. He's been seen regularly with Weber and one or two individuals, and I hope Fish will identify them. I've asked the question.'

'Any photographs?'

'We're working on it.'

'Please get a move on. I'm under a lot of pressure. Harry Price is on his way out here.'

'What for?'

'A progress report, but he has some intelligence for us. Might be useful. I damn well hope so, as we're going nowhere at present. We need a breakthrough, so get on it, James.'

Ernst was on the telephone when Tom and Roth arrived at the airfield. 'Telephone call for you, sir,' said Ernst.

'Thank you,' said Roth, taking the telephone with a questioning look. He spoke for nearly ten minutes. Tom tried to make sense of the conversation.

Roth handed the telephone back to Ernst, looking flustered. 'Good, God, Tom. You have arrived in a timely fashion.'

'Come on, what was that all about?'

'We need to work out a plan. Ernst, two black coffees. Make it three you'll need it too.'

'Right, here's the plot. That was Deruluft, my immediate boss in Berlin. We've a job to do, and I can't see how we'll do it. But we must. How much time have you got on the F.III, Tom?'

'About 50 hours. I'll need to check my logbook. That was on the Armstrong Siddeley Puma version, which KLM operates, so I was sitting on the right side of the engine.'

'Good. Moving onto the other side won't be a problem.'

'Why do you ask?'

'I had planned a slower introduction to our aircraft,

but that call makes things more urgent. Let me spell it out, and then we can work out a plan. The problem is we have one aircraft here, one in Moscow, broken down and the other on its way to Moscow.'

'How's that a problem?'

'Our masters have accepted a charter to take a "special passenger" to Moscow.'

'Where is he, or is it she?'

'Berlin.'

'We go to Berlin then,' said Tom with a shrug.

'Yes, but we have the mail run to do. We don't have enough aeroplanes.'

'Could we borrow or charter one?'

'It's possible, and one of us would need to do the Berlin trip and back here to do our normal route to Moscow. We would need to set off now.'

'Why don't we both go to Berlin, share the flight with one of us in the back to rest up with "Mr. Special Passenger", then take the mail on to Moscow with our passenger.'

'It's possible, Tom, but I'll be exhausted.'

'We'll be OK if we share the flying.'

'Yes, I see,' Roth said with a hand to his brow. 'OK, we'll try that. We better get it planned. Ernst, get the charts for a flight to Berlin. And see if you can get a forecast. The met' people should be in by now. Get the machine fuelled up to full.'

Roth rolled out the charts and drew some lines from

Königsberg to Berlin Johannisthal, routing along the coast as far as the River Oder, then south until a turn south west to Berlin at Osinów Dolny, where the Oder turns south east. He grabbed a pair of dividers, stepped off the route and measured a total distance of 600 km. He picked up his slide rule. 'If we use Königsberg and an airspeed of 130 kph, the trip should be about four and half hours in no wind. We'll talk with our met' man and see what the weather has in store for us. I'll do the leg to Berlin and you can bring us back, Tom. How does that sound?'

'Sounds good to me. I can get a good feel for the route out the window.'

'We've rigged up a system like your Gosport Tube so the pilot can talk to someone in the passenger cabin. We can chat en route. I don't need to tell you anything new about the machine, but I suggest you take some time on the ground in Berlin to get accustomed to the new cockpit layout on the left side. There's more of a swing on take-off from the big four-blade prop, and she climbs better. I can answer any questions when we get to Berlin. Hardly the best start for you.'

Tom did his best to keep awake on the journey. The monotonous, droning buzz in the passenger cabin was very effective at putting him to sleep. The weather was relatively calm, with fair weather cumulus clouds bubbling up by midday when they approached Berlin.

He recognised the airfield from many visits and became curious about their mysterious passenger. Could it be someone from the Reichswehr? That would be a stroke of luck. As he had had no contact with Alice or Harry for weeks, he had yet to learn if any progress had been made. He decided to concentrate on making a safe flight in this new aeroplane back to Königsberg and onto Moscow – a new destination for him.

Roth carefully parked the F.III so Tom could easily taxi off for their return journey. They climbed down onto the ground, both exercising their jaws to clear their ears of the racket of the past four hours. 'Good flight, Tom. Are you ready to do your bit now?'

'I think so. We should make it back by dark?' said Tom rhetorically.

'Yes, we haven't much time for a turnaround. I'll chase up the refuelling and get our Deruluft engineer to check over the machine. We usually need a couple of litres of oil. Can you see if our passenger is about?'

Tom walked over to the small terminal building and stopped abruptly. Two men were waiting, not just the one as they were advised, one tall and erect, the other small, older, with horn-rimmed spectacles. What struck Tom was their dress. It was noticeably extravagant with tan fedoras, heavy coats open to reveal expensively cut three-piece suits and colourful neckties. Also, they both sported pocket watches and chains and seemed to make a point of posing with their flashy black and silver walking canes. A porter waited beside them with two identical, beautifully crafted leather cases with bright copper corner pads. They could have walked off a film set. There was something markedly false about the pair, Tom thought. Dressed for the part is the expression that sprang to mind. What part? Once he overcame his surprise, he continued into the waiting room and introduced himself as the pilot for their trip back to Königsberg. 'Our other pilot will accompany you in the cabin to keep you informed about our flight,' he advised.

Both were travelling to Moscow on a tourist visit. 'See the sights now that the country is opening up,' the taller gentleman remarked The little group walked out to the aeroplane, the porter wheeling the cases behind in his trolley emblazoned with the Deruluft company logo. Two mechanics were completing their checks as Tom introduced the passengers to Roth who showed them aboard.

Tom transferred his attention to the flight back to Königsberg and scanned the sky to the northeast. He noted a heavy buildup of cumulus clouds, which would make for a bumpy ride. His experience with KLM had developed a respect for passenger comfort, which could be compromised somewhat as the machine could be buffeted uncomfortably in these conditions. Before long, the ground checks were complete, and Tom climbed into his cockpit, fastened his safety belt and pulled on his helmet and goggles. It was a relatively warm afternoon, but as they might be flying at two to three thousand metres, he stuffed his gauntlets by his side for later. Lastly, he put his carefully folded charts into cockpit pockets and wound the clock on the instrument panel.

The Deruluft staff at Berlin had provided two ground crew for the start, and the Eagle engine burst into life with an enthusiastic roar. A check of pressures and temperatures, and a power check against the chocks satisfied Tom that all was well, and he waved the chocks away before taxiing away from the terminal building. The aerodrome operators were operating a light system for take-off and landing clearance, and he spotted the green light from the control tower. Nevertheless, Tom checked the approach carefully for any other traffic before advancing the throttle and guiding the machine across the uneven grass. He was aware of the much heavier four-bladed propellor and was ready to counteract the swing as he raised the tail into the flying attitude; the big propellor disc acted like a gyroscope, causing the machine to "yaw". Roth was right, but the swing was controllable with the rudder, and as he accelerated over the uneven grass surface, a helpful bump projected the machine into the warm afternoon air.

The aeroplane flew just as he recalled in other marks of the F.III machine, and with some relief and growing confidence, he turned onto his heading of 045 degrees. He planned to follow the road that aligned with his track from Berlin to *Ahrensfelde, Werneuchen, Höhenland*, and *Bad Freienwalde*, where he expected to see the river Oder again. From there, he could follow the river north to the coast and then northeast to Königsberg. He had followed Roth's track on the flight to Berlin and hoped that all would be familiar.

The machine began to rise and fall in the turbulent air near the cloud base, and with minor adjustments to his compass heading, he climbed the machine between the clouds. He glanced out to the left with narrowed eyes as they soared upwards past the glistening, towering walls of cloud, a solid-looking bulbous body of vapour ballooning upwards with invisible thermodynamic energy. At 3500m, he cleared the cloud tops, and the turbulent motion settled down. He was sure his passengers would feel more comfortable in the stable air. He could just maintain sight of his road and realised that he was smiling; after all, he was back in his element.

CHAPTER THIRTEEN

'We lost him,' admitted Proudfoot sheepishly.

'What do you mean "lost him"?' Alice barked.

'We followed him to the airfield, parked our car, and couldn't find him in the passenger building. We don't know what flight he got or whether he got on a flight at all.'

'Do you think he knew he was being followed?'

'I don't think so. It was very busy, and we couldn't get too aggressive with the staff. You know, we couldn't make it too obvious with questioning and so on, so we just did a thorough search of the building, toilets and all.'

Alice put her head in her hands. 'I can imagine what Harry will think of this. It was a golden opportunity to see what Weber was up to and certainly where he was going. All we can do is maintain our surveillance. Get Dalton to come and see me. I hope he's got better news with Fish.'

Dalton's demeanour didn't inspire confidence. 'You wanted to see me?'

'Yes, I need some results to report when we see Harry Price tomorrow. You're going to tell me some good news on our man Fish. You are, aren't you?'

'Nothing yet, but I feel that he is getting somewhere.'

'What does that mean?'

'He says that he's seen many new faces in the building, and they often meet up with General von Mayer and Colonel von der Lang.'

'Good, but who are "they"?'

'He's trying to find out.'

'Well, that would be nice,' said Alice sarcastically. 'Does he think there is an increase in activity? Does he get the feeling that something is going on? Something unusual?'

'He's working on it,' said Dalton apologetically.

'Right. Let me know if anything interesting comes out from this contact, anything at all, Jim.'

'Will do.'

'Oh, and what happened at the airport? How could Proudfoot lose Weber?'

'It was just poor technique. They parked the car first and expected to catch up with him in the building. He just disappeared. I've spoken to him, and... it won't happen again.'

'Have you checked on what flights were leaving that morning?

'Not yet.'

'Well, are you?'

'I'll get it organised.'

'This is basic stuff, Dalton. Get a list to me before Harry Price arrives.'

'OK.'

'See if you can get passenger lists as well.'

‘How?’

‘I’ll leave that to you; just get them.’

Tom was enjoying the flight in perfect weather conditions. As they overflew Danzig with about an hour to go, he thought again about his passengers. Something didn’t seem right. He remembered suggesting that travel from Germany to Russia should be monitored for Reichswehr staff movement on potential Group R-related business. He recalled his earlier reaction to meeting the passengers and wondered if there was something familiar about the tall gentleman, but he could not place him.

They were all pleased to set foot on the ground once again at Devau. The smaller gentlemen looked very pale and waved gratefully from the taxi as they were transported into Königsberg for the night. Tom helped Ernst with refuelling, then plonked down on the seat in the office as Roth checked on the mail load for their departure the following morning. ‘Did you have much conversation with the passengers, Werner?’

‘A little. It’s a bit too noisy for much chat.’

‘What did you make of them?’

‘They maintained their story about being tourists and visiting the sights of Moscow.’

‘Why do you say “story”?’

‘They didn’t look or sound like tourists, did they?’

‘Sounds like you didn’t believe them.’

‘I didn’t. It’s none of our business, but I think I know

the tall gentlemen from my Air Force days.'

Tom tried to remain calm. 'Oh, who might that be?'

'A Mr Otto von der Lang. Quite senior in the military now if it was him, but it certainly wasn't the name on the passenger list, was it?'

'No, that was Hoffmann and Dessauer,' said Tom.

Harry Price seemed older and anxious. His usual sense of humour seemed to be absent when Alice cracked a joke to break the ice at their meeting. She briefed Harry on the recent blunder at the airport and apologised for the mistake. 'It won't happen again, Harry. I'll see to that even if I have to do the surveillance myself. We've subsequently checked all passenger records for departures on the day in question and the following day to be sure, and there is no record of a Weber on any flights.'

'He could be using another name,' Harry suggested

'True, but that doesn't really help us for now.'

'Just an observation.'

'Of course.'

'You need to be very careful, Alice. How's the disguising working out? Must be a pain.'

'I can deal with it. I only get dressed up when necessary. Dalton and Proudfoot do all the surveillance work.'

'Hmm. More effectively in future, I hope.'

Alice opened her file. 'Let me bring you up to date. First, Dalton's young girl in the Reichswehr, Herta Koch, was brutally murdered recently, which you know about, but there have been no further developments. We don't believe that a connection to us has been made. Perhaps she was found snooping about. At least we see no signs that anyone knew that she was in contact with us.'

'You need to be extra careful then. They might be waiting for you to do something that provides enough evidence. Then, there'll be a diplomatic incident and a clear out of embassy staff or worse. You know the routine.'

'Yes, that had occurred. Anyway, Dalton has another contact we call "Fish", who's starting to produce some material that's not of much use yet, but he's promising. He also confirmed the name of the man we've seen with von der Lang. The mysterious Mr Weber. We still don't know what the connection is.'

Harry opened his file. 'OK. Right, my brief - and this comes from the minister, is that we are to pull out all the stops on determining what, if anything, is going on between the Germans and Russians.'

'How? Does that mean we can have more resources?'

'Yes.'

'What?'

'Me.'

'I'm tempted to say, is that all?' Alice quipped raising a smile from Harry for the first time. So, does that mean you're staying out here in Berlin then?'

'Yes, and C gives his full support now to your, or shall we say our, operation. I should add that the suspicions you have voiced for some time now are fully accepted but we still need the evidence. I know I sound like a stuck gramophone record, but that's the fact of the matter. Are you in touch with Tom?'

'Haven't heard a dickie bird. Last I heard, he was hoping to start flying with another airline. A German/Russian company. I can't remember what he called it. It's in my notes, but we all agreed this could be useful if our German friends travel to Russia by air.'

'Let me know, Alice, if he gets in touch. I need to talk to him.

'Me too…'

Harry cocked his head to the side in a questioning gesture.

'Don't worry, Harry, nothing is going on.'

'Tom, concentrate,' Roth exclaimed with a note of frustration.

'Sorry, you were telling me about your plan.'

'We heard this morning that our aeroplane in Moscow is fixed, so we need to bring it back here. You can do it if you come with us and our two passengers. The mail load is relatively small, so we have the space.'

'Fine. Is your third pilot OK now?'

'Apparently not. So we have you, me and Anton, who you haven't met yet. He's out on the route so we might meet up at Smolensk or Kaunas.'

'So you fly the first leg to Kaunas, then we swap over?'

'Yes, give you a chance to size up our passengers.'

'You're the one sounding suspicious, Werner.'

'I suppose I am. Look, they're here.'

Tom had more time to talk to the passengers on the trip although they kept themselves to themselves at the night stop in Smolensk and stayed at a different hotel. Tom had seen von der Lang at a distance when in Berlin with Alice but could not be certain that their passenger was the colonel. The other smaller man, Dessauer on the passenger manifest, was unknown to both Tom and Roth. Tom knew that he needed to get to a telephone to communicate his discovery to Harry or Alice, but how? Certainly, any form of secure line was out of the question and he had no idea what conditions would be like in Moscow. He decided to consult Roth for advice on where he could make a telephone call home to his mother. That should work.

Hoffmann and Dessauer were effusive in their compliments about their travel with Deruluft and declared that they planned to make their return journey with them. They also enquired about regular services. Roth was delighted and explained that scheduled services to Moscow could be introduced later in the year.

Tom found the Moscow airfield remarkably well-organised and laid out. Called Khodynka Field, it was located on the northwest side of the city in an area formally used for exhibitions, civil festivals and military parades. He noted a number of low hangars surrounding a small central building with a control tower. Roth told him that a busy flying school was in operation and that the airfield was regarded as the cradle of Soviet aviation. Tom turned his attention to his telephone call.

'You could try a call from our office telephone,' said Roth. 'I can't guarantee you'll get through, though. Everything is a bit haphazard here in Soviet Russia. There's always the hotel, but you're welcome to try here first.'

The office telephone was in an open office, and any calls would be overheard. Tom decided to try later. 'I'll wait till we get to the hotel. We both need a good rest, that's important. Are we off tomorrow again?'

'You stay a couple of days, then take the repaired machine back with any mail, and I'll leave tomorrow. The weather might delay us,' Roth said as he studied the sky.

Tom was surprised at how the Muscovites were dressed. He could have been in any cosmopolitan European city, and the bustling chaos of motor vehicles, trams, buses and carts was very familiar. He was expecting the menfolk to be dressed in belted smocks and boots and the women in headscarves and dirty long skirts. On the contrary, fashionable dress was much in evidence. There were infrequent signs of military uniforms, and he found the manual, semaphore-type traffic control mildly amusing. Their hotel was on Theatre Square. He had been told of the propensity of historic buildings in the Russian capital, and he could see that he would not be disappointed. He found the language totally unintelligible despite his familiarity with German. He resolved to learn the rudiments at least.

'Here we are,' Roth announced as the taxi pulled up with the squeal of well-worn brakes. 'You'll like this place, lots of history. It's still being restored. The Bolshevik authorities used it after the revolution and all the guests were kicked out, but when the major European nations began restoring trade and diplomatic relations this year, I think the Bolsheviks realised that the hotels of Moscow would not provide Western visitors with a good impression of the new Russia. They didn't want ambassadors or businessmen to spend their visit in some austere hostel with shared bathrooms, humble furnishings, and limited services. They might think that Communism was failing! So, in order to signal success, the Bolsheviks kicked out the apparatchiks and began the restoration. You'll see what I mean. Welcome to the Metropol.'

'It does look like a building site.'

'We'll have nice rooms. The Russian bosses of Deruluft have seen to that. Remember, our company is Russian funded.'

Tom could see that the reception area was once very grand, and from Roth's explanation, it looked as if it could be again. He was more interested in the telephone facilities and his ability to make an overseas call. He reasoned that Alice would be based at the British Embassy in Berlin and decided to give that a try. Fortunately, the reception staff spoke good German and reasonable English. Tom was impressed until he was advised that the telephone system was very unreliable in Russia. 'I would like to make an overseas call,' he said, nodding hopefully.

'You can try, sir. Which country?'

Tom looked around to ensure that Roth was not listening. 'Germany.'

'Use the booth at the end there. I will ask the operator for a line to Germany then you will need to ask the German operator for your number if you get through.'

'Thank you. I didn't get your name.'

'Nikolai, sir. Nikolai Volkov.'

'Thank you Nikolai.

Tom tried twice without success before he sat down with Roth for their evening meal. 'They're going to keep trying until they get through. It'll probably happen in the middle of our meal.'

'Your call to Germany, sir,'

'Right, thank you,' Tom replied, noting Roth's puzzled expression. 'Excuse me. I shouldn't be long but don't wait. Don't let it get cold.'

Tom realised that he would need some explanation for Roth on his return, but the immediate requirement was how to make the call if he got through. He had to assume that the call was being monitored. He would need to talk in code. Something that Alice would understand. He also realised that she might not be there.

The German operator wanted a number and a location or business name. He provided both and waited. He noticed a few clicks on the line, which confirmed his suspicions that the call was being monitored.

'British Embassy.'

Tom decided to try the cover name Alice used in Hamburg.

'There is no one by the name of Andrea here.'

'Can you ask about please?'

'Certainly not.'

'I can wait.'

'No. Is there a message?'

Tom heard more clicks on the line and passed a quick message, the first thing that came to mind, then put the phone down in a hurry as though the handset was roasting hot or poisonous. He wondered if the message would get to Alice. But then what? How would she follow up the message? He wasn't contactable. He would need to speak to her at some point. Could he go back to Berlin somehow? Or find somewhere safe to make another call? Germany would be safer, so perhaps a call from Königsberg would be possible.

'Is your mother in Germany then,' said Roth as Tom

returned to the table.

Tom smiled innocently.

Roth winked. 'Ah ha. Not your mother then.'

'No, not really,' Tom mumbled, trying to figure out how to respond until Roth provided the answer.

'Must be a girl, eh? It is, isn't it?'

'You guessed,' Tom replied, desperately playing for more thinking time.

'That girl in Hamburg?'

What a good idea Tom realised. 'Yes, you guessed right. You should be a detective, Werner.'

'She took a flight with you to Berlin, I recall. Reuter, that was it?'

'You have a good memory. Yes Andrea.'

'Did you get through?'

'After all that detective work, no, I didn't. It might be easier in Germany.'

'Definitely. Try again back at Königsberg.'

The embassy post clerk scratched her head. 'AF? There's nobody with those initials on our staff.'

The telephone operator, clutching her notepad, looked down the corridor. 'It might be one of them. The ones we don't talk about.'

'You can try, but they say they are not to be disturbed.'

'I'll take the risk. It could be important.'

Alice and Harry were deep in discussion about how to make more progress with the project when they were interrupted by a knock at the door. Alice twisted around in her seat with a frown to see one of the embassy telephone operators looking worried. 'I thought I made it clear that we are not to be disturbed.'

'Sorry Miss, but we've just had a strange telephone call, and I was told that you might be able to interpret the message. The post clerk doesn't recognise the initials.'

Alice sprang to her feet and opened the door. 'What message? What initials?'

'It's for AF, whoever that is, and it said, "VDL is on the passenger list". Does that mean anything to you?'

Alice frowned. 'Yes, you're right. Thank you. Oh, was the caller male or female?'

'Male, soft-spoken, almost whispering. Sounded nervous. Strange now I think of it.'

'Any indication where he was calling from?'

The girl scratched her head. 'Yes, now you mention it. It was Russia.'

Alice turned to Harry. 'Russia? Could it be Drummond?'

'Does he normally communicate by telephone?'

'No.'

The door closed quietly as Alice pondered on the call. 'Wait, wait. Did you write the message down? Did you get everything that was said?'

The door eased open again. 'I wrote some of it down on my pad, here. I was a bit taken unawares, so to speak.'

'Look, come in here. Sit down and relax. You're not

in trouble. Just tell me exactly what was said. Take your time. You answered the phone. Take it from there.'

'He started by asking for a name I've never heard of. I just said that there was no one of that name here.'

Alice felt excitement rise in her stomach. 'And the name?'

'I cant remember. It was something like Anderson or...'

'I don't want to put words into your mouth but was it Andrea?'

'Yes, that's it, Andrea... Reuter.'

Alice nodded repeatedly. 'Yes, good. Now, this is very important. And the rest, what else was said?

'He wanted me to ask around for Andrea Reuter. I said I couldn't.'

'Yes, well, that's unfortunate now, but the full message was?'

The girl took a deep breath and spoke slowly and deliberately. 'He said, "This is a message for AF from TM. Just say that VDL is on the passenger list". I wrote that bit down.'

'You're sure that was all?'

'Yes, I think that was it.'

Good, you've done well. In future, if anything odd like that happens again, write it down. Make notes. It could be vitally important. You understand?'

'Yes, miss.'

'What's your name?'

'Elsa, miss.'

'Good, Elsa. Remember what I said. You could be the first one in this big organisation to hear something very important. Make notes, remember.'

'Yes, miss.'

The door closed a little more confidently this time, and Alice sat back. 'Well we know that was Tom, don't we?'

'Yes, a message for Alice Ferguson from Tom Munro, and I think he must be flying with that airline now.'

'Yes, I've checked my notes; it's called Deruluft.'

'And the VDL on the passenger list?'

There was silence in the room for a few moments then Harry and Alice looked straight into each other's eyes and spoke in unison, 'von der Lang.'

After Roth left, Tom spent a day exploring Moscow on foot, tramping over the very streets which Tolstoy, Dostoevsky and Chekov had walked. He feasted his eyes on the fascinating conglomeration of historical buildings, many within sight of the Metropol Hotel, and took time to stop and take in the contrasting shape, colour and design of the architectural masterpieces.

He spent several hours exploring the sights around Red Square: the red-walled compound of the Kremlin and the ominous solidity of the Great Palace, the nearby St Basils Cathedral with its colourful onion-shaped domes, and the colossal redbrick elevations of the State

Museum. Eventually, exhausted by his perambulations, he took a seat on a welcome bench in the Alexander Gardens to ponder on the splendour of his surroundings and how it contrasted with the confusion and brutality of the October Revolution and the Bolshevik creed.

He knew little of Russian history except to appreciate that despite the beauty and grandeur of these surroundings, the revolution had been a lengthy and bloody affair leading to a new Soviet Russia with dubious values, a worrying political doctrine and now, the possible collusion with an ambitious and dangerous Germany. He decided that a coffee and something to eat was in order and wandered off to find a coffee house. He found one with a seat in the sun but struggled with the language when trying to order a coffee the way he liked it. A voice behind interrupted his linguistic inadequacies.

'Allow me to assist.'

Tom felt relieved. 'Please do. I just want a white coffee with one sugar.'

The stranger, dressed smartly in a well-cut suit and polished shoes, turned away, rattled out the necessary words then caught Tom unawares as he sat down at his table. 'Can I join you?'

Tom wanted a little quiet time to watch the Moscow world drift by but didn't feel that he could refuse. 'Yes, of course.'

'What brings you to Moscow?'

'I'm a pilot. I arrived yesterday. Captain Tom Munro.'

'You are English, yes?'

'I am indeed but working for a new German/Russian company called Deruluft.'

'Where did you fly from?'

Tom felt that the conversation was turning into an interrogation. 'We fly from Königsberg.'

'What do you carry?'

'Just mail and parcels but we should be carrying passengers soon.'

'You carried passengers yesterday, yes?'

Now, Tom was fully on guard. 'You seem to know a lot about our company. I don't even know your name.'

'Ah, here's our coffee. Let me get these. My treat for our visitor. What do you think of our country?'

'I haven't seen much of it, but I suppose after your revolution, it will be very different from mine.'

'Yes, quite and a good thing too.'

Tom didn't respond to that remark but pressed on to find out who this gentleman was. 'You didn't mention your name.'

'You don't need to know my name.'

Tom shrugged. 'You must work at the aerodrome, Khodynka Field?'

'Why?'

'You knew that I had passengers on my flight.'

'You need to be careful, Captain,' the gentleman said menacingly. 'Careful about who you talk to. Things are different here, and we do not have time for certain people.

Keep yourself to yourself as you English might say.'

Tom was getting annoyed but maintained a cool determination to find out who this fellow was. 'I'm not sure what you mean by "certain people".'

'You should. I mean the academics, the intellectuals, the reactionary clergy and the bourgeoisie.'

Tom tried to ignore the angry tirade and noticed people leaving the café. 'Right, I understand. Are you a policeman?'

The gentleman stood to leave, throwing some rouble notes onto the table. 'Just remember what I said, Captain. I work for the GPU.'

'Thanks for the coffee. What is the GPU?' Tom asked, unintentionally cracking a smarmy smile.

'You probably know us by the old name, the Cheka.'

'Ah... yes, I know.'

'Good day to you, Captain.'

CHAPTER FOURTEEN

Tom returned to the Metropol without noticing much around him. His conversation at the coffee house had spoiled his day, put him on guard, and reminded him that everything was not what it seemed in the new Soviet Russia. He decided that he must suspect everyone until they earned his trust. Any spying activities would be hazardous. The GPU must have been watching out for his arrival at the airfield. Or were his passengers of interest? Were they being met? That would make sense if one of the passengers was Colonel von der Lang. And who was the other passenger? They seem to be travelling together.

Tom wandered up the marble steps to the reception desk, still deep in thought. Nikolai Volkov waylaid him as he reached the front desk. 'I should give you a guided tour of our hotel. It will be a while until it is restored to its former splendour, but I think you might be interested.'

'That would be very kind,' Tom replied hesitantly.

'This way then. We'll start in here.'

Tom was shocked at the state of the once opulent rooms and the stunning architectural features: furniture piled high, dust sheets draped carelessly, and inches of dust, dirt and cigarette stubs scattered across the floors. Walls once decorated with expensive paintings now blank except for the marks where these paintings once hung. The curtains were mainly removed, but those still in situ were stained and torn. A vast glass ceiling in the dining area was caked in several years of grime, casting a depressing, murky pall across the room. Nikolai said the hotel once boasted telephones and electric lighting in every room. Also, chandeliers and other large standard lights were either broken or cast indifferently across the floor. It was a depressing sight, and Tom couldn't understand why Volkov would want to show it to him.

'I wanted to speak to you privately,' Volkov whispered. 'Too many people are listening to conversations, and I saw you met one of these gentlemen this afternoon. I need to warn you.'

'How did you …'

'Sshh, quietly, please. I saw you at the coffee house with that Chekist.'

'Yes, he was very helpful at first, then it felt like he was interrogating me.'

'There must be a reason, but I will not pry. I just wanted you to know how things are here in Russia beneath the pretence, the charades.'

'I think you know that I am a pilot, and I will be flying into Moscow from Germany regularly.' Tom shrugged. 'I just need to be able to work here occasionally without any trouble.'

'Since the revolution and our new illustrious Bolshevik government came to power under Mr Lenin, it has become a very different place. They used to work from here at our hotel until they were moved on to the Grand Palace in the Kremlin. Do you know that the instructions to murder the Tsar and his family originated here in this hotel? And have you heard about the appalling famine in the Volga region? Lenin actually instructed the military to seize grain and other crops to feed the cities whilst the local people, mostly farmers, starved to death. At least the American Overseas Relief Organisation is helping now, but for how long, I wonder? The country is in a mess, and for what? Political ideals and Lenin's doctrine. He is too fond of the sound of his own voice if you ask me. But they are all the same. I'd be shot for saying such things.'

It was obvious that Volkov wanted to warn him of the dangers in Russia and unburden himself of his bitter frustrations. Tom didn't respond with any comforting words; he didn't have any, but he realised once again that any SIS activities in the country would be difficult, dangerous and potentially fatal. He mused on how Alice and Harry could conduct clandestine operations in this environment.

The F.III took some time to get airborne with the heavy load of mail and other cargo, but Tom was pleased and relieved to escape from the picturesque but chilling confines of the Moscow streets. He was even more determined to contact Alice so that he could emphasise how difficult it would be to monitor any German collusion with the Russian military. How would they move around with GPU eyes on every street corner?

He was just thirty minutes en route and settling down for his three-hour flight when suddenly, an object filled his view and flashed across in front of him, disappearing with a whooshing sound downwards and to the left. It was dangerously close. He followed it for a few seconds until it paired up in loose formation with another machine. They had no markings, but he recognised them instantly. 'They're bloody Fokker D.VIIs,' he shouted into the slipstream.

He turned his machine to keep sight of the aeroplanes. It was fortunate that there were no passengers on board as he turned in an almost vertical bank and dived downwards to follow. His fighter pilot instincts were kicking in. What were these aeroplanes doing here? Were they some of the machines that Anthony Fokker had shipped back from Germany? This may be the evidence we need. They were heading southeast. With his height advantage, he was catching them up.

He knew his machine wasn't armed but felt compelled to close on the enemy to get within firing range. His machine was screaming like a banshee, the wings vibrating as his speed reached the safe maximum. His jaw ached, his hands rigid on the controls. Then he took a deep breath, saw sense, and slowly pulled away. He shook his head to banish the fighting instincts and slowly turned back to his original heading. He glanced over his shoulder to see the Fokker duo slip away into the distance, realising he had made the right decision. His F.III machine was very distinctive, with bold registration lettering and emblazoned with the Deruluft logo. He would be easily traced and identified. 'Damn, I should have a camera,' he mumbled as he drew a circle on his map to record his position.

'We've got three more machines, Tommy,' Roth proudly announced as soon as Tom's propeller juddered to a halt.

It was late summer, and the temperatures at altitude were falling. Tom tried to speak through numbed lips. 'What machines? Where are they?' he said, looking around and into the hangars.

'The Fokker works in Amsterdam.'

'OK.'

'You don't seem pleased. And I've got three more pilots joining us. You can help me give them the once over. And the news gets better.'

Tom dragged his helmet off and wrapped his arms around himself to control his shivering. 'God, I'm frozen, Werner. Just tell me the whole story,' he said.

'Let's get you into the office. I've got a nice coal fire going. Get you warmed up.'

'Great idea.'

The glow from the small coal stove was pure heaven for

Tom. He opened his flying coat and stood as close as he dared. 'That is just wonderful. We've got to enclose our cockpits, Werner. What's it going to be like in the winter? I remember our winter patrols at twenty thousand feet. I don't know how we managed it.'

'We were younger then.'

'Not that much. I tell you what warmed us up.'

'What?' said Roth, expecting some new-fangled technical device.

'Fighting you buggers, that's what.'

'True. Look, there is more news. Two of the machines are to go to Berlin.'

Tom's tired eyes sparkled a little more. 'Are we starting a schedule from there?'

'Yes, and with passengers. I just heard today. Our masters seem to think that the time is right.'

'Where do we fly to?'

'Moscow via here at Königsberg and the current route via Kaunas and Smolensk. Maybe Petrograd in future.'

'Can I volunteer to fly from Berlin? Be based there. That would be bloody marvellous.'

'I thought you might say that. Anything to do with the lovely Andrea?'

'Could be,' said Tom, looking coy. 'I assume that they will be more F.IIIs?'

'Yes, for now, but we might get some Junkers F13s as well eventually.'

Tom thought he would see if Roth could shed any

light on the mysterious aircraft he encountered. 'You've just reminded me. Just after I left Moscow, about 30 minutes into my flight, I nearly had a collision with two machines heading southeast. We were lucky we didn't smash into each other. What do you think they were doing?'

'What were they?'

'Fokker D.VIIs. No doubt, but they had no markings. A bit suspicious, don't you think?'

Roth's face reddened. 'Hmm. I've heard rumours amongst some of my old air force friends, but I don't want to guess.'

'What rumours? We should know about flying activities where we will be flying. I don't want that to happen again. Thank goodness I didn't have any passengers. They would not have been pleased about being thrown around like that.'

'Just rumours about our Reichswehr and the Russians doing deals over military equipment.'

Tom was getting bold. 'What, dodging the Versailles Treaty? Deals on equipment supply, aircraft?'

'Look, it's not something we should concern ourselves with. God knows what some people are up to. This Rapallo Treaty is opening up opportunities for us and our airline. We should concentrate on that. We could be operating a hundred machines before long and bigger machines and more passengers and more routes. That's what you and I should concentrate on. If the governments want to play games, that's up to them. I've had enough fighting and want to concentrate on our airline, Deruluft.'

Tom felt relieved at Roth's reaction. 'Spot on Werner. My feelings entirely. Both of us know what war is like. It's time to look forward to a peaceful Europe connected by our aeroplanes. I just hope to God that the peace can be sustained.'

'I'll drink to that.'

Roth arranged for an F.III to ferry Tom and two new pilots to Amsterdam and for the three new aeroplanes to be ferried to their new bases: two to Berlin, Johannisthal and the third back to Königsberg. Tom worried about how Drukker would receive him. He decided to stick with the other Deruluft pilots, who seemed determined to visit the red-light district that evening.

When Drukker met Tom with his companions, his usual smiling demeanour was totally absent. He usually had a joke up his sleeve, but not on this occasion. Obviously, he was trying to hide his anxieties, but Tom played along.

'The machines should be ready tomorrow,' Drukker advised. 'Will you be ready to leave with them?'

Tom nodded to his fellow pilots. 'Yes, certainly. We can be here at 8 am if that is convenient.'

'That will be good. We will be ready for you. I have arranged your accommodation in Amsterdam and transport. I will have the taxi collect you at 7.30 tomorrow.'

One of the pilots nudged his friend. 'Some fun tonight, eh?'

Tom didn't want to be unsociable, and the four pilots walked the mile to the Oudezijds Voorburgwal, the canal running through the centre of the De Wallen area, better known as the red-light district. They piled into the first bar they encountered and gulped down their beers as if looking for a dose of "zelfvertrouwen" or Dutch courage. In a jolly state, they spilled out onto the street and took a slow stroll past the numerous brothels, the scantily clad girls displaying their wares behind windows. Two of the pilots nodded at each other and disappeared up the steps and into a little hallway dimly illuminated by the ubiquitous red lights. They were met by one of the girls who stepped out into the corridor from the window. Tom was not inclined to partake, and with Anton, they tried another bar.

After an hour or so of discussing the future of aviation, they took to the street again. As Tom stepped outside, he stumbled on the step, and the cool evening air made him realise how tipsy he was. He grabbed hold of the door frame, righted himself and stepped onto the street. He turned to speak to Anton, but before he could hear an answer, he felt a heavy blow on the side of his head. The punch hit him like a hammer. He dropped to the pavement, and the world went black momentarily.

When he came to, three men he didn't recognise were standing over him, and he saw Anton's legs sprawled out next to him. He sensed a small crowd clearing a space around them, and he copied Anton as they both staggered to their feet.

As expected, one of the attackers lunged at Tom, but he parried the blow and caught the fellow with a solid punch as he went past. The men were tall but gangly and slow to react, probably drunk. Tom recovered his senses and went into boxing mode. Some bystanders laughed at his stance, how he presented his fists and the position of his feet. The laughs changed when he felled a second man with a vicious uppercut. His fist smashed into the man's chin, his head snapping back, his knees folding like hinges. Anton was holding up too and his attacker was off up a side street. Two men stood their ground, and it was now one on one. Better numbers, Tom thought as he glanced across at Anton, who nodded encouragement. Distracted, Tom took a blow to the cheek, which penetrated his defences. This fellow knew his stuff. Tom pranced about and irritated his opponent with his taunts. That was Tom's idea: get him annoyed, make him lose his temper. One of the golden rules in boxing is not to lose your temper. Tom continued to evade the man's blows and waited his moment. The man staggered off balance after his punch missed its target, and Tom landed a heavy blow on his victim's right cheek. He spun around and fell head-first against the wall. He had nowhere to go, and when he turned around, Tom finished him off with another straight punch to his nose. A spray of blood seemed to knock the fight out of the man, and he held both arms up in front of his face as Tom pulled his fist back for another blow. The man turned and ran up a dark alleyway, followed by Anton's opponent.

Tom stood back, breathing heavily as he watched their attackers stagger off. He spotted a figure emerging from a doorway and recognised him. It was Heinrich Wolf, he was sure. Tom shot off up the alleyway like a runner off the starting blocks but was wrenched to a sudden halt with a strong hand on his collar.

'Let him go, Thomas,' said Anton. 'They've had enough. We don't want to get jumped again.'

Tom tried to pull away. 'I've got to get that bastard.'

'Which bastard?'

Tom slowly calmed down, realising that Wolf was gone and Anton would not know the significance of the man who had emerged from the shadows. 'You're right. I just got a bit mad with these characters.'

'Well, enough for one night, eh, Tom?'

'I suppose you're right. I was just getting back into the swing.'

'Were you a boxer then?'

'Yes, in the distant past, though.'

'They picked a fight with the wrong pair, didn't they?'

'Why?'

Anton raised his fists in a boxing pose. 'I was a boxing lad at school. Still do it when I get the chance.'

Tom clapped him on the back. 'Good man to go out on the town with then!'

It was during the war that Tom last flew an aeroplane in formation and his F.III bobbed up and down to the left of Anton's machine as they climbed away from Amsterdam en route to Berlin. Roth had agreed that Tom and Anton would operate the Berlin service. Tom spent as little time as possible at the Fokker works and was pleased to get away. One way or another, he would settle his score with Wolf. He couldn't confide in Anton or anybody other than the SIS team. He had managed to get a message to Alice to advise of their expected arrival time but assumed that to maintain his cover, he would need to share accommodation with Anton. How much could he say about Alice? Just preserve the story of her working in the embassy. That should be harmless enough.

As forecast, the weather started deteriorating, and Anton's machine frequently flew in and out of clouds. They had agreed to separate and make their own way if conditions prevented their loose formation. They had been flying for nearly two hours and had covered about half the distance to Berlin when Anton's gloved hand pointed downwards, indicating that he wanted to land. Visibility was deteriorating rapidly, and Tom assumed that Anton decided that it was too dangerous to carry on.

Tom raised a thumb and followed Anton's machine down into the murk. He relied on Anton to find a field but kept a wary eye on what he could see ahead of time, trying to guess which field Anton was choosing for a landing. He decided to watch Anton land, fly overhead and position his machine for a landing alongside Anton. The pair of machines carried on for some time, the fields below too small for a landing, let alone a take-off. Tom was getting tired, peering into the grey mist, keeping a safe distance from the machine ahead and trying not to lose it. They would need each other's help to get started again and needed to stick together. Eventually, Tom sensed that Anton was slowing for a landing and his machine was beginning a slow descent. Tom slowed his machine and watched Anton's machine drift downwards, crossing a low hedge and bumping down onto the field. Tom eased on the power to circle the field and watched the landing machine slow to halt. As Tom turned across the field, he caught sight of Anton's machine standing on its nose. 'Damn it,' Tom uttered, assuming that the ground must be too soft for their machines.

He had to decide whether to attempt a landing or try another field. But they must stay together or within easy walking distance to help with the engine starts. He flew over adjacent fields, which looked much the same. Anton was out of his cockpit and signalled something. It looked as if he was pointing out a safe landing area.

Tom overflew for a better look and confirmed that Anton was pointing out a better position for landing.

The mist became particularly thick as Tom tried to stay in sight of the area Anton pointed out. He made his approach as slowly as possible, preparing for soft ground. They didn't need two wrecked aeroplanes in some muddy German field. He could imagine Roth's reaction. He crept his machine across the boundary hedge and held the machine off until the last possible moment. The F.III shuddered and dropped positively onto the grass, Tom holding the stick well back to avoid Anton's mishap. The machine stopped rapidly, and Tom shut down where he was to avoid running into any soft ground. Time to survey the field later, he thought.

After two hours in the air, the silence was deafening but very welcome. Tom saw Anton's machine still perched precariously on its nose, looking very forlorn. Anton was nowhere to be seen as Tom scanned the field. Eventually, Anton appeared from the hedge row, beaming a wide grin of achievement or, in his case, relief. 'I sure as hell needed that.'

Tom understood the situation immediately. 'I know what you mean, two hours is a long time, four hours impossible. We need to get your machine back on its feet again. Was the engine running when you put the nose in?'

'No, I just managed to stop it so it should be alright.'

'OK, let's have a look.'

The weight of the two men brought the F.III's tail back onto the ground with a soggy thud. The mist had become much denser, hugging the ground like a thick grey blanket, so there was little choice but to spend the night in the field.

'Where are we?' said Anton.'

'You should know, being the lead machine.'

'I can tell approximately. We were approaching Hanover, but I was distracted when finding a field. They're all so small.' Anton peered across the field. 'Do you think we'll get off again?'

'We should pace it out before dark.'

The mist was thick, grey and clinging. Everything, the wings, the fuselage, and the tailplane, dripped silver globules of water onto the grass. If they stood perfectly still, they could hear the drip, drip, drip against the occasional muffled sounds of distant birds. 'Eerie, isn't it? said Tom. 'Can you remember the direction of the longest run across the field?'

Anton shook his head. 'Let's leave it until morning. The visibility can't be more than ten metres.'

Tom peered into the murk. 'You're right. Let's just rest up for the night. Have you got any food or water - anything?'

'I've got some drink, no water. I'll have a look in my bags.'

'Me too.'

'It's going to be a long night, but at least it's getting light at five or so.'

Anton pointed to his aeroplane, opened the cabin door and gestured with an open hand. 'Would you care to join me, sir?'

'I don't mind if I do. I'll fetch my luggage,' Tom replied, playing along.

The passenger cabin of both machines was of the highest quality. At the rear of the compartment, a three-seat leather chair with armrests and lap-straps occupied the entire fuselage width. At the front, facing rearwards, a two-place seat comprised what should have been a congenial travelling experience. The cabin walls were lined with leather to half height with a sky-blue papered surface above and over the ceiling.

Neat floral curtains adorned the windows, and a small drinks cabinet was positioned between the seats opposite the entrance door. Wall lighting with twin lampshades and two ceiling lights cast a cheerful ambience in the cosy cabin. Ample space behind the rear seat provided storage for luggage and other cargo. Anton sprawled across the rear seat, hands behind his head, and Tom did the same on the two-seater.

'We shouldn't drain the batteries,' said Tom, switching off the ceiling lights.

Anton dug into his bag. 'Let's see what we have. Ah, most important,' he said with relief. I remembered to top up my hip flask.'

'That's a good start. I have the same for this eventuality.'

‘I’ve got some very dry bread and some cheese. What about you, Tom?’

‘Not much better. A couple of apples and some cheese.’

The F.III cabin resembled an old English public house, and Tom felt quite at home. The smell of leather combined with their drinks completed the sociable ambience of the tiny space.

‘Cheers,’ said Tom, raising his hip flask.

‘Anton responded in a similar gesture. ‘Zum Wohl!’

‘I don’t know much about you, Anton.’

‘Not much to know. Born and raised in Hamburg. I joined the Luftstreitkräfte, our Air Force, in 1917 and my Jagdstaffeln, “Jasta Boelcke”, at the end of that year. We were combined into what you would call a fighter wing, Jagdgeschwader III, in 1918. We flew the Albatross.’

‘You must have been very young?’

‘Yes, just a boy. Only eighteen.’

‘I joined our Royal Flying Corps at the same time in 1917, but I had been persuaded to stay on at university, so I was twenty when I joined. I ended up on a Bristol Fighter squadron. Roth and I may have had a fight. He was flying the Fokker D.VII. I wanted to fly the Sopwith Camel, but I eventually mastered the Brisfit.

‘Yes, we were very wary of the Bristol Fighter.’

Tom wanted to move on from the war years. ‘Now all I want is to make civil flying a success. There is so much to do to develop airlines. We could be flying around the world before long. And anyone will be able to fly, not just the rich.'

Anton took a big slug of spirit from his hip flask, reached into his bag, and topped it up from his bottle of *Himbeergeist*. 'I want to return to flying real machines, the military.'

'I don't suppose that's possible now.'

'Yes, the bloody armistice. The politicians and the Jews betrayed us; we call them the "November Criminals". Then, the Versailles Treaty denied us our military. What shame for us.'

'Why betrayed? Tom asked.

Anton's face reddened noticeably. 'By our political masters and the Jews. We could have won the war.'

'Well, that's all history now, Anton. We should look forward, eh?'

'We will be looking forward. We will have our time, and those who profited from our blood will be the ones to suffer.'

Tom wasn't sure he wanted to continue the conversation, but his curiosity got the better. 'Who profited?'

'The communists and the fucking Jews. They made money from the war and then persuaded our masters to surrender. We should *never* have surrendered. We will have our day again. Mark my words. Just mark my words.' Anton sprang up, jumped from the cabin, and strutted off into the mist.

Tom paused, ran his hand through his hair in exasperation, then followed. 'Anton?'

An abrupt voice emerged from the mist. 'Yes?'

'We need to forget that bloody war. Learn from it, yes, but it mustn't happen again, ever.'

'We'll see. You should listen to a new man in our midst. He speaks sense.'

'What does that mean?'

'I mean Adolf Hitler; he's just become the leader of our National Socialist German Workers Party. They get my vote. Just wait and see, Thomas.'

Tom collected his bag and made off to his machine for the night. 'Night Anton. Maybe we'll feel differently in the morning.'

Anton shrugged, climbed into his machine, and slammed the door closed.

Tom didn't get much sleep. He twisted and turned on the three-seater in his machine and Anton's rant surprised him. Who was this man Hitler, and what did Anton call it? The National Socialist Party? He wondered what Anton did immediately after the war and what influenced his worrying views.

Before drifting off, Tom decided he might need to explore these questions further, but he would need to pick his moment, not when they had been drinking. Maybe it was the drink that set him off. The silence in their cold, lonely field eventually dowsed his muddled mind with sleep.

CHAPTER FIFTEEN

Alice had decided to meet Tom at Berlin's Johannisthal airport and wore her disguise out of necessity but also for some amusement. She wondered if Tom would recognise her. Her plan was scuppered when the aeroplanes didn't arrive, and she was surprised at how disappointed she was.

'Do you know when he is expected now?' Harry asked when she had returned to the embassy.

'There's been no communication from them, and the people at the airfield don't know anything either.'

'Are you worried?'

'Not really. Tom can look after himself. He's a marvellous pilot. Everybody says so.'

'I want us to meet with everyone once he's back. A workshop. We need to formulate a plan of action. We could wait forever for information from Fish.'

'Are we in contact with Drummond? It's time to fire him up and get him focused on what we really want. He sends reports on famine, gulags, and regional problems. We want him to focus on something more concrete: our operation.'

'The question is, where do we send him? Geographically, I mean. It's a big, bloody country. We need to give him some steers.'

'That's why we need to pool our knowledge. Decide

if we know anything substantial, definitive to put him on the right track.'

'I don't think we're there yet, but let's see what we know when we put our heads together.'

'Are you going out to the airport again, Alice? I'm really keen to hear Tom's news. That flight to Moscow, for example.'

Anton was in a better frame of mind as they consumed what was left of their meagre rations. They also found some berries in the hedgerows. Anton had the bright idea of collecting the dripping water in a can, and by morning, they had collected nearly half a pint. The mist remained dense at dawn, but the sun became visible as a hazy yellow orb peered through the thinning miasma.

Tom tidied his aeroplane and readied it for flight. 'We should carry emergency rations, Anton. This won't be the last time we have to land out,' he shouted as he completed his pre-flight inspection.'

'Good idea.'

'We should talk about starting the engines. It'll need some planning as there are only the two of us,' Tom shouted as he continued his inspection.

'Yes. We need to chock the wheels and tie back the stick as we will both be needed to swing those big props.'

Once all was ready with both mainwheels on each aeroplane firmly chocked and the sticks tied back to prevent the aeroplanes from jumping the chocks, they went through the carburettor priming routines and set the throttles. They started with Anton's machine with the clear understanding that once it started, he would run around, climb into the cockpit, and warm the engine. With arms linked, they pulled the engine through a compression or two to complete the priming, but despite a good muscular swing, Anton's engine refused to start. They tried again. It coughed and spluttered, which was promising but wouldn't keep going. They re-primed, set the throttle and tried again and again before sitting down, puffing from their exertion.

'What do you make of it, Tom?'

'Let's look around the engine. Ensure the intake is clear, and there are no obvious issues, such as loose plug leads, ignition connections, and so on. The plugs might be oiled up.'

'That's a lot of plugs to clean!'

'Let's hope it's not necessary. Everything seems OK. Let's try my machine; give this one a chance to think about it,' Tom quipped, although he often felt that his aeroplanes were conscious beings. They seemed to know when to be particularly unhelpful. 'It might feel differently when mine starts.'

Tom's engine started at the first pull, and he rushed to the cockpit as the machine's wheels pushed into the chocks. He settled the engine to a fast idle, let it warm up, and then checked everything at a higher power setting. He gave a thumbs-up, set the engine to idle and secured the stick fully back with his lapstrap. 'Let's try yours again,' he shouted to Anton as he jumped down from his cockpit.

Anton's engine started without any repeat of the earlier reluctance. They both shrugged at each other before Anton climbed aboard and completed his checks. They had agreed that Tom would take the lead on the last leg to Berlin, and after setting engines at idle, they carefully pulled the chocks away, watching for any movement of their machine, then tossed them into the cabin. With some relief, they climbed aboard, strapped in and taxied to the end of the field.

It was a bright, still autumn morning, with just a hint of the earlier mist hovering over the ground, when the two Fokker F.IIIs broke the silence, the throaty roar of Rolls Royce Eagle engines echoing across the landscape, chasing the local crow community from their perches. In turn, the machines rushed across the field, the heavy dew spraying into the air in their slipstreams. They just cleared the trees at the end of the field, the leaves dancing in the blast of air from their passage, the two machines turning east towards Berlin and a new beginning for Deruluft.

Alice was sifting through the many photographs that Dalton and Proudfoot had taken of personnel coming to and going from the Bendlerblock. They had identified several individuals often seen with the colonel and the general.

An excited Dalton burst into their office. 'They've arrived. Tom and the aeroplanes.'

Alice's expression brightened immediately. 'Excellent. I can't wait to hear what Tom has to say. We will need to let him go to his accommodation. I assume that Deruluft will organise that, and he will probably need to stick with the other pilot. We need to take his lead, but we will arrange our meeting as soon as he can attend.'

Tom managed to make contact the following day. Alice grabbed the phone as if her life depended on it. 'Where are you?' she said.

'I need to be careful. I've been in meetings with the Deruluft bosses and my pilot friend, Anton Baehr. We'll need to watch him. I'll explain. I told Werner Roth about you. A "girlfriend" in Berlin. He remembers you from Hamburg. He doesn't suspect anything, but I'm unsure about Anton. I'll need to make some excuse about going off alone in Berlin. When can we meet?'

'We're totally flexible. H is here and looking forward to seeing you. Can we meet here at Wilhelmstrasse… you know?'

'Yes, I don't see why not. Look, let's say tomorrow morning at eleven. We're getting a day off before we start flying again.'

'OK, eleven it is unless we hear from you.'

'What name did you use when talking to Roth?'

'Andrea. I hope that's OK?'

'I suppose so… I'm looking forward to seeing you too, by the way.'

'That's nice to hear. Must go.'

Tom turned up at the embassy an hour late as Alice and Harry were ready to give up.

'I couldn't shake off Anton. Not sure why he wanted to stick with me, but we agreed to meet up back at our digs this evening to do the town.'

Tom shook Harry's hand and wanted to give Alice a big hug. He sensed that Alice felt the same, but they resorted to a more formal handshake. They looked into each other's eyes, a kind of knowing look that lasted a few seconds until Tom picked up on Harry's impatience. 'How are you both? This job is not getting to you, I hope?' Tom asked.

Alice and Harry glanced at each other before Harry answered. 'We need to make some progress. I'm out here permanently until we get to the bottom of this. C is on my back almost daily, and we're both struggling to see a way ahead.'

Tom felt the need to be more positive. 'We need to review where we are. I have some interesting developments to report and…'

'I want to get Dalton in on this,' said Alice. 'Proudfoot is out at the Bendlerblock, but we want to put our heads together on this project and devise a plan. We've been thrashing around somewhat.'

Harry butted in. 'I need something concrete to report to C. At the moment, we know something is going on, but not exactly what or where. We need the damn evidence that C keeps hectoring about.'

Alice went to the door. 'Very true. Let's get a coffee, and I'll get Dalton in.'

Alice and Harry had been using a large meeting room for their work. A substantial oak table sat in the centre of the room, covered in photographs, papers, and files. A curtained notice board filled one wall and provided space for sketches, drawings, and other diagrams, which looked like an attempt to piece together their puzzle. The room had no windows, but bright walls and overhead lights created a classroom-like space. Tom scanned the board and noticed one particular photo. 'That's him.'

'Who, what?' Harry exclaimed as they sat down.

'This fellow was the other passenger on my flight to Moscow along with von der Lang. The colonel used an alias, Otto Hoffman, and this chap was called… Dessauer, Hugo Dessauer.'

Harry looked pleased for the first time. 'That's Weber and the first decent piece of intelligence we've had in weeks. Why was he travelling to Moscow with von der Lang?'

'And posing as tourists,' said Tom, tapping one photograph on the board. 'And if von der Lang used a pseudonym, Weber was also travelling under a false name.'

'Something to hide, obviously,' Alice added.

Dalton joined the meeting, and Tom was introduced, feeling a little tension between Alice and Harry. Harry made a point of taking the lead and spent thirty minutes reviewing the status of their investigations then concluded his review. 'So, we need to identify who von der Lang and von Mayer are working with and if they are related to whatever is happening in Russia. Tom's identification of Weber travelling to Moscow is the first real evidence that the Reichswehr is up to something with the Russians. Once we find out about Weber and why he is travelling to Moscow, we will know what they are up to.'

Alice turned to Dalton. 'When is Fish going to produce some useful intelligence? Can he not identify some of the people we're seeing with the colonel and the general?'

Tom put his hand up like a schoolboy. 'Can I add something? I forgot to mention that when we arrived, von Mayer was at the airfield to meet the Deruluft people and see our machines. We've been told we will start a new passenger service from Berlin to Moscow within weeks and may provide charter flights.

'Wow,' said Alice. 'Now we're getting somewhere. We can monitor these flights, pin down people of interest, and get leads on what's happening. You will be in an excellent position to see who takes the flights, Tom.'

Dalton spoke for the first time. 'Yes, but thinking ahead now, what happens in Moscow and in Russia? We'll need to tail our targets. How do we do that?'

Tom nodded. 'Good question. I won't be able to tail anyone. It would be too obvious, and I won't have the time.'

'You can make the time. Take a break, a holiday, see the sights,' Harry added flippantly.

'I know you're not serious, Harry, but I haven't reported on my more recent encounters with Wolf.'

'Have you seen him again?'

'Not just seen him, I believe that he's tried to have me killed… in Amsterdam.'

'You said encounters?'

'Yes, this is a good time to update you.

Tom described his inadvertent swim in the canal and the attack in Amsterdam whilst with Anton. 'You see, it's obvious they are on to me. So, to be of any use, I must play my part as the honest, reliable pilot flying for Deruluft. I can report on passengers, but any chance of me tailing people in Russia is out of the question - for now at least.'

Harry shook his head. 'I see. I was hoping that you would be able to track these people.'

'We'll need to use Drummond,' said Alice.

'Remember that Fokker might play a part in this game. I saw drawings of new fighter aircraft at the Fokker Works and a host of D.VII aircraft. That's why Wolf has been after me. Oh, and I nearly forgot: on my return flight from Moscow to Konigsberg, I saw two D.VIIs flying southeast; they were completely unmarked. Where were they going, and why were they there? Fokker has a hand in this affair, I have no doubt.'

'Sales of aeroplanes to Russia. What's wrong with that?' Dalton added cynically.

'Possibly, but why do I get attacked?'

'Did you see who ran you into the canal?'

'No.'

Dalton shrugged. 'It could have been an accident then?'

'I doubt it, but possible. But I saw Wolf in Amsterdam when Anton and I were set upon. Fortunately, Baehr can handle himself. In fact, he held me back when I tried to chase Wolf in the alleyway. I'm going to have it out with that bastard one day.'

Harry attempted to bring the meeting to order. 'Right, I think we've had enough discussion. Let me draw things together. We need to identify the people working with the general and the colonel in the Bendlerblock; that's down to you, Dalton. We know of Weber but not what he does. Tom can monitor the passengers travelling to Moscow, particularly when they are travelling with Reichswehr staff, and we get Drummond set up to monitor and tail targets in Russia when we alert him to who is travelling to Moscow. How does that sound?'

'Fine by me,' said Tom. 'Can I have a camera and

film? Maybe the little Kodak pocket camera I had before. I can get some shots of my passengers surreptitiously or even happy tourist snaps.'

'I'll keep working on Fish and continue with our monitoring of the Bendlerblock,' said Dalton.

'Leave Drummond to me,' said Alice. 'It's vital we get our system set up in Russia.'

Harry closed his file. 'Thanks, everyone. Let's get some results. I'll return to London directly and keep in touch with you, Alice. Let me know if any of you will be in London so that we can catch up. Good hunting.'

CHAPTER SIXTEEN

Tom's introduction to winter flying on the Moscow route was dire. Incessant snowfall, weeks without flying and very few passengers. Europe seemed to be in hibernation, although Berlin's nightlife kept him amused. Anton proved to be a good companion, and there was no repetition of his outburst. However, Tom still retained some reservations about him, as he couldn't forget the mention of Adolf Hitler, who seemed to feature all too often in the Berlin newspapers.

Roth flew in for a few days, and they caught up on Deruluft's plans. More aeroplanes and bigger machines, too, but these improvements were unlikely to be of much benefit during the restrictions of winter operation. Contact with the British embassy in Berlin was rare, and he concluded there was little further intelligence on their project. He met up with Alice frequently, and they slept together on occasion. Alice didn't say too much, almost as if she had been instructed to keep quiet. He still felt a little used by her, but the attraction remained. On balance, he probably used her too.

His exposure to operating aeroplanes in extreme weather conditions reinforced his view that suitable airfield surfaces and some form of blind flying aids in the cockpit would be needed. He had had too many near misses with flights in poor visibility and clouds.

On one occasion, he became very disoriented, similar to his experience during the war in his Bristol Fighter.

He managed a two-week break back in England in February as there was little flying to do. Airfields feet deep in snow, and the aeroplanes safely tucked away in hangars whenever possible. This gave the mechanics time to catch up on their work without the constant pressure of keeping the aeroplanes in the air, so Tom willingly grasped the opportunity.

Much of his break was taken up travelling from Berlin to Amsterdam via Hanover in uncomfortable, decrepit trains with dilapidated coaches full to bursting point with passengers who seemed to be travelling with all their possessions. The ferry directly from Amsterdam to the Harwich Parkston Quay at the London docks didn't fit his schedule, and he stopped in Amsterdam to reach London on the fourth day of his travels. He did not risk a visit to the Fokker works but felt tempted by the possibility of a quiet word with Drukker. He was sure he would tell him something of interest if he could get him away from his office.

It felt strange to be back in Salisbury. Typically, his mother was out, having found a welcome independence following the death of Sir George Foster, just after her engagement to him. Tom admired his mother for her fortitude after this tragedy and her informal mothering of Louisa in their joint loss. He eagerly awaited Louisa's arrival as she planned to return for the weekend.

He opened the door when the taxi arrived and was shocked by Louisa's appearance. Short, practical hair, drab, careworn coat and a little hat, more appropriate for someone twice her age; such a shame for a young woman who could look quite stunning. He kissed her on the cheek and hoped his surprise didn't show. 'It's marvellous that we could meet up,' he said, taking her small bag and stuffing it under the hall stand.

Louisa was always good at reading people's thoughts. 'Hello, Tom. I'm sorry, I must look like a mess. I'm a bit exhausted, and I'm just pleased to be home.'

'It's nice to hear you say that.'

'What?'

'You said home. It's nice to think you see this as your home now, but didn't you buy a little house somewhere in Salisbury?'

'Yes, I did, but I need a favour before I forget. Is your mother around?'

'No. Anything to help, just say,' Tom said with a frown. He felt like buying her new clothes, sending her off to the hairdresser and just looking after her. So much had changed. Why?

'Oh, let's have some tea.'

'Of course. Mother is out, so let's catch up. It's been a while.'

Tom got the fire going, which was still warm from the

previous night. Its flickering warmth seemed to cheer Louisa up. He poured the tea and offered Louisa a rather soft, tired looking bun hastily retrieved from the pantry. So, you need some help.'

'Yes. Sorry to bother you with this. I'm sure you are ready for a rest too. I look forward to hearing your stories, but this is urgent.'

'Just tell me how I can help. You know I'm always here for you, Louisa.'

'Well, it's Uncle Robert.'

'God, that man! I can't say I'm surprised. What's he up to?'

'Told me that the trust can't afford my fees. My medical college fees. I've still got at least two years to go.'

'Have you spoken to the other trustees? I am trying to remember their names, but they should be able to enforce the terms of the trust.'

'I was advised badly. Foster's Engineering needed money for a project, and I agreed to the loan based on a good interest rate. Mr Brankstone, you remember he's our bank manager, said it was safe, a solid investment. I didn't take too much interest; excuse the pun. I was up to my eyes in my studies and work at the hospital. Then, I was told that repayment was impossible when it fell due. Mr Brankstone retired, and the new bank manager was appointed as a trustee.'

'Something smells here. What does Mr Starkey say? He's your solicitor, isn't he?'

'He says it's a financial matter that should be resolved by repaying the loan, but Robert won't play ball. I've had to sell my house to keep paying my fees.'

'Bloody hell, Louisa, this is terrible. I understand that times are hard after all the war work disappeared, but I'm sure Robert must have other irons in the fire. You wouldn't know, but I saw him in Amsterdam, at the Fokker aircraft factory where I worked. I'm not there anymore, but that's another story. In fact, I have so many stories I wouldn't know where to start. But, back to your problem, how can I help?'

'You know I've never trusted Uncle Robert, and recently, I have been visiting the factory to demand the loan be repaid and generally snoop around. He always finds some excuse for not seeing me: "important meetings, must go out", that sort of thing. It would be helpful if you came along. I don't suppose he will find it quite so easy to fob you off.'

'Is Bill Franklin still there?'

'He left the company about two months ago, just after Christmas.'

'Damn, he might have been helpful. Someone we can trust. Do you know where he went?'

'No idea, he just disappeared.'

'Right, let's pay Foster's Engineering a visit. We can use the Morris if your mother isn't using it.'

'Talk of the devil, here she is.'

Mary looked as proud as punch as she breezed into

the hallway, tossing her goggles over a coat hook. 'You're back, both of you. Splendid, time for tea.'

'Hello, Mother, you're looking well,' Tom said insincerely, thinking she looked older and a little pale. Mary was not one for hugging and made straight for the kitchen and the kettle. She had never been reluctant to speak her mind. 'You look as if you need cheering up, Louisa, and a new coat, perhaps. What's the matter?'

'I'm just tired,' said Louisa, resorting to a simple, diplomatic reply. 'And looking forward to a break.'

'Have you finalised the sale of your wee house?'

'Yes, all done now.'

'Are you going to see that Robert? Get your money back? If only your father were still around.'

'Yes, and Tom will help.'

That seemed to satisfy Mary, so she turned smartly and marched off to the kitchen. 'Good, now let's have some tea.'

When Mary retired for the evening, Tom and Louisa took the opportunity to catch up. He put more coal on the fire and coaxed the embers into life. 'Why don't we just turn up at Foster's? We shouldn't allow Robert to run off or find excuses.'

Louisa sighed. 'He won't be pleased and might not be there.'

'That's too bad. We'll just take the chance. I have little time. If he is up to something, we might catch him out.

'Other than the money he owes me, I have no real reason to take an interest in the company, but I find it hard. It was my father's pride and joy. He lived for that business, and I used to spend many days there as a child, getting under the feet of the staff. I find it so hard to see it occupied by Uncle Robert, sitting in my father's office. He doesn't deserve it.'

'Does Sir Reginald Ferris take much interest in the company? He does own it, after all.'

'I don't know. I saw Sir Reginald there once. Robert has taken the business off in other directions. The aeroplane business has gone, although the motor car work is returning.'

'If I remember correctly, Sir Reginald was interested in storage space. What was that for? I plan to meet Daniel Ferris; he should know what Ferris Shipping is up to.'

'And see his pretty sister too, no doubt?'

'Oh, Louisa, do I detect a hint of jealousy?'

'Of course not. Let's go to Foster's tomorrow.'

Tom was impressed with the condition of the Bullnose Morris. Mary had arranged to keep it under cover behind a shop on Blue Boar Row, and the radiator cowl was polished just as Sir George used to like it. Mary still used Sir George's old goggles, and Louisa grabbed them off the hallstand before they set off down Endless Street. 'I want to wear these, for old time's sake.'

Tom felt that he was in a parallel world. One day,

he was in Berlin, then travelling through Europe, and now he was driving through Salisbury with the girl he had fallen for during the war. Salisbury traffic on the market day was a chaotic mix of motor vehicles, horse-drawn carts, bicycles and wayward pedestrians; the discordant jangle of a street organ and trader's cries added to the mayhem. The hubbub ensured that Tom had to concentrate on his driving, particularly when a butcher's boy on a bicycle, complete with an overloaded basket, swerved in front of his car. They drove down Minster Street, past Poultry Cross, the Little Ben clock tower and along Fisherton Street, where Louisa pointed her finger at the Infirmary in a reflective gesture. Young men, aged by trauma in blanketed wheelchairs, were still conspicuous along the pavements near the Infirmary. Empty sleeves and trouser legs tucked up and neatly pinned. Tom nodded understandingly, as this was where Louisa had been first introduced to the world of medicine as a VAD. They negotiated the tortuous conflagration of roads at the railway station, then headed west on the Wilton Road to the factory near Fugglestone St. Peter. Louisa's old family home, Fairview, stood proud at the end of its private drive, and Tom sensed her nostalgic reaction to the poignancy of the moment.

Tom slowed the Morris as they approached the entrance gates to Foster's Engineering, its name still proudly announced in steel over the double-gated entrance. He, too, was feeling nostalgic as this was where he first mastered the very same Morris he was driving into the factory. They parked in front of the main office buildings and found Sir George's former secretary, Annie, now retained by Robert Foster but probably much less happy with her appointment.

Her reaction shocked Tom and Louisa. Rather than the usual friendly welcome, her mouth dropped, and she said nothing. She looked at Robert's office door.

'What's wrong, Annie?' said Louisa, shocked at the reaction.

Annie stumbled over her words. 'You mustn't... They're not expecting you. You can't...

Louisa's expression changed as if she was about to go into combat. 'That's the idea. Is he in?'

Annie froze at her desk and put a hand to her mouth as Louisa barged across to Robert's door, knocked loudly and marched in, her face a picture of determination.

Tom was caught off guard by Louisa's pre-emptive sally but quickly caught up and followed her into the office.

Two gentlemen sat poring over a desk covered in papers and drawings, two cigarettes balanced on an ashtray, trailing smoke into the blue fug. They turned in unison, mirroring each other with the look of naughty boys caught in an illicit endeavour.

Robert stood abruptly, spilling papers across the desk and barged to the door. 'Bloody hell. Get out of here. Out,' he bawled hysterically as he crashed into Louisa.

Tom caught Louisa as she was projected backwards. 'Steady on Robert. What's got into you.'

'Just get out of here!' Robert bellowed, spitting his words like a machine gun.

Louisa tried to continue with her objective as she fell backwards into Tom's arms. 'I want my money,' she bawled. Tom just managed to stay upright and they looked at each other as the door slammed shut, the mortise lock clunking into place lock as a clear indication of some sensitive, secret shenanigans on the other side.

'I'm sorry,' said Annie, rising from her desk.

Tom pulled Louisa to her feet and straightened his tie. 'What's going on, Annie?'

'I can't say anything, Nothing.'

Tom raised an eyebrow. 'You know who that was with Robert?'

'He did look familiar.'

'More than familiar. That was Daniel's father, Sir Reginald Ferris.'

'I suggest we pop into town and talk this through,' Tom suggested as they returned to the Morris. He looked puzzled as he scanned the factory grounds. 'There isn't much activity. I can't hear any machines in the workshops, and no girls sitting on the wall during their tea break. I'd love to have a look in the sheds. Should we take a look in the window? Won't do any harm.'

Louisa nodded in the direction of the workshops.

'That looks suspicious.'

Tom followed her nod. 'Oh, I see. The windows, you mean.'

'Yes, they weren't painted out the last time I was here.'

Louisa climbed into the Morris as Tom sauntered nonchalantly across the courtyard, a brief glance over his shoulder. He didn't get very far.

'What do you think you're doing, Munro?' Robert bawled from his office window.

'I was just going to peek into the old sheds, for old time's sake.' He pointed at the central workshop building, one of three. 'I recall this one was where the aircraft parts were made for Sopwiths, and British & Colonial. I ended up flying the Bristol Fighter, you know.'

'We don't do anything like that now.'

'Right, nothing of interest then?'

'Not for you two, Munro. I suggest you take yourself off. Go on, off with you!'

Being market day, they were lucky to get a seat in the Limetrees Tearoom, a popular spot in Salisbury. They navigated their way to a table around the generous hats and similarly generous ladies. 'This'll do,' said Louisa, feeling inappropriately dressed in her motoring coat and hat.

'Can't say that was very successful,' said Tom, taking his seat.

'I didn't expect anything more. Uncle Robert's a bastard.'

'New medical terminology?'

'Well, it's true.'

'Do you think there's any mileage in meeting with your bank manager and solicitor? Your only chance is to appeal to the trustees. They could outvote Robert. Surely, they can approve a gradual repayment of your money?'

'You would think so.'

Tom shook his head. 'I'm bloody suspicious. If he is that tight on money, the business must be on its last legs. What was Sir Reginald Ferris doing? It's his company now. I should arrange a visit to Daniel. He would know.'

'But would he say anything, and did you see that thing in the office?'

'What thing? I was too busy catching you.'

'I don't know. Long black thing like a gun.'

Tom sat bolt upright. 'A gun?'

'I suppose so.'

'Now look, this could be important. Describe it to me.'

'For goodness' sake, Tom. I just caught a fleeting glimpse of it. I was charged off my feet, remember?'

'Ok. Sorry, but it is important. Do your best. Think back. What did you see? Your reward is one of these,' said Tom, pointing at the two-tier cake stand.

Louisa took her "reward" as she attempted to remember the details of the black shape propped up in the corner of the office. There was silence for a few minutes as they tucked into the tasty selection of cakes. Tom dabbed at his mouth before speaking. 'Something is going on out there. I know it, and I can smell it. Why paint the windows? What did you see, Louisa?'

Louisa mimicked Tom and used her napkin for thinking time. 'Right. I suppose it was a long tubular thing like a gun with a rifle butt and a round drum thing on top.'

Tom's eyes lit up. 'Yes, anything else?'

'About three or four feet long.'

Tom sat back, looking pleased with himself. 'That's a Lewis machine gun. I know it well. The question is, what's it doing in Robert's office?'

I need to snoop around the Foster's factory after dark and see what I can find. There wasn't much security, and I'm pretty adept at snooping these days.

'What do you mean?'

'Oh, nothing. Another story.'

A visit to Daniel Ferris and a surreptitious visit to Foster's Engineering while Louisa tackled the trustees were agreed upon as the most sensible course of action for Tom. Mary was getting irritated about the loss of her motor car. 'I'll only be around for a few more days,' Tom reassured with his easy smile. It always worked on his mother. But first, a snoop around Foster's Engineering could provide some answers, although he couldn't use his mother's car.

He decided that an early morning jaunt, around 1 a.m., would be best as he didn't expect any night shifts or other work at that time, judging by the relative inactivity they'd observed. It was too far to walk, so his old bicycle would need to be returned to service. 'Need some exercise,' was his excuse to his mother as he dug the elderly machine from the shed at the bottom of their small town garden. It was probably five miles to the factory, but once he cleaned up the machine, pumped up the tyres and applied oil liberally to the moving parts, he conducted a wobbly trial run around the market square until he felt confident of making the trip.

Dressing quietly, Tom pulled on his overcoat, grabbed a flat cap from the hallstand, and moved to the front door. He stepped cautiously down to the pavement with his bicycle, clenching his jaw tight as if this would help make his exit more silent. He heard a soft voice just before he closed the door behind him.

'Be careful.' Louisa whispered, her head just visible over the bannister at the top of the stairs. 'Let me know when you're back.'

'Will do,' Tom replied as he closed the door. His final preparation was to strap his Orilux trench torch with its leather pouch and Sam Browne belt across his chest before setting off down a dark, wet, Endless Street en route to Wilton.

The market square was deathly quiet, the scudding

grey-black clouds occasionally revealing the crescent moon, which winked at him as if it knew his plans. A dark shape moved on the pavement, a tramp seeking dubious comfort by a shopfront, Tom's coat flip-flopped on his knees as he peddled on in the dark.

CHAPTER SEVENTEEN

Dalton looked down at his hands and fiddled with his pen, his cheeks as red as a radish. Harry and Alice waited for his report. 'You don't seem very confident,' said Harry.

Alice was less patient. 'Come on, Dalton, let's have it. I can see that you don't have good news. Has Fish produced anything? It's weeks now since you predicted he would have useful intelligence.'

Dalton flared up. 'OK, right, I misjudged the situation. I got him wrong. He's bloody well disappeared. I haven't had any contact with him for, let's see, two and a half weeks.'

'So, are we writing him off?' Harry said, raising his hands in frustration.

'I don't know. All I have to report is Fish has disappeared,' said Dalton, reaching down into his bag by his feet. 'But there is this, in the dead letter box,' he added with a hint of a smile. 'Might be significant.'

Alice took the sheet of tatty paper that Dalton slid across the table. She read the words and looked up. 'Junkers and Fokker' she said. 'Is that it?'

Harry frowned. 'How long have you had this?'

'I collected it yesterday, which means it could have been there for a week.'

'These are names of German aeroplane companies.

Did you arrange another meeting?'

'No, I just left a chase-up note in the dead letter box. That's what I got back.'

Harry looked at the note again. 'Is this his writing? Do you think anything has happened to him?'

Dalton shrugged. 'It's his writing but I just don't know what's happened. I'll keep trying to make contact. I just hope he hasn't gone the same way as Herta.'

Harry looked worried. Alice suspected that unless he got results, he'd be recalled. She had ideas on how to proceed and wanted to help Harry make their project successful. If he was replaced, she dreaded the thought of some acerbic, arrogant operative being put in charge; some London arsehole, she thought!

'I've got to return to London,' Harry announced dramatically. 'C wants a face-to-face report. I might not be back. I can't report anything concrete, so you lot will need to produce results or face the same fate. The SIS is under a lot of pressure since Lloyd George's embarrassment over the Treaty of Rapallo. Finally, someone in government is suspicious; he wants to know if anything is going on under the cover of Rapallo.'

'Thank God. Perhaps now we'll get more resources. Could you be replaced with some pompous ass?' said Alice.

'Who knows? If that happens, I'll do my best to get someone suitable, but it won't be my decision.'

Alice tried to be positive. She could work with Harry,

trust him. She was worried now. 'You'll just have to explain the difficulties to C and devise a plan.'

Harry shrugged. 'That's the problem, a plan. I'm running out of ideas.'

Alice tried to be positive. 'Look, Harry, we can put our heads together and develop something; at least, we can report what we know so far and the way ahead. You can present it to C and get back here to get things moving. Let's get to it.'

Tom felt vulnerable as he pedalled through Salisbury and onto the Wilton Road. His bicycling experience in Amsterdam had generated a feeling that he was being watched, even in Salisbury. He had never established whether his collision with the car and his unplanned swim in the canal was accidental, but it had clearly affected him. He pedalled harder in an attempt to quell his unease, frequently glancing behind at the deserted black streets, wet and shining under the occasional gas lamp.

It was pitch dark as he left the outskirts of Salisbury, and his solitary journey stimulated thoughts and memories of the war which he had all but forgotten: the German soldier, the boy in the crater, his face, the bayonet. He had been pedalling hard for about ten minutes when he sensed a yellow glow behind him. It grew in intensity - a vehicle behind. He wondered if he should dismount and wait till it passed. As the lights got closer, he decided to keep going and be ready to dismount. As the road brightened around him, his giant shadow thrown onto the trees ahead, he decided to stop and watch as the vehicle passed. It didn't pass. It slowed and stopped a few yards behind him. He couldn't see much in the dazzling headlights, but he glimpsed a silhouetted figure passing the beams and walking towards him. He could feel his heart pounding like a steam engine.

'Evening, sir, and what might you be doing out here at this time of the night?'

Tom had not planned to meet up with a policeman and wracked his brains for a convincing response. He blundered out a hesitant reply and cringed at his words. 'Yes, a bit strange, officer, I know. Still got the shell shock, you see. Can't sleep, and I've found that the only way to cope is to get on my bicycle. I ride to Wilton and back if I get my dreams, the visions.'

'Hmm. Where do you live?'

'Salisbury, Endless Street, but I work in Berlin. I'm a pilot. Had some bad times in the RFC.'

This seemed to impress the police officer. 'Well, I'm damned. I was in the RFC. Just a mechanic.'

'Not "just" a mechanic. We relied on you, chaps.'

The conversation continued for some minutes, and Tom started to relax. 'I'm just off to Wilton, then I go back. A sort of routine that seems to settle me.'

'Right, you are, sir. Just take care on these dark roads.

Someone, half asleep, might run into you.'

'OK, officer, good to chat.'

As Tom expected, the Foster's works was dark and deserted. He made straight for the office block to look in the window at Robert's office. As Louisa had said, the narrow beam of his Orilux easily picked out the object propped up against the wall. It was definitely a Lewis gun. It was very careless to leave it lying around, he thought. Typical Robert.

He crossed to the three workshops, which triggered memories of his guided tour with Louisa's father, Sir George Foster. During the war, the main business was making aeroplane parts. He remembered the heady smells of wood in the machine shop, the girls sewing up linen coverings and the sickly-sweet aromas of dope applied to tauten the linen over skeletal structures, which gradually took shape before final assembly. He smiled affectionately at these memories before the piercing light of his torch indicated mostly empty spaces in two of the workshops. He tried to see through the painted windows in the third workshop, but it was impossible.

Having come so far, he wouldn't be put off and searched the building for an open or broken window. He even tried doors but without any luck. There was no alternative but to break in, and he made his way to the darkest, most remote corner of the buildings, took a final look around and listened for any sign of a guard. The factory seemed deserted, and finding a small rock, he took off his coat, smothered the window and tapped as gently as possible. The breaking glass sounded deafening, echoing inside the building. He cringed, paused and listened carefully, looking over his shoulder, his eyes darting about for anyone or anything. Nothing, just a soft rustling of the wind in the nearby trees.

He carefully cleared the pane and remaining shards of glass and jumped up using a convenient oil drum for additional height. Scrambling over the frame, he dropped to the floor, cushioning his landing and bending deeply at the knees for a silent arrival. He stayed in a crouched position as if ready to pounce; there could be a nightwatchman or guard. He listened intently for a moment before creeping over to a stack of large wooden cases visible in the moonlight.

He could smell oil, grease and wood and just a hint of the dope from days gone by. Feeling sure there was no one about, he switched on his torch, swept the Orilux beam around the building and stopped at a large stack of crates, which were the size of a small car. He paused to study the markings, walked closer, and stood up with a broad, knowing smile, his curiosity immediately satisfied. 'Well, what have we here?' he mouthed, tracing the letters with his finger. 'Napier Lion 450hp Aero Engine'. He thought immediately of Robert's visit to the Fokker factory and design drawings in the design office.

He turned his attention to the smaller cases, which

revealed equally startling evidence. The stencilled markings clearly indicated the contents: Air-cooled 0.303-inch Vickers Machine Gun and the other cases, Birmingham Small Arms, Lewis Machine Guns. He mumbled to himself again, 'I can guess where they're going. No wonder Robert was agitated.'

Moving along the stack of boxes, he eventually found paint pots, brushes, and stencil plates. Also, his torch beam found that some of the boxes and crates had been re-marked to read "Farming Equipment" or "Farming Machinery—Spares".

Alice eyed the door, feeling the tension in the room as she, along with Dalton and Proudfoot, waited to meet the new man.

'What's he like,' said Proudfoot.

Alice shrugged. 'I've no idea. A new recruit, I believe.'

Dalton shook his head. 'A new boy on something this important? He better be good.'

Alice scanned the report that Harry had hand-carried back to C at SIS HQ and wished they could report more progress. She had received a message from Tom that he was returning to Berlin to resume the Deruluft service to Moscow now that the weather was improving and that he had something interesting to report. She cursed under her breath, wishing that she knew what it was. It could be helpful with the new man arriving. What was his role going to be? How would they get on?

He came with little or no reputation, but she assumed he had been dispatched with C's blessing. That didn't help her guess what he might be like.

The door opened abruptly; a confident entrance, Alice thought. Her immediate impression was of a tall, erect military type in a smart three-piece suit, with a square jaw, short black hair neatly groomed, and someone who could look after himself. He was rather attractive, too. For some reason, they all stood.

'Morning all, do sit down. No need to be too formal.'

Alice took the lead. 'Good morning to you. I'm Alice Ferguson, in charge of this project, and this is Jim Dalton and Raymond Proudfoot.'

'Good to meet you all. My name is Colonel Freddie Ross, and with immediate effect, I'm taking charge of this project.'

Alice noticed a cultured Scottish accent but was more preoccupied with what she had just heard. She sat back with a sigh.

'Something wrong, Ferguson?'

'Well, yes. It is my understanding that I am in charge of this project. I spent over a year convincing the powers that it was necessary.'

'So I understand,' said Ross, canting his head. 'But not much to show for it, unfortunately.'

Alice clenched her fists on top of the table, took a deep breath, nearly responded in a way she would regret, held back and spoke slowly with apparent control. 'Right,

I can't say I am too pleased about that.'

'You will need to accept it, Ferguson, or else you'll be off the job. You and your team will be very valuable, so I hope you all accept the changes.' Ross looked around at Alice, Dalton and Proudfoot in turn. 'Can I assume your full support?'

Dalton and Proudfoot were quick to acquiesce, and Ross's cold blue eyes returned to Alice. 'And you Ferguson?'

Alice took another long breath. She knew that she desperately wanted to find out what was happening in Russia, but they still knew so very little. If she had to accept the new boy, then so be it. He didn't seem all that bad so far. He could be worse. 'Very well, you're the boss, colonel,' she mumbled impudently, her gaze averted.

'Good, but you can drop the colonel,' Ross replied, narrowing his eyes, taking his jacket off and pulling a secret file from his briefcase. 'I've read Price's report, but I want to summarise how I understand the story. Correct me if I've got it wrong and fill in any details if I'm missing anything relevant. I'll be brief, and then we can get on with plotting a way ahead. This is a top priority back in London. All eyes are on us, so we need to get results and fast. Even if our findings just indicate what might happen in the future. In fact, that's probably more important. But we need evidence, rock-solid evidence. So, here's how I see it.'

Alice raised a finger. 'Just before you start, do you

appreciate that much has happened that is not included in Harry's recent report?'

'Yes, so that's where you can fill in the details as I go along.'

'Ah, right,' said Alice.

Alice felt that Ross's recap of the story to date was reasonably accurate. She filled in the details of their encounters with Wolf, Colonel von der Lang, and General von Mayer. Ross seemed perturbed about Tom's involvement with the project.

'So, tell me about Munro. Is he dependable?'

'Very,' said Alice. 'And he could be even more useful. He has some more intelligence, which he should bring to the table when he gets back to Berlin.'

'Tell me a bit more about him.'

Alice sighed. 'You should know that he was brought onto the SIS strength a few years ago and has been providing intelligence ever since. He's now flying for Deruluft, the German/Russian airline on the Moscow route from here. He's a war hero and an ace and is reported to be an exceptional pilot. He has already reported von der Lang travelling to Moscow. That's all in Harry's report.'

'Hmm. That doesn't make Munro a good spy. Get him in when he gets back. I need to meet him.'

Tom removed his leather helmet, tucked his gauntlets

under his arm and smoothed his hair as best he could without a mirror. He thought about the car mirror, but it was too late. The heavy front door opened with a ponderous groan, a member of staff in pretentious tails appearing with a look of mild disdain. It seemed appropriate for the ostentatious surroundings at Branley House, the Dorset seat of the Ferris family. Tom decided on a surprise visit to Daniel Ferris for a bit of fun but also for more serious reasons: to detect any unusual reaction to the enquiries he planned. Would he know about the trade which his father was involved in? He was working in the Ferris shipping business, so he should know.

'Can I see Mr Daniel Ferris, please?'

'Is he expecting you?'

'Afraid not, just visiting on the off chance.'

'Who can I say is calling? Do you have a card?'

'No card, I'm afraid. The name's Captain Tom Munro. We're old friends.'

'Very well, sir, if you'd like to wait in the hall, I'll see if he's available.'

Tom sat on an over-stuffed chair beside a semi-circular table with a colourful display of spring flowers. He glanced around and decided there had been little change since his last visit some 12 months before. He wondered if Daniel's sister, Fran, would be in. He fiddled with his helmet, stood and removed his overcoat and peered into the ornate mirror at the end of the hall.

'You don't look all that bad, Thomas,' said Fran, posing like a model on the curving stairway. She liked making an entrance from the stairway.

'Fran, hello there. I was hoping to see you. How are you keeping? You look well, very well, in fact.'

'Oh, so so,' Fran replied with little enthusiasm as she descended the stairs with practised grace. 'Father just keeps arranging meetings with eligible young and not-so-young men,' she announced, swiftly kissing Tom on the cheek and taking his hand. 'Come through. Frazer will take your things. I suppose you're here to see Daniel.'

Tom took to her gentle, convivial manner and felt instantly warmed by her charm. 'Yes, is he in? I just took a chance before I go back to Germany.'

Fran's demeanour changed noticeably. 'Oh, when?'

'As soon as I can. I'm flying from Berlin now. It's quite exciting, particularly as I fly into Russia.'

'Isn't that dangerous? After the revolution.'

'I don't see much of that. I fly in and fly out again. I am staying in a marvellous old hotel, the Metropol. It's a ruin but being refurbished to its former glory. I should be able to see this happening. I'm told it was a marvellous place in pre-revolutionary times.'

'Captain Munro,' said Daniel. 'Wonderful to see you. What a surprise. You should have given us some warning. We could have arranged a bit of a do.'

Tom and Daniel shook hands warmly, and Tom gave

him a brotherly hug. 'Yes, great to meet up again.'

'Would you believe it, Daniel? He's off to Germany.' Fran lamented with a shrug. 'He pops into our lives all smiles and cordiality, then disappears again. Whoosh, gone in a jiffy,'

Tom felt a little guilty. 'A man needs to earn a living, Fran. I'll come and see you again when I'm back in England. So, Daniel, how has the Foster Engineering business been doing since the acquisition?' Tom asked, wanting to get to the point. 'I visited Fosters yesterday with Louisa. Robert has stopped her allowance from her trust. Says he can't afford it. Your father was there too. Do you know what's happening? Why Foster's should be in financial trouble?'

Daniel's countenance transformed. His radiant smile faded away, and he appeared worried and serious. 'I don't believe the company is in financial trouble; it's just a matter of cash flow. Once the project is completed, all will be well. These days, there isn't much engineering work to be done; it's mostly about sourcing equipment for shipping overseas. I'm currently working with the Ferris Shipping business.'

Tom was curious to know more and wanted to see if Daniel would provide any specific details before he asked his burning question. 'Oh, I see. What project is this, and what equipment are you working with?'

'Not sure; I get the weights and measurements, then arrange shipping.'

'Surely, you must know what you're moving to complete the shipping documents. Where are you shipping to?'

Fran butted in. 'Tom, you sound like a barrister questioning a criminal. What's the matter?'

Tom realised that he was getting too pushy. 'Sorry, just curious. I'm concerned for Louisa and her ability to continue her medical training. It's not right that she should be deprived of money that's rightfully hers. Can you do anything about it, Daniel? It isn't fair, is it?'

'Let me see what I can do. I'll have a word with Father. He is up to all sorts of ventures, which I'm not party to. He keeps them very close to his chest.'

Tom realised he couldn't mention that he had seen the engine and gun cases, as he would be admitting to the break-in. His knowledge of the consignments could compromise his innocent and legitimate interest in helping Louisa. 'Thank you, Daniel. I'd appreciate it. I don't want to cross swords with your father, but Louisa will meet with her bank manager and solicitor to seek guidance on releasing her money. I feel a brother's responsibility for her.'

Daniel smiled again. 'Is that all?'

Fran looked askance at Tom.

Tom replied with a hint of irritation. 'Yes, that's all, Daniel. You know that.'

Tom's drive back to Salisbury provided time to consider

his visit to Branley House. As he passed through Blandford and headed back towards Salisbury, he ducked down behind the windscreen for its meagre protection, wiped his goggles with his gloved hand, and prepared for a soggy drive home. He recalled how Daniel had reacted to his questions and remembered Fran's retort. Perhaps he was a little robust in his questioning, but he had good reason - two in fact. He felt sure that Daniel knew more than he was letting on. It was only natural that Daniel should protect his father's interests, and poor Fran was caught in the middle and probably did not appreciate the tone or substance of the conversation. Also, Louisa's situation was very much in his mind. If anything, this was the most overtly legitimate reason for his questions. Daniel and Fran should be able to see that as well.

As he approached Salisbury, his thoughts returned to the next challenge, his travel back to Berlin. A journey to be endured with little room for enjoyment or a traveller's thrills: a rough Channel crossing, (it was always rough), multiple gruelling train journeys on hard, cramped seating in carriages more suited to cattle and the inevitable delays and uncertainty of dilapidated railway systems. If only he could fly. To have control over his journey, weather permitting. Now there's an idea, he thought with heavy sarcasm and a knowing grin.

'You've had a telephone call,' Mary announced before

Tom could hang his damp coat on the hallstand. 'And don't put it there; you're soaking,' she added, grabbing the coat and his other motoring accoutrements to march them into the kitchen for drying by the range.

'Was there a message?' said Tom, noticing that his mother was getting prickly and irritable, her usual behaviour when he was about to leave home. He knew that she never found it easy; a throwback from the war days, he assumed.

'It was another of your female friends. She just said that you must meet when you return to Berlin. It's very urgent, she said. She'll be at work, whatever that means.'

'Right. Thank you. I know what she means.'

'Who is she, Tom? Does Louisa know about her?'

'I don't suppose she does, mother. She's a work colleague and nothing else. You mustn't worry about these things.'

'You know I don't like you going away. When will you be back?'

'I'm not sure, mother. My flying will get busy now that the weather is improving. It's a new route, and my bosses will be keen to prove the service and build the business.'

'Why can't you fly closer to home, in England and nearby Europe like you used to?'

'That would be nice, but the wonderful British government won't help. They refuse to subsidise our airlines like the French and Germans do, so our airlines can't compete. I have to go where the work is, and that's

Germany for now.'

Tom detected Mary's watery eyes and gave her a hug.

'I just don't like you being so far away,' Mary sniffed, reaching for her handkerchief.

'I understand that. I'll get back soon,' said Tom.

CHAPTER EIGHTEEN

Alice could not see how Harry's successor would blend into the Berlin community. He looked so uncompromisingly British and a British army officer to boot. His German was accurate and correct but *too* correct and totally lacking in the subtleties of the language. He certainly would not pass as a local.

In the grand surroundings of the British Embassy in Berlin, they had spent some days poring over the evidence of German skulduggery, and it was time to take some action, according to Ross. He stood for no nonsense or backchat, and Dalton and Proudfoot were well under the thumb in Alice's view. As to *her* relationship with Ross, she would not take any nonsense or bullying, which she expected from his brusque and arrogant manner to date. Alice stood in the at-ease position in front of his desk. She wondered why she should be so subservient and relaxed her stance. Sitting on his desk crossed her mind, but that would be a clumsy provocation.

'When are we going to meet him?' Ross barked as if he were addressing one of his subalterns, his usual angry expression evident. Alice had never seen him smile.

'Any time now. You know what it's like travelling here from England.'

'I want something definite. If Munro has something

to offer, as I'm led to believe, then I want to hear it now. We need to get this project moving.'

Alice was getting red in the face. 'I'll do my best. We should remember that Captain Munro has a job to do, and it will be very useful to us. We don't want to put his work at risk, or him, for that matter.'

'So you keep saying. Just get Munro here in the next few days.'

'Very well,' Alice replied, resisting a more robust response.

Tom approached the embassy, somewhat overawed by the building. He was about to see Alice again, generating the usual nervous excitement, but he put it down to the uncertainty about his reception. She had referred to difficulties with Harry's replacement, which added to his pensive mood. The journey to Berlin took three days, and he was due to fly to Moscow the next day following a three-week break. He wondered if his flying would be up to his usual standards.

As he waited for a response at the embassy doors, he turned and gazed skywards, looking for signs of the weather to come. He knew how unpredictable conditions could be on the route to Moscow, particularly in the spring. The weather was often capricious in the birth of the nascent new year. It could be reluctant to abandon the cold winter blanket, the iced-up aeroplanes, engines refusing to start, the impenetrable curtains of snow, then it might tempt the unwary with a sample of summer: melting snows, blue skies and puffy cumuli, only to hit back with frosts, freezing rain and waterlogged airfields. He knew that his weather fate was very much in the hands of the good Lord. Weather forecasters, if available, seldom knew much more than the pilots who developed a close and personal relationship with the weather demons which plagued their routes.

'Good morning, sir. Can I help?' a tiny man announced.

Tom turned from his study of the heavens and looked downward, hoping his gesture was not too noticeable. 'Ah, yes, I believe I'm expected. Captain Munro to see Miss Alice Ferguson.'

'Yes, indeed, sir. You can leave your overcoat over here.'

Tom noted the heavy oil paintings decorating the hall as he followed his escort. They turned left, then right and left again before descending into the bowels of the building. He felt the temperature drop. The dim lighting along the final corridor created a gloomy sense of foreboding as they finally arrived at a heavy oak door. He could hear a voice barking out commands and some arguments, which seemed to be quelled with more barks. His escort looked cautiously. 'Are you ready, sir?'

'Of course.'

The room was blue with cigarette smoke. Tom's eyes smarted as he peered into the fug. The occupants turned to observe his entrance; the mood felt less than cordial.

'Captain Munro. I believe you are expecting him,'

the little man announced.

'Yes, yes, come in, Munro,' snapped Ross.

Tom had worn his Deruluft uniform, thinking that it might add a degree of authenticity or authority. He liked the silver wings. He nodded at Alice and was about to sit beside her.

'Over here, Munro,' ordered Ross, gesturing to a seat next to him.

Tom felt he should say something to shut Ross up, who was irritating him already. 'Good to be back in Berlin and meet with you all again.' He made himself comfortable and pushed Ross's ashtray with an associated column of smoke away from under his nose.

This didn't go down well, Ross making his repositioning of the ashtray obvious. 'Right, Munro, we've been waiting to hear your summary of the situation as you see it.'

Tom took a few notes from his pocket.

'I trust you will leave these with us. Sensitive material, I imagine. Classified even. I expect you to take care of security matters. Is that clear?'

Tom nodded; the only acknowledgement he could manage in the hostile atmosphere Ross seemed determined to create. He decided to bide his time but realised he must face up to this character. The tension in the room was palpable. Alice clutched her fists and reddened noticeably, Dalton and Proudfoot studiously avoided eye contact with him, their eyes cast downwards. Tom stood. 'Can I use the blackboard?'

'Yes, go on.'

'Right. I'll describe how I see things and what I've learnt recently under the following headings.'

'Well, let's see,' Ross interjected, taking a long drag on his cigarette.

'Right,' Tom acknowledged tight-lipped whilst he wrote his list on the board.

von der Lang,
Reichswehr,
Fokker and Wolf
Deruluft,
Foster Engineering/Ferris Shipping
Russia Operations

'So, recapping a little, Alice and I confirmed that some form of cooperation between the German military and Russia is taking place. My visit to von der Lang's flat nearly a year ago now and Alice's meetings with von der Lang confirmed our suspicionsThe problem in the past has been the lack of solid evidence. My photos in von der Lang's flat didn't develop sufficiently, and Alice met with her accident, probably due to her altercation with Heinrich Wolf. We know Captain Heinrich Wolf is an officer in the Reichswehr and von der Lang's right-hand man. Clearly, he's also quite adept at… '

'Alice are you certain that Wolf was the man you

encountered on the ship?' said Ross.

'No, I have very little memory of that night.'

'Hmm. Carry on Munro.'

'We eventually confirmed that the Ferris ship was carrying Fokker D.VII aeroplanes and engines and that Sir Reginald Ferris was probably aware of the consignment. He denied it, and the cases were conveniently marked as agricultural machinery. We now know this shipment was only a small part of a larger consignment of aeroplanes and engines shipped from the Fokker works at Schwerin in Germany, to the new plant in Amsterdam. In effect, Fokker bought and shipped his aeroplane assets back under the noses of the ICC inspectors, thus avoiding a loss of the cargo which would have been confiscated under the terms of the Versailles Treaty.'

'I know all this, Munro.'

'Very well, but my information builds on these activities, so it is important to recap.'

'I'll be the judge of that.'

Tom had had enough. 'Colonel Ross, I understand that you are new to this project and feel the need to move ahead, but I would appreciate the courtesy of listening to my evidence.

I am here to help uncover what is happening in Russia and how the Germans are involved. Like you, I have fought a war and am determined to ensure it will not happen again. The least we can do is to advise our masters of what is going on. I think we are getting close.'

Ross looked a little chastised. 'Not my view. We'll get to it when you've finished, but we need to get into Russia, get active, get out there, find the evidence.'

'And stop it,' Alice mumbled under her breath.

Ross didn't hear her and continued. 'We've spent too long chasing our tails, pussyfooting around. It's time for action, now!' Ross sat back and took another draw at his cigarette, his hand shaking, aware that his diatribe was probably excessive. 'Carry on, Munro.'

Tom welcomed this first sign of human frailty. 'Thank you, Colonel. In that, we agree.'

'Yes, yes, go on.'

'More recently, I have been working at the Fokker works at Veere and Amsterdam, and Anthony Fokker continues to advance his interests in developing new machines and new markets. He is quite prepared to push boundaries, and a few months ago, I was instructed with moving, some would say steal, an F.II machine from Schwerin to fly it back to Holland. Unfortunately, I didn't quite make it and crashed due to engine failure in Dutch territory, fortunately.'

'Is this relevant?'

'I'm getting there. Activities at the Fokker plant have become ever more suspicious. First, I saw Wolf and was warned off. That's an obvious link with the Reichswehr. Second, I met up with Robert Foster, the general manager at Foster's Engineering, during his visit to the Fokker Works. He was extremely agitated when he recognised me; I was flying the KLM service to Amsterdam, Schiphol. At this point, I should bring you up to date. Recently, I had cause to visit the Foster Engineering Works for reasons irrelevant to this meeting. I arrived without notice to find Sir Reginald Ferris of Ferris Shipping and Robert Foster in conference. When I deliberately waltzed in, unannounced into Robert's office, they looked like two shocked schoolboys caught in the act. I also noticed a Lewis gun parked in the corner of the office.'

Ross sat back, folding his arms. 'I can't see anything particularly suspicious here, Munro.'

Alice interrupted. 'The plot thickens if you'll just listen, Colonel.'

Ross looked as if he were a lion about to pounce, but he decided otherwise. 'They could be simply involved in some commercial business. Nothing wrong with that but carry on.'

'I agree, but the look on their faces betrayed something a little more suspicious. After I was unceremoniously expelled from the meeting, and on my way to the car, I noticed one of the workshops had its windows painted out, so I decided to return for a closer look after dark. The long and short of it is that I found a hoard of packing cases in that building: brand new Napier Lion engines and Lewis guns.'

Dalton shook his head. 'They could be going anywhere. Sir Reginald Ferris is in shipping, and Foster

Engineering could be sourcing and consolidating the goods.'

'That's possible, but there is so much secrecy. So, in my last few weeks at Fokker's, I decided to have a snoop around there as well and nearly got caught. To cut a long story short, I found drawings of a new advanced fighter, the Fokker D.XIII and the engine ⊠ the Napier Lion. A power output of 450hp. I estimate this machine will have fabulous performance, 150 mph plus.'

'Who are they for? Who's the customer?' said Proudfoot.

'I didn't find that out. I was nearly discovered but managed to slip away until I was run off the road and into a canal on the way back to my flat.'

'Who was it? Who did that?' said Alice.

'Don't know, but I can guess.'

Alice nodded knowingly. 'Wolf. I bet it was Wolf; it's got all the hallmarks of his handiwork.'

'Yes, possibly. When I turned up at Fokker's the next day, my boss, Drukker, looked like he'd seen the proverbial ghost. 'Shortly afterwards, I was shipped off to KLM to train their pilots on the Fokker F.III, probably to get me out of the way.'

Ross was listening more intently now. 'So, Fokker is up to something, and the Wolf link suggests that the German military could be involved.'

'Yes, indeed. Sometime later, Drukker announced an opportunity to fly their F.III for the new German/

Russian airline Deruluft. By complete chance, an old flying acquaintance of mine, Werner Roth, asked for me by name. So off I went to Königsberg to start the new route to Moscow. I was keen on this as it would be a legitimate reason to be in Russia—for you people.'

Ross was getting interested. 'That will be helpful. More of that in a minute. Go on.'

'That's when I was ordered to do the special flight to Moscow, and I encountered Colonel von der Lang with the little chap we've seen here in Berlin. Hugo Dessauer was the name on the passenger list. We have now identified this man as a fellow called Weber. We need to find out what this man Weber does. Significantly, von der Lang was travelling under an assumed name, as was Weber so they have something to hide. Why is he being accompanied to Moscow?'

Alice was getting excited. 'Our attempts to find a mole in the Bendlerblock have failed. Poor Herta murdered and now Fish has disappeared. We need to get someone on the inside. We could end up chasing any number of people across the city. We need to identify the right targets.'

Ross was re-arranging his papers as if he was preparing to make a speech. He was. 'Right, I've heard enough. You won't know, Munro, but we are calling this project "Operation Shadow", and it's time we took the action I spoke about. I've heard what we know so far. We are onto something, and it's time to get out there and find that bloody evidence. We need to get our operations into Russia. Follow the trails of the Reichswehr people. They'll lead us to their layer or layers.'

'Operating in Russia is going to be difficult and dangerous,' Alice said sceptically. 'Tom is the only one with a legitimate cover. What about the rest of us?'

'Correct. You and I, Miss Ferguson, will join the British Trade Delegation and Dalton and Proudfoot will get that spy in the Reichswehr and get that working.'

The meeting fell silent for the first time. 'We should use Drummond,' Alice suggested. 'He's already well installed in the country. I don't know what he's doing at the moment.'

'Good idea, Ferguson, get Drummond in for a briefing. If he's so well established in the country, he can arrange accommodation if the Trade Delegation isn't that organised. Any other ideas are welcome. Munro, you're going to be key to this. You need to monitor your passengers flying into Moscow and report anything or anyone of interest. We'll get you some photos of the people we're monitoring. Make sure he's kitted out, Ferguson. The usual stuff: a camera, a radio, a handgun, a knife and so on.'

'We're going to need some clandestine means of communicating in Moscow and Russia, said Alice. 'How is that going to work? And much of the travel from Germany will be by train. That will need monitoring – at both ends. The same for flights.'

Tom went quiet as Ross continued to dole out his orders and instructions. He clasped his chin and shook his head. 'Can we just think about how we'll move around the country? We'll need freedom of action without raising suspicion and rock-solid, legitimate reasons for our movements and for being there, along with appropriate papers. There is no doubt we will be tracked and challenged by the GPU thugs. Our stories must be watertight.'

'That's where the trade delegation comes in for Alice, me, and Drummond, probably,' Ross explained unconvincingly.

Tom shook his head again. 'That won't work, will it? It might get you into the country, but you'll be tied to meetings and visits with little flexibility to search for the clandestine activities we suspect. How would you react to being challenged out in the country? Snooping around some military installation? We need more freedom. I have an idea. It might not go down well in some quarters, and a degree of diplomacy will be necessary.'

'Well, let's hear it, Munro,' said Ross reluctantly.

'Well, you'll have heard about the famine in Russia, concentrated in vast swathes of land in the southeast around the Volga and Ural Rivers as far south as the Caspian Sea. The British newspapers were full of it when I was home. It's also in the German newspapers. Dreadful conditions, even reports of cannibalism. During the civil wars, all sides, the Bolsheviks, the Whites, and the Anarchists, provisioned themselves by seizing food for their armies. Eventually, the Bolshevik government and Lenin in particular, were persuaded in 1921, following large-scale peasant uprisings, that action was required. The writer, Maxim Gorky, issued an appeal in his open letter to "all honest European and American people to give bread and medicines".'

Ross looked incredulous. 'Where do you get all this stuff, Munro?'

'I read the newspapers. I often sit around for days, waiting for the weather to clear. It's a good time to catch up.'

'OK, so what's your idea?'

'Well, Lenin finally capitulated, and last year, aid was accepted, primarily from the American Overseas Relief Organisation, the AORO, and the International Feed the Children Fund, with a major contribution from the British Feed the Children Fund. It might seem cynical, but if we could pass as relief workers in some way, we could travel extensively without challenge. If we were to be assessors, charged with identifying needs and organising transport for relief workers, that could be ideal. I thought Deruluft might be tasked with flying in aid or relief workers. That's a bit fanciful, I know, but we could try. What d'you think,' said Tom, sitting back in his chair and waiting for a reaction.

There was silence for a few moments. 'That could work,' said Alice. 'Yes, it could, damn it.'

Ross shuffled in his seat and fiddled with his papers. 'Hmm. I suppose it might work.'

Tom still had to finish. 'If we can persuade certain

people in the Foreign Office to provide some funds to help with aid, those funds could be channelled into transport and logistics, including by air.'

'What? Are you a salesman for your airline too?'

'Why not? If I'm flying into these regions, I can keep my eyes and ears open. And the odd unscheduled and totally innocent emergency diversion could be helpful. I see it as an opportunity to help get aid into Russia while sniffing out what the Germans are up to.'

Dalton spoke for the first time in a while. 'But the activities of interest to us, the military activities, won't necessarily be in the famine regions.'

Tom nodded in agreement. 'That's true, but I have a hunch it could be. Remember my sighting of the Fokker D.VIIs heading southeast of Moscow? They were heading towards the famine regions.'

There was silence again and many long, thoughtful drags on cigarettes. Tom stood to stretch his legs and paused at the window. 'I would add that there have been some mutterings in the newspapers which report a reluctance to save Bolshevism from self-destruction. This sentiment is also voiced in the US, so getting funds won't be easy. Perhaps C could pull a few strings. At the very least, we should be able to get appropriate accreditation and identification documents.' Tom paused for a smile and nodded at Ross. 'You'll need to dress down just a tad to fit into the new socialist Russia, Colonel.'

Ross smiled for the first time.

CHAPTER NINETEEN

Khodynka Field, Moscow's rudimentary airfield, basked in hazy morning sunshine as the Deruluft F.III aeroplane pierced the mist layer, which hugged the ground in an ethereal wafer of glistening moisture. A pair of young eyes watched the machine flare to land, the wings whisking the mist into a cloudy vortex. The vortex quickly settled into a mist again as if reluctant to relinquish its short life over the field.

The noise of the Eagle engine, thrashing the air with its big 4-bladed propellor, came to a shuddering stop, relieving the early morning air of its rude awakening. There was little movement on the airfield save for Dima Kuznetzov, an enthusiastic Deruluft recruit spotted by Tom for his enthusiasm and passion for anything aeronautical. A lone bent figure, he pulled his hand cart out to the morning arrival. The stationary engine ticked its cooling song as the door opened in the fuselage, the helmeted figure in the cockpit taking time to come to terms with the transition from his airborne existence to the normality of ground-borne life. It was more likely that he was close to being frozen solid. Four hours at below-freezing temperatures took their toll.

Dima lifted a wooden step from his cart and positioned it carefully just as the cabin door opened. The first passenger squeezed through the narrow aperture to take unsteady steps onto Mother Russia. Four passengers stepped down from their aerial chariot, stretching and twisting to dispel the stresses of many cold hours in the noise and vibration of a fabric-covered aluminium box.

The silence and tranquillity of the early morning and the extreme contrast with the previous hours encouraged the passengers to linger around the aeroplane. Dima busied himself, unloading the baggage and humming an unrecognisable tune. The pilot, Tom Munro, eventually extricated himself from his cockpit. In common with all F.III pilots, he was hot and bothered down his right side from the proximity of the engine and frozen on the left. His face was frozen to the point of being unable to form words, and he had to apologise for his condition as he tried to chat with his passengers. 'I'll weecower in a foo minutes,' he mumbled.

His German passengers had kept themselves to themselves during their delayed flight and were distinctly reluctant to engage in any conversation during their overnight stops. Finding overnight accommodation was probably the most challenging aspect of the journey for Captain Munro during their many diversions. Still, at least in this respect, his German passengers had been very helpful.

The two Americans were quite different, and Tom learnt that they worked for the American Overseas Relief Organisation (AORO) and were heading for the Volga famine zones.

'A reliable machine?' said one of the German passengers.

Tom was pleased to converse at last. 'Yes, well built, easy to fly, although I would like better protection from the elements. A closed cockpit.'

'Yes, I can understand that. I see you have a little frostbite.'

'Oh, where?'

The man touched his cheek before walking around to the nose of the F.III. 'What engine?'

'A Rolls Royce Eagle. Deruluft opted for the larger engine rather than the Armstrong Siddeley Puma, which had less power.'

'And take-off weight and payload?'

'About 2000 kg take-off and 400kg payload depending on fuel load. You seem very interested in our machine.'

'Oh, just find aeronautics rather interesting. Transport of the future. What cruise speed?'

'140 kilometres per hour or thereabouts.'

'And range?'

'Five or six hundred kilometres,' Tom replied abruptly. He remembered his role. 'You must fly with us again. Do you have business in Moscow?'

'Tourists, just tourists. Thanks again for a safe arrival. You had to earn your pay these last few days. Goodbye.'

'Ah, yes, goodbye. We look forward to flying you gentlemen again,' Tom replied as the two Germans marched off, following their luggage piled high on the baggage cart.

Tom was puzzled by the abrupt departure of his German passengers but was happy to be distracted by the contrasting communication skills of his American passengers.

'Boy, that was some journey. You're a hero, Captain Thomas.

'I'm glad you think so. It was a hard day's work, or three days, to be correct.'

'Might use your good offices again.'

'Only too pleased to help. Where are you going?'

'We're off to the famine regions to assess the needs for the AORO support. On my last trip, we took three days by train and eventually a donkey cart. God, Tom, it's hell on earth. You do not want to go there. You can't imagine the desperate plight of these people. At least we're making some progress now.'

Tom's joint commercial and spying interests were combined for once. 'Would it help if we could fly you in? It would save so much time.'

'That would make our life easier, and we could take vital supplies and other volunteers. I don't expect you to have any regular services. We need to get to Samara and Saratov, which are pretty much central to the famine areas on the Volga River.'

'It would be a special charter. I'd have to speak to my boss. I'm not sure about refuelling in the region if everything is so bad. We might have to carry extra petrol, which would limit our range and payload.'

Tom saw the two German passengers again as they were met. A large black vehicle was visible through the stylish arch into the aerodrome. It looked very official. Tom wished he could follow them; his suspicions were aroused.

'Hello, Captain. Are you still with us here? You seem to be in another world.'

'Oh, sorry, just making sure my other passengers are alright. You can't be too careful.'

'Yes, the GPU guys are on our tails all the time. Where do you stay in Moscow?'

'The Metropol.'

'Us too, at least until we ship out to Saratov.'

Tom had spent the first few months of the new year proving and improving the Deruluft service from Berlin to Moscow via their base at Königsberg. Frequent engine failures and aircraft structural defects encouraged him to take the lead in setting up maintenance facilities at their bases along the route and at Berlin and Moscow. He enjoyed getting his hands dirty and slowly developed his Russian language skills. He persuaded the Deruluft owners to allow the recruitment of two young locals to help with baggage handling and general aircraft maintenance. Dima and his friend Andrei Belov could not be faulted for their willingness and enthusiasm.

His contacts in the AORO met at the Metropol Hotel, where they jointly developed a taste for vodka. In their alcoholic haze, they solved many problems, but the most significant was the agreement that the AORO could fund occasional relief flights from Moscow to Saratov. Tom had obtained an agreement with Rolf that an additional F.III pilot was based at Khodynka Field for that purpose. This was a conditional arrangement based on the machine being used at least twice a month.

Merv Jackson and Bobby Bernstein, the two AORO workers, announced their plans in late April. Merv tended to do all the talking. A tall, lanky fellow with piercing blue eyes, a hooked nose and a pockmarked complexion, Merv spoke his Russian with a noticeable Texan drawl. A committed Christian, he wanted nothing else but to help the starving in the pitiful Volga farmlands. Although Tom was relieved that he could also be himself in Russia with no need to play some dubious cover game, he was very aware of the suspicious glances and the ever-present GPU spies who inhabited every nook and cranny like an infectious plague.

Tom wondered when he would hear from Alice, Ross, or Drummond. Still, his Deruluft work was demanding enough to hold his attention and prevent undue diversionary thoughts about his other role in Russia.

Tom was in the Metropol lobby awaiting transport to the aerodrome. He planned to continue working on a draft maintenance programme for the F.III and its RR Eagle engine and direct Dima and Andrei on some maintenance activities. He was often distracted by the comings and goings in the hotel lobby, a much busier environment now as the hotel refurbishment neared completion and more customers were attracted. There was always a GPU flunky loitering in the shadows. They were so obvious, and he realised that they would need to be careful when and if Alice, Ross and the team arrived. On many occasions, these Chekists would pounce on some unsuspecting victim who would be dragged off and bundled into a waiting car. for no apparent reason. Tom noticed that victims were often well dressed and had a professional or superior air. At night, a beating was not unusual under the convenient cover of dark. He checked his watch. His car was late.

'A note for you, sir,' said the receptionist, now smartly dressed in the Metropol's house uniform. Tom's instant reaction was to check if the GPU fellow was watching. He wasn't. Tom took the note, rechecked the lobby, and unfolded the crumpled paper. He recognised the handwriting. It felt magical, like a note from Father Christmas. She had been to the hotel, but she hadn't made contact. His heart thumped with expectation.

We've arrived
Not R just Me & D
Be in the lobby tonight
8pm
A x

He reread it. There was little to read. He looked for the GPU fellow again. He'd gone. After a third perusal, he searched the lobby and stuffed the note in his pocket. He sat back, smiled, took a deep breath and reflected on the moment. He had been waiting for the contact for over a month. Now what, he wondered. The care and the secrecy implied by the note said it all. He knew they would need to be careful. He had legitimate reasons to be in Moscow, in Russia, but the others? It would be a deadly game. He reasoned that the note meant that Ross had remained in Berlin, a relief, and Alice and Drummond would be alone. How would it all work?

'Captain Munro? I have the car for you. For the aerodrome.'

'Ah, right, thank you. You're late. Let's get going.'

CHAPTER TWENTY

After a long day at the airfield, Tom enjoyed a hearty meal at the Metropol's Boyarski restaurant. He chose *Pelmeni*, a dumpling-like dish with ground meat and grated onion filling wrapped in thin, unleavened dough. Accompanied by generous portions of boiled cabbage and potatoes, he felt unable to manage a dessert and was happy to wash his dinner down with a local beer.

Feeling replete after his dinner, Tom waited again in the lobby amongst the palm trees. Well-dressed diners headed for the Boyarski, their footsteps on the marble floor competing with their echoing chatter. He looked down at his baggy, careworn suit. He felt distinctly underdressed and shifted his attention to his 8 p.m. appointment.

Who would collect him? Would it be Alice? Just after eight, a small, scruffy man in a long black greatcoat and a tatty hat shuffled his way up the steps into the lobby. He looked around momentarily until his gaze fell on Tom with a furtive nod of recognition. 'I'm Danya Chernoff. I am to collect you for a meeting.'

Tom noticed the hotel receptionist marching purposefully across the lobby. 'Is he bothering you, sir?'

'Ah, no, thank you, Nikolai. I'll deal with it.'

'Very well,' the receptionist replied as he backed away hesitantly.

Tom wondered if he could trust the man and ever watchful for the GPU he spoke quietly, 'I don't know you. Where are you taking me? Who am I meeting?'

'If I mention the name *Ferguson*, would you be happy to come with me?'

Tom paused and responded in a whisper with a hint of a smile. 'I think I know you. It's Drummond, isn't it?'

'You noticed. I must be losing my touch.'

'Pretty good, nevertheless.'

'This way.'

Tom followed Drummond out of the hotel and down the steps, where he stopped in mild shock as Drummond cranked the reluctant engine of a dilapidated truck into life. Drummond fanned the air with an impatient wave. 'Quickly, we need to go.'

Tom glanced left and right in his usual search for Chekists, then scurried down the steps to his tatty transport. He opened the door, which groaned in complaint and sat down hard on firm seating. A cursory look around revealed that the only meagre attempt at comfort on the wooden bench seat was damp straw in a dirty grey pillowcase. With a jolt and prolonged shudder, which reverberated through the entire vehicle, they were on their way. 'God, this is what I call travelling in style, Drummond.'

'It's Danya, Danya Chernoff when I'm here in Russia,' he shouted over their rattling, chugging progress. 'We can't travel around in some swanky limousine. The trappings of wealth and position would attract too much attention. So, we have this jalopy for now. Thank your lucky stars that we've got pneumatic tyres on this heap. We're not likely to get much better.'

Tom shrugged. 'Oh well, whatever works for us. Where are we going?'

'It's better you don't know. Just enjoy the scenery.'

As they left the city centre, a pair of overloaded trucks crammed with young men and banners pulled out from a side street. Chernoff brought his vehicle to a halt with a painful squealing of brakes, their trailing exhaust plume engulfing them as they waited. Tom coughed his hand fanning to clear the fumes. 'What's their problem?' he said as the trucks passed, the men bellowing repeated, aggressive-sounding chants.

'Propaganda trucks. You'll see them all over the city and propaganda stations erected in the train stations. This is just one way the party faithful can spout their Bolshevik rhetoric. It's best to stay well away.'

Dodging trams, some of which were horse-drawn, Chernoff navigated his truck south across the Moskva bridge. It was balmy evening, and the locals were still bathing in the river. 'Quite a bold bunch, aren't they?' Tom commented when he spotted that many swimmers were doing their aquatic exercise in the nude. 'I can just see that happening on Bournemouth beach,' he quipped.

Moving into the Moscow suburbs, Tom noticed how

the locals dressed very differently. Quasi-military garb seemed the norm: brown and often dirty belted smocks and rough leather knee-length boots, all topped with soft skipped caps. Many children scampered about in bare feet, but they seemed happy enough. Unlike the city centre, where women sported European fashions, those in the suburbs became progressively less fashion-conscious, dressing in full ankle-length skirts and headscarves. The clear impression was one of a tough, hard life of work and little play.

Tom caught sight of a small band of men trudging out of a railway station. Their weather-beaten features seemed oriental, and their dress stood out from the locals. These fellows wore animal skins on their feet, which were roped up for security. They seemed to carry all their belongings, including hand tools, fire-stained pots and pans, and rough bulging sacks.

Chernoff noticed Tom's curious study of these people. 'Peasants arriving for work. They come in droves and probably from the famine areas.'

After nearly an hour, Tom was starting to regret his beer when the truck turned along a dusty farm track just as the light faded. He spotted a clutch of rudimentary farm buildings nestling at the edge of a small pine forest, with faint flickering lighting showing through the ground-floor windows. He couldn't believe he would meet Alice in this remote spot. Why here? This scruffy, dusty hole in the middle of nowhere? It just didn't seem right.

Chernoff seemed to read his thoughts. 'It's not too bad. We need to talk. You need to understand the … Well, as I say, we must talk. Alice will explain.'

The heavy wooden door to the farmhouse opened slowly as the truck's engine stopped with a reluctant kick and hiss. Chernoff looked across at Tom apologetically, then shrugged, stepped down, and strolled stiffly over to the door. A small woman only just visible and silhouetted in the farmhouse glow met Chernoff warmly. He turned and called out to Tom, now equally stiff from his journey, as he walked around the front of the truck. 'Come,' he called. 'Meet Yelena.'

Tom shook her hand gently.

'You will be Thomas,' said Yelena in stilted English. 'Come in and meet your friends.'

The front door led directly into a large room with a wide, open fire at one end and a rough farmhouse table and six chairs at the other. Rugs littered the floor, and the fireplace was surrounded by stacked logs and buckets of kindling on either side of the hearth. Two big armchairs were positioned either side of the flickering fire where a generous log spat and sparked its presence. Two figures slouched in the armchairs, and Tom instantly recognised Alice as she rose with some difficulty from the depths of the chair. The other figure remained seated.

'Thomas,' Alice sighed. 'At last, we meet up again.

And here of all places.'

Tom was lost for words. He wanted to clutch her close, like a long-lost friend or someone special. Her hair was much shorter than he remembered, and from what he could see of her clothing in the dim, smoke-infused light, she was dressed like a Westerner, but she didn't look well. 'Hello Alice,' Tom mumbled, reserving anything more personal for later until he was introduced to the other person in the room. He looked down at the figure in the armchair who had remained seated. Tom felt this was rather rude and probably sounded irritated. 'Am I to be introduced?' he said impatiently.

'Yes, of course,' said Alice. 'You may recognise our friend.'

Tom moved closer to the seated figure and watched as he rose from his seat. The tall fellow stood slowly, his large frame and rounded face rising well past Tom's 5-foot-9-inch height. He thrust out his hand.

'Do you remember, my friend? We have met before.'

Tom noticed Alice grinning. He sighed. 'Go on, tell me. You have me beaten.'

Alice stepped forward, picked up a paraffin lamp and illuminated the big man's face. You didn't see much of him in that field. Remember the field at Kamenka when you left me behind.'

Tom nodded. 'Yes, Mikael or something, if I recall.'

'Correct,' said Alice. 'Can I introduce Mikael Heikkinen.'

Tom shook Heikkinen's hand, feeling the same guilt he had felt when he had collected the agent, Drummond then, in Western Russia on his first mission for the SIS. 'I still feel bad about that.'

'Yes, but it ended well,' said Chernoff.

'I know what threw me,' said Tom. 'You had blond hair then, I'm sure.'

Heikkinen drew his fingers through his hair. 'Just a little disguise. We think my blond head would be a little too obvious in this part of the world.'

Yelena fussed over a polished brass samovar to the right of the fireplace. 'You must be tired after your journey. What you need is a good strong *Zavarka,* our tea. Maybe with some sugar for your delicate tastes.'

'Go on. Give it a try. It'll wake you up if nothing else,' said Alice.

'I'll stick with my beer,' said Mikael, raising his glass before flopping back down in his armchair.

Tom noticed Chernoff walking behind Yelena and his friendly clutch at her waist. 'Sorry, ah, yes, I'll try the tea, thanks, then something a little…

'Alcoholic?' Chernoff suggested with a smile.

'Yes, exactly. I assume that we are not going back to Moscow tonight?'

'Correct,' said Chernoff to Tom's noticeable relief.

Tom endured the tea and quickly switched to a local vodka, which Yelena splashed liberally into five glasses grouped together for rapid dispensing from her ceramic jug.

Alice made a point of being next to Tom as they sat around the table. The yellow light of the paraffin lamp cast long shadows and generated a sickly look amongst the group. Tom leaned into Alice. 'You're not looking your normal picture of health. Is anything wrong?'

'Nearly two weeks on trains, buses, and Chernoff's truck took their toll. I picked something up in the process. I'll be fine. I just need a few days.'

'You should stop that,' Tom admonished, nodding at Alice's cigarette. He waved in the air. 'Look at the atmosphere in here.'

'You can blame Mikael for that. He got me onto this.'

'I had a brief encounter with the pipe during the war but gave it the push, thankfully.' Tom admitted as he looked around at the others, chatting noisily over their vodka and cigarettes. 'Look, can we talk freely here?' Tom asked quietly, gesturing towards Yelena and Mikael.

'Certainly. They both have good reason to despise the Bolsheviks. Yelena's parents, both academics, were murdered by the Cheka and Mikael, well, he likes causes and hates the Chekists. He lost many good friends fighting for the White Russian cause.'

'Very well. I have some news which may help us track our German friends.'

'Good. Our boss seems reluctant to get his hands dirty and prefers to do business from the comfort of the Berlin embassy.' Alice banged the table with her glass.

'Can we do a little business before this hooch dulls our senses to the point of collapse?'

The chattering noise subsided gradually with one voice, Mikael's, still booming away. Eventually, he too fell into line and sat back obediently.

Alice had clearly learnt a few tricks from C and, copying his technique, waited until there was a complete, expectant silence before speaking. 'We have much to discuss, and above all, we need a plan. I have some ideas, but Tom tells me he has good news.'

'I believe so. We all know that tracking our targets is the key to finding out what's going on. First, we need to know who these people are, and in addition to the Reichswehr officers von der Lang, von Meyer and Wolf, we now know of Gustav Weber. We have no other suspects to track, although we carried two German passengers in today who seemed to take a distinct interest in our aeroplane. Who knows, they may be of interest too. So, how do we track or follow these people? How will they travel to Russia, and how will they travel when they're in Russia?'

'We're closely monitoring these officers in Berlin, and we suspect they will travel by air and train,' said Alice. 'But Russia is another matter.'

'That's where I can help. My company, Deruluft, is now offering regular service from Berlin to Moscow, and now, thanks to two recent passengers from the American Overseas Relief Organisation, we have been engaged to fly special routes from Moscow to Saratov.'

'Are you suggesting that we could use these flights?' Chernov asked.

'Yes, and Saratov may be the direction for our search. Remember that I saw the unmarked Fokker D.VIIs southeast of Moscow.'

'What facilities?' said Mikael.

Tom sighed. 'Exactly. We still don't know what is happening apart from the possibility of some aviation facilities to the southeast of Moscow. But the question is where? That's why our tracking activities are key.'

'What do we do then? I mean, when we find these mysterious facilities?' Mikael continued.

'We photograph the evidence that proves what the Germans and Russians are up to. Then we report it up the chain,' Tom replied.

Mikael frowned. 'Is that all?'

'Perhaps not,' said Alice. 'But for now, that's all we are authorised to do. Find irrefutable evidence of the German/Russian military cooperation we already suspect.'

Tom looked puzzled. 'So, we can detect the movement of our targets from Berlin, but when they get to Moscow, how do we take up the surveillance?'

'Yes, and how do we know they are on their way,' Chernoff said, looking less than convinced.

Alice nodded. 'Now you are starting to see that good communication is vital. That's the problem. We need to be able to communicate with Berlin, who can alert us to a target's departure by train or air. Tom can confirm he has a target on his flight so that we can pick up and follow the target when they arrive in Moscow.'

'We need a location in Moscow with a telephone,' Chernoff suggested. 'Berlin and Tom can phone through, but after we get on the tail of our target in Russia, we will be on our own. I suppose someone can man the telephone in Moscow, be a control point, and relay messages as and when.'

'We can agree to phone regularly, at prearranged times, to tell if something is wrong.'

'I can see that going to the dogs,' said Mikael.

'So can I, but besides having radios, I can't see an alternative.'

Alice stood and wandered around the table as the others argued about communication. She stopped behind Mikael and put her hands on his shoulders. Mikael looked around with a self-conscious smile, then glanced at Tom, whose eyes locked quizzically onto Alice amid a brief hush in the room. Chernoff sensed the awkward silence and jokingly mentioned pigeons as a means of communication.

Alice removed her hands from Mikael's shoulders and continued her tour around the table. 'I like the idea of a Moscow telephone. A kind of control centre to keep us all in touch. I can't think of any other ways. We could have a dead letter drop as a backup and an agreed signal for a collection. Danya, is it likely the GPU will monitor telephone calls somehow?'

'Only if they target someone or suspect something.'

Alice returned to her seat and made brief cryptic notes. 'Right, so we must keep the location beyond suspicion and ensure our telephone conversations are guarded. Danya, I want you to find a suitable location, and we will need the phone monitored.'

'I could do that,' said Yelena.

'Are you sure?' said Chernoff. 'It'll be a boring job.'

'We could agree hours. I'll need to get out sometimes.'

Tom re-engaged with the conversation. 'Yes. Why don't we arrange for Yalena to split her watch? We have two or more. Do shift work.'

Alice completed some notes and tapped a thoughtful finger to her lips. 'Good idea. Now, Mikael, you and your people will tail targets in and around Moscow and hand these targets over to continue the surveillance away from Moscow. It could be by road, rail, or air. That's where Chernoff and I will step in with Tom, who will be responsible for targets travelling by air.'

'I won't be able to tail people once I've reached my destination,' said Tom. 'I'll be too obvious.'

'I agree. So when a target is to travel by air, one of us must travel under our "Feed the Children" cover.'

'Time to eat,' Yalena announced, carrying a large bowl of borscht, a sour soup of meat stock and vegetables. She placed it centrally on the table, clouds of steam picked out in the light from the oil lamps. This was followed by Stolichniy rye bread pulled into chunks and piled high on several plates dispersed around the table. A large slab of butter was on a wooden platter, followed by crude knives scattered alongside.

After a breakfast of kasha, a buckwheat porridge with a dollop of jam, and steaming hot mugs of tea from the busy samovar, Tom returned to Moscow with Chernoff in his truck. He had said his convivial goodbyes to Alice, Mikael and Yelena but remained a little stunned by Alice's affection towards Mikael. He admitted that this was not a complete surprise to him as he had long ago decided that Alice was her own person. An independent spirit who would not be tamed that easily. He decided to concentrate on his flying and, where possible, helping with the efforts to identify what the German/Russian game was all about. He still found this fascinating and longed to get to the bottom of the mystery.

Chernoff seemed reluctant to talk as he crunched his way up and down the primitive gearbox with the odd curse. Tom reviewed what had been decided at their gathering. His travelling companion was going to be busy. A safe house with a telephone and drop letter box for communication was to be organised. Tom was to report any movement of potential targets from Berlin to Moscow by air so that Mikael, Alice or Chernoff could tail them to their destination. Dalton from the Berlin embassy would report targets travelling from Berlin to

Moscow by rail. Tom was to report any plans for travel from Moscow by air with Deruluft, and one of the team would be aboard his flight for surveillance at the final destination. He decided that would be difficult, if not rather dangerous.

As they encountered the busy outskirts of Moscow, Tom recalled that he would need to remain vigilant during his flights for any other signs of military activity on his routes. Would he see the Fokker D.VIIs again? He might spot military airfields. Alice had agreed to provide cameras, pocket pistols, and details of the safe house and communication procedures. He wondered how this would be done, but Alice advised that he would find out and be contacted.

CHAPTER TWENTY-ONE

Tom sat in Moscow's Deruluft office, forearms on his lap, staring absently at the ground and fiddling with his leather helmet. His thoughts strayed to Alice and her plans for their clandestine activities in a wounded, troubled country. Surrounded by the bustle of pre-flight activities as Dima and Andrei piled luggage onto their hand cart outside his office, he shook himself back into the present and looked up to give his team the thumbs-up as they towed their cart to the aeroplane. Dima was pulling whilst Andrei prevented the pile of luggage from tumbling onto the grass. The F.III was rocking gently in the gusty wind, tugging at its tie-down ropes and pressing impatiently at the chocks.

Tom watched the low, ragged stratus cloud streaming downwind in truculent swirling tufts scudding along with impatient energy as if racing to some distant destination. Although the wind was expected to abate within his limits, he knew his passengers were in for a rough ride. Tom instructed his young mechanics to ensure that the pots were ready to hand under each basket seat in the passenger cabin.

As he assembled his maps and notes for his flight, he leaned on the chart table and glanced across the airfield again to check on his charges. Andrei and Dima had finished loading and were fussing around the machine:

touching, checking, and polishing it with the care and attention of children with a new toy. This brought a smile to Tom's face as he had been teaching the lads how to conduct a pre-flight inspection. He was pleased to see that they were using a checklist.

Now, all that was required were his passengers, who had disappeared to the airfield restaurant for some last-minute Dutch courage. He checked his watch, pushed the office door open against the wind, and shouted into the blast, 'Call the passengers, Andrei; we'll start in ten minutes.'

Tom returned his attention to his charts but was interrupted. 'I have a telephone call for you, Captain Munro. It's your office in Königsberg.'

'Thanks. I haven't much time,' Tom said as he rushed through to the front office. 'Captain Munro speaking.'

'It's Ernst, Captain. We have a charter for you. To Saratov.'

Tom gritted his teeth. 'Excellent timing,' he mumbled sarcastically. 'When will the passengers arrive? Do you have names?'

'I'm working on that. They're on their way on today's flight out of Berlin, so they should be with you the day after tomorrow.'

'OK. I am about to take off for the return flight. Can you arrange for a pilot to take this flight at Smolensk? Actually, no, Kaunas will be better. I can jump back on the flight back here to Moscow and take the charter onto

Saratov. Do you understand, Ernst? Otherwise, there will be no pilots here to do the charter.'

'I think so. I hope there is space on the flight to Moscow.'

'So do I. I must go, my passengers have arrived. Goodbye.'

Alice travelled to the safe house with Chernoff. She worried about his choice, which he described as being a mile from the city centre.

Chernoff explained his rationale: 'It's near *Komsomolskaya Square*, which has three main railway stations. In particular, the *Kazansky* station, which serves the southeast and the Volga region. Tom felt that this could be where they should be searching.'

'Hmm. That was just a hunch,' said Alice, wary of any guesswork.

'Nevertheless, if you are supposed to work for Feed the Children, this is where you would normally take a train to the Volga famine regions. Tom also saw his Fokker aeroplanes flying to the southeast, so this would be a good start. We can always move. This way, we stand the best chance of getting on the tail of our targets if they take the train.'

'All right, I understand. Have you decided on a dead letter drop?'

'I'll show you. It's nice and simple, behind the station, by the sidings. It's normally deserted and impossible to detect unless you know about it.'

'Good. Is Yalena in the flat? I assume it's a flat?'

'Yes, and with a good friend. Someone who also hates the Bolshies.'

'I hope you're right, Danya. We can't afford any slip-ups. You know what will happen if we fall foul of the Chekists.'

'Yes, I know. And the same applies to Mikael's people. They need to be solid and trustworthy, too.'

'Of course. I'll look after them.'

Chernoff slowed his vehicle before entering the square. 'Here we are. We'll drive around the square. It's always busy, and it's easy to hide amongst the traffic and pedestrians if you are following someone. I'll park around the back of the station and go on foot to the flat.'

Tom spent much of his flight to Smolensk and Kaunas wondering how he would get a message to Alice about his passengers travelling to Saratov. He had yet to be advised of the location of the safe house, a telephone number or even a dead letter box. He decided to leave a coded message with Nikolai at the Metropol and work out how it would make sense if Alice or Chernoff were to make contact. And passenger names? Hopefully, he will get that information at Smolensk. The passengers may not be of interest to their Operation Shadow, but at least the Saratov flight will be helpful to learn the route and watch out for the mysterious D.VIIs.

'I don't know the names. We haven't been able to get through to Berlin.' Ernst reported on a bad line from Königsberg. 'The lines are down. A storm or something.'

Tom shook his head. 'Damn it. Nothing at all? The number of passengers? Anything?'

'I heard that there were three passengers for Saratov. Two Germans and an American.'

'All men?'

'Yes, and the American is with some organisation. I need to remember the name. The American something.'

'That's not terribly helpful, Ernst. Could it be the American Overseas Relief Organisation? The AORO?'

'Could be, something like that.'

'Well, I'm here at Smolensk. Have you managed to get a pilot to take my flight and my two passengers back to Berlin from Kaunas?'

'Yes, that's…'

'Ernst? Ernst, can you hear me… Damn it,' Tom shouted down the telephone slamming the receiver down in frustration. 'How can we operate like this?' he muttered, thinking as much about their SIS work as operating an airline.'

Tom slept in the Deruluft hut at the remote Kaunas airfield. A couple of small bedrooms were provided. Hardly luxurious but clean and comfortable. Breakfast would be available in the airfield café, a "malen'koye kafe" he had learnt. Getting transport to town was more trouble than it was worth, although Deruluft had arranged a small bus for his passengers. He was keen to be at the airfield to meet the passengers for Saratov and crossed his fingers as he settled back for the night. He hadn't been warned of anyone of interest, but anyone travelling to Saratov must have a good reason, given the dreadful famine conditions still existing in the region.

Tom was happy to breakfast on his growing favourite, kasha and jam, although he couldn't quite work out the jam flavour. He tried asking the cook with sign language and heard something unintelligible. He just nodded with a smile. Some ten minutes later, the man returned and pointed to a raspberry in the palm of his hand. Tom nodded gratefully, then paused, listening intently as he detected the distant sound of an aero engine. He looked at his watch. 'Early for a change,' he mouthed before swallowing the final spoonful of his porridge.

The machine taxied briskly, and Tom wondered who the pilot might be. His question was answered almost immediately as Anton removed his helmet and waved enthusiastically. Tom stepped out onto the airfield with a nod of thanks to the chef as he left the café. He felt like he was waiting for the results of an exam as his gaze locked onto the aeroplane's door where the passengers would be revealed. It seemed to take an age before the first of four men stepped down onto the wooden step. The first he assumed was the spare pilot to take his machine onto Berlin, although he didn't recognise him. He had the look of a pilot; whatever that meant, he mused. The second looked Germanic and military as well. But again, he didn't recognise him.

The third man seemed familiar. He was almost too busy to notice or register the final man to emerge from the F.III. He did a double take and stared for a moment, his mouth agape.

'Hiya, Tom, ma boy,' Bill Franklin yelled.

Tom was distracted by Bill Franklin's presence and tried unsuccessfully to monitor the two German passengers as they made their way to the Deruluft building. 'What are you doing here, Bill?' Tom exclaimed, looking over Bill's shoulder. 'This is quite something. Are you following me? Are you the AORO passenger on the flight?'

'One thing at a time, Munners.'

'God, don't start that name again. We left that on the airfields in France.'

'True. But you know what I always said. You need someone to look after you. Someone to watch your tail. So here I am.'

'That's true, but why the AORO?'

When you see my luggage, you'll understand.'

'Come on, spill the beans. I never saw you as a charity man.'

'I'm doing some photography for them,' said Bill, leaning in. 'And a little friend of yours worked her magic.

She said you might like a friend to help you out. So here I am, a registered photographer with the AORO, to get photographic evidence of the famine conditions for the home audience. Many don't believe what's happening, and the British press is particularly scathing of the Feed the Children funds being used for foreign problems.'

'So you're going to get the evidence?'

'Correct, and you may appreciate my services too. So, off to the Volga. I can't say that I look forward to the conditions there from what I've read, but I have a job to do—probably two jobs,' said Bill with his trademark wink.

Anton strutted over from his aeroplane, stretching and twisting to relieve the stress and strain of his day's flight from Konigsberg. 'Hello Munro, I hear you need a lift back to Moscow?'

'Hello Anton, I assume you two have been introduced,' said Tom.

'Yes, we had a brief chat at Konigsberg. He tells me he was your gunner in your Bristol Fighter. It was a tricky machine for us, but we learnt fast. You don't follow a Bristol in a dive. That was one lesson.'

'What did you fly, Anton?' said Bill.

'Albatross. It's a fine machine, but it had a habit of folding its wings, right? Our next machines will be better—unbeatable. You'll see.'

Bill looked askance, and Tom changed the subject. 'I'll be in the back for your flight to Moscow, Anton. I've been allocated the new route to Saratov. Taking your two passengers and Bill.'

'Why Saratov?' said Anton suspiciously.

'For the AORO and other charities like Feed the Children. They're providing aid for the famine regions, I believe.'

Anton nodded in the direction of the buildings. 'They're hardly the charitable type.'

'That's what I thought,' said Tom. 'Have you had a chance to talk to them? Maybe ask them why they're going to Saratov.'

Anton shrugged. 'None of my business.'

'He didn't seem to want to talk to me,' said Bill. ' My American accent, probably.'

'Can I see the passenger list, Anton?'

'Why?'

'I'm just curious. I think one of them travelled with me before. And I will take them on to Saratov, so it's good to know.'

'The small chap is called Weber, and the other is Hofmann, a military man. His bearing and manner say it all. He is the type we will need soon.'

Bill couldn't resist. 'What do you mean, Anton?'

Tom stepped in. 'Let's get some food. You've had a long day, and we need to take you and your passengers to their accommodation and my flight off to Königsberg.

Tom, Bill and Anton had food and drink at the Malen'kiye kafe. Tom spent much time trying to divert Bill from his apparent desire to interrogate Anton on his views on a future for the German military. He had suspected Anton for some time and wondered if he had other interests. They would need to keep any hint of their other activities secret from this fan of the new Germany and the National Socialist Workers Party. They eventually shuffled off to their respective bedrooms, Anton looking particularly tired after his long day.

As planned, Tom made his way to airfield operations, an aggrandised term for a small hut with a telephone, green, red and white signal lamps, a desk and chair and a single bare electric light bulb swinging from the ceiling in a constant draught. The office was permanently manned primarily for the telephone, which Tom planned to use to leave his message at the Metropol. He reached reception after trying to get a line for half an hour. Nikolai detected his frustrated tone.

'Hello, Captain. Are you all right?'

'Oh, yes. Yes, of course. Can you hear me, all right?'

'Yes, it's a surprisingly good line. What can I do for you?'

'Can I leave a message? Write it down, please.'

'OK, this is for anyone who wants to contact me or know where I am. The message should read that I am flying back to Moscow, arriving tomorrow evening with three passengers for Saratov. This is a special charter flight, and I plan to depart in the next few days. I will be staying at the Metropol tomorrow evening. That's it, Nikolai. Oh, and do you have bookings for two German gentlemen, Weber and Hoffmann?

'Let me check… yes, we do.'

'Good, thank you. I will see you tomorrow, all being well.'

CHAPTER TWENTY-TWO

Bill leant back in his chair. 'These guys keep watching us, Tom.'

'Did you get to talk to them on the way from Berlin? Did they say anything at all?'

Bill looked unusually dapper in his three-piece suit. 'They kept very much to themselves. The big guy acted like a bodyguard at times, a bit protective, and they didn't seem to talk much between themselves either. It was too noisy to chat in the aeroplane. God, what a racket. You should provide earplugs or something.'

'We do; they're in a pocket by the seats.'

'Nobody told us. Talking of which, where's our pilot? The other big German.'

'Good question. I've no idea. We need to watch that one.'

'Look, Tom, we need to talk about what you're up to out here. I did get an inkling from Alice, but I should know more. I don't want to put my foot in it.'

Tom leant across the table. 'What do you mean, from Alice?'

'Didn't you know? I assumed that she'd tell you that she approached me.'

'How, why… when?'

Bill leant forward, elbows on the table, mimicking Tom's posture. 'Which one would you like me to answer first, buddy?'

'Don't mess me about Bill, this is serious. I had no idea Alice was talking to you.'

'Right, I get you. I don't know how she knew, but I got laid off from Fosters and got a message from her. One of her notes, you know.'

'Yes, I do, and then what?'

'Well, we met up in Salisbury, all secretive-like, on a park bench when she told me you could do with a reliable sidekick. Then she goes on to tell me that they want photos. Just like before. Evidence and you'll know what's required. So here I am, complete with all my camera gear and ready to watch your tail like the old days.'

Tom sat back and blew a long sigh. 'God, she's a one.'

'One what?'

'Oh, that's just an expression I reserve for Alice. It's something my father used to say. I just don't know what she's going to do next. She's inscrutable, mysterious, enigmatic. Take your pick.'

'Right.'

'How did you get your AORO accreditation?'

'Alice arranged it through a buddy in AORO by the name of Jackson.'

'Merv Jackson?'

'That's the man. Must be a US government flunky. Like you guys.'

'I know him. They were on my flight a month or so ago. We shared a few vodkas ⊠ too many, I recall.'

'OK. As I said, I'm out here to photograph evidence of the famine, so I'm also at your disposal for your games.'

Tom managed to crack a smile. 'Well, that could be very helpful.'

'So what's the plan?'

Tom looked pointedly at Bill. 'You recall the Official Secrets Act you signed a couple of years ago?'

'Yeh.'

'It's still in force; it's in force forever.'

'OK, I got that. What're we getting into?'

'Right, just remember this is very sensitive. All "need to know".'

'Oh, get on with it. I get all that stuff. I'm here to help.'

Tom nodded across the restaurant at the two Germans. 'We're going to follow these two. See where they go and hopefully get some clue what they're up to. In general, we're looking for Reichswehr people who travel to Russia to follow them to their place of business. In that way, we hope to discover what the German military is doing in Russia. We suspect some military cooperation, but not exactly what.'

'You can't swan around Russia in your swanky Deruluft uniform.'

'I'm not. That's for Alice and her cronies,' Tom said, chucking his head back in derision.

'You don't seem too impressed with the "cronies".'

'Hmm. We'll see, but we'll need photographs once we

get something interesting—locations, people, documents, anything that will provide identifiable and convincing evidence of their games.' Tom took a long sip from his glass. 'Enjoy the wine, Bill. It's not very common around here. The Metropol seems to have found a source. The Soviets discourage the consumption of alcohol.'

Their meal arrived just as Tom emptied their first wine bottle into their glasses. Clutching the bottle, he nodded to the waiter, who seemed to get the message.

'God. I'm ready for this,' said Bill. 'What is it?'

'I thought you'd appreciate one of my favourites, ' Tom said, checking the menu. salmon coulibiac is a pastry pie filled with salmon, rice, eggs, dill, and a lemon butter sauce.

'Hey, Munners, you've been living well.'

The waiter returned with another bottle of wine balanced precariously on a silver platter with a folded note. 'A message for you, sir.'

'Thank you,' said Tom, nodding appreciatively. 'I can guess what this is... Yes, as I thought. She got my message. She's off to Saratov by train. She'll pick up these two and tail them when we arrive.'

Alice and Heikkinen agreed to travel separately to avoid suspicion. She had not admitted it, but suspected Mikael might draw attention. Even with his dyed hair, he didn't look like the typical Russian. The AORO and other charities frequently used the train route to Saratov, so foreigners were a familiar sight. They both had their Feed the Children accreditation papers and were hopeful they could reach Saratov without being accosted by the GPU.

The grand edifice of the Kazansky railway station couldn't fail to impress with its four-level, tiered structure, tall spire and many adjacent structures with elaborately decorated windows and arches. To Alice, the whole impressive edifice looked as if each individual and distinctly different element of the building had been added over time, with scant regard for the earlier iterations. Indeed, she felt each building was trying to outshine its older brothers and sisters. She stood for a while, taking in the sight, coat over one arm and her soft carpet bag in the other hand. She spotted Mikael striding determinedly through the central arch, oblivious to the building features that had impressed Alice. She shrugged and made her way to the entrance and the growing sound of steam trains belching and hissing their presence in the resonant space within the station concourse.

Mikael indicated their carriage with a surreptitious nod and rather obvious thumbing towards the correct door. Alice acknowledged and noted the Cyrillic coach numbering before walking along the platform to view the locomotive. She walked past the line of flat-bed wagons, stacked precariously high with foodstuffs destined for the famine region, most marked boldly with "American Overseas Relief Organisation". The hot steaming monster at the head of the line seemed to be straining at the leash. She noted a bold red star on the smokebox door and a strange wheel configuration, "0-10-0". She remembered the Whyte notation taught by her father when they used to make their frequent visits to London, St Pancras station after church. The configuration definitely struck her as odd. She turned about to board her coach at a brisk walk, which broke into a run as the train moved off.

As the train slowly gathered pace under its considerable load, Alice watched central Moscow's solid and proud buildings change to tattered, dilapidated structures and people equally shabby making their way in the early morning sunlight. The buildings became more scattered, and within forty-five minutes or so, the train chuffed its way into the open countryside. Occasionally, small towns and hamlets drifted by, and the people looked increasingly malnourished, their pleading eyes staring into the passing carriages as if willing help to come. A couple of loaves of bread tossed from the train caught her eye, so the townspeople clearly knew that the occasional offering might be forthcoming from passing trains.

The journey was scheduled to take eight to ten hours, arriving in the early evening, but Merv Jackson, the AORO contact, had warned that it could take twice as long. That would be painful, Alice thought. Merv had also prepared her for the famine region, and she remembered his bleak warning.

'You need to be prepared,' he had advised. 'You need to understand the devastation the famine has caused. I know what you're doing out here, at least the basics, and I don't need to know any more, but you should be aware of the conditions in the Volga area.' Alice remembered his unusually grim demeanour.

'After the war, all sides in the civil war, that's the Bolsheviks, the Whites, the anarchists and seceding nationalists, provisioned themselves by taking food from the farmers and giving it to their armies. Then, the Bolshevik government requisitioned supplies from the peasantry for little or nothing in exchange. Our AORO offered aid to Lenin in 1919, but he refused what he regarded as interference in Russian affairs. The situation became so desperate that some of the population resorted to cannibalism. I'll spare you the details, but it became so organised that ten butchers' shops were eventually closed in Samar for selling human flesh. It became dangerous to venture out after dark, particularly for children.'

Alice remembered shuddering after this remark and felt she had heard enough, but Jackson seemed determined to tell his story.

'Eventually, in 1921, during the worst famine in history, Maxim Gorky appealed in an open letter to "all honest Europeans and Americans to give bread and medicine". The AORO and the British Feed the Children Fund became significant contributors, and now we have the famine under some degree of control. However, if you venture out into the more remote areas, you are likely to encounter chronic undernourishment and starvation still, and you could face attacks from desperate people. I'll ensure you have a truck for your "work", and you can take Bill Franklin and one other. The truck can be loaded with food and medicines and Bill's cameras. After the derogatory comments in your Daily Express, we want photographic evidence of the conditions. That's Bill's job, but we recognise that he may be helpful in other ways for you. I don't need to know that. The Feed the Children people in Saratov are advised that you are working for the British Government to report on the current conditions in the famine regions and to obtain photographic evidence. I guess we can say that any others you bring are for safety, bodyguards. You'll stay in the AORO hostel in Saratov, but elsewhere will be up to you.'

Alice mulled over Jackson's remarks as she lifted her head to return her gaze to the passing countryside; she jumped, startled…

'*Vashi dokumenty*,' said a gruff Russian voice as the uniformed figure appeared beside her.

Alice froze for a few moments as she stirred from her reverie.

'*Vashi dokumenty, bystro*,' he repeated, an ancient rifle sliding off his shoulder and into his hands.

Alice noticed that Mikael was watching, his tight-lipped expression self-explanatory. The fellow was probably GPU and certainly not a railway official, she thought whilst digging around in her bag. Her Smith and Wesson handgun was secured in a pocket within the lining, but a determined search would find it. She turned and gave the man the warmest smile she could muster. On reflection, she felt that it was more of a grimace. *'Konechno, ser,'* said Alice in her best Russian. She found her papers, including her British passport and Feed the Children accreditation, and handed them over with a more convincing smile. The man surprised Alice with his questions in passable English.

'Where you going?'

'I'm staying with the train until Saratov.'

'Where you staying in Saratov?'

'I believe in a hostel. I don't know where it is. I hope I will be collected from the station.'

'Why you here? We don't need British in Russia.'

'I am here to help with the famine relief effort. I am a volunteer with the British Feed the Children charity.'

The GPU man, dressed more like a soldier, studied Alice's documents, looking around suspiciously.

'Your bags?'

Alice pointed across the carriage. 'On the rack there.'

'Get it.'

Alice dragged her bag from the rack, placed it on the seat beside her and waited. She tried to look unperturbed, hands on her lap, looking ahead, avoiding eye contact. She noticed Mikael watching and resisted any response. The man rootled around in her bag and turned to look at her with a skin-crawling leer as he encountered her underclothes. She smiled back with a shrug.

Finally, he appeared satisfied with his search and dumped the bag on Alice's lap, followed by her papers. '*Budte ostorozhny, eto opasno dla zhenshchin,*' he said abruptly.

Alice interpreted his words as a warning of the dangers for women as he marched off, looking at the other passengers until he reached Mikael. She saw the rifle slide from the man's shoulder again, a standard technique obviously, but she couldn't hear what was said. Mikael jumped to his feet, knocked the soldier onto another passenger and grabbed him by the throat. Alice froze; she could not react or move. She would give herself away. The tussle continued for a few seconds until Mikael seemed to realise his mistake. He stood, his hands raised apologetically, while the man grabbed his rifle again and marched his prisoner back along the carriage towards Alice. She froze, avoiding eye contact with the soldier. Mikael stared ahead, and the pair disappeared through the connecting door to the next carriage.

Eventually, Alice dared a glance over her shoulder but saw nothing unusual and no sign of Mikael. She pondered her next action and decided that she should do nothing, hoping Mikael could deal with the situation alone. She could do something at Saratov and certainly keep watch for Mikael. As she exhausted her options for responding to the situation, she heard a door bang behind her, and Mikael swept past, adjusting his clothing before plonking down on his seat to the enquiring looks of their fellow passengers. He looked around with an unusually ashen complexion, then returned to his book.

CHAPTER TWENTY-THREE

A low industrial haze hung over the airfield at the Moscow Khodynka field. Tom had risen early and pored over his calculations, maps and other information in the Deruluft office for his flight to Saratov. His south-easterly course would take them over barren, featureless countryside, and his navigation would rely heavily on dead-reckoning and railway lines with course checks at Ryazan and Serdobsk and little else. He took some comfort in knowing that when his calculated five hours thirty minutes were up, hopefully at Saratov, he should see the Volga River. Once there, he should be able to identify his position and, if off course, find his way along the river to his destination. The AORO people had provided a sketch of the landing field, which was considered suitable for his machine. They had also undertaken to supply petrol. Anything else would need to be carried on the flight. He had made a telephone call to Yalena at their "safe house" so that she could advise Alice of their estimated arrival time at Saratov.

The F.III was a good load-lugger with a maximum take-off weight of 2000 kg, but his flight would test the machine's carrying capacity to the limit. He had three passengers, including Bill Franklin and his photographic equipment, and a flight of nearly five hours over a distance of 450 miles. The temperatures had been forecast to reach 30 degrees Celsius in the current heatwave so take-off could be a struggle at maximum weight. He rechecked his figures and felt cautiously confident that the generous take-off distance of 1400 meters at Khodynka would be adequate.

When a local pilot mentioned a military airfield on his route Tom's ears pricked up. He was told that the town of Lipetsk had an airfield, and once found on his map, this airfield was almost halfway to Saratov. He decided to route via this airfield despite the warning that it was military and that civil flights were not permitted. That advice was the carrot that Tom needed to investigate further. Routing via Lipetsk would mean turning south at Ryazan and leaving the navigational security of his railway line, launching off into uncharted territory. He had plotted the only reliable features on his map, large lakes, but wondered if his adventure was too risky. Eventually, he found a route from Ryazan to Tambov and from there to Lipetsk. He felt more confident with that, although the advice that he could be shot down if he flew too close to the Lipetsk airfield didn't fill him with confidence. This alerted him to the possibility that the mysterious Fokker D.VIIs might operate from there. He started considering a feigned engine problem and an emergency landing to see what was happening at Lipetsk.

The two Deruluft ground crew trundled their loads to the machine, weighed the luggage, and then stowed it carefully at the rear of the passenger compartment. Tom watched with interest, noting the weights on the load sheet. 'We'll be right on the limit,' said Tom as he stowed his maps, a bottle of water and a cheese roll in his cockpit. He made a mental note to visit the toilets at the last minute; five hours was a long time. He was now sure that he would land at Lipetsk but kept this to himself.

The passengers appeared in good time, the Germans looking refreshed after a break from their travels. Bill was never a morning person, and his appearance reminded Tom of their early flights in France when Bill had over-indulged the night before. As Tom did his pre-flight inspection, each passenger stepped on the scales before climbing aboard. Bill carried one of his cameras, which caused one of the Germans to cast a questioning eye in his direction. Bill shrugged and climbed aboard.

'How does it look?' said Tom, reaching for the completed load sheet.

'Two thousand three hundred kilos, Captain.'

'Hmm. Right. A bit overweight. I'll need the entire field length, then. Let's get started.'

Tom taxied to the airfield's far boundary, noticing the limp windsock and the increasingly hot and humid conditions even at seven in the morning. He dabbed his forehead, pulled down his goggles and turned the machine into what little wind was on offer. Taking a deep breath and swallowing hard, Tom advanced the throttle lever until it was hard against the stop to get maximum power from the RR Eagle engine. He could feel the sluggish acceleration and kept the machine running straight with judicious use of the rudder. He noted his slowly increasing airspeed, checked the oil pressure and temperatures, and raised the tail into the flying attitude, countering the familiar swing with his feet on the rudder pedals.

The machine rumbled and bounced over the grass surface, the speed holding worryingly steady at 80 kph. He needed at least 90. The end of the field materialised all too soon in the haze as the airspeed speed needle shuddered reluctantly up to 90. A mental picture of his aeroplane in a smoking heap in the next field flashed into Tom's mind. The tree line filled his view. A glance at the airspeed showed just under 90. He coaxed the machine into the air. The machine felt loose and unresponsive. He could feel the wings clawing at the air, the humid airflow burbling its reluctance through the controls.

He held the machine steady, flying level, the wheels still rumbling along the ground, reluctant to leave Mother Earth. Tom held the machine down, the wheels just off the ground. It accelerated but reluctantly. The field boundary was on them. He eased the controls back just enough to rise over the trees. The foliage brushed the underside of the aeroplane as it sank back towards the ground. The following field provided a little more room as the machine continued complaining under the weight. Tom wondered about the accuracy of their weighing scales as his hands clamped rigidly around the controls. The field just below continued to rush past, but at last, he could feel a more positive response from the aeroplane. The machine maintained its critical 90 kph as Tom sensed the aeroplane was balanced between flight and the stall when it would pitch back down to the ground in a welter of pieces. He felt the sweat run into his eyes just as he was able to coax the aeroplane into a climb. He noticed his hands shaking and made a determined effort to relax whilst daring a gentle, shallow turn to get on the course as soon as possible; his altimeter indicated 200 meters. For the first time, he noticed the RR Eagle engine alongside him thrashing away at maximum RPM, the big four-blade propellor fulfilling its side of the bargain. He breathed at last as he sensed a positive rate of climb, his altimeter needle creeping around the instrument face in the right direction.

It took nearly twenty minutes to reach 1000m, and he sensed a sigh of relief from the engine as he pulled the throttle back to cruise revs and adjusted the fuel/air mixture for maximum range. The reluctance of the aeroplane to take off convinced him that they must have been significantly overweight unless the engine was not performing properly. He knew the more powerful Rolls Royce Eagle engine did not provide any increase in cruise speed, but he did expect better take-off and climb performance. He knew the high temperature would not help.

Tom estimated a flight time of two and a half hours to reach the mysterious airfield at Lipetsk and had decided to set a course to try to land there. His curiosity was aroused, and he pondered how he would convincingly justify the need to land at Lipetsk. A fake misfire would be possible by switching the magneto switches on and off. If he was challenged or intercepted in the air, the misfire would be seen with smoke puffing from the exhaust. Also, his passengers would be able to attest to the misfire. The view over the nose of his machine and the gradual build up of clouds in the distance offered another possibility. Hot, humid conditions often generated cloud build up and the possibility of thunderstorms making a weather diversion another plausible reason for a landing.

As Tom's calculations indicated that Lipetsk should be visible soon, he peered through his windscreen whilst ducking down to avoid the impact of heavy rain. He started to wish that he had not even considered the possibility of thunderstorms as a weather diversion as he descended to avoid the colossal development of a single cumulo-nimbus, which now filled his view. The storm was immense, and he knew that flying around it would be unrealistic. Turning back into unfamiliar territory with no hope of a landing site and the lack of fuel was also out of the question. The threatening cloud was a blessing in disguise; it would be the Lipetsk airfield or landing out in some uncertain field. As his clock indicated he should have reached the Lipetsk he began a gradual turn and a search of the ground barely visible in the murk. It was as dark as night under the cloud, which was now generating worrying turbulence. He empathised with his passengers for a few seconds before continuing his search.

If only he could find the town and feel confident that he was only a few miles off track. He had managed to get some information about Lipetsk from a geography book back in Moscow, and he knew that a large lake, with a name which he couldn't pronounce, was positioned to the east with a river and smaller lakes close to the town to the southeast. If only he could find the town! After over twenty minutes of circling in heavy rain, Tom started to consider an alternative plan. He could continue on his track to Saratov, but now, his time searching for Lipetsk would mean they might not have enough fuel to reach his destination.

He decided to search a little longer, and for no other reason than pure speculation, he levelled his wings and pushed further north. The dull grey light grew more menacing. He had to descend further to maintain sight of the ground. He knew his altimeter was useless, as the pressure would have changed dramatically from his setting at Moscow, so he relied on the sight of the ground to judge his height.

After ten minutes of fruitless searching, all thoughts of finding Lipetsk, let alone the airfield and spying for the SIS, had left his mind. Survival was now the only remaining objective. The storm continued to roar and buffet his machine. He was now down at almost tree height. He decided to land at the first opportunity. All he needed was a large, flat field; was that too much to ask?

A field appeared to the left, which might meet his desperate needs. He turned across it. The machine was down at tree height now. It drifted dramatically, skidding across the mottled green landscape. He thought the wind strength must be over thirty knots. They must land into the wind. He turned again to position for a landing, the machine rushing downwind, bouncing around in the turbulence kicked up by the trees surrounding the field. 'Why are there always bloody trees around the fields I pick? Tom hissed.

During the final turn to line up with his chosen field, the machine seemed to stop and hover in the air. Tom glanced at his airspeed, which was 80 kph and was OK for landing. They made little progress towards the field. He lowered the nose and increased power to drive the machine into the gale. The field boundary moved slowly underneath as Tom fought the bucking machine down under as much control as he could manage. At least the wind would shorten his landing run. They seemed to hover, almost stationary, over the grass as Tom flared the aeroplane into a landing attitude. He wrestled with the controls in response to the gusts. Finally, they were down with a firm bump, stopping almost instantly in the furious wind.

From the corner of his eye, Tom saw Bill bursting out of the passenger cabin with the chocks, which he pushed into place at the wheels. Tom kept the engine running while struggling to keep the machine level. Finally, Bill appeared again at the machine's left side, making signs to indicate the chocks were in place. He looked shocked and pointed into the rain squall.

Tom glanced in the direction of Bill's desperate gestures to see the ethereal sight of a line of soldiers, rifles held diagonally across their chests and charging towards them out of the rain. He blinked hard and stared again at the bewildering sight.

As he stopped the engine and began his climb down from the cockpit, Bill was bundled to the ground face down with the soldiers standing around him, boots on his back and rifles levelled at his head. The remaining soldiers dashed across to Tom as he stepped unsteadily onto the grass, not knowing whether to feel relieved or terrified. He, too, found himself similarly pushed to the ground with frantic yelling in Russian. He looked up to see the same treatment meted out to the two Germans who were dragged unceremoniously from the aeroplane. The big fellow bellowed in Russian, which seemed to get the soldier's attention. They stood back in shock, then gingerly pulled the two Germans to their feet, dusting them down and mumbling something which seemed to be an apology.

Tom and Bill were then dragged to their feet with considerably less care, and their arms were then pulled behind their backs and secured with rope. Tom marshalled his limited Russian. 'What have we done? Why are we being treated like this?'

'*Zatknis.*'

'I think that means shut up,' Tom mumbled as he took another shove in the back.

Bill seemed transfixed by something in the distance as the rain showers cleared through. 'Look, that's an airfield, ain't it?'

'Good God. That must be Lipetsk. We landed just beside it. No wonder these boys seem a bit upset.'

'Zatknis, zatknis!'

It was a long trudge across the airfield towards a motley collection of buildings and hangars. Some old Russian aeroplanes were parked outside one of the three hangars, and Tom searched keenly for anything of interest. He hoped to see his Fokker D.VIIs as another rifle prod in his back reminded him of their predicament. As they reached a small brick-built building to the left of the hangars, one of the soldiers beckoned the two Germans forward and escorted them through a passageway and out of sight. Bill and Tom were forced to the ground. Tom thought he could hear voices speaking in German but could not make out the conversation.

'Captain,' said the tall German in perfect English.

Tom recalled that his name was Hoffmann, but that was all he knew. 'Yes?'

'We need to speak. In here. This American can stay where he is.'

Tom pulled himself to his feet with some rough assistance from a soldier. He walked along a short passage, following Hoffmann with a soldier following up at the rear. They turned left into a large office with desks down each side manned by uniformed men and women busy at typewriters. They all stopped their work as the group walked to the end of the room and into a well-appointed office. A more senior officer in Russian uniform sat behind a large oak desk with the small passenger, Weber, sitting alongside, looking smug. Tom was beckoned to one of two seats in front of the desk and was seated next to Hoffmann. The officer behind the desk nodded an instruction to the soldier, who promptly cut Tom's rope bonds. He blew a sigh of relief and rubbed the welts on his wrists.

Hoffmann spoke in English. 'I've explained that we are travelling to Saratov, and I have assumed that we landed in the field in an emergency.'

'Thank you,' said Tom. 'You are quite correct. It is entirely coincidental that we should be close to this place. If I had seen it, I would have landed here.'

'Very well, but you should not be here. I have spoken to the commandant, who has agreed to get our machine onto the airfield so we can set off tomorrow.'

'That will be very helpful. Can you please convey my thanks to the commandant?'

Hoffmann turned to the officer across the desk and spoke at length. He then turned back to Tom. 'Will we require petrol?'

'We certainly will, and again, that would be most helpful.'

Tom and Bill didn't see any more of their German passengers after Tom was escorted without further explanations from the office. They were taken by their usual escort to a remote bunkhouse some way from the main airfield buildings. They were escorted up the wooden stairway and pushed into the room. The door slammed behind with the sound of a door lock echoing in the unfriendly space. Bill and Tom looked at each other, shrugged, and explored their accommodation. It didn't take long. Their small wooden hut had four beds, a table with a large jug, and a bowl of water. A paraffin lamp and a stove were encouraging in the centre of the room, but there was no fuel. Bill looked curiously at a cupboard-like structure in the far corner of the room, which he proceeded to explore.

'Yeh, it's the "John". It reminds me of our RFC huts,' said Bill.

Tom wandered around the room and peered out of each window in turn. 'Yeah, hardly the Metropol.' He stopped at one window. 'We have a guard. They are hiding something. We can't pass up this opportunity. We need to have a look around, particularly in the hangars.'

'You can't be serious. We won't get a hundred yards before we're spotted. And we don't have any light, a torch or something.'

'We'll have moonlight tonight, I think.'

'It'll be suicide. Look how we were treated. They'll shoot us on sight, is my guess.'

'When will we get another opportunity? We'd probably be shot down any other time if we try to fly in here. We were damn lucky.'

'Maybe we can get a look around tomorrow before we leave?'

'What, please, can we look around your hangars, general, or whatever rank he was? I don't think so! I suppose we could fly into some neighbouring field some other time. Hop over the fence and sniff around when we're better equipped and more organised, you know, torch, camera… that sort of thing.'

Tom continued his examination of the hangar buildings, his face squashed up against the window. 'They're building new hangars and more buildings,' he said as he worked his way around the hut, trying each window in turn. 'Here, look, we can get out of this window. Right, that does it. I want to give it a go tonight. If I'm caught,

I want to check our machine and get some clothes or something. You can stay here if you want. I'll go on my own.'

'What and break my promise to Alice? She'd never forgive me.'

'Good. We should leave it till the wee small hours.'

'Another of your father's expressions?'

'Yes.'

A rattling of keys in the door interrupted their conversation. The door burst open to reveal a soldier and two others holding trays. They stomped up the steps into the room and placed the trays of bread, water, and cheese on the table by the door. A waft of kitchen smells accompanied the men, who avoided eye contact, and all three left the hut. The door banged closed, followed by a rattling of keys and the clunk of the lock.

'Feels like we're in prison, Bill.'

Bill surveyed the food. 'I wonder how our German friends are being treated? Pretty different to us, I guess.'

'Yes, that's significant, eh? It supports our view that some sort of cooperation is afoot. We better get some rest before our little survey of the local facilities.'

Tom sat up, swung his legs off the bed, and stretched. He leant across and shook Bill awake. 'It's time.'

'Time for what? Oh, that.' Bill mumbled as he struggled to shake off the sleep.

Tom pulled on his uniform jacket, pulled up the collar, and tried to cover up his white shirt where practical. He opened the window, gave Bill a thumbs-up, and looked for any sign of the guard before gingerly lowering himself onto the grass. He gestured to Bill to wait and crept along to the front of the hut. The guard was asleep on a ground sheet and propped up against the hut.

'It's OK, Bill. Come on, let's go.'

They moved across the open ground towards the building complex adjacent to the hangars, appreciating and cursing the moonlight in equal measure. 'The hangars first,' Tom whispered.

Their F.III, now parked outside the first hangar, glistened in the moonlight and provided convenient cover en-route. When they reached the machine, Bill grabbed Tom's shoulder. He pointed towards the hangar. 'Guards!'

Two guards stood chatting between the first and second hangars. A puff of smoke drifted in the breeze as they continued their conversation. Bill shrugged with a questioning, open-hand gesture. 'What now?'

Tom ducked down under the aeroplane's fuselage and watched. 'We wait until they move off. We should get to the rear of the hangars. There should be some easier access there.'

'Should we grab our guns?' Bill asked.

'It would be the end of us if we use them.'

'Might be the end if we don't have 'em.'

'Torches would be more useful.'

'Good idea. There's one in the cabin by the door. Hope it works.'

Bill carefully opened the cabin door and pulled the torch from its clamp. 'Look, Tom, the guards are off towards the other hangars.'

'OK, quickly, down the side of that one. You go first. Make for the rear. Any door you can find.'

Tom watched Bill skulk across the grass and concrete surface in front of the hangar until he disappeared into the shadows. The guards were barely visible now, so Tom followed, keeping low. When he reached Bill, he found him lying flat on the ground, gesturing to Tom to do the same. 'More guards, look,' Bill mouthed.

The buildings behind the hangars were more heavily guarded, and at least three men were visible. There were two doors to the rear, and when the guards moved out of view, Tom crawled along to the first door. He reached up, tried the handle, and shook his head. At the next door, there was no handle, but it was slightly ajar. Tom slid his hand into the gap but stopped when he noticed that lights were on inside.

Bill joined him, squatting down to watch for the guards. 'Give it a try.'

Tom eased the door open outwards and stopped abruptly as it emitted a loud creaking noise. 'Damn it.'

They waited, then tried again, opening the door just enough to get a head in. Tom leant through then looked back at Bill. 'Wow!' he mouthed.

'What? Can I have a look?'

'Yeah, but quiet. Don't move the door.'

Just as Bill peered into the hangar, a bird disturbed by their movement fluttered noisily, banged against the door, and escaped into the night.

A voice echoed in the hangar. '*Wer ist da?*'

'He's German,' said Tom out of the side of his mouth as he backed away from the door. He froze, standing flat against the back of the hangar, shielded by the door that opened outwards. 'We can't be seen.'

Footsteps echoed noisily within, getting louder, ever closer.

'What now,' Bill whispered.

The door creaked open; light spilt onto the ground.

Tom gripped his torch ever tighter. 'He mustn't see us,' he muttered through clenched teeth as a head peeped out into the night.

The man looked the other way just as the torch landed on his head with a dull thump, whereupon his body flopped out of the door, falling face down onto the grass. Tom raised the torch for a second blow, but there was no need; the body lay still.

'Let's go. We saw what we wanted,' Tom whispered, pushing Bill along the back of the hangar. 'Quickly before he wakes up. Back to the hut.'

There was little sleep in the hut that night. 'How many did you see, Bill?'

'Four. I only got a quick look.'

'Yes, that's what I saw. They were all Fokker D.VIIs, and they looked brand-new. They had the same colour scheme as the machines I saw near Moscow.'

'So what are they doin' here?'

'That mechanic was German. From what we've seen, our German passengers are being treated fairly well. My guess is that this is, or will be, a training base.'

Bill did not look convinced. 'So, the Russians have bought some machines to set up a flying training base for their air force. There's nothing strange about that if it's for training Russian pilots. You think it's for training German pilots, don't you?'

Tom took a gulp of water. 'Correct. A clandestine training facility away from the prying eyes of the Inter-Allied Control Inspectors. Dodging the Versailles Treaty restrictions. It all makes sense.'

'We'll still need to prove that. Oh, don't tell me: photographs,' said Bill.

'Do you think you could get something tomorrow… actually today?'

'All my stuff is big and heavy. It would be too obvious. I'd be shot on sight.'

'We could make it official. See if we could get a posed group photograph.'

'I can't see that working.'

'Hmm, yes, I agree.' Tom held up a finger in a moment of inspiration. 'I've got my little Kodak Vest Pocket

Autographic. It's in my bag in the aeroplane.'

'What, the one that failed to take any photos in von der Lang's flat?'

'Don't be smart, Bill. You know that was due to the poor light. It'll be perfect lighting today… I hope.'

'So what's your plan?'

'Simple. During all the hubbub before our flight, you return to the machine, dig out my camera, and get shots from the cabin. It's got a film in it. Improvise, play it by ear. I'll keep everyone busy, even a distraction of some sort.'

Bill still looked unconvinced. 'There may be nothing to photograph.'

'I agree. They will keep aircraft hidden in the hangar when we're around but get anything: the buildings, our German passengers and any important-looking people at the airfield. We might not be able to identify them now, but we can do it later if we've got the shots. It'll help our case. You never know what might be useful.'

'I guess that will work,' said Bill.

Tom glanced out the window as he stretched out on his bed. 'It's getting light. We ought to get some rest. I have a three-hour flight tomorrow, and you have some camera stuff to do.'

Tom thought he had just fallen asleep when the hut door banged open, shocking him into consciousness. He attempted to clear his eyes as he saw another tray placed on the ground. The soldier spoke gravelly as if he had been cheering too much at a football match.

'shyest' cha-sof oot-ra.'

Tom checked his watch, noticing that it was six o'clock. 'Bill, breakfast is served.'

Bill opened one eye and focused on the tray. 'Bread and water! You'd think we were prisoners.'

'We are.'

Tom tried to smarten himself up as much as possible, but this was difficult with his 24-hour stubble and crumpled uniform. 'We should see how things are in the wider world.' The door wasn't locked, and it opened freely onto a bright morning with little activity other than local birds, which rose into the sky when Tom jumped onto the grass. 'Our guard has gone. We should go to the office where we were taken last night.'

'Why don't we go to the aeroplane? That would look normal,' said Bill. 'I can grab the camera and you can do your checks.'

CHAPTER TWENTY-FIVE

Tom and Bill strolled across the Lipetsk airfield in the early morning sun, the smell of warming grass pervading the air. They felt like they were on holiday until a small group of soldiers jogged towards them from the airfield buildings.

'Here we go again,' said Bill. 'Do you think we'll get the handcuff treatment this time?'

'We'll soon find out.'

The lead soldier, an NCO, told them to stop. Tom gestured to their aeroplane. 'We need ben-zeen, ben-zeen.'

The soldier looked around at his squad and then pointed with an open hand towards their aeroplane.

Tom beckoned to Bill. 'Looks like we can carry on. I tried asking for petrol. Let's see what happens. The German Hoffman speaks good English, so let's hope he can sort it out for us. You'll find the camera in a small internal pocket in my bag.'

Bill opened the cabin door and climbed in as they got to the aeroplane. Unfortunately, the soldiers were too interested to allow Bill to search for the camera, so he merely looked for Tom's bag. He moved the bags around and smiled casually at the soldiers who were at the door and looking in curiously. He rearranged the bags so that Tom's was on top and easily accessible.

‘I’ll get these chaps to help push the machine onto the hard standing in front of the hangars, said Tom. That should give you some time, Bill?’

With appropriate sign language, Tom assembled a team of four soldiers and pushed the F.III some fifty metres onto the concrete fronting the hangar they had investigated during the night. The main doors were still firmly closed. Once parked, Tom looked around for any other activity or his German passengers. Bill was still ensconced in the Fokker cabin and Tom wondered if he had found the camera and taken any photographs.

‘Bol’shoye spasibo,’ Tom said with a wave, pleased to use one of the few Russian expressions he had learned. He then checked the fuel contents on the level gauge on the bulkhead behind his seat, took his chart, and measured the distance to Saratov. He decided they would only have enough fuel to reach their destination but no reserves. This was not a healthy situation, and getting a top-up of petrol was essential. He was sitting at the cabin door when Hoffmann appeared.

‘Good morning, Captain. Are we all ready?’

‘Good morning, sir. Not quite, we will need more petrol.’

‘Oh. I thought that you planned for a direct flight to Saratov. You must have enough?’

‘I’m afraid our route is much longer now that we’ve landed here. We spent a lot of time looking for a safe place to land, and we have used a lot of fuel.’

'I will ask.'

Tom turned to Bill, who had stayed in the passenger cabin. 'Have you got some photos?'

'Just a few.'

'It will be good to get Hoffmann and Weber at least. I don't suppose we'll see any aeroplanes. And get the buildings in the background so that we can identify the location somehow.'

'I got Hoffmann. Are we getting any fuel?'

'We're trying. It will be very marginal if we don't. Look, here's Hoffmann.'

'No fuel, Captain.'

'Did they give a reason?'

'No. Can we make it to Saratov or not, Captain?'

Tom looked thoughtful. 'Just about.'

'Yes or no, Captain. That's all I need to know.'

'Then, yes.'

'Good, let's get going.'

'I need to call my office first.'

'That could be difficult,' Hoffmann mumbled.

'My office could be organising a search at this very moment. The last time I was in contact was when we left yesterday. They would be expecting to hear about our arrival in Saratov.'

'I will speak to the people in the office. Wait here.'

Tom could just make out Bill in their aeroplane, snapping away. If only the D.VIIs were visible.

‘Quickly, in here,’ said Hoffmann. ‘You are not to mention where you are. No talk of this airfield, do you understand?’

‘Of course,’ said Tom, trying to decide what number to call. The safe house would be best. That’s where Alice would call. He needed to advise her of their time of arrival. Once in the office, Tom advised a clerk of the number to call. He crossed his fingers that Yalena would answer. She did, and Tom found it difficult to get a word in.

‘Yalena, listen, we had to land in bad weather. We are taking off now and expect to arrive in Saratov just after midday.’ Tom glanced at Hoffmann. ‘We are short of fuel, so wish us luck.’

Hoffmann took Tom’s telephone and slammed it down. ‘Right, now we go, yes?’

‘Not quite. Are there any maps here that I could use? My map is ancient. I assume that pilots flying from here have up-to-date maps.’

Hoffmann sighed. ‘Damn it, Munro, we need to get to Saratov.’

‘Well, a reliable map will help, and if you really want to guarantee getting to our destination, we need more fuel.’

Hoffmann was getting red in the face. ‘I thought you said we can get there.’

‘You rather forced me into saying that. We may run out of fuel. So, you decide. There must be fuel here, so why can't we refuel? I have money for this eventuality.'

Hoffmann turned away again and barged through the outer office, brushing Weber aside and into another office at the rear of the building. Tom could hear much discussion in Russian, and with his hands behind his back and humming a song, he attempted an innocent stroll into the outer office following Hoffmann. A squadron badge was prominent when looking around the office. Tom smiled at some of the staff, who looked at him like he had just landed from outer space. His scan of the office found something of even greater interest. He shuffled nonchalantly towards the desk for a better view of a file. It was titled in German. *Wissenshaftliche Versuchs-und Personalausbildungstation* (WIWUPAL). He translated as best he could, hiding a tantalising desire to grin and punch the air; *Scientific Experimental and Personnel Training Station.*

Hoffmann appeared from the back office, closely followed by a senior Russian officer who seemed to be competing with Hoffmann for the reddest face; he was puce. With little of the courtesies one would expect for a visitor, Tom was bundled out of the office. 'There is no fuel for us, Captain,' Hoffmann said.

Tom shrugged. 'We have to take our chances then.'

Tom briefed Bill and Hoffmann on the engine start, and the two of them swung the big four-blade propellor to bring the Rolls Royce Eagle engine to life, scattering the birdlife and shattering the peace on the airfield. A few people gathered to watch them depart.

The aeroplane was off the ground and on course within minutes. Tom knew that he would have to conserve fuel as much as possible, and he climbed on course, levelling off at 1000m, adjusting the engine controls and cruise speed for maximum range. It was another still, humid morning, and a storm buildup was a distinct possibility. He expected to reach Saratov just after midday and hoped the fuel would last. If the weather and clouds permitted, he decided to let the aeroplane drift higher so that he had the maximum amount of time to find a field if the tanks ran dry before Saratov. The wind was light and variable, so there would be little help from that quarter.

On the better maps he had seen at Lipetsk, he could identify a helpful railway line running east-west from Voronezh to Saratov and expected this line to converge on his track from the right. As he had decided, the Volga River, running through Saratov, would be his backstop. If Saratov was not visible, he could find the river and fix his position.

After two hours, he rechecked the fuel gauge. It wasn't necessary, as he had repeatedly checked the fuel contents since they got airborne. It indicated empty now; the engine running on fresh air. The road to Saratov was now visible a few kilometres to his right, so he felt confident about finding the airfield. He had worked his way up to 1500 meters, but the cloud would be problematic as it was forming at the same altitude. He peered over the nose towards the horizon and spotted what might be Saratov, but he couldn't be sure. He rechecked the gauge in a fingers-crossed gesture, but the needle bounced around the empty mark. He hoped the bouncing needle would continue to bounce for a few moments longer when the engine spluttered. Was it his imagination? Yes, it maintained its rhythm.

Tom was holding his breath now whilst peering into the distance to pick up the airfield. The visibility was poor under the clouds. A few minutes later, it happened again; the engine coughed, picked up, and coughed. It was struggling to suck the dregs from the bottom of the fuel tank. He looked again over the nose and thought he could see Saratov. The railway line was now just off to his right, so he decided he was close. The haze prevented a good view of the ground, and he turned off course to see what was below on his track. There it was, a town, he was sure. Just at that moment, the engine faltered and then died, the big propellor shuddering to a stop. The comforting noise of the engine was replaced by the soft but disconcerting whistle of the airflow over the machine.

Tom lowered the nose, trimmed for best glide speed, and searched for the airfield. He knew where it should be but couldn't see it. He headed to the north side of the town where the airfield was located. The machine was descending fast, now down to 1000 metres. He scanned the land below for an airfield. Any big field would have to do. He cursed the Lipetsk people; perhaps they wanted him to have an accident. Down to 500 meters now, and he picked a field just off the nose to the left. A field fire indicated the direction of the wind. He was relieved to see that the wind was light.

He kept his chosen field just to the left of the nose and judged his height by experience. The field looked good, his height also. He turned crosswind, noticing his rate of descent relative to the field, and lined up for a landing. At the last minute, he spotted a windsock and started to breathe again. Perhaps he had found the airfield after all. He flew down to a smooth landing, his heart still pounding as the machine rolled to a halt.

All was quiet apart from the sound of some movement in the cabin. *I wonder what they're thinking*, Tom wondered. He breathed a long sigh of relief and paused a little longer to savour that relief then pulled his helmet off to climb stiffly and gratefully to the ground.

Alice had been waiting at the airfield since 6 am and was relieved to see the insect-like shape of an aeroplane appear in the distance. 'I hope that's him,' she said to Mikael, slumped in the back of the truck. Merv had left them with a vehicle of sorts: a well-worn Fiat 15 with a canvas-covered tubular frame over the cargo area. With two seats in the front, Mikael seemed quite happy, stretched out in the back on the journey to the airport.

The aeroplane descended to the grass runway and came to a halt, its propellor stationary. 'That's not right. Look, it's just stopped,' said Alice.

Mikael had roused himself by now and climbed out to observe the activity. 'Hmm, strange. We better keep an eye on this. The two Germans may set off at any time.'

It was some ten minutes before there was any movement, the Fokker F.III looking lost in the middle of the field. 'That must be Tom,' Alice said with a tinge of emotion. 'Yes, it is, look, that's him climbing down from his cockpit. And look, a truck is making its way onto the airfield. I think they're going to tow it in. They must have had engine problems.'

'We better be ready. You're driving?'

'Why me?' Alice said with a frown.'

'Cos I can't drive.'

'That's great, you could have told me,' Alice moaned, turning to watch what the Germans were up to. 'Look, they're transferring luggage to that car. They might be going. You can have the pleasure of cranking this old girl into life.'

Mikael poised at the cranking handle. 'Ready when you are.'

Alice set the controls and nodded. 'OK, wind away.'

The engine started at first go, and they sat ready for the Germans to move off.

'Looks like they get the plush vehicle, whereas we

get a bloody ancient truck.'

'Merv says that we will blend in better in our Fiat. Look, you're right; they're on the move. I hope we can keep up.'

Alice and Mikael turned away as the Fiat 501 cruised past, the two Germans sitting in the rear seats looking like royalty. Once the car was on the road, Alice crunched her truck into gear and moved off with a judder. 'This'll take some time to get used to,' she huffed

The 501 maintained a slow yet steady pace as it wound its way into Saratov, leaving a helpful dust cloud. Alice worked hard at changing gear. The non-synchronous transmission required double declutching techniques to avoid grinding the gears. 'I'm glad they're slow; I can only just keep up.'

Mikael monitored the progress through the dust. 'They're going right. 'They could be going to their hotel. We'll just have to see what happens. I don't suppose they'll be staying at our hostel.'

After some ten minutes, the 501 pulled up outside a hotel in the centre of Saratov. The driver lugged the cases into the building while the two Germans followed, dusting themselves down. 'Now we wait,' said Alice. 'I hope they carry on to their destination. That's what we need right now. You can climb into the back, Mikael. We can take turns keeping watch.'

Mikael had just climbed into the back, under the canvas flap, when Alice spotted a man walking down the steps from the hotel. He had the unmistakable gait and dress of the Cheka, now the GPU, the Soviet Secret Police. They tried to blend in with the local population, but this fellow was failing miserably. They didn't have a uniform, but his man was wearing what seemed to be the typical fashion amongst the Chekists: a leather jacket, jaunty cap, boots and belted trousers. As he approached Alice, she saw he sported his Cheka commemorative badge. This was the last person in the world she needed. As he sauntered along the street towards Alice, he glanced left and right casually as if looking for trouble - targets, anyone who might look suspicious and prove worthy of interrogation. She knew they were to be avoided at all costs, but there was always the risk of encountering a Chekist. 'Not now, please,' she mumbled through tight lips. She turned and spoke through the canvas. 'Wake up, Mikael, we might have a problem. We have a Chekist heading our way. We're going to need your Russian skills. What's our reason for being here? Lost, Resting?'

'I'm coming. Don't say anything.'

Mikael slipped out the back of the truck and attempted a nonchalant stroll to the front, slipping in beside Alice. They had raised the windscreen previously to hide from the road dust, and the mucky glass served as a convenient way to hide. Mikael glanced at Alice and patted his pocket. She knew what he meant. 'That's a last resort,' she said.

'What are you going to say? Why are we here?'

Mikael shrugged. 'I'll see what he asks. We're working for the Feed the Children, yes?'

'Yes, of course. We could be looking for somewhere to get petrol.'

'Good idea, I'll try that.'

'Look,' said Alice. 'He's off after someone else, thank God. What's he saying?'

'Something like "halt, stop where you are."'.

That's a relief. That could have been tricky. Look, our German pair are off. Get on the handle, let's go.'

'I'm going to teach you to drive this thing,' said Alice after following the Fiat for nearly half an hour. 'It's bloody tiring; the steering is so heavy.' They were on the outskirts of Saratov, and buildings were few and far between. Still, trails of emaciated people were heading towards town. Some held their hands out as they passed.

'Not so long now, look, they're turning off the main road. Hang back or drive past. There's little traffic around now. They might spot us.'

'Sounds like you've done this before.'

'Right, drive past. They're stopping by that building. Looks like a factory compound of some sort. Keep going. Did you bring the binoculars?'

'Yes, in my bag. Down there,' Alice said, gesturing to the floor.'

'We should park a little further on, by that building. Hide the car.'

Alice studied the building. She had just focused her binoculars when she felt a tugging at her sleeve. 'What the devil? There are dozens of 'em!' Michael exclaimed as they were quickly surrounded by a crowd of starving people; men, women, and children.

'God Mikael, we don't have anything, do we?'

'No, there's nothing in the truck.'

'Can you explain that to them?' said Alice, gesturing wildly. 'They want my binoculars.'

'We need to go. Let's drive past the compound and see what we can. We can't do anything with this lot around us.'

Mikael had to push and shove his way to the front of the truck and eventually made enough space to crank the engine into life. Alice sat ready at the wheel, having a similar struggle to ward off the crowd's desperate attention. When the engine burst into life, Mikael pushed his way back and climbed aboard just as Alice drove off, the rear wheels kicking up dust and debris into the faces of the crowd. As soon as she could, she turned the truck around and eased her way through the crowd to turn down the side road and past the building where the Fiat had disappeared.

Alice stopped the truck one hundred metres past a high wall topped with barbed wire and kept the engine running. The wall running away from the road retained its height and vicious wire. The sturdy gates through which the Fiat had disappeared looked secure and purposeful, designed for tight security. No signs were visible, which might indicate the establishment's purpose. 'The camera's in my bag. Take some shots. Don't make it too obvious.'

'Look, the gate's opening.'

Alice slammed the truck into gear. 'OK, we're going. It's too obvious sitting here.'

After a kilometre, Alice stopped the truck. 'It's difficult working in these conditions. We were so obviously up to no good. That place looked very suspicious. It was designed to be very secure. What's hidden behind those walls?'

'Why don't we go back and turn down the road along the other wall, see if we can drive all the way around? It looks quite big. I can get some photos if we're not observed.'

'OK, let's do that. Did you see what came out when the gates opened?

'It's just another vehicle. Not the Fiat. It was a truck stacked with, I don't know, bottles or small tanks. I'm not sure.'

Alice turned the truck around and was about to set off when a man appeared from a small hut by the side of the road.

'Vy chto-to ishchete?'

Alice stopped the truck. 'What's he saying?'

'He wants to know if we're looking for something.'

'Hmm. Ask him what that building is used for. What goes on there?'

Mikael rattled away in Russian for some time, and the man responded with a shake of his head and cautious expression, which intrigued Alice. 'Well?'

'He says he doesn't know, but he sees a lot of coming and going and military people. If he walks nearby, he is usually chased away.'

'That's not much help. How long has he lived here?'

Mikael tried again.

'He says not long. Nobody wants to live here. He says he got his hut for free because some people died here and most others moved away. He pointed at these other shacks, which are all empty, apparently.'

Alice looked around at the bleak surroundings. The compound stood alone, apart from the deserted buildings and the man's little house. 'Let's go. Have you got the camera?'

'Get moving, and I'll have it ready.'

Alice turned left along the compound, where little was to be seen except the high wall. There was no road or path along the back of the compound, but the roofs of what appeared to be warehouses and factory-type buildings could be seen. Several chimneys were belching pale grey smoke. 'We need to investigate this place further. Why else would the Germans be visiting?'

'Not going to be easy getting in there.'

'Yes, we need to think about that. Let's get back and see Tom. See if there's any news and work out how to get into this place.'

CHAPTER TWENTY-SIX

With Merv's help, Tom found hotel accommodation on the banks of the Volga just downstream of the train ferry berth. Alice tracked him down to a small bench overlooking the river. 'Penny for your thoughts?'

Tom jumped. 'Alice, you gave me a shock… Have a seat. I could watch this river for hours; it's very therapeutic. Have you seen how they get the coaches across? They should build a bridge. And that's a food barge. Merv said they ship flour and other foodstuffs upriver to *Volsk* and *Khvalynsk*.'

'My, you have been doing your homework,' Alice quipped. 'I hear you have a hotel.'

'Yes, just behind us. Pretty comfortable, I must say. I've seen your cosy dormitories. Warm and dry, I suppose,' Tom teased, ducking at Alice's mock swing to cuff him about the ears.

'We followed our two Germans to their eventual destination. It looks like an industrial compound, very secure and in a rather isolated out-of-town location. There's no indication of what goes on there, but I mean to find out.'

Tom rubbed his hands together, 'I've got some news for you.'

'Go on then, what is it?'

'OK. We had an unscheduled landing on the way

here. Well, it was planned in a way, but I need to brief you on what we saw. And I have a letter for you from Harry. It's to be delivered to you by hand. It came via the Berlin Embassy.'

Alice stood. 'Then let's go and see it.'

Tom put his hand inside his pocket. 'No need, I have it here.'

Alice looked about, 'God, Tom, is that safe out here?'

'Just as safe here as anywhere.'

'Don't you believe it? The Chekists are everywhere. If you were searched, you'd be in deep trouble, believe me.'

'OK, I believe you. Do you want to go back to my hotel, then?'

'No, give it here, I can't wait.'

Alice peeled back the flap, pulled out the letter and after a hopeful glance at Tom, started to read. Tom watched her reaction. Her serious expression gradually warmed to a grin, then a smile, and finally delight. She looked as if she just received very good exam results.

'Well, what's it say? Good news, I assume.'

Alice looked about again. 'I can't quite believe how significant this is after what we saw today. I'll read it. It says, *It is very probable,* which we know is intelligence speak for

"I'm not absolutely sure", *that the gentleman in the photograph is Mr. Gustav Weber,* the name Herta wrote in lipstick, and the man that Fish identified. It goes on to say that *Weber was heavily involved in the introduction of chemical weapons during the war. He was an assistant to Fritz Albrecht, Germany's Chief Scientist and had a hand in the first use of chlorine gas on the French positions in Ypres in 1915. Weber was one of chemical warfare's earliest casualties as he was blinded in the left eye when a chlorine cylinder exploded.'*

'I thought he looked a bit odd.'

'Yes, and this is the very man we followed today. It goes on: *After the war, cleaning up the battlefields provided Weber with an opportunity. After French government workers failed to successfully clean up Germany's chemical weapons stockpile at Lüneburg Heath, the German government hired Weber to take over. He is still working on this project and has devised rather dubious methods for disposing of the stockpile. Loaded chemical munitions and bulk stored poison gases have been sold outright to the US and Swedish firms, and other items have been transported to Weber's company, Chemische Fabrik Weber, near Hamburg. Useable chemicals and weapons have been stored for possible future contracts. Anything too dangerous has been dumped, we believe, in the North Sea, and incredibly, it is reported that some material has been allowed to sink into the peat bogs around his factory.*

Last year, Weber received a commission as chief engineer for Spain's newly constructed La Maraosa mustard gas plant. Spanish mustard gas bombs have been used already in Spain's fight with rebels in Morocco. Your reports of contact between Weber and Colonel von der Lang are worrying. The question is, are attempts being made to resurrect Germany's capability for poison gas production? If so, where?

Alice paused again and turned over the letter. 'Could that be here in Saratov? Harry's letter goes on to say… *given the recent Rapallo Treaty, you are to step up the surveillance of Weber and the senior Reichswehr officers to identify if any clandestine operations are ongoing with a foreign power, notably Russia. We have been monitoring Weber's activity, which the IMCC has reported as posing a potential threat to European and world peace. Consequently, we must be informed of any other attempts to spread chemical weapon capabilities to other nations, particularly to those of an unstable or despotic regime. Our government is striving to take a measured response to reports of German actions to circumvent the VPT provisions, but nevertheless, we need to know the facts. Keep up the excellent work, and keep me advised.*

Alice tossed the letter onto her lap and shook her head incredulously. 'A measured response,' she mouthed. 'No chance of that if I have my way.'

'Do you think that the site you found today is a chemical weapons factory of some sort?'

'Don't know, but the fact that Weber was going there with…?

'Hoffman.'

'Yes, so it's a powerful clue on what's happening in the compound.'

'This is great news, but how do we get the evidence, the hard facts that C and our government need to take action on?'

Tom shrugged. 'We need to get into this compound of yours.'

'Exactly, but how? We need to talk to the others.'

Tom paused and looked skywards.

'What?' said Alice, narrowing her eyes.

'I wonder if we could get some photographs from the air. If they're manufacturing or experimenting with poison gas, one of our scientists might be able to identify equipment, structures, or something else that could indicate what's going on.'

'Could you do that?'

'You know that Bill has brought his cameras. If questioned, we are doing an aerial survey of the famine region. Looking for… I don't know. Merv can help with that?'

'It's worth a try, but there will be no substitute for getting in there. You're getting good at snooping around.'

'How did you know?'

'Know what? I just meant from your shenanigans in Berlin. You know, searching von der Lang's flat.'

'Oh, that. Well, I have done a little more snooping. On the way to Saratov, we had to land in a field due to the weather, and by pure luck, I picked a field next to an airfield at Lipetsk. I was told of this airfield and warned to stay clear. That was enough for me. My curiosity was aroused, so I planned to get in there somehow. It was on our route, and I thought of feigning engine problems, but ultimately, the weather turned nasty but, in our favour, and I had to land.'

'What did you find?'

'Well, Bill and I had a "snoop around", as you call it, and we found, locked away in a hangar, four Fokker D.VIIs, the aeroplanes I spotted near Moscow. And what's more, I spotted a file in their ops room. Roughly translated, it meant something like Scientific Experimental and Personnel Training Station. Obviously, it was in German.

Alice leaned over and hugged Tom. 'This is wonderful news. We have now found two probable examples of German/Russian military cooperation, just what I always expected.'

'Now the difficult bit; how we get the evidence?'

The hostel was buzzing with activity, with charity workers returning from their shifts in the local country kitchens and feeding centres. Merv also explained that they had constructed a disinfection facility to deal with the hordes of children infested with lice, a carrier of typhus. Tom found Merv and his colleague Bobby Bernstein in the canteen. 'Hello, Merv. Is there somewhere private that Alice and I can meet with Mikael and Bill?'

'You could use our office, but I can't guarantee you won't be disturbed.'

'That should do fine, thanks.'

Alice kicked off the meeting, Mikael, Tom and Bill sitting around the little room lounging in some old armchairs. 'We're pretty secure here. Tom and I have just brought each other up to date, and we have two locations of interest: the factory here and the airfield at Lipetsk, which Tom and Bill have seen. The priority now is to investigate the Saratov factory, and Tom has suggested that we could get some aerial photographs for our scientists to examine. Seems like a good idea, but don't make it too obvious.'

Tom knew they couldn't circle the factory or spend too much time overhead. 'We'll do a single flyby and possibly one more on a return leg. If anyone queries us, we can just say we were asked to photograph some of the AORO sites and deny any knowledge of the factory.'

'Good, but I'd also like to get into that compound,' said Alice determinedly. 'We suspect it's involved in poison gas manufacture or research or both, as we followed our man Weber there. He's a German poison gas specialist, so I'm sure we're on the right track.'

'How secure is this factory?' said Bill.

'That's the problem. It's very secure from what we've seen,' said Mikael.

'Why don't we start by looking at this place from the air? ' Tom suggested. 'The problem is we only have a few days until I need to fly my passengers back to Berlin.'

Alice tutted. 'We need to get a move on. Bill, have you got suitable equipment for this?'

'I've got just about everything with me. I can even develop the negs. In fact, I've developed the shots we took at Lipetsk. There's a great photo of you, Tom, chatting up the Germans. Hoffman and Weber are in it.'

'Anything else of interest? said Alice.'

'Not really, other than they prove we've been there.'

Alice shuffled in her seat and closed her notebook. 'Look, let's get some aerial shots of this factory. Can you do it tomorrow, Tom?'

'Yes, providing I can get fuel. I need to speak to Merv. He said he was organizing it.'

'Good, let's do it tomorrow. I'll apologise now for the transport. It'll be a truck, and at least one of you will have to go in the back.'

Mikael raised his finger. 'Can I suggest that we should put a watch on the factory? Remember, Alice, we saw several deserted buildings close to the compound. We could put someone in there to keep a 24-hour watch on the place. That way, we might be able to figure out the best way in.'

'Good idea. Are you volunteering, Mikael?' said Alice

'I suppose so. Why don't you come too?'

'I will. They'll be playing with their aeroplane,' Alice quipped nodding at Tom.

CHAPTER TWENTY-SEVEN

'God, has this thing got springs,' Bill cried as the truck bumped its way to the airfield.

'Just look after your cameras, Bill,' Tom replied from the relative comfort of the front bench seat. 'I've been thinking about our flight; we should use our Gosport system. We'll need to be able to talk to each other. I think I've got a spare helmet.'

'That's a good idea. I can keep a lookout for the "Hun in the sun" and let you know if there's anyone on our tail.'

'Hardly. The air is deserted around here.'

Tom carefully inspected his aeroplane. He knew it had been left unattended for some time, and the Saratov airfield was insecure. As the machine had been refuelled from twenty-litre cans, he also took a fuel sample to check for water contamination.

'All looks good, Bill. Are you ready?'

'Yep. I've rigged my cameras on the left side, but I'll talk you in for our photos.' Bill replied. 'Look, we've got some spectators. I'll need some muscle to help with the start.'

'Good plan.'

The start went well, Tom blowing a sigh of relief. He was never quite sure how the RR Eagle engine would behave. It was a warm, humid morning, which was always helpful when starting. He watched Bill handing out a few coins, but food would have been better received.

One of the helpers had been briefed on removing the chocks by sign language, so Tom hoped for the best. He did the engine power checks while on the chocks, then throttled back to idle, giving the pre-arranged sign for the chocks to be removed. Thankfully, Bill had instructed the boy to walk in and away from the side of the aeroplane.

Tom climbed the machine to the northeast after a wide circuit of the airfield. Merv had provided a sketch map of the local area, the factory's location and his food kitchen on the Volga near a town called Marks. Merv planned to take Mikael and Alice on a run to his kitchen and drop them off at their hideout. 'If we're stopped, we say that we're on the way to replenish the kitchen,' he had said.

'Are you ready in the back?' Tom shouted above the noise of the engine.

'Yep. Give me a few minutes' warning and put the factory down the left side.'

'Will do. I'll only do one pass, but we'll return this way. Is this height OK?'

'What's the height now?'

'Eight hundred.'

'OK, three hundred meters will be good.'

'Right, a minute or so to go. I can see it. Stands out like a sore thumb. Just to the left of that L-shaped wood. I can see the buildings where Alice will be staying.'

Bill squeezed his head against the side window, peering into the morning haze. 'I can see it. Can you turn 10 degrees to the right...that's better; just hold that heading.'

'Feels like we're back in France,' said Tom.

'Concentrate. Ten degrees right now. I'll ask you to bank left in a moment.'

'OK.'

'Bank left now. Hold it there and hold it, hold...got it, I hope. Strange looking place.'

'OK, we'll head north up the Volga towards Marks. That's where the food kitchen is.'

Tom felt able to fly a few orbits around the Marks' food kitchen until Bill had bagged his photographs. They came down low to get the best shots.

'Can we get this low when we return to the factory?' said Bill.

'We can, but it might look a bit obvious. Could invite trouble.'

'OK. Let's have the same height again, all nice and innocent-like.'

Bill concentrated on getting another selection of factory shots. He felt pleased that he had captured all the required details. When pulling back from the camera viewfinder, he caught sight of something to his left and behind—a fleeting glimpse. He looked again and could not see anything. He thought it must have been the tailplane.

He started packing his camera equipment away to keep it safe for the rest of the flight and the landing back at Saratov. Just as he finished stowing his gear, he realized he had seen something. 'Fuck, do you see him, Tom?'

'What?'

'A bloody pair of Fokker D.VIIs are taking an uncomfortable interest in us. They're behind and to the left.'

Tom leaned out into the slipstream and peered under the wing. 'Shit, I see them now. The visibility in this thing is terrible.'

'What are they doing?'

'They're just sitting there. I think these machines are from Lipetsk—the machines we saw in the hangar.'

'I'm going to climb up for some height. See if they can stay with us. We're pretty light. The Eagle engine gives us a decent rate of climb. Watch them, I can't see a damn thing behind us.'

'They're staying with us, Tom.'

'OK, I'll just continue back to the airfield. They may land there and... we can have a chat.

'They're overtaking us now.'

'Give 'em a wave.'

The two D.VIIs gradually pulled ahead on the same heading, taking Tom back to Saratov. They were almost invisible within five minutes, and Tom started to relax.

'Can you still see them, Tom?'

'Yes, excitement over they've just flown off towards Saratov. Oh, hang on, no, they're turning back towards us, and they've split up. One's coming back. Fuck, he's coming straight at us.'

Merv frowned as Alice and Mikael unloaded their bag from the back of the truck. 'Are you going to be OK out here, you two? Do you have everything you need?'

'We'll be OK. We're not going anywhere. We'll just stay in this building and watch. Can you pick us up at the same time tomorrow evening, yes?'

'OK, just don't do anything I wouldn't do.'

Alice waved. 'We won't, bye.'

The dilapidated cottage was about three hundred and fifty metres from the factory compound, which was more like a small walled town. The cottage provided the ideal vantage point with two windows at the back of the building overlooking the compound. Alice stood at the front of the building, by the track, watching the lights of Merv's truck grow faint and disappear into the gloaming as Mikael carried their bundle of blankets and makeshift bedding inside. She turned and walked in the front door, which faced away from the compound. Mikael was moving around, exploring their accommodation for the night. 'Looks like they left in a hurry,' he said softly, which created a dull echo in their dank surroundings.

'There's a meal of bread and cheese in here. The mice have been at it. I'd say they left a month or so ago.'

Alice joined him in his search of the building. 'There's a bit of a nasty smell,' she murmured, walking outside. Ah, that's why. There's a dead dog up against the front wall. But there's another smell. I can't quite identify it.'

'Well, we won't be here for long. We better get ourselves organised before it gets dark. We can't show any lights, but if we need to use our torch, we can use the small room at the front. That shouldn't be visible from the compound. I wonder what scared them off.'

Alice arranged their blankets into two makeshift beds at the back of the room, which overlooked the compound. 'What makes you think they were scared off?'

'They've left almost everything, the things you would take with you like furniture, pictures, and clothes; their possessions and the unfinished meal all abandoned. This little chest is still full of clothes and meals; in a famine area, they wouldn't leave food, would they?'

Alice finished making up the beds. 'Yes, a little mysterious, but I'll take the first shift. Shall we say two hours? We should keep our cameras ready. We won't get any pictures at night, and it's too dark now. I assume that Weber and Hoffmann will stay in the town and return in the morning; they might be still in there. We must get a photo of Weber entering the compound and watch out for vehicles going in and out and people too. I've left a notepad with the torch in the room by the front, so make any notes ⊠ events, timing, that sort of thing. Then the next priority is to see if there is any way we can get in.'

Mikael interrupted with a wink and a nod at the bedding. 'What about a quick, you know?'

'Oh, come on ⊠ *here*? Oh, wait, we have some action. A truck has arrived.'

Alice watched intently as the driver walked to the main gates. She could hear him banging at them and felt excited at the first activity since they had arrived. Mikael joined her at the window.

The truck driver waited patiently, looking around for signs of life. Alice concluded that the entrance was not manned or guarded, at least not very effectively. She used the delay to examine the vehicle: a medium-sized flatbed truck much like their own that was loaded with cylindrical objects. Her binoculars were not good enough to read the markings, and she cursed under her breath. 'Damn it, we need to get closer,' she muttered. 'Look, he can't raise the guard. See, I can't believe no one is awake in there. He's been waiting a good five minutes.'

'The gate's opening now,' said Mikael, reaching for his telescope.

'I didn't know you had that. Can you read what's on the drums?'

'Oh, let me see. Right, they're not drums. They're like metal bottles or cylinders. The labelling is in Cyrillic. It says Khlor, I think,' Mikael paused, then frowned uneasily at Alice as the truck disappeared from view. 'It means… chlorine.'

'Look, the Fiat's leaving. It's stopped. Use your telescope. Someone left the car.'

Mikael focused his telescope. 'That's Weber. He's inspecting the things in the truck. Get a photo. This could be our only chance.'

'It's too dark, but I'll take one. We're still not close enough, but we might be able to blow it up. We must get them in the morning.'

Mikael took his eye from the telescope and gave Alice a suspicious look. 'Blow what up?'

'I mean the photograph, stupid.'

Alice was still watching the compound well after darkness had fallen. The lighting at the gates illuminated the entrance effectively and was bright enough to provide some light in the cottage. 'That might be the way in.'

'What, how?'

'Stow away in a truck somehow. They seem to arrive and leave quite frequently in the hours of darkness.'

'I guess they're hiding something.'

'Could we hang on underneath? The guards don't seem to take much notice. They're not searching the vehicles.'

Mikael looked askance at Alice. 'It would be better to just get in the back. Some of them are covered. We could jump in when we find out where they come from and what routes they take.'

'Actually, this is a good time,' Alice suggested as she pointed at the waiting truck. 'It's stationary, and the driver is busy banging on the gate.'

'Then they open up and say, "Hello, nasty spy person; what're you doing here?"'

Alice jabbed Mikael in the ribs. 'Possibly, but can you think of any other way to get in?'

'What about banging the driver on the head, taking his truck and driving in?'

'Hmm, that's a bit risky too. We don't know the routine, and we'd be suspected straight away. If we do that, it would have to be you. You know the language but look at you.'

Mikael was taken aback and pretended to look down at his attire. 'What's wrong?'

'You are hardly the typical Russian truck driver. You'd never get away with it.'

'Probably right. We'll need to think about it. You take the next couple of hours, and then I'll take the graveyard shift.'

'What's that?'

Mikael forced a mock scowl. 'two till four.'

Mikael drifted into consciousness noticing dust particles dancing in the sunbeams, which penetrated the cracks in the building. 'Have I overslept… Alice?' he muttered, throwing off his blanket and sitting up, rubbing his eyes and stretching the sleep from his bones. He looked at his watch. 'God, it's six o'clock. Where are you? Did anything happen on your shift?'

There was no response. 'Alice?' Mikael whispered, getting increasingly concerned as he checked the other rooms. He fully expected to find her curled up in a ball, but there was no sign of her even outside.

'For God's sake, where are you?' He whispered fruitlessly, now convinced that he was talking to himself. He wondered if she had found somewhere private for nature's necessities and scanned the other dwellings. He saw nothing. Where was she? He looked over at the compound, and his heart sank. She wouldn't try to get into the compound on her own would she?'

'Yes, he's coming straight at us,' Tom yelled. 'Hold on, Bill, strap in!' Tom rolled right, the D.VII flashing past down his left side. 'That was bloody close. The other machine is holding off. I hope your camera stuff is secured. We could be in for a rough ride if he keeps up this game.'

'Hold steady for a moment. I'll tie it down.'

'I'm turning back after him. I need to keep him in sight. There he is. He's coming back.'

'Gimme a sec!' Bill bellowed.

'Hold on,' Tom barked into the Gosport tube. The D.VII was head-on now. He waited till the last minute, then pushed the nose down, pitching Bill onto the cabin roof; he hadn't managed to strap in!

As the negative g-load relaxed, he crashed back down onto the floor as Tom recovered from the dive and pulled his machine around into the tightest turn he could manage.

Bill crawled back to his seat and fastened his lap strap, thinking that the machine was not designed for violent manoeuvring. He plugged his Gosport tube back in. 'I'm strapped in now. I'm not sure my camera gear will stand up to this.'

'Can't help it. It's either that or this bugger will smash into us.'

'Maybe that's the plan.'

'He's coming back again. I'm going down low. See if I can sucker him in.'

'What'ya mean?'

'Just hold on,' Tom yelled as he pitched his machine into a dive. 'Try to keep an eye on him. Visibility in this old girl is not designed for combat.'

'I'll try. He's' following us down. About 50 yards back.'

'OK, tighten that strap. This is going to be rough. I hope this old bus can take it.'

'God, Tom, we're going to hit the ground.'

'Yep, that's the idea… him, not us.'

Bill gritted his teeth and gripped the arms of his seat until his knuckles turned white. He watched out the side window as ground, trees, bushes, and buildings flashed past. He estimated the height at ten to fifteen feet. "In the weeds", as Tom would say. The engine blared at maximum RPM. He heard Tom yelling as he manoeuvred, a kind of primitive war cry as he flew his machine like a madman. The D.VII was clearly visible to Bill, jinking from side to side, in and out of view as it followed Tom's crazy flight path. It was only feet behind, its propeller close enough to chew up their tailplane.

The low flying continued for what felt like an eternity to Bill until he was violently pushed down onto his seat, his jowls dragged downwards as the machine pitched up to the vertical. It hung there for a few moments, engine blaring, then rotated about its axis like a cartwheel. Then, it was pointing straight at the ground. Bill didn't get airsick, but this was challenging his usually tough constitution. He heard the engine note change; he knew that Tom would be throttling back to avoid overspeeding the engine. Then the g-force came on again, along with the power as Tom levelled off, almost touching the ground.

The D.VII caught up quickly and continued harassing the F.III.

The engine was blaring at maximum RPM. Bill squeezed his head against the window. He could see a tall barn-like building rushing up in front of machine. Tom seemed to be flying directly at the building as he cried out, 'Where is he?'

'Right behind. Bloody close!' Bill yelled.

'Perfect.'

Bill felt their wheels rumbling along the ground.

He gritted his teeth. Then a sudden violent pull-up generated enough g-force to crush Bill into his seat, nearly blacking him out. He felt their undercarriage scuff something, but they were still in the air, still flying but pointing vertically at the clouds.

Tom throttled back, reducing engine power, and looked for his adversary. He wasn't behind. He scanned the ground and spotted him or what was left of him. The Fokker D.VII was now a smoking wreck in the side of the barn.

Tom punched the air, puffing and panting, sweat running into his eyes as if he had just completed a 100-metre race. 'I haven't done that for a while,' he yelled, his entire body shaking from the exertion.

He looked around for the other D.VII and spotted him far off and high up, heading back in the Lipetsk direction. He relaxed his shaking hands on the controls. 'You alright back there?'

'Fuck a duck, Munners. What the hell was that all about?'

'Getting rid of the Fokker on our tail,' Tom said with a grin.

'Where is he?'

'Down there, look,' Tom declared, turning steeply to reveal the remains of the D.VII smashed into a burning building, its column of oily smoke sending its gruesome message into the morning sky. 'Get a photo.'

CHAPTER TWENTY-EIGHT

Nothing of note happened throughout the day other than the coming and going of the occasional truck and women and children begging for food. The beggars were usually chased away, although, on one occasion, a guard took pity (or was it for his entertainment?) and chucked a piece of bread into the air. The resulting scrabble for this morsel was not a pretty sight. Mikael wasn't bothered about the arrival and departure of trucks anymore, and his stomach was knotted up with worry about Alice. He felt responsible and remained puzzled. He could only think that she must have ventured into the compound. Searching the scattered cottages and hedgerows nearby was not an option; he would undoubtedly be seen from the compound.

When another truck arrived, he was becoming blasé about these routine movements until the kerfuffle that broke out caught his attention. A man, probably a peasant judging by his clothes, jumped to the ground and made a desperate dash away from the compound. A guard followed nonchalantly from the back of the truck. He stopped, casually took careful aim and fired. Mikael knew his weapons and recognised the standard Russian army issue Mosin-Nagant rifle the extended trigger guard giving it away. His binoculars provided a close-up view of the effects of the rifle shot, the round bursting through the man's chest, exiting with a gouty spurt, and pitching the man onto the ground. Mikael was surprised to see the man still moving. But not for long. The guard calmly strolled up to his victim. *'On nay prineset nam nikakoy polzy,'* he shouted with a sickening grin. The guard then looked around for an audience, exercised the rifle's bolt action, grinned then shot the peasant in the head.

Mikael flopped down onto the floor, his back against the wall, and dropped his binoculars onto his lap. He had understood the Russian's cold statement and wondered what was meant by, *not being any good to us*. The body was left lying in the dirt until five more similarly scruffy men were forcibly dragged from the truck and made to carry the body into the compound, trailing a red smear in the dust. The truck then turned around and sped off as the gates closed with a bang.

Mikael spent a long day observing much the same kind of activity as he had seen with Alice; trucks and vehicles came and went with a variety of cargo. He had some film left in his camera, which he had kept in reserve for anything noteworthy. This was a sensible precaution as one uncovered vehicle arrived crammed with artillery shells, stowed menacingly with their noses pointing skywards. Also, more trucks with peasant-like men and women arrived; what service did they provide? These unfortunate people were treated like cattle, and there were no more escape attempts.

He was getting desperate for Merv to collect him but was still very worried about Alice. After churning over all possible explanations, Mikael decided that she must have gone into the compound. *God help her if she is caught. What would they do to her?* The Chekas were notorious for their brutal interrogation and torture. He shook his head, not daring to imagine how she would be treated. The thoughts chilled him to the bone. He knew that he must get back to the hostel as soon as possible and, with the others, decide what they should do. If Alice talked, they would all be in danger. He sniffed and wiped his nose as another truck emerged from the compound. 'I don't need any more bloody photographs, and I certainly don't need a fucking cold,' he mumbled.

It was getting dark as Mikael transferred his attention to the road. His heart thumped rapidly as he spotted headlights in the distance. The truck was familiar. 'It's Merv, it must be,' he mumbled hopefully. The truck pulled up, and he hurriedly gathered his things and stood at the front door.

'You must be getting a bit bored out here,' said Merv. 'Jump in the back.' He looked around, searching the landscape. 'Where's Alice?'

Mikael paused, wondering how he should break the news. 'She disappeared in the middle of the night. I searched everywhere. I assumed in the end that she must have got into the compound somehow.'

'My God, are you sure? Didn't you try to get her back?'

Mikael climbed into the back of the truck and took a deep breath, his face a picture of anger and frustration. 'What the fuck could I do? Knock on the gates and ask for Alice?'

'I suppose you couldn't be sure she was in there,' Merv replied in an attempt at contrition for his remark.

'She was keen on using one of the trucks to get in. They were coming and going throughout the night, so I can only guess that's what she did. I can't think of any other explanation.'

Merv cranked the truck into life, then climbed aboard. 'Let's get back to the hostel. See what the others think. Decide what we should do.' He jammed the truck into gear and moved off with a shudder. 'What the hell was she thinking?'

The Saratov hostel was buzzing as the shift change got underway. Merv managed to get Mikael to his bunk. 'Have you seen those marks on your arm? On your face, too?'

'What marks?'

'On your skin, your face and arms. I'll get the doc to have a look at you.'

'I've just picked up a cold. I need a good sleep.'

Mikael was asleep. 'In here, Doctor,' said Merv. 'He's

exhausted, but I think there's something else going on. I'd just appreciate it if you would have a look at him.'

The doctor gently shook Mikael. He woke slowly, allowing the doctor to conduct the examination, looking barely conscious. When he had finished, the doctor turned to Merv, looking bewildered.

'What are those marks on his skin? He says he feels like he's got a cold. Look, his eyes are watering,' said Merv.

The doctor looked even more baffled. 'Let me have another look. I need to be sure.'

After a more comprehensive inspection of Mikael, the doctor stood back. 'I need to wash my hands quickly. Have his clothes removed and burned. Whoever does that must wear gloves and a mask if possible.'

'Doctor, please, what's wrong with him? Is it typhus?'

'It's a long time since I saw these symptoms but I feel fairly certain. Where has he been?'

Merv felt that he had to be careful about what he said. 'Out in the country.'

'Can you be more specific?'

'I'm not really sure. Please, doctor, what's wrong with him?'

'The doctor took a deep breath. 'I think he's been exposed to a poison of some sort and probably mustard gas. He's probably had minor exposure, but we'll know in the next 24 hours.'

'My God. Will he be OK?'

'Has he vomited? Any diarrhoea? Pains?

'Not that I know of.'

'Right, that's good. Give him a good bath or shower and burn anything he's been in contact with, such as clothes, blankets, pillows, and so on. The next few days will be telling. If the skin markings develop into blisters, he may be in trouble, but I think he'll be alright. I'll look in tomorrow. Let him rest after a wash, top to bottom.'

Merv steered the doctor out of the dormitories and outside. 'Are you absolutely sure, doctor?'

'Unfortunately, I am,' the doctor said in a hushed voice. 'The last time I saw that was back in 1919 when the British and the White Army were using it against Trotsky's mob, the Bolsheviks.'

Tom and Bill arrived at the hostel with their own stories to tell, but their experience with the Fokker D.VII paled into insignificance when they heard about Alice. Tom was the first to react to the news. 'Do we know for certain that she's in the compound?'

Merv shook his head. 'We're just going on what Mikael has reported. She disappeared when Mikael was asleep during the night, so he's guessing.'

'Where else would she go, and why would she leave the cottage?' Bill asked.

'We've tried to address all these questions. There's no easy answer.'

Tom made to ask more questions. 'What…?'

Merv sighed loudly. 'Before we go on, there is another troublesome development.'

'Go on, what?' said Tom.

'Mikael has returned with mild symptoms of exposure to Mustard Gas.'

'Well, why am I not surprised?' said Tom, rolling his eyes. 'If Weber is working in the compound, we must assume they're playing around with poison gases of one sort or another.'

'I'm all for steaming right on in there and getting her out,' said Bill.

"Steaming in there" is not quite how I'd put it,' Tom said, 'but we've got to do something.'

Merv still looked puzzled. 'I can't understand *why* she would go in there.'

'She's determined to do more than just find out what's going on between Germany and Russia,' said Tom. 'She is, and has been for some time, convinced that much military activity is going on in the shadow of the Rapallo Treaty. And maybe civilian business as well. We expect to see this growing in the coming months and years, and she is required to report this activity, that's all, but Alice wants to stop it altogether.'

There was a hush in Merv's office until Bill asked, 'How do we get Alice out of that place if she's in there? We need to put on our thinking caps.'

CHAPTER TWENTY-NINE

Tom organised a meeting in Merv's office with Bill and Mikael, who was incoherent and needed a strong coffee to rouse him.

Tom sat back on the desk as Bill and Mikael slouched on two armchairs. 'I've called our Moscow safe house, spoken to Yalena and left a message for Danya Chernoff. I've told him to get here as soon as possible. He's the best man to pass as a Russian and is fluent in the language. I'm sure we're going to need him. Also, I haven't included Merv in our chat. It's best that he doesn't know much, but I've told him we'll need transport.'

Bill was like a bulldog on a lead. 'We need to go get Alice outa there.'

'Agreed, Bill. Any suggestions on how we do that?'

Mikael looked as if he was experiencing the worst of a cold. 'We can't just go crashing in there. The guards are well-armed, but from what I saw, they're a slack bunch. Also, how do you say it? They are happy with triggers?'

'Trigger happy,' said Tom. 'We could try an innocent approach. Bang on the door and ask if they've seen Alice, say that she has gone missing. Remember, she has all the documentation that verifies her association with Feed the Children.'

Bill didn't look convinced. 'But we assume that she got in there unofficially. She sneaked in. How would she explain that?'

Mikael was starting to recover from his malaise. 'We don't know what she said if she has been captured. My guess is that she was.'

Tom knew they had to act quickly. 'Any more ideas? I favour the innocent enquiry about Alice's whereabouts. I'll go with Mikael; I'll drive, and we could have a backup if it all goes haywire.'

'What backup?' said Mikael. 'There is no backup. I can get some, but it'll take days, maybe a week, for them to get here.'

There was silence in the room. 'When are you flying the Germans back to Moscow?' said Bill.

'I'm not sure. They said they would be here in Saratov for a few days. They will leave a message at the hotel. I suppose they think I will be just sightseeing, a tourist.'

'You're certainly sightseeing,' said Bill.

'Right,' Tom snapped. 'We'll try the diplomatic approach. Me and Mikael visit the compound. Your Russian is pretty good, yes?'

'So, so, but it'll do for this.'

'Bill, you keep watch and… I don't know, use your initiative.'

'We go armed, I'm thinking,' said Bill.

Tom was getting impatient. 'Of course. We go at 1 pm, and for now, let's get some rest.'

Tom's voice broke the silence in the hostel dormitory.

'Let's get going. Merv lent us one of his trucks, which has the AORO and Feed the Children signs, so that will help us look legitimate.'

The roads were relatively clear in the day's heat except for the odd oxen and cart, which allowed Tom to brief his companions on their plan. He felt that he had covered everything when Mikael shouted. 'Stop.'

'What's up?' said Tom as he skidded the truck to a halt.

'Did you not see?' Mikael said as he turned around in his seat. 'Look.'

All Tom could see was an old peasant shuffling along at the roadside. He raised his hands in a puzzled gesture. 'I just see an old woman or man, I don't know…'

'We should check it out,' said Mikael knowingly.

'We have little time. What's the point?'

'Patience,' said Mikael as Tom struggled at the heavy steering to turn the truck around. He stopped at the roadside, a cloud of dust enveloping them.

The bent figure straightened up and then collapsed.

Tom's mouth dropped. He looked at Mikael for confirmation and then stared incredulously at the figure. 'My God. It's Alice, quick.'

Back at the hostel, Alice was in no condition to answer the many questions left hanging in the air for later. After drinking several mugs of water and consuming a cheese sandwich, she was put to bed as if she had not seen food for days. Tom and Bill returned to their hotel, receiving a message from Tom's German passengers who wanted to return to Moscow the following day. 'Damn it, Bill, I won't be able to see Alice.'

'You just want to interrogate her, or is there more to it?' Bill joked, shoving his elbow to Tom's ribs

'Well, there is that, but I want to see she's OK.'

'Did you see? She had the same skin problem as Mikael, kinda blister-like marks.'

'Yes, I saw that. Look, I'll have to get the Germans to Moscow and decide how to get back here.'

'Yeh. At least that gives me time to see if I can print off those negs of the compound. They look pretty decent. I'm dying to hear Alice's stories.'

'So am I but get the doc to have a look at her.'

Tom's return flight to Moscow was without incident, although his German passengers seemed surprised yet relieved that he was able to make the flight. Tom wondered if they knew anything about his encounter with the Fokker D.VII. Was the intention to bring his aeroplane down? There was little logic behind that objective. Perhaps the purpose was to scare him off, let him know he was being watched. When he reached Moscow, Tom was ready to put his feet back on the ground. His flight had been just minutes short of 5 hours, and on refuelling his machine, it was evident that he had little reserve fuel left when they reached Moscow's Khodynka Field; he was lucky to have a following wind.

Anton was there to welcome him. 'Welcome back, Captain Munro. Have fun in Saratov? Who are the passengers? I'm to take them back to Berlin.' Tom could not get a word in. 'Are they good company for overnight stops?'

Tom was not in the mood for casual conversation but didn't want to appear rude. 'Hello, Anton. What I need now is a long hot soak.'

'Look who I have with me?'

Tom was pleased to see Werner Roth, now the chief pilot at Deruluft and someone he could trust. 'Werner, good to see you. We have some catching up to do.'

'What are we to catch?' Werner replied, putting an arm around Tom's shoulders.

'Oh, sorry. It's just another of our English expressions. I mean that we have a lot to talk about.'

'OK, I understand. If you are not too tired, let's have dinner together. This is my first visit to the Metropol.'

'Great idea. I'd like to hear how Deruluft is getting on and news of civil aviation in general. I've been a little isolated from the real world here in Russia.'

'Das ist gut. Let's say 7 o'clock.

Tom started with borscht soup, which he found much too filling. He elected for something a little lighter to follow. 'Wow, that was quite something.' He turned to the waiter who had been teaching him some Russian. Wait, Let me try, Mozno li sashlik.'

The waiter looked impressed and replied in heavily

accented English. 'Very good sir, the Sashlik'

'*Da, spasibo*,' Tom replied.

'Werner looked impressed. 'Getting to know the language, Tom?'

'Well, just the basics.'

Anton ate his meal, leaning on the table with a forearm, shovelling his food as if he had not eaten for days. Werner looked on with a scowl.

Tom ensured that they were well plied with vodka and wine.

Werner updated Tom on developments in Deruluft: 'We are looking at more and larger aeroplanes and have nearly decided on a Dornier machine, the Dornier Merkur. It will carry up to ten passengers.'

'Is it a single-engine machine? We really should move towards twin engines. Much safer.'

'No, I'm sorry to say the Merkur is a single-engine design. We need to get Anthony Fokker to work on a twin-engine machine. It's the cost. We need to fill the seats to afford bigger machines. Now I know an English expression: "one step in the time", eh.'

'You've nearly got it. One step at a time.'

'Of course.'

Tom continued on one of his pet aviation subjects. 'From my experience with the Vimy, the next generation of twin-engine machines should be able to maintain altitude on one engine. That would make it very safe. Does the Merkur have an enclosed cockpit?' said Tom.

'I don't think so, but we are also looking at the Junkers F.13, which has an enclosed cockpit.'

'Yes, I've seen one on my travels.'

Anton was getting quietly drunk. 'Why the enclosed cockpit, Thomas? Getting soft in your old age?'

'It just makes sense. It won't be long until we're flying higher and faster, and if we want to fly through the winter months, the pilots will need protection.'

'*Ach was*,' Anton replied, getting red in the face.

Werner nodded at Anton. 'He's a little drunk.'

Tom was getting irritated with Anton's belligerence. 'Just wait. When new military machines are designed, they will have enclosed cockpits too. They will be faster and have much greater overall performance.'

'We'll see, and very soon. The new D.XIII has an open cockpit. That's a new machine—*Flugzeug der Spitzenklasse*, even if it has one of your bloody Napier engines.'

Tom made a remark that he initially regretted, but it proved very timely. 'You're not likely to find out. You don't have an air force.'

'We bloody well do.'

Tom was starting to think Anton knew something interesting. 'What's a D.XIII?' he asked.' It sounds like a Fokker design with that numbering.'

'You will find out soon enough.'

Tom continued to play along with Anton. 'Right. Where is this air force?'

'Right bloody here in Russia. I hear you landed there.'

Werner stayed quiet but looked puzzled.

Anton leaned across the table, his face inches from Tom. 'And we will be building machines here too.' He leaned even closer and looked behind in a mock display of secrecy.

Tom couldn't believe what he was hearing. He tried his luck and pushed for more information. 'Are you still in this Air Force?'

'I will be.'

The meal ended abruptly when Anton stood, tipping his chair to the floor with a bang, the other diners' heads turning in response. He continued with his display of annoyance and dumped his napkin on the table. He went to stomp off, thought the better of it, turned back, and grabbed the half-empty bottle of wine with a bad-tempered flourish. His dramatic departure provided some entertainment for the other diners as Anton finally took his leave of the Boyarsky.

'Don't bother about him, Tom. He's had too much to drink. He dreams of a new Germany. I don't know where he gets his ideas from.'

'I can guess, he told me. The National Socialist German Workers Party.' Tom wondered if he could confide in Werner, and if so, what could he say? He thought he might mention the attack by the D.VII, at least fish for an explanation. That would seem normal and detached from his *secondary duty*.

'I should tell you about an incident we had on the

way to Saratov. You are the chief pilot, and so on. It does have safety implications.'

'Oh, what was that?'

'I didn't want to mention it in front of Anton. I don't trust him. He has some worrying ideas. He has spoken about it before.'

'So, what happened.'

Tom paused as if having second thoughts. He was, but he knew he had gone too far. 'We were doing aerial photography for the AORO; they chartered us for the flight to Saratov. They also asked us for aerial photos of their feeding stations and other facilities. They'll pay, don't worry.'

'Good, we need to make this charter work pay as well. So, what happened?'

'We were returning to the airfield at Saratov, Bill Franklin in the back. He's a photographer for the AORO. Anyway, I fitted him out with a Gosport helmet, and we spotted a pair of Fokker D.VIIs.' Tom waited to see how Werner reacted and note his demeanour.

'What? What would they be doing in Russia?'

'I don't know, but to cut a long story short, one came at us as if spoiling for a fight. Thankfully, he didn't seem to be armed; at least he didn't shoot at us, to the best of my knowledge.'

'What do you mean "spoiling for a fight"? I don't understand the English expression.'

'Well, he flew directly at us; we nearly collided. I think

he wanted to collide with us; at least, it felt like that.'

'And then?'

'He latched onto our tail, and I did everything to shake him off. I did all kinds of manoeuvres, but he hung on. I was uncertain that our machine would stand the loads. It's not designed for violent manoeuvring, as you know. Then I tried some low-level stuff, flew at a barn-like building, and pulled up at the last minute. I can tell you it *was* the last minute because I felt our wheels touch the roof. Our friend in the D.VII wasn't so lucky; he didn't react quickly enough and flew smack into the barn. He wouldn't have survived that.

'*Donnerwetter. Ich glaub mich knutscht ein Elch!* And what happened to the other machine?'

'He flew off.'

Werner shook his head in disbelief. 'I just don't understand. I've no idea why that should happen. Why should these machines be in Russia?'

Tom sensed that Werner was genuine. 'Well, we survived, obviously.'

'You didn't have your passengers on board, did you?'

'No, just Bill Franklin. He was taking his photos for the AORO. Remember, you met him once. He was my gunner on my Bristol Fighter.'

'Yes, you introduced us in Hamburg.

'That's right. Changing the subject, is Anton flying the German passengers back to Berlin?'

'I think you should do that, Tom. Get you back to

civilisation for a few days. Anton can stay here and take any more charter flights to Saratov. I'll take the scheduled flight tomorrow.'

Tom realised that Werner might think he was doing him a favour. He wanted to return to Saratov but realised this was more to see if Mikael and Alice had recovered. That could wait. They were safe, but he could not wait to hear how Alice had got into the compound and, more importantly, got out!

His thoughts turned to his current situation. He could use the safehouse to communicate with Alice, but Anton would be about.

'Tom, did you hear me?'

'Sorry. OK, I'm happy with that. Do you know when they want to return to Berlin?'

'They have notified us that they will be in Moscow for several days.'

Tom realised he had an opportunity to follow the Germans, but Anton was always present. He would have to shake him off somehow. 'Right, well, I'm not going anywhere. I can be contacted through the hotel here as usual.'

'You seem to be in another world, Tom.'

'Just thinking about what I'll do in Moscow. I suppose, as you say, I'll have the pleasure of Anton Schultz for company,' Tom said with a sarcastic upward nod and roll of his eyes.

'Time to get to know him better.'

CHAPTER THIRTY

Tom managed to shake off Anton and took a stroll to familiarise himself with the route to the Lubyanka. He could not mistake the large yellow brick building with its neo-Baroque façade. Nikolai, his Metropol confidant, advised that it was built in 1898 for an insurance company before being appropriated for government use following the Bolshevik revolution and now the home of the GPU, the successor to the Cheka. Tom suspected that this would be Weber and Hoffmann's likely destination. Clearly, they would recognise him, so any tailing would need extreme care. He also knew the area could be a hornet's nest of GPU troops and guards.

On what could be his last opportunity to tail the Germans, he positioned himself in a tucked-away position in the Metropol reception. He chose to keep watch after an early breakfast when he expected to avoid Anton. He would take his time, having enjoyed a late night at his favourite seedy nightspots.

Tom took a small book, dressed in a suit, which was the hotel's dress requirement, and waited interminably. He checked that his camera was to hand. He had taken to leaving his S&W Hammerless in his room for fear of being searched. He made himself comfortable, entertained himself with people-watching, and waited some more.

It was nearing 9 am when he spotted the Germans chatting animatedly and walking out of the hotel reception and down the steps onto Teatralny Proyezd. They were similarly dressed in the obligatory suits, and Hoffmann carried a briefcase. Tom waited until they had turned towards the Lubyanka, then followed about a hundred yards behind, screwing up his eyes against the bright morning sunlight. He was determined to get a photograph of them entering the Lubyanka, and this, combined with a similar photo of their entry into the Saratov compound, would seal that link, a link to whatever might be going on in the compound. He could do little more than that and would feel pleased if he managed to get the critical photo. He didn't know if Alice and Mikael had photographed the Germans entering the compound but kept his fingers crossed. The trams, horse-drawn carriages and occasional motor vehicles provided excellent concealment as Tom moved along the busy roadway. He realised he would have to close up to his target to get a decent photograph. He estimated where they would be on the other side of the road and sped up to intercept them as they entered the building.

Suddenly, as he emerged from the cover of a tram heading for the Lubyanka he ran smack bang into the two Germans still talking ten to the dozen. He couldn't turn away and ignore them; that would be much too obvious, so he acknowledged them. '*Guten morgen*', he said, explaining that he was out and about for some exercise. They seemed to accept that, doffed their hats, and continued.

Tom hoped his shock was not too obvious and turned away, trying to look nonchalant but feeling that he might be ludicrously overacting like a Laurel and Hardy performance. He shrugged off this thought with a smile, gave his target some time to get ahead, and continued toward the Lubyanka building. He was just in time to see the Germans enter and, following a surreptitious look around, took his photograph.

Tom's return flight to Berlin via Königsberg was somewhat protracted due to weather, as the autumn conditions had started to take effect. Squally showers, a hint of snow at altitude and a weakening of the sun's warmth. Tom dreaded the thought of enduring another winter flying over Eastern Europe. He managed to have short conversations with Hoffmann and Weber during the journey but steered away from anything contentious. As Roth had suggested, returning to Berlin's relative civilisation was a treat. After a good night's rest, Tom ventured out of the comfort of the Adlon hotel to the British Embassy for updates or mail.

'What are you doing here?' was the best Tom could say when he was surprised to encounter Harry Price.

'Come to see you and Ross,' said Harry unusually detachedly. 'I have some important information for you. Let me get Ross. He's been briefed, but hearing my news once more won't do any harm. I also have a letter for Alice; it's in code, but you will be able to understand its contents once you hear what I have to say. And there's another letter for you. I don't know how it found you.' Tom recognised Louisa's writing, which gave his heart a flutter. Reminiscent of his wartime correspondence, he recalled.

Mikael, Alice and Bill squirrelled themselves away in Merv's office. 'How did you do it, Alice?' said Mikael.

'Just as we discussed, I jumped in the back of a truck in the early hours. It was empty, so it was easy peasy.'

'It could have been full of the peasant folks. But what happened when you were in the compound?' said Bill.

'Well, I peeped out the back of the truck once inside and could see stacks of crates and small tanks in one corner of the compound, which is massive, like a small town. I saw brick buildings, warehouses, and what looked like a manufacturing plant. I couldn't see much further into the place, but it extended half a mile or so away from the main gate where I came in. When the coast was clear, I checked around, jumped down, and dashed over to hide behind the crates.'

Mikael remained mystified. 'What were the guards doing? They must have been asleep.'

Well, that's the thing: in the middle of the night, everyone, including the guards, was trying to get their heads down. They're a slack bunch but never reluctant to dish out a beating or a shot in the head. My driver just parked his truck and disappeared into a barrack-like building to get some sleep, and I waited for this particular truck to leave as my passage to safety.'

Mikael looked on incredulously. 'Why did you do it? It was near suicide. You've got some guts. If you'd been caught, you'd have been tortured by the Cheka. I can't think what they would have done to you.'

'Look, someone had to get in there. Find out how it can be done. I know the layout of the place now. I managed to get some photos at first light, and my pictures will confirm what that place is like. We could do some real damage if we get in there. If we make a big bang, perhaps people will listen.'

Bill shook his head in disbelief. 'God, Alice, you've got some gumption. Did you see what happened to the people who were trucked in? What were they for?'

'I don't know.'

Bill continued. 'Did you get around inside any buildings or look into them, maybe see through some windows?'

'Only for a short excursion when I could see what looked like laboratories and classrooms. I didn't get as far as the factory buildings. Oh, and I found where they were keeping those people. It was a small room but crammed to bursting point. I estimated about twenty people. They were guarded, but the guards looked asleep too.'

Mikael puffed and shook his head at Alice's gall. 'How

are you feeling?' His expression changed to a frown as he pointed to Alice's arm. 'You've got some blisters, look. I had the same.'

'It's just a heavy cold like you. I can't say I noticed these,' Alice admitted, pulling back her shirt cuffs to reveal her forearms.

Mikael, looking off-colour, sat beside Alice and took a deep breath. 'I'm afraid it's more than a cold. We've been fortunate. I pressed our doctor. He has an ear to the ground, a local man, and apparently, the rumour is that the cottages we were hiding in had been used for experiments.'

'God, I hate to ask, but what experiments?'

'Poison gas and the people you saw being trucked into the compound are probably "guinea pigs". The locals were evacuated, probably forcibly removed, from the surrounding houses so that they could be used for these experiments. As you know, they are tucked away in the forest, so ideal cover for their experiments where they won't be noticed.'

'So, we were infected, if that's the correct term, by poison gas.'

'Exactly, mustard gas, to be specific. The doctor has seen it before. Apparently, the British used it against the Red forces during the revolutionary wars. Anyway, you need a good wash, preferably a bath, and you need to burn these clothes. Only time will tell how much we will be affected.'

Harry looked worried. Once he returned with Ross, Tom had to nudge the conversation into action. Harry seemed reluctant to reveal his news.

'Let's sit down,' Harry said, his hand open, pointing to the desk. 'I'd like you to hand carry this letter to Alice, Tom. For your sake, Tom, in a nutshell, the Germans' surveillance and cooperation with the Russians are being called off. Alice is to return to London for a new assignment. I can't say what it is, but it is not associated with her current work.'

The room fell silent. Ross sat back in his chair and watched Tom shake his head. 'No… you're not serious, Harry? Why when we are getting results? This is ridiculous. We are close to exposing the most significant military activity in Europe since the end of the war. Is nobody interested in what could prevent another war?'

Harry looked embarrassed. 'I can't begin to defend this decision; clearly, it is way beyond my authority to do anything but implement these instructions. They are orders.'

'God Harry, we and particularly Alice have risked our lives to bring solid evidence to our government which shows… *proves* that Germany is colluding with Russia to re-build and resurrect their military capability in blatant contravention of the Treaty of Versailles.'

The Colonel was equally flabbergasted. 'Has any reason been given for this dramatic change of direction, Harry?'

'Nothing formal.'

'What does that mean? Sounds like you have a view on the matter?' said Tom, now standing to pace around the table.

Harry pointed angrily at Tom's chair. 'Sit down, Tom, for goodness' sake.'

'I think better when I'm on my feet. What do you think Harry? How do you see it?' You're close to the Foreign Office and their machinations.'

'It's not official, but there is a thought that Germany has suffered enough and that a slow return to normal relations might be the better course. Also, there is a view that Germans are helping to hold back the tide of Bolshevism. Needless to say, the French are not taking that view.'

Tom sat down again in a reluctant display of acceptance. 'I don't blame them.'

'I'm sorry, Tom. It's completely out of my hands. But please ensure that this notification, this order, gets to Alice. Hand it to her yourself. And for her own good, get her home, back to London, as soon as you can. She can even travel on your airline. How's that?'

Tom entertained Harry and Ross at the Adlon that evening, but the atmosphere was flat and stilted. Although Harry tried to lighten the conversation with tales of his family and young children, little could cheer Tom. Ross was a little more jovial, as he was also required to return to London, a decision which he clearly favoured.

Harry worked hard at maintaining the conversational flow. 'When's your next Deruluft flight, Tom?'

'I need to check in, but it's probably the next scheduled run, the day after tomorrow.'

'Does that go as far as Moscow?'

'Yes, but not to Saratov. That's where Alice is with Mikael.'

'Right, well, I'm sure you'll get to see Alice as soon as possible,' Harry quipped with a wink. Harry's little joke didn't really land that well.

Tom thought about the passengers he might have and if there might be some "interesting" people, but then he quickly realised that he should not be interested any more. He and Alice had spent years following this trail, analysing the Reichswehr's activities and following their key actors. They couldn't just drop it! Alice would not accept her instructions. He knew that. Finish the job was the phrase that came to mind. He decided they should decide collectively how they should proceed. He knew he wouldn't be able to stop Alice. The question was, what would she do?

Tom was introduced to his passengers in Berlin and was becoming used to presenting a professional, welcoming approach—all the techniques that would be appropriate and normal when meeting new passengers. The airline business had developed these service techniques to make passengers feel unique and safe, but Tom found this unusually challenging on this occasion.

Tom's passengers were none other than Colonel Otto von der Lang, with the gentleman whom he had accompanied to Moscow on an earlier trip, plus Captain Heinrich Wolf, the Reichswehr officer who had doled out the brutal interrogation of himself and Bill in Berlin some years before. Tom observed the introductions with interest. The Colonel would recognise him from his earlier flight, and so would Wolf. They shook hands, and their eyes made contact. Did he recognise Tom? Undoubtedly and was that a look of disdain he detected. Tom continued with his usual spiel on the passenger compartment and safety precautions, including using the lap strap and the potty for those not "feeling quite themselves". He stood back to leave the passengers to climb aboard, still in mild shock at seeing Wolf. Where was he going? And why?

All three passengers were travelling all the way to Moscow, and it was advised but not confirmed that some may wish to travel on to Saratov on special charter. Tom felt excited and deflated in equal measure. This could be a unique opportunity to expose the Reichswehr's plans, but the opportunity now seemed meaningless. They were being offered the prize but were not allowed to compete. The silver cup was sitting on the table, and they could win it, but not if they were to sit on the sidelines. He knew what Alice and Mikael would say.

What would he do? They were orders, after all, as Harry had pointed out.

The three-day travel to Moscow via Danzig, Konigsberg, Kaunas and Smolensk was surprisingly trouble-free. The weather behaved, as did the aeroplanes, and the passengers were most courteous and complimentary about the trip. Tom noticed that the constant throbbing of the RR Eagle engine seemed to render the passengers a little hard of hearing after the long legs of the trip. He had recommended earplugs, but they did not seem to bother. Heinrich Wolf was the exception at stopovers. He seemed preoccupied, distant and reluctant to engage in any way. He knew that Wolf had recognised him. As a result, Tom became increasingly wary and cautious and somewhat perturbed by the proximity to someone who had threatened his life and probably nearly killed Alice.

When they reached Moscow, all three passengers were booked into the Metropol, which was awkward for Tom. Despite the recent change in priorities, he still felt determined to follow von der Lang and his companion. Tom recalled that this mysterious companion was very interested in the aeroplane on his earlier trip to Moscow.

CHAPTER THIRTY-ONE

Tom waited again in the Metropol reception, feeling he was becoming part of the furniture. He was appreciating the breakfast smells, adding to the fresh morning air which wafted in the front doors, and then he started in surprise as Danya Chernoff walked past. He only just recognised him after a double take as, for a change, he was dressed in a suit. 'Danya,' Tom hissed, suppressing his voice to avoid attention.

Chernoff turned with a blank look, then mild shock. 'Good gracious, Tom, I didn't expect to find you here.'

'Bloody convenient, I can tell you. What a stroke of luck.'

'I thought you were at Saratov,' Chernoff said softly, looking about. 'That's the latest I got from Yalena.'

'Well, here I am. Can you get a vehicle?'

'When do you need it?'

'Like now? I need to follow some people, some Germans?'

'You're in luck; I have a motor car. I managed to get one when I arrived a few days ago; I have some other business to attend to. When do you want to follow these gentlemen?'

'I'm waiting to see if they appear this morning. We flew in yesterday.'

'Were they on board your flight?'

'Yes. They may be having breakfast. It's still quite early.'

'Have you checked the Boyarski?'

Tom stood, his eyes darting around the reception area. Before walking off, he spoke quietly: 'Yes, I'll have a look again now. I was worried I would miss them. Keep an eye out. They might come down from their rooms. Grab me if you see them.'

Tom had only reached the breakfast room when he caught sight of von der Lang and his companion. They carried briefcases and looked as if they might be heading off. Tom turned away, attempting to be inconspicuous. Once they were walking out of the Metropol, Tom joined Chernoff. 'OK, let's go. Are you parked nearby?'

'We'll need to teach you a thing or two about spying, the tradecraft. You stood out like a sore thumb back there.'

'Let's forget about that for now. Where's the car? They've gone. Quick.'

'This way, we're just around the back of the hotel. But hold on, let's see what car they're in. They might be walking.'

'There they are,' Tom said, grabbing Chernoff's arm. 'It's a black Fiat.'

'They're all black. You wait here to watch their car. I'll get mine.'

Tom's eyes remained glued to von der Lang's car for as long as possible. The wait for Chernoff seemed endless. The Fiat disappeared into the distance and out of sight around a corner just as Chernoff arrived. Tom jumped in, pointing, 'That way, but I've lost them.'

'I'll just head that way and hope we can pick them up. They're heading west.'

Tom glanced at his driver. 'I'm not sure that helps us much.'

Chernoff ignored him and raced off with a squeal of tyres, dodging in and out of tramcars, trucks trailing noxious exhaust fumes and horse-drawn carts. 'I still can't see them.'

'Just keep going. We'll just have to trust lady luck. I think they turned left here,' said Tom, pointing.

They had been driving for at least five minutes. 'I think we've lost them,' said Chernoff, his driving relaxing to a more sedate pace.

'Keep going. You never know. Where are we? Do you know Moscow?'

'Reasonably well. I have *worked* here before,' Chernoff said, his eyebrows shifting upward. 'There they are. Look, they just turned left. I thought so.'

'Yes, I see them. What do you mean, I thought so?'

Chernoff's expression changed. He looked pleased with himself. 'I think I know where they're going,' he said.

'And?'

Chernoff kept Tom waiting; he wanted to be sure. Yes, damn it, I'm right.'

'Oh, God, Danya, where?'

'The Russo-Baltiiskii Vagonnyi Zavod motor car factory at Fili.'

‘’That’s a mouthful. How do you know?’

‘It’s my business to know these things, and I’m told that there might be more than cars being built there.’

‘You really are dragging this out,’ said Tom, increasingly irritable.

‘I’m right. Here we are,’ Chernoff proudly stated. That’s the factory entrance.’ The car shuddered to a stop and pulled into the roadside. ‘We should stop here, hold back. The security has been tightened up in recent months.’

‘I should have talked to you before, Danya.’

‘Perhaps you should have.’

‘What else can you tell me? And how do you know about this place?’

Bill strutted about the room irritably as Alice sat on her bed, her cheeks red and puffed up. ‘We should get in there and blow the fucking place to pieces. If that’s not evidence of German/Russian military collusion, what is?’

‘Sit down, Bill, you’re getting on my nerves. But, yes, that’s not a bad idea,’ said Alice, inspecting her legs. ‘We should blow the place up.’

‘Don’t be ridiculous,’ said Mikael as he pointed out some traces of blisters on Alice’s legs. ‘Look there. They’re not too bad. Let the doc see you. Anyway, I thought your instructions were to report on your findings?’

‘Now we’re here; we should do something about it. We’ve got to stop these bastards from using that stuff again. I remember my brother describing the effects.'

'Was your brother in the army?'

'No, an RFC pilot. Killed like all of my family. Let's blow it up. Can you get explosives, Mikael?'

'That's a tall order, Alice. We can't blow up the whole place. You described it as a small town, remember? What do you think, Bill?'

Von der Lang and his companion drove in through the gates at the Russo-Balt motor car factory. 'Well, there is no doubt about that,' said Tom, lowering his camera. 'So, what do you know about this place, Danya?'

'It's a motor car manufacturing plant, but I have heard that Junkers has signed an agreement to construct aeroplanes here. That other man was probably from Junkers.'

'Do we know what type of aeroplanes they plan to build?'

'Not yet? I have a new contact. What do you want to know?'

'Are they military types and is this some sort of agreement under the Rapallo Treaty?'

'I'll work on it.'

'OK. We better get back. I expect that I will be making the trip back to Saratov. I need to check if that character, Heinrich Wolf, wants to continue his journey to Saratov. I'm assuming he will. You should come too. I don't know what Alice is up to. I fear the worst. I don't think she will rest at gathering intelligence. I'd better check in with Yalena, too. See if there are any messages.'

'Yes, we're not going to get much more out of this little jaunt,' Chernoff said, nodding towards the hotel. Let's get back, and I'll tell you what we know,' he said decisively, executing a neat U-turn just missing a tram.

'Why haven't you reported this?'

'Look, relax, Tom. I've just heard from an informant. He works there. He is a new man, so his information may not be sound. It could be a stroke of luck. We'll see. I'll work on him.'

As they pulled up behind the Metropol, Tom took a deep breath. 'Danya.'

'Yes?'

'I need to tell you something. Have a think about it before you answer.'

'Go on then, spit it out.'

'The operation has been called off. I'm carrying written orders for Alice.'

Chernoff dropped his hands from the steering wheel, his head turning slowly with a puzzled look. 'You can't be serious, Tom. After all our work, some people have died.'

'I know, I know all that... We should finish the job and get as much as possible from this visit. Alice can at least write a convincing report based on what we have now. It's up to the powers that be to decide what to do. We're just the minions taking the risks.'

Chernoff shook his head. 'This is what frustrates me

about this business. We take risks, live a life looking over our shoulders, sleeping rough at times and then… it's cancelled, just like that. No discussion, no room for our point of view. What we uncover here is vitally important for peace in Europe, if not world peace. I can feel the way this is going. All the talk is about a resurgence in German military power. They want to set the record straight after WWI and much worse. There is talk of a superior Arian race, a cleansing of the true German peoples. Have you heard of this man, Adolf Hitler?'

'Yes, Anton mentioned him,' Tom replied letting Chernoff have his rant. He felt exactly the same. Danya worked full-time at the spying game. His work was dumped like useless rubbish. 'Look, let's get inside and freshen up. It's time for a good meal and bottle of wine in the Boyarski.'

Yalena was enthusiastic when Tom called in. 'It's you. Good timing. They want you back as soon as possible,' she said. 'They have plans and need your help.'

Tom bit his lip. He imagined Alice bubbling with energy and grand plans and dreaded the thought of breaking the news. 'Anything else?'

'No, but they need to know when you will come?'

'I don't know yet, but I'll let you know soon. It should be tomorrow.'

'Right, thank you. Bye.'

Tom was pleased with how Yalena played her role;

she had mastered saying very little but conveying much more. Wondering about Alice's plans, he walked through the reception to join Chernoff for dinner in the Boyarski. He suspected that she would want to do something about the Saratov poison gas plant, but that would be well beyond her remit. But when did that restrict Alice?

Chernoff was ordering when Tom took his seat. Chernoff nodded to something across the other side of the restaurant. 'Do you know them? They stick out like a sore thumb.'

'Damn it. That's Wolf, an officer in the Reichswehr, and Anton is one of our pilots. How did they get together? It doesn't surprise me; they will be blethering about a Third Reich. Anton is extreme right in his views. I had to control myself when he started spouting his poison.'

'Will he be flying us to Saratov?'

'I bloody well hope not. That would be a kick in the nether regions if that happens,' said Tom, leaning in. 'I've had a message from Alice, and she needs my help. I don't know what it means, but it scares me when she says that. And I've got to give her the letter, her orders.'

'Yes, she wants me there as well. I agree; she scares me, too. She is much too adventurous for my liking.'

Tom tucked into his marinated meat grilled on a skewer called Shashlyk. He took a long, slow drink from his wine glass to observe the Wolf's table. 'He's coming over,' he said.

'Who,' Chernoff replied, feeling it best not to look.

'Anton.'

'Good evening, gentlemen,' said Anton, pulling up a chair, turning it and sitting astride it as if riding a horse. 'I'm having a fascinating conversation with Heinrich over there. You should join us.'

Tom felt cold, a shiver running down his back. 'We're fine here, thanks, Anton. I'm flying tomorrow on the Saratov flight. Taking your friend and Danya here.'

'We haven't been introduced. I'm Anton Schultz.'

Tom continued to feel nervous about this introduction. He wasn't sure why and tried to look relaxed while thinking of a reason for Chernoff to travel to Saratov. He didn't feel very creative. 'Can I introduce Danya Chernoff? He's travelling to Saratov. He's involved with the "Feed the Children" people working to relieve the famine around the Volga. He's an interpreter.'

'*Ah, Gut.* So you speak this awful language.'

'*Da, imenno tak.* Yes indeed.'

Anton stood and rubbed his chin thoughtfully. 'Mmm. I was thinking I should do that flight to Saratov. I haven't been there before. We should have at least two pilots familiar with the route and the airfields.'

Tom struggled to come up with a good reason that he should fly to Saratov. He made a stab at it: 'I've planned it. I'm all ready to go. I think familiarity with the route is important. It is marginal for our range, and carefully leaning the fuel/air mixture is crucial to minimise petrol consumption. I nearly had to land out on my first trip.'

Tom took care to leave out his landing at Lipetsk.

Anton looked suspicious, and he was obviously thinking of a counterargument. 'I could go in the back. Maybe fly the return leg.'

'Someone's got to fly the other machine back to Berlin. Were you not down to fly that service.'

'Hmm, I suppose I was,' Anton said. 'You could fly it. Yes, why not?'

Tom was searching for another reason. 'The Saratov flight should be flown by the most experienced pilot. That's me, Anton.'

'Maybe we let Rolf decide. He's our chief pilot, is he not?'

Tom couldn't find any more arguments in his favour. 'Get in touch with Werner Roth then, but I'm on the rota, so I don't see why it should be changed.'

'OK. I'll try him now if this antiquated telephone system works,' said Anton, springing to his feet to march off to the telephone booth with a wave to Wolf.

'I'll want to speak to him if plans are changed,' Tom shouted after Anton.

Tom shook his head. 'He's a bugger, that one. Always pushing the boundaries. I just hope Roth doesn't change the plans. What do we do if Anton is with us in Saratov.'

'God knows, Chernoff said. 'Depends on what fun Alice has in mind.'

'We won't be able to shake him off. And we don't know for sure if Wolf is going with us. According to the passenger list, he must be, although he isn't mentioned by name. There is just one passenger to Saratov in addition to you now. I've fixed that.'

As expected, Tom could see Anton mouthing in his usual aggressive delivery as he argued with telephone operators. It was nearly thirty minutes before his arm appeared, thrusting out the telephone booth with a thumb up. After a few minutes, the thumb morphed into a finger pointing and then waving, clearly directed at Tom.

'Shit,' Tom uttered as he pushed himself to his feet. A big sigh followed as he marched off towards the telephone booth, his negative body language clear for all to see. That included Wolf, who wore a grin.

'Tom, good evening. I trust all is well there in Moscow?' said Captain Roth.

Tom had to be careful with his response as Anton stood beside him with a big smile followed by a wink. He composed himself, took a deep breath, and glanced at Anton. 'Yes, all is well, as long as the plans are unchanged. I feel it's important that I make these flights to Saratov. Although a good pilot, my friend Anton needs more experience before taking the Saratov route.'

'I tend to agree, Tom, but for harmony amongst our pilots, it would be a good idea if Anton went along with you. There are no booked passengers for the return flight to Berlin, so I can afford for him to tag along in the back.

I'll leave it to you to decide if he flies the return leg.'

Tom realised that Roth's solution would be the best compromise. 'OK, Werner. We'll do that. Do you want to speak to Anton again?'

'Yes, put him on. But you're in charge of the entire flight. I will make that clear to Anton.'

Tom handed the telephone to Anton. 'Werner wants a final word.'

Back at the table, Tom enlightened Chernoff. 'He's bloody well coming with us. God knows how we will operate in Saratov with him hanging around.'

Chernoff was more positive. 'I'm sure we will come up with something. We could always poison him, a small dose, put him out for a while,' he said flippantly.

Tom looked more serious. 'Now that might work. Let's see what Alice has in mind.'

CHAPTER THIRTY-TWO

Anton tumbled out of the F.III passenger cabin at Saratov as if released from a lengthy stay in a prison cell. *'Oh mein Gott, es ist so laut in der Kabine.'*

Tom climbed down slowly from his cockpit. He exercised his arms and touched his toes for a long creaking stretch before pulling his leather helmet and goggles off with a long, exhaled breath. He completed his post-flight ritual by running a hand through his hair, exercising his jaw, and finally, giving a grateful pat on the aeroplane's engine cowl. 'Yes, that flight is much too long. Two or three hours is quite enough.'

Anton was recovering. 'Why don't we use our airfield for God's sake?'

'Our airfield. What airfield?'

'You have landed there already. On your last trip. Lipetsk.'

'I wasn't aware that it was *our* airfield. It's a Russian military airfield. We were not welcome, tolerated yes, as it was a weather diversion, but our visit was not appreciated.'

Anton backed down, carefully retracting his statement. 'Well, it may be useful in the future. Where are you staying?'

Tom pulled his bag from the passenger cabin. 'We're roughing it at the AORO hostel. What about you?'

'With you lot, I suppose. And you, Heinrich?' said Anton as Tom waited intently for the reply.

'At the factory,' Wolf replied abruptly.

Anton looked puzzled. 'What factory? Why don't you stay with us?'

Tom stepped in. 'I don't think there will be space. I'm not sure about you either, Anton. Your visit wasn't planned, as you know.'

Anton shrugged. 'I can sleep anywhere; it shouldn't be a problem.'

As Tom listened to the conversation, he noticed their truck arrive to ferry them into town. 'Oh my God,' he muttered through clenched teeth as he spotted Alice in the truck. Wolf would recognise her? Tom ducked down as if to hide, glanced at Danya with a pleading look, and then back to Alice. He breathed a sigh of relief as he could see that Alice had spotted the predicament and had made a smart about turn to disappear behind the airfield huts. Tom smirked at Alice's sense of humour, tiptoeing out of sight like an absurd cartoon character.

'Are you all right, Tom?' said Anton.

'Just checking our transport. I see it's arrived. Have you got transport organised, Mr Wolf?'

'*Ja.* It should be here by now. We wait in the buildings, yes?'

'Yes. Have you made arrangements to be collected? Did you say you are staying in a factory?' Tom said quizzically.

This irritated Wolf, who spat out his words: '*Ja*, yes, I have.'

Tom was now sure Wolf recognised him. He looked embarrassed and reluctant to make eye contact. 'If you want to wait in the airfield buildings, there should be a log fire. It's getting chilly now that…

'*Ja, danke*,' Wolf mumbled and walked off to warm up.

The tired-looking group had to wait thirty minutes for Wolf's transport to arrive. Alice stayed hidden until Wolf had been collected. There was little conversation in the hut, and Tom took the opportunity to warm up. Wolf waved reluctantly as he left, and Anton rushed after him.

Tom watched them discuss something. It appeared to be serious, but their animated behaviour indicated a disagreement. Anton then waved dismissively and stormed back into the hut.

'Are we off then?' Anton said, looking irritated.

Tom stood and grabbed his bag. 'Let's go.'

Alice appeared from nowhere and plonked down in the driver's seat, much to Anton's surprise.

'Where did you spring from, young lady?' Anton said with a broad grin.

Tom stepped in. 'This is our driver for today. They work for the AORO, the American Overseas Relief Organisation.'

'I guessed that, but a young woman in these miserable conditions.'

Tom could see Alice ignored the remarks and just smiled as she navigated around the potholes, carts, and vehicles. How would they deal with Anton? He would get in the way. Tom noticed Alice had that look about her again. Something was brewing, he could tell.

'We need to talk, Alice,' Tom said when Anton was out of earshot. 'We should have some privacy; he's off to find somewhere to sleep.'

Alice pushed Merv's office door open. 'In here. Why did you bring him? What's his name?'

'Anton Schultz. I know, he's a bloody nuisance,' said Tom, closing the door. 'He's one of our pilots. He's on this trip to familiarise himself with the route.'

'We can't have him around. Not with our plans.'

Tom's eyes narrowed. 'We'll get around to that, but first, you must read this.'

Alice opened the envelope, glanced at Tom as if looking for his reaction, and unfolded the paper marked SECRET. She read slowly, her expression changing from mere curiosity to disbelief and then anger. She stood up straight, looked at Tom without comment, then returned to the letter. 'The bastards. I don't believe this, Tom. How can they do this? What did Harry say? Did you speak to C?'

Tom took a deep breath. 'I don't expect you to take this very well, but Harry was also disappointed and annoyed. I got an *orders are orders* response when I challenged him. Ross was there, too, but he was just pleased that he was going home. He didn't object but understood how much effort you had put into the operation.'

Alice slammed the letter onto Tom's chest. 'Well, I'm ignoring this, Tom. I can tell you. I have a plan, and we will go out with a bang. If the powers that be won't listen and don't want to believe what's happening in this country, that's their problem. We're going to do something that will make people sit up and listen. Something that will draw attention to Germany's intentions.'

'Alice, what the devil are you planning? We can provide a convincing report on our findings to date. We have some good photographs to support our claims. I've seen some of Bill's negatives. We can make out the locations and the people, and I'm getting closer to more evidence. Danya and I followed von der Lang to a place called Fili on the outskirts of Moscow, a motor car plant. One of Danya's informers says that Junkers may be building German-designed aircraft there…'

'That's all fine, Tom. I can see this wonderful, detailed, convincing report in a bottom drawer, gathering dust. No one is interested any more. We can't allow another war.'

'Just because Germany is attempting to re-establish their military, it doesn't mean there will be another war.'

'Oh no? From the language I've heard from people like von der Lang, that's precisely what they intend.'

Tom took a deep breath. 'Yes, I know. You'll hear

the likes of Anton Shultz talk the same way, but it's no guarantee, so why take more risks? All you're required to do is complete that bloody report.'

'I'm sick of reporting. As Bill said, we should go out with a bang.'

Tom sat down behind the desk, elbows on the table, head in his hands. He shook his head and looked up at Alice, standing on the other side of the desk, flushed in the face and hands on hips. 'God Alice, what the hell does that mean?' Tom knew that he couldn't change her mind. Even if he refused to help and flew off back to Moscow, she would do something and probably something dangerous. Tom hesitated and didn't want to ask the question. He tilted his head. 'What's this bloody plan then, Alice?'

'You will help, won't you?' she said, smiling for the first time in a while. 'I know you will.'

'God, just tell me what you're planning, for goodness' sake.'

Alice stood tall and cupped her hands together as if to pray. 'Right. In a nutshell, the idea is we get into the compound, blow up some of the critical buildings and release the guinea pigs'.

Tom leant forward on his desk. 'I understand the blowing-up bit, but what are the guinea pigs?'

'We're pretty sure that the peasant folk I saw being trucked into the compound are used for experiments with poison gases. Mikael thinks they are brought in from the Gulags.'

Tom was still stunned by Alice's simple plan. 'OK, let's run it through. First, how do we get in, and who are *we*?'

Alice replied confidently, 'Right, we know that the peasants are trucked in mostly at night when many guards are asleep at their posts. So, we play the role of one of these trucks. Chernoff drives as he speaks the language fluently, and we are in the back dressed as peasants, armed and with the wherewithal to blow something to smithereens.'

'How many guards are there, and what do we blow up?' Tom asked.

'I think about 20 guards, and we go for the laboratories.'

'There are only four of us, assuming Bill and Mikael are up for this exploit. And what arms do we have, and where do we get explosives?' said Tom.

'Mikael can get some of his old fighters from the revolutionary wars. They're on their way here now?'

'How many?' said Tom.

'Four at least,' said Alice with an increasingly furrowed brow.

Tom continued with his questioning despite Alice's demeanour. 'And arms, and explosives?'

'Mikael will supply arms. We'll need to get Chernoff onto the explosives. There are mines in the area.'

Tom paused for a moment. 'We could just set fire to the place. We have lots of petrol cans.'

Alice's frown transformed into a smile. 'Now you're getting interested, Thomas. That's a great idea and much easier to arrange.'

'We have a couple of other problems,' Tom said ruefully. 'Wolf and my pilot friend Anton. Wolf is OK; he will be at the factory, but Anton will be hanging around here.'

'We will deal with Wolf if he appears during our foray into the compound. Do you have any thoughts on Anton?' said Alice.

'I don't know what you planned, but we could get him out of our hair with Merv to visit some famine-feeding sites.'

'Do you really think he would be interested in that?' Alice asked doubtfully.

'No,' Tom said with a sigh, his expression changing as an idea formed. 'If you'll play along, Alice, I have an idea. I'll need to speak to Merv first.'

'Tell me more,' said Alice with a sideways glance.

Anton took the bait. 'If you'll drive, Alice, I'll come and see the AORO facilities,' he said. 'Do we have to stay overnight?'

'Yes, it's too far for a day trip.' Alice said. 'The countryside along the Volga is wonderful, but you need to be prepared for some dreadful sights amongst the population. It's much better now, though, but there are pockets of starvation which we need to log. Part of this trip is to survey more areas we haven't been to recently. So it's not just a tourist outing. You do understand that?'

'Yes, of course,' Anton said with a smirk, which Alice found unnerving.

* * *

Merv played his part perfectly, along with Alice's stand-in, Bobby Bernstein. Alice's truck sat fully loaded in the autumn mist in the hostel courtyard. Anton threw his bag in the back enthusiastically and jumped into his seat, looking like he was off on holiday. Who knew what he had in mind, but Tom watched with fingers crossed. Bobby approached the truck with his bag, and Anton's expression changed.

'Are you coming too?' Anton asked.

'Alice is ill. She's been sick all night. She must have picked up a bug. I'm your driver. Settle back and enjoy the ride,' Bobby shouted as he cranked the engine into life and jumped aboard. Before Schultz could have any second thoughts, Bobby crunched the truck into gear and shot off, Schultz's mouth agape.

Alice emerged from hiding as the truck disappeared down the road in a dust cloud. 'He took the bait, eh Tom?'

'He sure did. Let's wait until we are sure he doesn't force Bobby to turn around.'

Alice looked up the road as the dust settled. They

waited a good ten minutes, then shook hands. 'I think we've done it, Tom. Now, where's the rest? I want to meet Mikael's bunch of thugs. I hope they do as they're told. We'll have a pow-wow as soon as everyone is back. And where's Danya?'

'He's out to find a truck and a dozen cans of petrol,' said Tom.

'Mikael is getting what arms he can organise,' said Alice. It's bound to be old Russian stuff, but we have little choice.'

'We've got our Smith & Wessons. Have we got plenty of ammunition, and what about clothing? If we are to be peasant like...'

'I'll get a box of ammo each. We've got plenty of peasant clothing here in the hostel stores. Can't guarantee how hygienic it'll be,' Alice said with a twist of her mouth.

'Good grief, Alice. What have you got me into now?'

'Extremely unhygienic peasant apparel.'

CHAPTER THIRTY-THREE

Alice looked up from the clothes she was sorting, a headscarf carefully secured around her nose and mouth. She noticed a shape at the door from the corner of her eye. She dropped the clothes, threw her arms around Mikael's neck, and kissed him fondly. 'Mikael, it's so good to see you. Have you brought some of your friends?'

Mikael pulled her arms away gently, with a guilty glance at Tom. 'Yes, here I am, and here are my willing warriors, all good, trusted fighters from the White Army days. They don't need any excuse to get into a fight with the Bolsheviks. They've seen the effects of poison gas and can't wait to destroy any factory making the stuff.'

Four rough-looking men nodded and responded to Mikaels' introduction differently, mostly nodding or waving furtively. They removed their bandoliers and stowed their old M1891 rifles by the wall. One big man carried a Lewis gun and an open bag of forty-seven-round, pan-type magazines for his Lewis.

Tom noticed they were also armed with handguns, British Army standard-issue Webleys. Bill would identify which mark. Their large knives in leather scabbards looked like American trench knives with their distinctive brass knuckle hilt. They were a frightening bunch, he thought. They were probably just what we needed. 'Do they understand English?' Tom asked abruptly.

'Enough,' Mikael said. 'You should know their names.' Mikael pointed at his motley crew, one at a time. 'We have Sergei, Vlad, Dima, and Aizel ⊠ all great fighters,' Mikael advised proudly.

'Thanks, Mikael. We're very grateful for your help tonight,' said Tom. 'One thought: it will be very dark and difficult to distinguish friends from foes. We need something unique to identify us—a red scarf, for example.'

'Nothing red,' said one of Mikael's men.

Tom responded quickly to his error. 'Of course not. Any suggestions?'

Alice held up a dirty white sheet. 'How about these?'

'Make us a good target,' said Mikael.

'Stop us shooting at each other,' Tom suggested as he looked around the store. 'What about that yellow material. We could make up neck scarves. That would be much more distinctive.'

'Good idea,' said Alice with a smile. 'And, Tom, Bill, you need to select your evening dress. Something from this pile if you please.'

Danya Chernoff appeared at the door, looking tired but with a look of pride. 'I've got them. A big enough truck and plenty of petrol. It cost me a fortune.'

Darkness had fallen when Alice's team gathered in a storeroom at the back of the AORO hostel. All were dressed in their peasant garb, and appropriately, they looked like escapees from the Gulags.

Alice drew a diagram on the ground. 'This is the layout of the compound. I only know some details about the factory compound, but there are large buildings, probably for gas production. Our objective is to set the place alight as much as we can and free the guinea pigs imprisoned here; let's just call them the "guineas".'

Alice finished her diagram. 'The first buildings look like administrative offices, with staff accommodation at the back. I guess that's where the sleeping guards will come from. We should torch these, but we'll probably bump into guards aroused by our kerfuffle. Further in, there are three laboratories. We must set them alight. If we can get further in before we are noticed, we must get as much of the factory as possible.'

'How many petrol cans do we have, Danya?' said Tom.

Chernoff counted around the room. 'There are enough for one each plus some more. There are nine of us. We have twelve cans.'

'OK, we take one each and more if we can get to them at the end,' Alice said.

'What do we do about guards,' Bill asked, to which one of Mikael's men drew his hand across his throat.

'We will be going in with our truck. Danya driving and Mikael in the front,' said Alice. 'We will be posing as delivering more guineas—that's us in the back if the guards get to look in,' she said with a grin. 'Surprise is essential, and we want to get the petrol on the buildings before any rumpus starts. So, Mikael and Sergei, you deal with any guards. If there are more than two, we'll have to deal with them from the rest of us in the back. We must be silent as long as possible. And, Danya, can you position the truck for a quick getaway?'

'What do we do with the guineas?' said Bill.

'Let them go. It's up to them. It's every man for themselves. Direct them to the gates. Make sure they're open, Danya.' said Alice.

Bill looked fired up by the thought of the action. 'Once this gets going, the rest of the guards and whoever feels like a fight are gonna appear. It could be quite a night. Do we know how many we're up against? And do we have enough arms?'

Mikael nodded and glanced at his men, who displayed various signs of agreement. Bill looked as if he didn't need to ask further. Mikael then looked the others up and down. Other than his men, he looked disappointed. 'You don't look ready to me, he said, bending down to dig around his bag. 'Take these,' he said, handing out the knives in belted leather scabbards. He nodded at Tom's handgun. 'I think you'll need more than that.'

'I'll have a Webley if you've got one,' said Tom.

Bill put out his hand. 'Me too.'

'Here' said Mikael. 'I've even got a belt and holsters.'

Alice took a long breath. 'Right, just one last thing from me. I suggest we divide and move down each side of the compound with a petrol can each. Obviously, make sure you have something to set the petrol alight. Get as far into the compound as the factory buildings at the end here. Then work back. This is where the guineas are kept, a kind of prison block, so don't fire this building, but as we pass it on the way back, let them out. This will help with the chaos.'

'Danya, you stay around the truck. Stop the guineas getting into the truck, get them out the gate,' said Mikael. 'Let's divide into Sergei, Vlad, Tom, and Bill down the left, and me, Dima, Aizel, and Alice down the right. How does that sound, Alice?'

'Sounds good to me,' said Alice. 'We leave at one am. Any questions?'

A group of sober-looking faces remained quiet; a short head shake was the only response as they settled down to wait; the difficult bit.

Finally, Mikael spoke from the back of the darkened room. 'And we agree that nobody gets left behind, OK? No matter what.'

'OK,' was spoken quietly by everyone.

CHAPTER THIRTY-FOUR

They took nearly forty-five minutes to reach the compound. Danya coasted the truck to a halt. The rest of the compound was visible as a spectral grey structure illuminated by a near-full moon. It was warm and dry, the air scented by the oak and birch foliage surrounding them. Mikael turned around. 'Are you ready in there? A minute to the gates. Sergei and I deal with guards.' Mikael nodded at Chernoff. 'Let's go.'

As the truck approached the gates, Mikael jumped down. He banged the wood and yelled in Russian, '*Otkroyte vorotato.*' He waited and tried again. '*Otkroyte vorotato.*'

'What's he saying?' Tom said impatiently.

'Just shouting for the gates to be opened,' Chernoff whispered. 'They're probably asleep.'

Mikael tried a hefty push, but unsurprisingly, they were secured from the inside. He tried another shout. At last, he heard a distant response; a man was running.

'*Khorosho, ya idu.*'

'Sergei, get ready,' said Alice.

From the back, they could hear Mikael chattering in Russian. The tone didn't sound very encouraging; it was more like an argument. The truck was still stationary, and the gate only just cracked open. Those in the truck held their breath. Then, a scuffling sound and a gurgling grunt broke the silence.

Mikael whispered as loudly as he dared. 'Sergei, give me a hand,'

Sergei jumped down to help push the gates open. Chernoff nudged the truck into gear to move slowly into the compound, leaving Mikael and Sergei crouching and scanning for other guards. Once inside, he drove in a wide circle, stopping with the rear of the truck facing into the compound.

Mikael skulked across to the truck. 'There was only one guard. I've dealt with him. So far, we've not been spotted. Quietly now.'

The rest of the team clambered down from the truck, lugging the heavy petrol cans, desperately trying to minimise their noise. Collecting their weapons and forming into groups, they set off in their allotted directions.

Tom went left with Sergei, Vlad and Bill. 'This way,' Tom whispered. 'I can see the passageway by the wall. That's the way.' Once in the narrow passageway by the administrative building, Tom felt relatively safe, although their careful footsteps seemed to echo loudly off the walls. He stopped his team with a raised arm for a breather before exiting into an open space, like a courtyard or parade square. They were looking for the laboratories when a dog barked. 'Shit, we didn't think about dogs,' said Tom.

Bill crouched behind Tom. 'Let it sniff around. I'll deal with it. Can you see a guard?'

Tom leant out from the corner of the building. 'Fuck, yes, a guard with a dog. A bloody big dog. On a leash.' Tom turned around. 'Bill, you get the dog. I'm on the guard.'

'OK.'

'Back up a bit,' said Tom, withdrawing his knife from its scabbard. 'Let them come into the passage. Use your knife, Bill.'

The dog was getting excited after picking up their scent. They could hear it getting closer. The guard chattered continuously to his canine companion. The guard stopped. More talking and barking. Tom wondered if the guard had spotted something. The others? Then he heard the sound of more excited barking and running. Tom ventured a peep around the corner. 'He's off. Must have spotted the others.'

'Let's go then,' said Bill.

'Wait, let me check it's clear,' Tom hissed, leaning around the corner of the building. 'OK, go.'

Bill set off toward the prison building, the rest following, with Tom at the rear. It was a full 100 yards across the open compound. Tom noted the lack of cover. He suspected a firefight on the way back. The guineas were visible through the barred windows—all asleep. Not for long, Tom thought. Whilst running across the courtyard, he looked for access doors to the prison block. He could not see any. They had not considered how to get the guineas out.

As they were about to pass the prison block, Tom heard

shots ringing out. 'It's started,' he said, fearing the worst.

Bill was off like a whippet again. 'Let's get going,' he panted. 'That building, look. That's the laboratory, and there's the factory buildings.'

Just as they reached the factory, more shots rang out, and a flickering appeared in the dark sky where Alice and Mikael's team would be doing their bit. Bill had found a window into the factory. He quickly opened the top of his can and thrust it through the window with a crash. He paused with a wicked smile, then followed his can with a match. They waited. Bill's grin turned sour. 'Another match, Bill!' Tom shouted when a loud whoosh with an encouraging flash of yellow light confirmed the result they wanted.

'The laboratories next!' Tom yelled as he rushed off with his petrol can, which seemed to be getting heavier. He found a window in the closest laboratory building. He smashed it with the can, loosened the top, then launched it through the window. Shots started to whizz around his head. He ducked down, looking for gun flashes. He saw shadowy shapes appearing from the admin block and pulled his Webley from its holster. 'Bill, give me some covering fire. I need to set this place alight.'

'I see 'em,' Bill roared. 'Our surprise is gone.' Bill fired a few shots with his rifle, which seemed to quieten things down. Tom finally managed to ignite the petrol now spilling across the laboratory floor. With the now familiar whoosh echoing across the compound, the laboratory lit up with a flash, then a flickering yellow light which helped to show up the guards as they rushed out of their accommodation.

'We've got to get the guineas out,' Tom shouted as he dashed towards the prison block. 'Cover me!' he shouted.

He crouched down again before venturing around the corner of the prison block. He could see a group carrying someone off and out of sight. He knew it must be Alice's group. He thought no more of it and peered into the darkness to find out how they could release the guineas. More shots rang out, and Bill, Vlad, and Sergei joined him, crouching to work out the next step.

More guards were piling out of the accommodation block, and Vled and Sergei lay down to take measured shots with their rifles. Several men tumbled to the ground with their accurate shots. The remaining guards got the message and took more care before launching into the killing zone. Tom spotted a familiar shape at the door. He was sure that it was Wolf.

Once they reached the prison block on the other side of the compound, Mikael and Alice bashed on the doors to awaken the guineas. The doors didn't seem to be guarded. Alice yelled, 'It's padlocked.'

'Use the rifle, shoot it off!' Mikael bawled between his shots. 'Set the Lewis gun up, Aizel. Put it down here.'

Rounds continued to zip past as they lay at the corner of the prison block in full view of the guards. 'Keep down,'

Mikael cried as he saw movement out of the corner of his eye. He looked left to see Alice spreadeagled face down on the ground. He checked whilst firing another couple of shots from his Webley. 'Alice is hit. Cover me, Aizel.'

Mikael put a hand to Alice's back. She didn't respond. He rolled her over to reveal a pool of blood soaking into the dust, a small but pulsating river of life running from underneath her motionless body. He crouched down, shots still whizzing overhead. 'I'm going to get her to the truck. Give me covering fire.'

Tom could see that the rifle shots from Sergei were decimating the feckless guards who tried to rush them at one point. The Lewis gun at the other side of the compound discouraged any heroics and seemed to be finishing off any remaining guards. Tom could see that Wolf was trying to get them more organised, but he was failing. Tom raised his Webley, lined his sight on Wolf and fired. He missed. Wolf ducked down instinctively. Perhaps he knew that Tom was on the end of the shot that just missed. Tom fired with his rifle, taking slow and careful aim. He could still make out Wolf's dark bulk. This time, his target jerked and fell forward.

Tom stood for a better view.

Sergei shouted. 'Get down!'

Tom ignored the warning and set off on a slow, crouching walk towards the tangle of bodies, his pistol levelled at the ready.

Another guard took a shot. Tom ducked, the bullet zipping past his head.

Sergei fired. It was the guard's last shot.

As Tom approached where he saw Wolf fall, the ground was littered with bodies. There seemed to be no resistance now. Finally, he reached the fallen shape, the lifeless body he'd shot.

'They've all had it,' Tom yelled, waving his arm towards the entrance. 'Get back to the truck, everyone. I'll be with you in a minute.'

The noise of gunfire had stopped; now, the predominant sound was the crackling of burning buildings and the last of the guineas, the injured ones, chattering and hobbling across the square to the exit. Everything was brightly illuminated by the fierce fires raging in the factory and laboratory buildings, the flames as tall as the buildings, licking the low cloud and smoke plumes lurking over the compound. The pungent smells of the infernos were overpowering. Tom coughed as he stood over Wolf's body. He had mixed feelings: pity, fulfilment? He wasn't sure. He reached down to turn the body over when suddenly his legs were pulled from under him. He fell backwards, smacking the ground hard, taking his breath away.

When Tom regained his senses, a man, was on top of him. He was sitting astride him, pinning him and his arms to the ground. It was Wolf.

Wolf had a bullet wound in his chest and must be

weakened. Tom thought. He was a heavy-set man and difficult to move. Tom thought he had a chance until Wolf grabbed his Luger P08 and pressed it against Tom's temple. Tom couldn't move. He waited, screwing up his eyes, waiting for the end. *Not like this*, he thought.

He twitched in reaction to the next thing he heard: a loud click. The gun was empty. Tom used Wolf's shock to his advantage and wrenched his right arm free. He strained to reach his knife. He could reach it. Wolf realised what Tom was doing and tried to grab Tom's arm. This put the German off balance, and Tom's upward thrust at the hips finally dislodged him. Within seconds, Wolf had scrambled to his feet and staggered off into the building.

Tom shook himself and followed into the darkness. He stopped and listened to the sound of running echoing inside the building. It sounded like steps; Wolf was on a stairway.

Tom moved slowly towards the stairs, switching on his Orilux trench lamp strapped to his chest. He spotted the stairs and crept forward, his ears pricked up like a rabbit. Could he assume that Wolf had no more rounds in his pistol? Tom decided not and touched his trench knife to check that it was still there.

The torch beam swept the stairway, and after a dozen careful steps, a short passageway came into view. There were four doors off the passage. He would have to check each. Tom clutched the Webley in his right hand, the knife in the other. A check of the first and second rooms revealed nothing, but smoke was beginning to fill the passage; the building was alight.

As Tom approached the last room, his torch beam caught Wolf as he rushed at him from a doorway, knocking Tom to the ground. When they recovered, they stood facing each other like a pair of animals defending their territory. Wolf raised his knife and lunged. Tom parried the thrusting blade, which overbalanced Wolf. He hammered into the wall, falling heavily to the floor. He rolled over, blood dribbling from his mouth, his eyes vacant and pleading.

Tom now had the chance. He raised his Webley and fired. Wolf kicked out at the right moment, sending the round wide. He fired again. A loud click said it all.

Tom tossed his pistol away, drew his knife and jumped on top of Wolf, who was tiring fast but he managed to squirm under Tom's weight, his hand scratching and hitting out wildly. He cried out. 'Gnade!'

Tom raised his knife and paused.

A loud bang by Tom's ear brought him to his senses. He looked around, his ears ringing to see a Webley's smoking barrel only inches from his head. He looked down again to see Wolf. He lay flat on his back with a neat bullet hole where his empty eye socket had been, a river of blood flowing across the floor.

'I wasn't sure you'd do it, Tom,' said Bill.

Tom nodded and dragged himself to his feet. 'I

suppose I should say thank you but I was going to do it. I was. He deserved it.'

Bill grabbed Tom by the elbow. 'No time to hang around; this way.'

Tom took one last look at Wolf as the flames licked ever closer. 'OK. Where's Alice and the rest?'

'They're all in the truck. Just you now,' Bill barked, noticing that Tom was still dazed. 'Come on, let's go.'

Tom took a last look at Wolf, slid the knife into his sheath and dashed after Bill. 'Are the guineas free?' Tom wheezed as they ran into a dense cloud of smoke.

'Yes. There were only twenty or so,' said Bill. 'They got the message pretty quick, like.'

When they reached the truck, Danya stood ready for a quick getaway with one foot on the driver's step. 'Start her up, Vlad!' Danya yelled as Tom and Bill bundled into the back.

Tom glanced around as Bill pulled up the tailgate. The light was poor save for the flickering yellow illumination provided by the inferno now raging in the compound. 'We're all here then?' Tom shouted, smarting from the stink of smoke-soiled clothing. He peered around the dim interior, which darkened as the truck pitched and lurched its way out of the compound. Narrowing his eyes, he thought he could see Mikael wedged into the front left corner and another shape sitting opposite. 'Mikael?' Tom shouted.

'I'm sorry, Tom. He's gone,' said Bill.

‘What? How?’ Tom stuttered as he switched on his trench torch. Its beam picked out Mikael’s lifeless shape slumped in the corner, Sergei holding him in place. Tom nervously swept his torch beam across to the other side, fearing more bad news. Its fading beam picked out Alice, Dima’s arm around her shoulder, his other hand pressing on her stomach. Tom sprung from his seat and scrambled along the floor. ‘What happened?’ Tom asked.

‘Shot in stomach,’ Dima replied in his deadpan voice.

Tom pushed in between Alice and Dima. ‘I’ve got her. Thanks, Dima. I’ve got her.’ With an arm around her shoulder, Tom felt carefully for the dressing and gently applied pressure and watched for any reaction in her pale expression, but it remained still and almost lifeless. ‘Alice? Can you hear me? We’re going to the doctor. Hold on. It won’t be long.’ Tom’s stomach churned just as he remembered when flying into battle. But now he was helpless, and for one of the few times in his life, he uttered a prayer. He kissed Alice’s forehead, a long, desperate kiss. At that instant, he recalled his mother’s mantra, which would solve his all too frequent minor scrapes, ‘There, there, all better now’. He drew back, his torch light now fading to nothing, but he was captivated by what he saw. A single glistening tear emerged from Alice’s eye. He watched its progress, transfixed by its poignancy as it ran down her cheek. Was she saying something? He looked for some sign. Her face seemed untroubled, serene and almost at peace.

Tom was shocked by this serenity and rushed to find a pulse. It was there, but only just; it was faint and irregular. 'Alice. We did it; the factory's an inferno. They'll not be making anything there now. Hold on. Not long now. The doc will see to you. You'll be fine. Fit as a fiddle in no time.'

The journey seemed to take forever. Tom held onto Alice for the entire journey, cushioning her from the truck's bumping and bucking on the unmade roads. There was no light now from his torch, but he peered at Alice regularly to detect any change in her condition. He could see little and relied on feeling her shallow breathing. Tom's relief when he heard Bill's cry was palpable.

'We're nearly there,' Bill shouted from the back of the truck. 'Is she still OK?'

'Only just,' Tom replied with moist eyes.

Tom waited alone in a small room to await the outcome of the doctor's examination. He sat at a small desk, head in hands, his stomach knotted in despair. He feared the worst as he occasionally peered at a picture on the wall in front of him. He realised that he was tracing the shapes in the picture without recognising the subject. He took some comfort from recalling some of the happier times with Alice and meeting up again after mourning her loss. In his heart, he didn't feel that she would be so lucky this time. Their love had been occasional but wonderful; he realised that he was smiling. He was still reminiscing when Bill appeared quietly at the door. Bill didn't do anything quietly. It put Tom even more on edge.

'Tom?'

Tom turned and looked up with reddened, pleading eyes, one elbow still on the table, a hand on top of his head as if trying to keep a lid on the painful emotions trying to burst forth. 'Yes, Bill,' he sniffed.

'The doctor asked me to speak to you.'

Tom took some time to respond. 'What does he have to say?'

Bill shook his head. 'I'm so sorry, Tom… She didn't make it…'

Tom closed his eyes momentarily, exhaled through pursed lips and looked down disconsolately at his hands flat on the desk. He paused for some time, then took a deep, quivering breath. 'Can I see her?'

'I should think so. Do you want me to come with you?'

'Thanks, Bill, but no, I'd like to see her alone.'

CHAPTER THIRTY-FIVE

'It's all there, everything we found. You've got the negatives, too? It's all in the file.' said Tom, looking up at the trees in Green Park. Now devoid of leaves, the trees dappled the winter sun, which barely provided enough warmth for sitting outdoors. He turned his coat collar up and looked at Harry, who sat alongside him on the park bench. Tom tried to smile, a sad smile, the kind of smile that is a precursor to tears.

Harry felt the need to say something. 'I think we always felt that Alice would go off on her own. She was too passionate and personally involved. The possibility of a resurgent military in Germany was too much for her to bear.'

Tom sighed. 'If only she could have seen sense. I take it our foray into the Saratov gas factory will be… forgotten?'

'Yes, it never happened.'

'At least this time, I know there was no SIS ruse. I know for certain that my lovely, spirited Alice didn't make it. The dear girl. I loved her, but in the end, I could see how much of a free spirit she was. We buried her quietly in a cemetery in Saratov. I'll go back there one day to say goodbye properly. In my own time,' Tom explained with watery eyes.

Harry put his arm on Tom's shoulders and gave him a little shake. 'She was almost destined to come to grief.

She took more and more risks. C was going to withdraw her from active service. Too much of a loose cannon. I don't suppose she would have accepted that, either. And you lost another of your men at the gas compound? I don't suppose those details are in your report?'

'Yes, big, big-hearted Mikael. He tried to get Alice to safety but got caught crossing open ground. I didn't see it. I was too busy hunting Wolf down.' Tom took a long pull of the cold air, his outward breath quivering. 'And Alice was getting fond of Mikael. He was feeling guilty. He knew I was fond of Alice, too. Anyway, they're close now,' Tom quipped, shaking his head. 'We buried them beside each other.'

Tom swallowed, blinked hard and sighed. 'Did Fritz Uittenbogaart, our man in the Netherlands, ever find out what Anthony Fokker was up to?'

'Apparently, Fokker had won a contract to build fifty Fokker D.XIII, supposedly for the Argentines, but we rather suspect that they could be for the facility you describe at Lipetsk. But we can't be sure... yet.'

'And the Napier engines are in the same order as the D.XIIIs?'

'Yes, but there was nothing illegal about Foster Engineering's activities.'

Tom glanced at Harry; his eyes still swimming. 'And why was the operation cancelled?'

'As I mentioned, there is a general feeling that Germany has suffered enough, and that cooperation is the way forward. However, the French and Belgians don't agree with this view. They've just occupied the Ruhr Valley to force reparations out of the Germans.'

'Bloody hell, Harry, that'll just make the Germans even more determined and resourceful, as we've seen already. Our people in this country should know about this—I mean, what's happening in Russia.'

'They will eventually, Tom, but not by my hand. Did you hear about the failed coup d'état in Munich? They're calling it the "Munich Putsch". Some two thousand National Socialists, as they call themselves, were confronted by a police cordon. Their leader was a fellow called Adolf Hitler.'

'Well blow me. Anton, one of our pilots, was spouting off about him, his hero, I think.'

'He was the leader of this new "Nazi" Party, the Nationalsozialistische Deutsche Arbeiterpartei or NSDAP. He was arrested and charged with treason. We don't think this man is going to lie down quietly.'

'That's our point. Germany and its military are not going to lie down quietly either. We've seen it for ourselves. We have witnessed the beginning of something significant. We ignore it at our peril.'

Harry clasped his hands together. 'Anyway, let's change the subject. Did you manage to sort out Louisa's financial woes?'

'She did it herself. The trustees understood her predicament and persuaded Robert Foster to release some funds.'

‘I bet you’re relieved about that. And what does the future look like for Captain Thomas Munro?’

‘I’ll keep flying for Deruluft for now,’ Tom replied, tilting his head. ‘But I’m interested in this new scheme to amalgamate the original British airlines. I had a letter from Daniel Ferris. Apparently, Sir Reginald Ferris is getting involved. Some committee has made recommendations for a consolidated airline comprising the survivors of our earlier attempts: it’s to be called the Imperial Air Transport Company, Daniel says.’

‘That’s good. That’ll open up new horizons for Captain Munro, our man on the ground or, in your case, our man in the air.’

‘No, Harry. Let’s have no more of this “our man”, no more of your shenanigans. I just want to fly my aeroplanes. Make something significant of this airline business. I don’t really want any more of this spying lark.’

Harry paused, a twinkling of understanding in his eyes. He smiled, put his arm around Tom’s shoulders and winked. ‘Oh no?’

Manchester Guardian 3rd December 1926

"An aeroplane factory has been built by the Junkers' Works in Russia for the purpose of manufacturing military aeroplanes for German as well as Russian use. Arrangements for erecting chemical works in Russia to manufacture poison gas for both countries were also made by German and Russian military experts. These activities began at least five years ago but have been going on ever since. To make the necessary arrangements, officers of the Reichswehr have travelled to and from Russia with false papers, visaed by the Russian authorities. General von Seeckt, until recently Commander-in-Chief of the Reichswehr, was on the best of terms with the Russians, particularly with officers of high rank in the Soviet Army. It seems that he was not unaware of the facts mentioned above."

* * *

Manchester Guardian 6th December 1926

"The Junker Works in Moscow were a preliminary to further production, to manufacture a hundred aeroplanes. Almost the entire expense of fitting out works, dispatching and maintaining experts, providing material, and constructing aeroplanes was borne by the Germans. The construction program was to reach 300 aeroplanes yearly, of which the majority were to be for German use."

ACKNOWLEDGEMENTS

Writing any novel is a major undertaking, and with this, my third novel, I have found that successfully marketing and selling the work is equally challenging. Time will tell! As before, my writing would not happen without the unwavering support and encouragement of my wife, Elisabeth. To her, I owe an enormous debt of gratitude yet again, and I hope that our efforts will be worthwhile in the end.

Rapallo's Shadow is the third novel in the Tom Munro series of aviation/spy stories and is also based on real events in post-WWI Europe. Writing is a team effort, and editing is key to obtaining an independent view of the story and for sourcing constructive feedback with which to knock the story into shape. On this occasion, I would like to thank Jo Lane at *Reedsy* for her helpful editing and for copyediting my cousin, Anne Fernie. Thanks also to Maree Walker for stepping in with very timely proofreading and to my cover designer, Paul Palmer-Edwards, who has produced an excellent, lively and colourful cover image yet again.

Thanks also to my Beta Readers for their invaluable input and feedback. Their perspectives have been crucial in shaping the narrative. And, of course, not to forget Elisabeth, who, for a change, actually got to read the manuscript with little prior knowledge of the content.

I think she enjoyed it, too.

I have made much use of many works and articles, but the following stand out and continue to be valuable reference documents: *The Vickers Vimy*; P St John Turner, *British Airways, The Imperial Years*; R E G Davies, *Aerial Transport*; G Holt Thomas, *Early Birds*; Alfred Instone, *Transforming the Skies*; Peter Reese, *Travellers in the Third Reich*; Julia Boyd, *MI6, 1909 – 1949*; Keith Jeffrey, *Diamonds in the Sky*, Kenneth Hudson and Julian Pettifer, *Great Britain, Germany and the Soviet Union, Rapallo and After, 1922-1934*; Stephanie C Salzmann. *Fokker – The Man and The Aircraft*; Henri Hegener, *Croydon – The Peaceful Years;* Mike Hooks.

Other extracts and works which were particularly informative include: *Devils Bargain, Germany and Russia Before WWII*; James S Corum, *Rapallo Re-examined: A New Look at Germany's Secret Military Collaboration with Russia in 1922;* Gordon H. Mueller, *Sowing the Wind: The First Soviet-German Pact and the Origins of World War II;* Ian Johnson, *The Faustian Pact: Soviet-German Military Cooperation in the Interwar Period;* Ian Johnson, *Hugo Stotzenberg and Chemical Weapons Proliferation;* Benjamin C. Garrett, *The Save the Children Fund and the Russian Famine of 1921-23;* Linda Mahood & Vic Satzewich, *Documentary Film and the Volga Famine: Save the Children's Famine (1922);* Jeremy Hicks

My acknowledgements must not neglect *Wikipedia's* amazing role as an initial source of reference for almost any subject. As a frequent user of this valuable source of information, I would like to make a special note of this wonderful modern research tool.

AUTHOR BIO

William Fernie is an aeronautical engineer, pilot and author of the Tom Munro series of historical fiction novels.

Rapallo's Shadow is the third book in this series.

Following a short spell in the merchant navy, Bill read aeronautical engineering at university and served for sixteen years in the Royal Air Force, completing his service in the fascinating world of military intelligence.

After his military service, Bill formed his own company and combined his marine and aeronautical skills in what proved to be his most fulfilling work. If you subscribe to Bill's newsletter, you can find out more about this third career. Drop Bill an email if you want to be included.

Throughout his working life, Bill satisfied his aviation and maritime interests through sailing and flying classic aircraft. His most recent aeroplane is a de Havilland Chipmunk, which he enjoyed flying until this year (2024). Sadly, it was time to hang up the "headsets", and now Bill concentrates on his sailing in CENTAYNE III and his writing.

Bill is married with two grown-up daughters and lives in West Hampshire in a wonderful old farmhouse with his wife Lizzie. Watch out for the fourth book in the Tom Munro series, which is currently churning around in Bill's imagination but should be published next year.

Keep in touch via Bill's website, www.ferniebooks.com and find him on Facebook/Meta @billferniebooks. Alternatively, you can always email on bill@ferniebooks.com

AUTHORS NOTES

For further information about the subjects raised in this and other William Fernie novels, please visit "Author's Notes" on the William Fernie website at **www.ferniebooks.com**

BOOKS IN THE "TOM MUNRO" SERIES

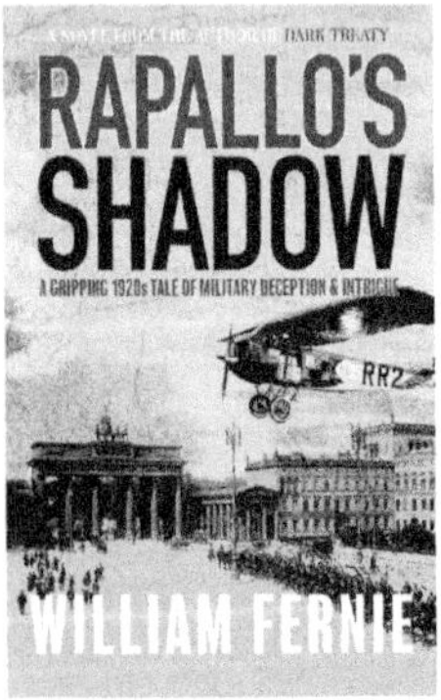

Printed in Great Britain
by Amazon

45250303R00248